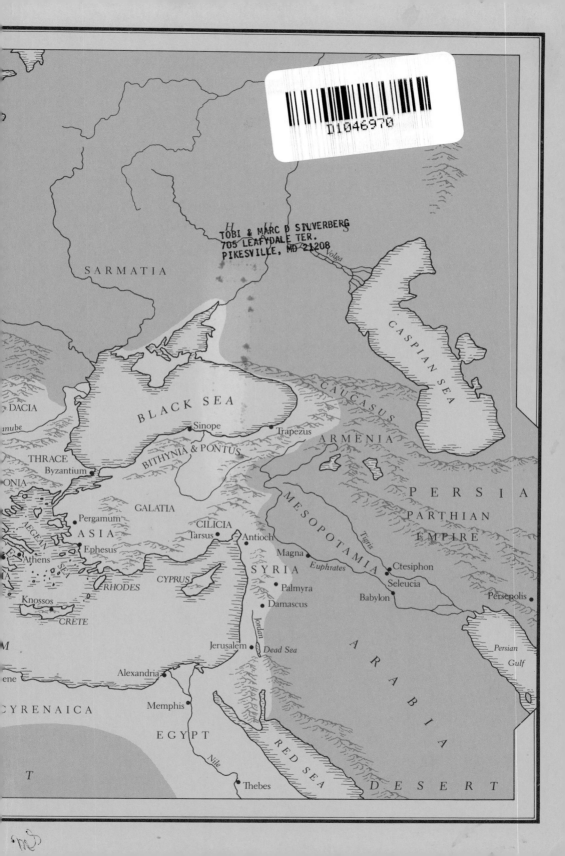

SARMATIA

Volga

CASPIAN SEA

DACIA

Danube

BLACK SEA

CAUCASUS

• Sinope

• Trapezus

ARMENIA

THRACE

Byzantium •

BITHYNIA & PONTUS

ONIA

GALATIA

PERSIA

MESOPOTAMIA

PARTHIAN

Pergamum •

CILICIA

Tigris

EMPIRE

ASIA

Tarsus •

• Antioch

AEGE

• Ephesus

Magna •

Euphrates

• Ctesiphon

Athens •

SYRIA

Seleucia

• Persepolis

RHODES

CYPRUS

• Palmyra

Babylon •

Knossos

• Damascus

CRETE

Jordan

Jerusalem •

Dead Sea

A

R

A

B

I

A

*Persian
Gulf*

M

Alexandria •

ene

CYRENAICA

Memphis •

EGYPT

RED SEA

Nile

T

• Thebes

D

E

S

E

R

T

SOUL FLAME

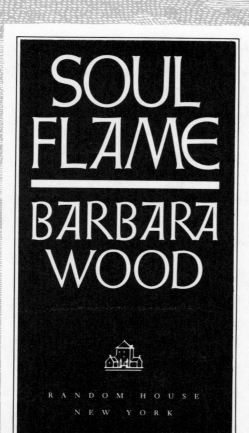

SOUL FLAME

BARBARA WOOD

RANDOM HOUSE
NEW YORK

Library of Congress Cataloging-in-Publication Data
Wood, Barbara.
Soul flame.
I. Title.
PS3573.O5877S6   1987   813'.54   86-3893
ISBN 0-394-55571-6

Manufactured in the United States of America
9 8 7 6 5 4 3 2
First Edition

Typography and binding design by J. K. Lambert

This book is dedicated, with love, to

J O H N   M A K A R E W I C H

Thanks are in order to some very special people: to my mother, who always believed a certain gypsy fortune-teller; to my husband, George, and to my father, both of whom encourage and support me; to Betty Vasin, who saw this coming years ago and who has always had faith in me; and to Kate Medina, the greatest editor in the world, and to Harvey Klinger, the greatest agent in the world.

A special warm thanks to Denis Keating for coming to my rescue with each crisis of the typewriter!

A Note of Explanation

The ancients had their own names for many of the plants and herbs mentioned in this book, but for easier identification I have chosen throughout to use those by which they are commonly known today—"henbane" instead of the Latin *hyoscyamus,* for example.

I also introduce the historical figure Lucius Domitius Ahenobarbus as Nero, a name he was not in fact known by until he became emperor.

—B. W.

SOUL FLAME

The day had been so full of omens that even before the healer-woman heard the frantic late-night knock upon her door, she knew that this night was going to be one that could change her life forever.

She had been reading the portents for days. There had been her own auspicious dreams—of snakes, of the moon running red with blood—and the dreams of those who came to visit her: women, full with child, dreaming of giving birth to doves; and young virgins seeing disturbing visions in their sleep. And then the two-headed calf had been born in the Bedouin encampment to the south of the city, and the ghost of Andrachus had been seen walking the streets at midnight, headless and yet calling out the names of his assassins. So many signs, they could not be ignored. But who are these portents meant for? asked the citizens of the desert city of Palmyra, as they cast glances over their shoulders.

They are meant for me, thought the healer-woman, not knowing how she knew.

So when she heard the urgent rapping on her door shortly after moonrise, she thought: *This is the hour foretold.*

She threw a shawl around her slender shoulders and, carrying a lamp, opened the door without first asking who stood outside. Other residents of Palmyra might fear a stranger's call, but not Mera. People came to her for medicines and spells, for relief from pain, for potions to ease their anxieties, but none came to do her evil.

A man and a woman stood in the windy darkness of the threshold. The man was silver haired, with noble features, and wore a blue cloak fastened with a gold clasp; the woman was not much more than a child, her swollen abdomen barely concealed by her billowing cape. The first thing Mera saw upon opening the door were two frightened eyes set in a pale face. The man's face. The girl's face was twisted in pain.

Mera stood back and let the wind usher them in. She had to fight to close the door, the lamplight dancing wildly on the walls, her long black braids flying out behind her; when the door was secure, she turned to find the young woman sinking to her knees.

"It is her time—" the man said unnecessarily, struggling to hold her up in his arms.

Setting down the lamp, Mera nodded toward the pallet in the corner, and helped him lay the young woman down.

"They said in town that you would help—" he began.

"Her name," said Mera. "I must know her name."

His eyes looked haunted. "Is it necessary?"

Mera could feel his fear, it washed over her like a winter rain. When she paused to look into his terrified eyes, Mera laid a hand on his arm and murmured, "No matter. The Goddess knows it."

So, Mera thought as she quickly set to work. *They are fugitives. Running from someone or something. Wealthy, by the look of their fine clothes. And they have come a great distance, strangers to Palmyra.*

"She is my wife," the man said, standing in the center of the room, uncertain what to do. He was studying the midwife. When he had come to this house on the outskirts of the city he had expected to find a crone. But this woman was beautiful, and of an age he could not guess. He waved his hands helplessly. Smooth hands, Mera noted in the flickering lamplight. Long and beautiful hands, like the man himself, who was tall and handsome and refined. Roman, she concluded. A very important Roman.

She wished there were time for the proper preparations, to read the stars, to consult the astrological charts, but there was none. The birth was imminent.

The man watched the healer-woman as she hastily prepared the hot water and linens. Back at the inn, the hosteler had spoken of her in reverent tones. She was a sorceress, he had said, her magic was more powerful than even that of Ishtar. So why, wondered the Roman as he looked around the small room, did she appear to live meanly? Without even a slave to answer a late-night knock at her door?

"Hold her hands," said Mera, as she knelt between the young wife's legs. "Which is her god?"

He paused before saying, "We worship Hermes."

They come from Egypt! Mera thought, nodding in satisfaction. She herself was Egyptian and therefore intimately acquainted with Hermes the savior-god, so she leaned forward and traced the sign of the Cross of Hermes over the supine young woman, touching forehead, breast and shoulders. Then Mera settled back on her heels and crossed herself as well. Hermes was a powerful god.

It was a difficult delivery. The young woman's hips were narrow; she cried out frequently. Her husband knelt solicitously at her side, pressing a cloth to her forehead, securing her hands and murmuring to her in the Nile valley dialect Mera herself had spoken many years ago. It fell now like sweet music upon her ears. *I have been away for too long,* she thought, as she braced herself for the arrival of the baby. *Perhaps before I die the Goddess will grant me a last glimpse of my green river* . . .

"It is a boy," she said at last, sucking gently at the tiny nose and mouth.

The Roman hovered close, his shadow falling over the baby like a protective blanket. The young wife, relieved of her labor, sighed deeply. After Mera had tied and severed the cord, she placed the baby at its mother's breast and said softly, "You must say his names now. Protect him, little mother, before the desert *jinn* try to steal him away."

With dry lips pressed to the pink shell of his ear, the young woman whispered her son's soul-name, the one known only to him and the gods. And then, aloud and in a weak voice, she said softly, "Helios," his life-name.

Satisfied, Mera returned to her task, for the placenta must be delivered next. But as the wind outside rose to a howl and the doors and shutters rattled, she saw in the oblique light something that alarmed her. A hand, tiny and blue-white, was emerging through the birth canal.

A twin!

Again signing the Cross of Hermes, and adding the sacred sign of Isis, Mera steadied herself for the second birth. She prayed the young woman had the strength to see it through.

It seemed now the *jinn* were indeed at the door, and trying to steal away the two new lives, so ferociously did the wind shriek. Mera's small one-room house was of solid mud-brick, and yet it shuddered and shook as if it would topple at any moment. The young woman screamed with the wind. Her cheeks were crested scarlet; perspiration dampened her hair to her scalp. In desperation Mera tied an amulet around the poor girl's neck, a carved jade frog sacred to Hecate, goddess of midwives.

Strangely, the infant boy, still cradled against its mother's breast, had not yet made a sound.

At long last Mera was able to guide the second baby onto the waiting sheets. With profound relief she saw that it lived. But as she was cutting the cord, she heard a sound outside mingle with the wind, a sound that should not have been there. Mera brought her head up sharply and saw that the Roman was staring at the door.

"Horses," he said. "Soldiers."

Then there was thunderous banging on the door, not of someone knocking to come in, but of someone trying to break it down.

"They have found us," he said simply.

Mera was up on her feet in an instant. "Come!" she hissed and ran for the narrow door at the end of the room. She did not look back, did not see the red-cloaked soldiers burst in; without thinking, she plunged into the darkness of the storage lean-to that abutted her house and, with the newborn baby girl clasped wet and naked to her breast, climbed into the corncrib, curling herself as small as she could under the husks. As she huddled in the dark night of the crib, her skin pricked by the corn, barely breathing, Mera listened to the stamp of hobnailed sandals on the hard-packed dirt floor. There was a brief dialogue in Greek, a staccato demand and a reply, the whistle of metal through the air. Two sharp cries and then: silence.

Mera shivered uncontrollably. The baby trembled in her arms. Heavy footfalls sounded around the room, with one foray into the lean-to. Through the cracks in the bin she saw a light: someone was searching with a lamp. And then she heard the voice of the handsome Roman, weak and breathy: "There is no one, I tell you. The midwife was not at home. We are alone. I . . . *I* delivered the child myself . . . "

To her horror the baby in her arms started to whimper. Mera quickly placed her hand over the little face and whispered, "Blessed Mother, Queen of Heaven, don't let this baby be killed."

She held her breath again and listened. Now there was nothing around her but darkness and silence and the moaning wind. She waited. With the baby pressed to her bosom, her hand over its mouth, Mera lay crouched in the corncrib for what seemed like hours. Her body began to ache, the baby squirmed. But still she remained in hiding.

Finally, after what seemed an eternity, Mera thought she heard another voice in the wind. "Woman . . . " it called.

Cautiously she raised up. In the gloom of pre-dawn, Mera could just make out a crumpled form on the floor of the room, and she heard the Roman call out weakly, "Woman, they have gone . . . "

There was pain in every joint and muscle of her body from crouching so long in the corncrib, and as she limped to the man's side she saw that he was covered in blood. "They have taken her . . . " he croaked. "My wife, and the boy . . . "

Stunned, Mera looked over at the empty pallet. To have dragged a woman fresh from childbed, and her newborn baby with her!

The Roman raised a trembling arm. "My daughter . . . let me . . . "

They came to slay the father, Mera thought, as she lowered the naked infant to the father's dying hand, *and yet they took the mother and son alive. Why?*

"Her names . . . " he gasped. "I must give her her names before . . . "

Mera brought the baby's head down to the level of his mouth and watched his lips form her secret name, the name that was a child's spiritual bond with the gods and which no mortal must hear because of its powerful magic. And then, out loud, he spoke her life-name: "Selene. She is Selene . . . "

"Let me tend your wounds now," Mera said gently. But he stayed her with a shake of his head. And she saw why: The Roman lay sprawled in an unnatural position. "Take her away from here," he whispered. "At once! Tonight! They must not find her! Hide her. Care for her. She comes from the gods."

"But who *are* you? Who shall I tell her are her parents, her family?"

He swallowed with difficulty. "This ring . . . give it to her when she is older. It will tell her . . . everything. It will lead her to her destiny. She belongs to the gods . . . "

As Mera slid the heavy gold ring from his finger, the Roman died, and in the same instant, the child Selene started to cry.

Mera looked down and discovered in shock that there was something wrong with the baby's mouth—a small birth defect. And then she understood: It was a mark of the gods' special favor on the child. The Roman had spoken truly: This little girl did indeed come from the gods.

BOOK I
ANTIOCH
IN SYRIA

CHAPTER 1

S elene was crossing the market square when the accident occurred. She was in a section of the city she seldom visited, the northern suburb, with its wide avenues and villas of the rich, and she was here on this hot July day to visit a shop that sold rare herbal medicines. Her mother needed henbane seeds for a sleeping potion. What Mera did not grow in her herb garden and what she could not purchase in the great marketplace in the lower city, Selene was sent to procure from Paxis the Greek. Which was how she happened to be crossing the market square the moment the rug merchant met with his accident.

Selene saw it happen. The man had been securing rolls of carpet to the back of his donkey and had bent to pick up the tail of the rope when the animal had suddenly kicked out behind and caught the merchant a ferocious blow on the side of his head.

Selene stared for a moment, then ran to where he lay. Carelessly dropping her basket and its precious contents, she knelt by the unconscious man and took his head into her lap. He was bleeding terribly and his face was turning a dangerous dusky color.

A few passersby stopped to watch in mild curiosity, but no one made a move to help. Selene looked up at those around her. "H-help!" she cried. "He's h-h . . . " She grimaced as she tried, to no avail, to push the words out.

The people standing around her only stared. She read their expressions. *Can't talk,* they were thinking. *The girl must be simple.*

"H-he's hurt!" she blurted, as blood from the man's wound flowed over her hands.

The bystanders looked at one another. "He's beyond help," said a cloth merchant who had come running from his shop and who was now eyeing the expensive rugs, wondering how he could get his hands on them. "The magistrate'll see he's buried."

"He's not d-dead!" Selene said, struggling to make herself understood.

As people started to turn away, losing interest, Selene called after them, to help, to *do* something. It was not right; they couldn't just leave him. And what could *she* do, a girl not yet sixteen, alone in an unfamiliar section of town?

"What's going on?" came a voice from the crowd.

Selene looked up to see a man pushing through. He had an authoritative manner about him, and wore the white toga of Roman citizenship.

"The d-donkey k-kicked him," she struggled to say as plainly as possible. "In the head."

The stranger stared at her. His eyebrows gave him an angry look—there was the beginning of a permanent furrow between them; but the eyes beneath seemed kind. He studied her for a moment, her eyes pleading for help, her mouth struggling with clumsy words, then he said, "Very well," and dropped on one knee to make a quick examination of the rug merchant. "Come with me. We might be able to save him."

To Selene's relief the stranger signaled to a companion, a large, brawny slave, who hefted the unconscious man over his broad shoulders. Then they headed off down the street at a good pace, with Selene, who was tall, keeping stride with the two men. She gave no thought to her basket back in the square, now claimed by a beggar who couldn't believe his good luck; and she did not think of her mother who was waiting down in Antioch's poor quarter, waiting for the henbane seeds she needed for the abortion she was to perform that afternoon.

They entered through a gate in a high wall and Selene found herself being led across a garden full of summer flowers. Never in her life had she seen a house so grand, with rooms so large and airy. Selene's sandaled feet had never set foot upon such fine floors, so highly polished and inlaid with mosaics, nor had she ever imagined walls could be so beautifully marbled or furniture so rich and elegant. She turned her head this way and that as she followed the gentleman and his slave through the atrium and finally into a room bigger than her whole house, sparsely furnished with couch, chair and gilt-legged tables.

When the unconscious rug seller was laid upon the couch, propped up with pillows at his back, the stranger removed his white toga and set about examining the wound.

"I am Andreas," he said to Selene. "I am a physician."

The slave began at once to open drawers and boxes, to pour water into a basin, to set out linens and instruments. Selene watched with wide eyes as the physician swiftly and deftly shaved the rug merchant's scalp, then proceeded to wash the bleeding wound with wine and vinegar.

While he worked, Selene stole a better look around the room. How unlike the room where Mera practiced her healing! In Selene's house, to which a well-worn path had been beaten by Mera's myriad patients, their one room was cluttered with the paraphernalia of her mother's profession: crutches were hung on walls, shelves were crammed with jars; herbs and roots dangled from the low ceiling; bowls were tucked inside other bowls and bandages were wedged into every available cranny. It was a comfortable and familiar haven for the sick and injured of Antioch's poor quarter; and it was the only home Selene had known in her nearly sixteen years.

But *this* room! Large and breezy, with a shining floor and sunlight streaming through a window, delicate tables neatly laid out with instruments and sponges, small jars standing in orderly rows. And in the corner, a statue of Aesculapius, god of healing. This was the treatment room of a Greek physician, Selene realized; she had heard how advanced and modern such doctors were.

When she saw Andreas expertly cut the rug merchant's scalp with a knife and pack it open with lint, she knew she had guessed correctly. This man might even have been trained in Alexandria!

Before proceeding further, Andreas paused to say to Selene, "You can wait in the atrium. My slave will call you when I am finished."

But she shook her head and remained where she was.

He gave her a brief, quizzical look, then addressed the task. "We must first determine if there is a fracture," Andreas said quietly, in a refined Greek Selene seldom heard in her own neighborhood. "And to find the fracture we apply this . . . "

As Andreas spread a thick black paste onto the exposed skull, Selene stepped up closer and watched in fascination. She saw that his hands were smooth, with long, slender fingers. After the paste had been left on a moment, Andreas scraped it off. "There," he said, pointing to a black line in the bone. "There is the fracture. See how it is indented, how it presses downward? The brain is under pressure here. I must relieve that pressure or this man will surely die."

Selene's eyes grew wider. In all her years of helping her mother, of

working at Mera's side and learning the ancient healing arts, Selene had
never seen a skull opened.

Andreas next picked up an instrument that looked very much like the
drill Selene and her mother used to start wood fires. "Malachus," he said
to the slave, "steady it for me if you will, please."

Selene stared dumbfounded as the drill did its work; Andreas' hands
went back and forth swiftly in a tireless, unbroken rhythm, and every so
often Malachus rinsed the wound with water.

Finally the drill came to a halt and Andreas laid it aside, saying, "There
it is, the egg that would have killed him or paralyzed him for life."

Selene saw it. The demon's egg, nesting between skull and brain, laid
by the blow from the donkey's hoof. She stared in awe. Whenever head
injuries were brought to her own house, Selene's mother made a poultice
of opium and bread and spread it on the victim's head like a hat. Then
she said a prayer, gave him a magic amulet and sent him away. Mera never
laid knife to scalp or opened the skull; and most patients with such an
affliction died. Selene now wondered, with racing heart, if she was about
to witness a miracle.

Andreas picked up what looked like a blunt trowel, gently slipped it
under the skull, and elevated the bruised bone off the brain. At once the
unconscious man let out a moan, his color improved and his breathing
grew deeper.

As Andreas worked, Selene studied his profile. In deep concentration he
looked stern, the brows lowered down over dark gray-blue eyes. He had a
large, arched nose that suited his angry look, his lips were set in a thin line
and his jaw, firm and square, was neatly outlined by a trim dark-brown
beard. Selene thought he must be about thirty years old, but there was a
hint of graying at the temples, an indication that Andreas was one of those
men who are silver haired by the time they turn forty.

The egg came out whole, but brought with it an alarming rush of blood.
Andreas worked on, calmly and silently.

Selene marveled at his calmness. His face was grave, but in concentration, not in fear. His eyes scarcely blinked; his breathing was cautious and
shallow. His hands kept up their continual work, while all the time Selene
thought surely he would at any moment throw down his instruments and
cry, "It cannot be done!"

But Andreas kept at it, his eyes, his hands, his whole being focused upon
his patient, as if nothing else in the universe existed; and his undaunted
resolve in the face of such odds filled Selene with respect.

Finally the hemorrhage began to abate. When at last Andreas did put
down his instruments, it was to rinse the wound with wine, fill the hole

with warm beeswax, and then bring the edges of the scalp together. Finally, washing his hands again, Andreas said to Selene, "If he regains consciousness in three days, he will live. If not, he will die."

Selene met the physician's gaze for an instant, then turned away, wishing she could put into clear words the many questions that crowded into her mind.

Suddenly, the man on the couch cried out in his sleep and started thrashing his arms. The slave Malachus, who had been bandaging the head, jumped back.

"A seizure!" said Andreas, running to the man's side. He tried to take hold of an arm but was thrown back. "Get rope!" he said to Malachus. "And fetch Polibus. We'll need help."

Selene watched as the rug merchant, still unconscious and whey-faced, writhed and bucked on the couch like a man tormented by devils. Andreas tried to restrain him, to keep him from throwing himself to the floor, but was kept away by flying fists. The poor man's head banged back and forth against the headrest, splitting the wound anew and starting fresh bleeding beneath the bandage. A strange growl came from his throat, and the cords of his neck stood out.

Malachus returned with a giant slave, and it took all three men to lash the rug merchant's arms and legs to the couch. But even when that was done the seizure continued, driving the injured man to fight against the restraints. Selene could hear his bones and joints creaking as if they were about to break. Andreas said darkly, "There is nothing we can do. He will surely kill himself."

Selene stared at the physician, and for a moment their eyes met and held, then she looked back down at the man on the couch. There *was* one chance . . .

Without a word Selene stepped forward. She closed her eyes and formed an image in her mind—the picture of a flame, a single golden flame burning gently up from its source; all around that flame there was darkness. Selene's mind filled with the vision of the steadily burning flame until she began to feel its warmth and could hear the soft murmur of its energy. Concentrating on the flame, the flame that burned at the core of her soul, Selene slowed her breathing and forced her body to relax. It was a process that felt as if it took hours, but which in fact took only moments—the gathering of her strength and the centering of it in that "flame."

To those who watched, Andreas and his two slaves, she appeared to have gone into a kind of sleep; her face betrayed none of the intense concentration inside her mind, there was no evidence of the centering of the forces slowly building inside her. They watched, puzzled, as the girl, with purposeful, even breath, slowly raised her hands and held them directly over the writhing body of the rug merchant. The hands hovered outstretched, palms downward, close but not touching the man, and they started to move, at first in small, searching circles, then gradually widening until they traced a path in the air the length of his body.

In her mind Selene was seeing the flame. Nothing else existed. Just as Andreas had directed his mind totally to the open skull, so now did Selene channel all her thoughts and power into the image of the flame. And when she "touched" it, the flame's heat went out from her mind, down her arms, and through her hands, radiating out over the half-reclining body.

Andreas watched in curiosity as the girl's slender form swayed slightly. He studied her face—the high cheekbones, the full-lipped mouth—which had, moments before, been shy and self-conscious but which was now strangely serene. She held out her long arms and outstretched hands until finally, by slow degrees, the tortured body of the rug merchant started to relax, then to toss and turn, then twitch, then ultimately recede into sleep.

Selene opened her eyes and blinked, as if waking up.

Andreas frowned. "What did you do?"

She avoided looking at him, timid once again. Selene was unused to talking to strangers. Invariably there was the look of surprise on hearing such faulty speech come from her lovely mouth; and then would come the impatience, and the expression on the face that said *simpleton.* She should be used to it by now, Selene often told herself, after all these years of being cruelly teased by other children, of being ignored at market stalls, of having people bark, "Speak clearly, why don't you!" Her mother had told her her affliction was a sign of favor from the gods, the tied-tongue she had been born with and which had later been corrected. Mera said it was the gods' mark that Selene was special to them. But why did other people not seem to see it as such?

And yet, to Selene's amazement, the handsome face of the Greek physician showed none of the usual reactions. She forced herself to meet his gaze, and looked into the dark eyes that were at once stern and gentle, and she thought she saw compassion there. So she ventured to say, "I sh-showed him the w-way to sleep."

"How?"

Selene spoke as slowly as she could. It was difficult to make herself understood; it took time, and so people usually finished her sentences for her. "It is s-something my m-mother taught me."

Andreas raised an eyebrow. "Your mother?"

"She is a h-healer."

Andreas thought for a moment, then, remembering the rug merchant's fresh injury, strode to the couch, removed the bloody bandage and commenced to repair the wound.

When he was finished he picked up the tip of a rusty spear and scraped it with a knife over the wound. "This rust will help the wound to heal faster," he said, seeing Selene's questioning look. "It is known that in copper and iron mines the ulcers of slaves heal faster than anywhere else. Although why this is, no one knows." He put a new bandage on the rug merchant's wound, gently replaced the sleeping head against the headrest, then turned to Selene. "Tell me about what you did to calm him. How did you do it?"

Selene looked down at the floor, overcome with shyness. "I didn't d-do anything," she said awkwardly. "I g-guided his en-en—" Her hands curled into fists at her sides. "His *energies* out of their con-confusion."

"Is it a cure?"

She shook her head. "It d-does not heal. It only h-helps."

"Does it always work?"

"No."

"But *how?*" he pressed. "How did you do it?"

Selene chewed on her lip as she studied the pattern in the marble floor. "It's an ancient technique. You s-see a flame."

Andreas's dark eyes contemplated her. The girl was beautiful. As he stared, an image came to his mind, the memory of a rare flower he had once seen, called an hibiscus. Selene's features were lovely, especially her mouth. What irony, he thought; that a mouth so perfect to look upon should be so imperfect in its function. She was not tongue-tied, he could see that when she spoke. Why, then, could she not speak properly?

When the rug merchant let out a loud snore, Andreas smiled and said, "Your flame worked magic, it seems."

Selene shyly raised her eyes and saw how the smile transformed his face. When the scowl faded, Andreas looked younger, and Selene found herself wondering about him.

And Andreas was wondering about her. The speech defect was possibly the result of a deformity corrected in childhood, but corrected at a late age and not followed by speech training. Andreas guessed what heartbreaks the affliction must cause the poor girl, because he could see how it governed her now—a beautiful girl, truly, but painfully shy, her posture apologetic, her gaze self-conscious and timid. Why didn't someone help her?

A shadow passed over Andreas's face and the furrow returned between his eyebrows—a premature crease in a man just thirty, the result of being too bitter for too long.

Why should I care? he asked himself, having for years now passed the point of no longer caring.

A breeze came through the window and stirred the gauze hangings. The hot breath of summer was layered with scents of woodsmoke, flowers in bloom, the green river creeping to the sea. The wind moaned through the house of Andreas the physician and brought him out of his thoughts.

"You'll need help with your friend," he said, signaling to Malachus. "My slave will assist you."

Selene gave him a puzzled look.

"I assume you want to take him home," Andreas said.

"H-home?"

"Yes, so he can recover. What had you thought of doing with him?"

Selene looked confused. "I-I don't know. I d-don't know who he is."

Blank surprise stood on the physician's face. "You don't know the man?"

"I was walking th-through the m-m—" Selene's hands flew to her mouth. "My basket!"

"Do you mean to tell me you don't know this man? Then why on earth were you calling for help?"

"My basket!" she cried again. "The l-last of our m-money . . . the m-medicine . . . "

Impatience crept into Andreas's tone. "If you don't know this man— and *I* certainly do not know him—then why are we here? And why did I"—he gestured toward the couch—"do *that?*"

Selene looked over at the bandaged head. "H-he was hurt."

"He was hurt," Andreas repeated incredulously, casting a glance at Malachus, who was looking amused. Andreas scowled. "A whole afternoon spent working on a stranger," he said. "What am I supposed to do with him now?"

Selene looked helpless.

Andreas's impatience turned to irritation. "You expected me to keep him here, didn't you? I do not keep patients in my house. That is not a physician's job. I have mended him. It is now the job of his family to see that he recovers."

The look on Selene's face turned to one of desperation. "B-but I don't know who his family is!"

Andreas stared at her. Did this child really care what happened to a total stranger? Why should she care? No one else in the world did. When was the last time he had met someone so utterly naïve? Not in years, not since his days back in Corinth when he had gazed at his own reflection in a pond and had seen a callow youth staring back at him, a smooth-faced boy on the threshold of disillusionment.

Andreas reined in his temper. This girl stood there now, just on the other side of that inevitable brink, still guileless, still unspoiled. She had stopped in the marketplace, a girl barely able to speak, to give aid to a man she didn't know.

Selene saw the look on his face and it brought back an old thought, one that had pricked her mind for as long as she could remember: the perplexing and apparently insoluble problem of *what to do with people.*

Selene witnessed it time and again at her mother's house: strangers appearing at the door for treatment and then having nowhere to go to convalesce. People who lived alone, widows with no friends, invalids who lived as recluses, all of whom Mera treated in their beds and who had no one to care for them afterward. And in the streets—oh, the streets! Especially in the squalid quarter that abutted the harbor, where children roamed in packs, where prostitutes gave birth in alleyways, where nameless sailors fell ill and died on the cobblestones. People lay where they fell because there was no one to care, nowhere for them to go.

Selene said, "P-please, can't you t-take care . . . "

Andreas regarded her for a moment, mentally chastising himself for his haste in getting involved—the greenest medical student knew to ask questions first! Then he felt himself give way to the look in her eyes. "Very well then," he said at last, "I shall send Malachus out to inquire in the marketplace. Perhaps someone there knows this man. In the meantime," Andreas scowled as he reached for his white toga and draped it over his shoulder, "he can recover in my slaves' quarters."

Selene smiled in gratitude.

Andreas looked at her a moment longer. There was an inexplicable magnetism about her, although he could not put his finger on why. She certainly was not from a well-to-do home—her clothes indicated a poor family. And how old could she be? Not yet sixteen, for she still wore a girl's dress that ended at her knees. But the day was not far off, he suspected, when she would receive the *stola* and *palla* of womanhood. His eyes were drawn finally to her mouth, which was almost hypnotic in its sensuality. It was a heavy, pouting mouth, like the tropical flower that once again came to his mind, the hibiscus opened on its stem. It lent to her face an exotic, seductive quality, and a haunting beauty. Andreas hoped the girl was not aware of the trick the gods had played, having bestowed on her a feature that was at once her most singular gift but also, ironically, her blemish. What a surprise it had been for him, as it must be for anyone who met her for the first time, to hear clumsy words tumble from those lips. It made a mockery of beauty, and he felt inexplicably moved by it.

On impulse Andreas said, "What was it you lost in the market?"

"H-henbane," she said, and held up fingers to indicate the amount.

Andreas turned to Malachus. "Give her what she needs. And a basket, too."

Surprised, the slave said, "Yes, master," and went to a row of jars.

The hardness returned to the physician's face, a dark brooding look that aged him, but his voice was kind. "Take care in the future whom you willy-nilly stop to aid. The next man's house might not be as safe as this one."

Selene blushed fiercely as she received the basket from Malachus, thanked Andreas in her clumsy way and hurried out.

He stood for a long time afterward, listening to her sandaled footsteps echo down the corridor. He shook his head. What an extraordinary afternoon this had been! First he had operated on a stranger who, in all likelihood, would never pay him, and then he had sent away the girl responsible for it well supplied with the most costly medicine. And he had received nothing in return—not even, he suddenly realized, her name!

C H A P T E R   2

There, do you see it, daughter?" whispered Mera. Selene bent close to look down the bronze vaginal speculum at the mouth of the womb. "That is the *cervix*," murmured Mera. "The blessed doorway through which we all make our entries into the world. Do you see the string I tied around the cervix months ago, when it threatened to open up before the baby's time had come? Watch closely what I do now."

Selene never ceased to marvel at her mother's knowledge; Mera seemed to know everything there was to know about birth and life. She knew the herbs that increased fertility in women who wanted to have children, or the ointments that prevented conception in women who did not desire pregnancy; she knew moon-cycles and auspicious days for conceiving and giving birth; she knew which amulets worked best to protect the baby in the womb; and she even knew how to perform safe abortions on women who must not, for their own reasons, bear a child. That very afternoon, Selene had watched Mera insert a sliver of bamboo into the womb of a pregnant woman whose health was so frail that childbirth would kill her. The bamboo, Mera had explained, placed in the mouth of the womb, would slowly absorb the woman's bodily moisture, and as it did so, it would expand, forcing the cervix open and releasing the tiny and as yet unformed child.

The woman whom Mera and Selene attended tonight, in her final stages of labor, was a young wife who had miscarried three times in the past year and who had begun to despair of ever having a child. Her young husband, a tentmaker who desperately wanted sons to carry on the trade, had begun to be urged by his brothers to think of divorcing her and taking another wife.

And so the woman had come to Mera's house, two months pregnant and afraid of losing this one, her last hope. Mera had done the reverse of what she would do for a woman requesting abortion. Instead of gently forcing the cervix open to dispel the baby, she had secured it closed by stitching a string around the opening of the womb, pulling it tight like a pursed mouth. Then she had confined the young woman to bed through the winter and spring.

Now the nine months were ended; the young wife lay on her bed, her swollen abdomen rippling with healthy contractions, her tentmaker husband kneeling anxiously at her side.

"We must be very careful now," Mera said quietly. "Hold the light steady, daughter. I will cut the string."

Selene committed to memory each word, each movement her mother made. Ever since she'd been three years old and able to tell the difference between the safe mint leaf and the deadly one of the foxglove, Selene had worked and learned at her mother's side. Tonight, when they had arrived at the tentmaker's house, Selene had helped her with the preparations: lighting the sacred fire of Isis, heating the copper instruments in the flames to chase out the evil spirits of infection, singing incantations to Hecate, goddess of midwifery, asking her to help this young mother tonight, and finally laying the sheets and towels out in readiness for the birth.

Then, first washing her hands, Mera had taken over. Her aquiline face seemed to be sculpted in sharp black and brown planes.

While the young woman moaned and clutched her husband's wrists, Mera steadily guided a long forceps over the groove of the vaginal speculum, and seized the free end of the string with the delicate copper teeth. Then she picked up the long knife and fingered it in deep concentration.

The womb did not lie still; it moved with life. Each contraction pressed the baby's head against an opening that was sealed shut. Once, the forceps lost the string and Mera grasped it again. The young wife cried out and tried to raise her hips. Selene had to reposition the lamp several times; she held the speculum steady for her mother. There was only a narrow wall of soft flesh between the knife blade and the baby's tender skull.

"Hold her steady," Mera said to the pale-faced husband. "I must cut now. I cannot delay any longer."

Selene felt her heart race. No matter how many births she had attended, she would never come to think of them as routine. Each childbirth was different; each brought its own element of chance, of wonder, of danger. This baby, Selene knew, was at risk of suffocating in the womb, of dying from the contractions and from the exhaustion of trying to be born.

The city beyond the walls of the tentmaker's house lay silent in the hot night. Antioch's half-million inhabitants slept, many on rooftops, while Mera the Egyptian healer-woman worked her magic once again.

The eyes of the young husband were wide with fear. His forehead glistened with sweat. Selene smiled, tried to calm and reassure him, touching his arm. Sometimes the men suffered as much as the women during childbirth; they were baffled and helpless in the face of this ultimate mystery. Selene had seen husbands faint at the bedside; most preferred to wait outdoors, in the company of friends. This young man was a good husband. Plainly distressed and clearly wishing he were elsewhere, he nonetheless stayed with his wife and tried to help her see the ordeal through.

Selene reached out again, laying a hand on his arm; he turned to face her, swallowed hard and nodded.

Mera kept her eyes steady. Her back was rigid, her chest barely rising and falling. One slip of the knife, now, and all would be lost.

Suddenly the womb relaxed for an instant, and she saw the brief retreat of the baby's head; she brought the long knife up and swiftly, cleanly, cut the string.

The young wife cried out, Mera hurriedly took the instruments away, and positioned herself for the birth. Selene moved around to the side, knelt by the young mother, and laid a moist cloth on her forehead. The labor came in earnest now; the contractions were so close together that there was no rest in between. Mera instructed the wife when to push, when to wait. The young husband, as pale as the sheets his wife lay upon, bit down on his lip. Selene placed her hands on either side of the wife's head, closed her eyes and conjured up the soul flame. She could not offer words of solace; she was not gifted with the facile, soothing speech of other healers. But in her silence her hands spoke for her. Her long, cool fingers conveyed reassurance, calm and strength.

Finally the young wife gave one last cry, and the child came into Mera's waiting hands.

He shrieked immediately, a healthy little boy, and everyone laughed, the young husband the loudest. Overcome, he gathered his wife into his arms and whispered private promises into her ear.

It was the second watch of the night when Mera and Selene returned to their own house. While Mera went to a cupboard to find something to drink, Selene began to wash the copper birthing instruments, and to replenish the medicines her mother had used from her medicine box.

Selene was tired but excited; her mind would not stay upon the jars of ergot and white hellebore, universal herbs of midwifery. Her thoughts returned instead to the villa in the upper city where, that afternoon, Andreas the physician had performed a miracle.

She could remember every detail, as if he stood before her now in the glow of the lamplight: the smooth curls of his dark-brown hair brushed down upon his high forehead; the gold trim of his white tunic and the well-muscled legs showing beneath the hem; his hands working on the injured skull as if it were a work of art. She was looking again into his eyes, dark blue and slanting slightly downwards at the corners, compassionate eyes overshadowed by angry brows. And she was again wondering if something had happened to Andreas to harden him so.

Selene glanced at her mother, who was busy at the cupboard in the alcove, and wondered if she could talk to her about Andreas. There was so much Selene wanted to know. She had never felt this way before; it confused her. She did not understand why she was unable to concentrate on her work—during the abortion that afternoon on the Lady Flavia, or tonight, during the birth of the tentmaker's son. No matter how hard Selene had forced her concentration upon the task at hand, the handsome face of the Greek physician had kept intruding.

Selene's experience with men was slight. Beyond helping Mera with male patients—the occasional sailor with gum problems, the dock worker with the broken leg—Selene rarely came into close contact with boys or men, and certainly was never alone with them for any length of time, as she had been with Andreas. The boys in her neighborhood, on this crowded little street of the lower class, ignored Selene. She was pretty, but they grew impatient with her when she tried to speak.

Selene watched her mother pour something from a jar and drink it. Mera knew everything, Selene thought; there was nothing her mother did not understand, could not explain. And yet . . .

Selene had never heard her mother talk of love, of men, of husbands and marriage. When she was little, Selene had been told about her father

—a fisherman who had died in a boating accident before she was born—but beyond that, Mera was silent on the subject. And although men did sometimes show interest in Mera, and Selene had seen them come to the house with gifts, her mother gently but firmly turned them away.

Selene returned to the instruments she was washing.

Marriage. She had never really thought about it before. Whenever she thought of her own future, she saw herself living the way her mother did, modestly and alone in a little house, tending a small herb garden, delivering babies.

Was Andreas married? Selene wondered as she dried and wrapped the instruments in a soft cloth and stored them away. Did he live alone in that big house? And why, when his eyes showed evidence of a compassionate soul, did his face seem to be molded in anger?

How patiently he had waited while she spoke, not finishing sentences for her, or ignoring her as other people did! Andreas. What a beautiful name. She wished she could say it out loud, feel it on her tongue. Tonight, when she went to bed, Selene knew she was not going to fall asleep but would lie awake instead and re-live every second of the extraordinary afternoon.

In the shadow of the alcove where they cooked their meals, Selene's mother watched her daughter and drank secretively from a jar. Drawing the back of her hand across her mouth, Mera set the jar down and closed her eyes. She could feel the strong medicine start to fill her veins, could imagine, even before it in fact arrived, the relief it would bring to the troubled part of her body. The pain would subside; for another night, Mera hoped, she would be free of it.

But, she thought, replacing the jar in its hiding place, *for how much longer?* Soon, she knew, she was going to have to increase the dose. And then it would be impossible to keep her illness a secret from Selene.

The wind whistling down the deserted street outside reminded Mera of another night, almost sixteen years ago, when such a wind had delivered a strange cargo to her door. She was recalling it with increasing frequency these days and she knew why: It was because the dreams had come back.

Those awful dreams that had plagued her sleep in the first days of her flight from Palmyra—dreams of red-cloaked soldiers suddenly bursting into the house, seizing Selene, dragging her out into the night. Sometimes, in the dreams, Mera saw them murder the girl. Other times, Selene was carried away into an inky darkness that swallowed her up. Each time Mera had wakened to feel her heart racing, her nightdress damp with perspiration. The dreams had stopped years ago and she had forgotten them; but now they had returned, and they were dreams of such intense realism that Mera was becoming afraid to fall asleep.

What did they mean? Why had they come back now, after all these years? Was it because Selene was soon to turn sixteen and go through the rites of womanhood? Were the dreams a warning from the gods? And if so, a warning against what?

As she stood in the darkness of the alcove, waiting for the medicine to ease the pain in her body, Mera thought about herself, about her life.

A tall and slender woman, still attractive after fifty-one summers, she had had a hard life, one filled with periods of rootlessness and roaming, of having to learn new cities, of knowing only occasional, impersonal love from men whose names she had forgotten; fifty-one years of wondering what her purpose was supposed to be, of waiting for the Goddess to reveal the reason why She had singled out Mera to be a healer of bodies and spirits.

And why had she been given this child? Had all her life been but a preparation for raising this orphaned baby? And Selene herself was a mystery. Although Mera was, in many ways, so wise and knowledgeable, she had not been able to fathom the enigma that was her daughter.

Mera had come away from that house in Palmyra with but a small legacy to pass on to the child when she reached maturity: a ring, a lock of the dead Roman's hair, a small piece of the linen sheet that had received the newborn twin brother. They were powerful tokens, and they were the sum total of Selene's identity.

What these tokens represented, Mera had never been able to unravel. But she had kept them against the day when she would pass them on to Selene; the girl herself must carry on the search.

Safely locked away in a small box was an ivory rose. It had been given to Mera years ago in the city of Byblos, payment from a grateful patient. It was a rose the size of a plum, carved out of the purest ivory, unblemished and perfect in every detail; it was hollow, meant to carry keepsakes. Mera had placed the ring, the lock of hair and the strip of linen into it and sealed it; over the years, she had taken the ivory rose out of its box and had shown it to Selene, not telling her of its contents but impressing upon the girl the value and importance of the rose, a value beyond measuring. Selene had asked what was inside the rose's secret heart, but Mera had said she must wait until she was older, until her sixteenth birthday. Then, like all girls, Selene would go through the ritual of passing from childhood into womanhood.

And what shall I tell her on that day? Mera asked herself, as she watched Selene putting away the medicine box. *I will have to tell her the truth—*

*that I am not her real mother. But when I take that security away from her,
I shall have no real parents to give to her, in my place.*

As the medicine finally started to work its spell, Mera thought again of
that night nearly sixteen years ago. She saw once more the hasty flight from
the house that had been her home for five years, bundling all she owned
—her herbs and medicines, instruments and magic scrolls—into a box and
striking north with the newborn baby girl snug in a pannier lashed to
Mera's old donkey. It had been a long and arduous trek, a lonely one and
fraught with fear. She had backtracked several times, to confuse her trail
in case any red-cloaked soldiers were following, stopping in towns and at
oases only long enough to rest, and then on again, joining caravans going
west, sharing water with desert Arabs, praying in the temples of strange
gods, until she came to the green city of Antioch nestled in the verdant
bosom of the Orontes valley. It was on the outskirts of this metropolitan
city that Mera had read the night sky and knew that her wandering was
over: The stars and planets had said that the child would be safe here.

And so she had been, safe and happy for nearly sixteen years, growing
and learning and bringing into Mera's lonely life the only real love she had
ever known.

Now all that was about to end. There was little time left, and Mera was
filled with an increasing sense of urgency. In twenty days the first ceremony was going to take place—the most important day in a girl's life, when
she officially laid aside the trappings of childhood, and put on the *stola,*
the long dress of womanhood. She would cut off one of her maidenly curls
and consecrate it to the household gods.

For most girls, the Dressing Ceremony ended with a great feast attended by friends and relatives; but for Selene there was to be one more
rite she must pass through. On the first night of the full moon after her
birthday, twenty-eight days from tonight, Selene would be taken by her
mother up into the mountains nearby and there receive her initiation into
the deeper Mysteries.

Mera had taught Selene everything she knew of the healing arts—
ancient skills that had been handed down from mother to daughter
through the centuries, just as Mera had received them from her own
mother. But now must come the passing on of the ultimate Secrets, in a
ritual Mera herself had undergone years ago in the Egyptian desert. It was
not enough to know the herbs and their preparations; a healer-woman
must also be joined spiritually to the Goddess, because from the Goddess
comes all healing.

Nothing must prevent that initiation from taking place, Mera thought as she watched Selene get ready for bed. *Not even,* she thought grimly, *my own death.*

Mera closed her eyes and tried to conjure the image of her soul flame, so that she might speed the opium to the troubled part of her body. But she was too tense; her mind was too set on the secular plane. She was worried about Selene, worried for her future. Mera was dying. Very soon, Selene was going to be alone in the world. Was she prepared? And how will she survive, she who is still afraid to speak, unable to communicate?

Selene had been born with her tongue frozen to the floor of her mouth, and it had not been until she was seven years old that Mera had been able to find a surgeon trained and skillful enough to cut it free. Until that day, Selene had never spoken; but even after the operation, she had had difficulty learning to speak properly. And then, over the years, because other children made fun of her and adults shouted at her to hurry up and say what she had to say, the speech defect had gotten worse instead of better. What little instruction Mera had been able to give had been repeatedly counteracted by the intolerance of the world outside. And so now, a scant twenty days before her Dressing Ceremony and official debut as an adult, Selene was burdened with a crippling shyness.

Blessed Isis, Mera prayed, let me live long enough to pass my mantle on to Selene. Grant me the time to see her through the rites, to deliver her into womanhood and independence. And please, Blessed Isis, keep my daughter pure until the day of her initiation into the Mysteries . . .

A dark look came over Mera's face as she recalled the agitated state in which Selene had returned from the upper city that afternoon.

The basket on her arm had not been the same one she had left the house with that morning, and it contained far more henbane than they had had money for. Selene had babbled out an incoherent tale about a man getting kicked by a donkey, a handsome Greek physician, a miracle cure. Mera had never before heard such a breathless run of speech from her daughter. "He b-burned his instruments in the f-fire f-first," Selene managed to say. "And he w-washed his hands fir-first."

"Yes," Mera had replied. "But was the fire gotten from a temple, for otherwise it will do no good. And did he burn no incense? What magic amulets did he wrap inside the bandage, what prayers did he recite, what gods were in the room?" It was all to no avail, Mera believed, to be the best trained physician in the world if one did not enlist the aid of the gods. And to use the knife! For the lancing of a boil, yes, or to cut a string from a cervix; but to delve beneath human flesh was arrogance, sacrilege. Mera placed her trust in herbs and spells; surgery was for charlatans and would-be heroes.

As she left the alcove to get ready for bed, Mera thought again of the look on Selene's face when she spoke of the Greek physician. It was a look Mera had never seen there before, and it had reminded her of the urgency of these final days. Selene must come to her initiation pure in spirit, in heart, in body. There must be no distractions, no mind to the flesh. There would be fasting and prayer and meditation, to bring the girl to cosmic consciousness. She would have to guard Selene in these last, precious twenty-eight days.

Mera lay down on her pallet and sighed wearily. It had been a long day. That morning she had set and splinted the broken arm of a fishmonger's wife, her right arm, as it almost always was with women. The woman claimed she had broken it falling on the stairs, but Mera knew the truth: The arm had been broken when it had been raised in defense against a raging husband. Threatened, a woman raises her arm to her face, and the arm then receives the blow intended for her head. Mera had seen the same injury countless times over the years.

After the fishmonger's wife, there had been a boil to lance, an infected ear to drain, herbs to grind and in the afternoon, Lady Flavia's abortion. Most of this had been done without the assistance of her daughter, who had gotten herself involved again in the misfortunes of a stranger.

Selene seemed to feel obliged to stop and help every unfortunate she encountered, no matter how futile or pointless the effort. As a small child, she had brought home injured animals, making little boxes for them, nursing them back to health before setting them free. Later, she had kept her dolls in beds and had wrapped their wooden arms and legs in bandages. Where Selene got this notion, the concept of a house where sick people dwelt together, Mera had no idea. And she half suspected that, if she could, her unworldly daughter would bring home and take care of every wretched creature under the sun.

Mera stared up into the darkness, and in that darkness she saw her immediate future—death. *I had thought I would have years to go yet, but fate bids otherwise.*

The lump in her side, not there one day but there the next, all of a sudden, and growing rapidly, brought home to Mera the immutable reality of life's brevity and of human mortality. Life had been rolling as predictably as the Orontes River; but now it was filled with a desperate urgency as the days seemed to rush by in a flood. *I will go to the temple and consult with the Oracle. I must know what future lies in Selene's stars.*

Mera felt a sharp stab in her side and realized, to her dismay, that the medicine was not working after all.

CHAPTER 3

They were in a tavern in Antioch's red-light district, the street by the docks where prostitutes hung red lanterns above their doorways to let arriving sailors know they were open for business.

Andreas and Naso the sea captain sat in a corner of the tavern, comfortably out of the way of the drunken crowd, idly watching a pair of naked dancing girls weave to the rhythm of cymbals and flute. Andreas watched with detachment. Although as a physician female nakedness was nothing new to him, he was nonetheless not beyond the seductive effect of swaying breasts and bellies. In his travels, Andreas had known many dancing girls. But tonight, try though he did to deliver himself into the spirit of merrymaking, he found himself maddeningly distracted. He could not get that girl out of his mind, the one from the marketplace.

There were mostly seamen crammed within the walls of Apollo's Cock, a rowdy, drunken bunch of sailors just come in from a long sea voyage or enjoying a final binge before setting sail. They came to Antioch's busy port, crossroads of the Roman Empire and beyond, from all over the world; men who spun out the most incredible tales, whose skins were tough as hides, whose eyes were washed colorless from the sun-glare on rolling seas, whose appetites were enormous but whose wants were simple and few. They were homeless, grizzled men, outcasts of society, and yet, ironically, a breed with whom the refined Andreas felt very much at home. Such as the gnarled, sun-blackened Naso, who boasted having the biggest nose in Syria and therefore in the world. Three times in the past, Andreas and Naso had entered into their peculiar contract, and they were here again tonight to work out the terms of a fourth.

The captain drained the last of his mug and signaled to the serving girl for another, noticing that Andreas, as usual, still nursed his one beer, hardly touching it. Despite their years of acquaintance and their various adventures together the quiet physician remained a mystery to Naso.

He had no idea what drew the man to ships and harbors in a regular and inexplicable cycle. Naso had witnessed the strange urge three times in the past, when Andreas had sailed with him. The physician would close up his house, send his patients elsewhere and buy passage on a ship bound for distant ports. When he boarded, Andreas would be aloof and self-involved, a curious, searching hunger in his eyes. He would spend weeks up on deck, staring out at the horizon, keeping apart from the crew, taking meals alone; and then, just when Naso would start to worry and think, *He's going to jump overboard*, Andreas would come around. He would start smiling, talking to the crew, dining with the captain until ultimately he would return home like a man purged.

It was in him again tonight, the captain knew. Naso had seen that look in Alexandria, in Byblos, in Caesarea—the port cities where the itinerant physician had lived. The poison was in Andreas's veins once more. When he had heard last year that Andreas had bought a house in Antioch, Naso had had hope for his friend. *He will settle down now*, the captain had thought, *he will marry*. But here was Andreas, after only a few months in his fine villa, haunting the docks once again for a ship.

What was it that periodically drove him to sea? Naso did not know and could never ask. He had heard the saying among medicos: "Physician, heal yourself." But the sea captain suspected that the wound piercing Andreas's heart was beyond the reach of balms and stitches.

"We sail at dawn, with the tide," Naso said, when he received his new mug of beer. There was a plate of sausages on their table; wrapping one in a round of flat bread and stuffing it into his mouth, he added, "Bound for the Pillars of Hercules this time, and beyond. That suit you, Andreas?"

Andreas nodded. He never cared where the ship was bound, only that it was going. He had told his slave Malachus that it might be six months this time, and Malachus, who was familiar with his master's strange need to go to sea from time to time, would take care of the house in his absence.

"You goin' take a girl tonight, son?" asked Naso, having already picked one out for himself. "Be a long spell before we see a woman again."

But Andreas shook his head. Women were the least of his needs now; what plagued him tonight was only one woman—one girl. The one with the basket, the one with the strangely afflicted mouth, who had saddled him with the rug merchant that afternoon.

Andreas frowned and studied the tavern crowd, trying to put her from his thoughts.

A Scythian trader was urinating against a far wall; two Mauritanian sailors, black as night, were engaged in a fist fight that no one paid attention to; and a dwarf, raised up on someone's shoulders, was scratching a graffito high on a bit of bare wall. *Why?* Andreas wanted to know. He had known many girls and women in his travels, and none had affected him as this one had. *Why her?*

Andreas scowled, disliking the battle inside himself. His heart said: *Because she is different*. His mind said: *No, she's not*. Women were ultimately alike the world over. As a physician Andreas knew it; as a man he knew it.

"You've caught that one's eye," Naso said, getting Andreas's attention. The physician turned to see, across the room, a young prostitute eyeing him with interest. He stared back at her. She was tall for a woman, with white skin and hair as black as Hades. And a red, red mouth. She reminded him of—

"Do yourself a favor, laddie," Naso urged, reaching for another sausage.

Andreas looked down at the table. That hypnotic, drooping mouth, which contained a crippled tongue, was haunting him. What was her name? *What was her name?*

He looked up to see the prostitute pushing her way through the crowd toward him, laughing as she evaded groping hands. Naso saw the greedy glint in her eyes before Andreas did; she clearly knew a prize catch when she saw one. Men like the physician, with his silky hands, white toga, and good looks, rarely came to this part of town. It was beyond Naso why the man was not married.

Andreas watched her as she drew near, and when she was close he felt himself fill with sadness. The whiteness of her skin was not natural but the result of rice powder dusted on her face to hide blemishes; the mouth was painted with rouge, the thin lips outlined to lend a fullness that was not there. His physician's eye read her life in a glance—the hardship, the abuse —and then it read her future: Something was eating the marrow in her bones. Was she aware, he wondered, of the shortness of her life, that her tomorrows would be measured in months instead of years?

Before she could hike up her dress and sit bare-bottomed on his lap, Andreas stood abruptly. With a formal salute to the captain he said, "I shall be at the boat at dawn." And he slipped a gold coin to the bewildered girl, the first her hand had ever held.

Outside, the night air was hot and heavy. It was summer and the Orontes rolled along sluggishly. Andreas looked right and left. It might be daylight on this red-lanterned street, so bright were the cressets and lamps in windows and doorways. Pulling his toga up onto his shoulder, Andreas struck off along the waterfront, knowing from experience to stay to the lighted and populated streets. He had known many harbors in many ports of the Roman Empire—they were alike the world over.

He withdrew into his thoughts as he walked.

Yes, the restlessness had come over him once again. But this time, it had come a little sooner than usual. Andreas had in the past been able to go two or three years before the poisons built up and needed to be cleansed on the open sea. This time it had been only a year since his last sail with Naso. It was because of that girl.

After she had left his house and Andreas had transferred the unconscious rug merchant to the slave quarters, the physician had found to his chagrin that he could not get the girl out of his mind. That afternoon, as he had stood and watched her beautiful mouth struggle pathetically to form words, Andreas had felt briefly moved. But his heart, conditioned against tender feelings, had quickly shored up the weak spot. The hard heart, he knew, was the safe heart; the heart made of stone could not be bruised. So he had sent her away and had sent Malachus to inquire about Naso; if Naso could not be found, then another captain with a sturdy vessel would do, a vessel heading for distant ports. But Naso had by good fortune been in Antioch and was preparing to sail to Britain. Andreas was going to be on that ship come dawn.

A sudden cry followed by shouts brought him out of himself. He turned to see a man come running out of a nearby alley. He had blood on his hands.

"Help!" he cried, seizing Andreas's arm. "My mate's been hurt! He's bleeding!"

Suspicious, Andreas looked past the man's shoulder and saw in the shadows at the end of the alley, a man lying on the ground cupping a bleeding ear. "What happened?" Andreas asked.

"We was attacked! Me and my mate, we was taking this shortcut and somebody jumped us! He's hurt bad. They cut his ear off!"

Andreas looked into the man's face, which was gray with fear, then at the man lying in a pool of blood. He was about to turn away when a vision flashed in his mind: the tongue-tied girl pleading with passersby to help her with an injured stranger. Impulsively Andreas said, "I am a physician. I can help."

"And the gods bless you for it!" cried the man, turning and hurrying back down the alley.

When Andreas reached the injured man, he got down on one knee, saw at once that he was indeed seriously hurt, and said, "You'll be all right, friend. I am a physician. I will help."

Then the other man, still standing, said in a low voice, "Yeah, now you do like I say and you'll be all right, too."

Andreas looked up and saw the bloody knife, and he knew in that instant that he had fallen for one of the oldest tricks in the world, one that the greenest medical student knew to avoid. The man lying in the pool of blood had been the first victim, and then had been used to lure in a second.

Andreas felt his own blood run to ice. "You can have my money," he said as calmly as he could.

And then he saw the thief's arm go up and come down toward his face, and just before the blow fell, just before the stars and streetlights winked out of the night, Andreas thought: *So it's finally come, after all these years* . . .

CHAPTER 4

Mera mentally scolded herself as she followed the linkboy and his lantern down the dark street.

She had not wanted to leave the house tonight; she was deep in preparations for Selene's Dressing Ceremony and for the initiation eight days following. Time was running out and Mera was racing against it. But when a familiar face had appeared at her door, a skinny little girl Mera had treated for pneumonia last winter, begging the healer-woman to come to the harbor because Naso the sea captain needed her, when Mera had seen the big eyes and felt the tug of the hand on her dress, she had relented. First and foremost she was a healer; and she had made sacred vows to the Goddess.

The prostitute's room was down by the river, in one of those hastily built *insulae* that were unstable and overcrowded and frequently collapsed with everyone inside. The linkboy with his lantern guided Mera up the narrow stone steps to the third floor, where the girl was waiting. Behind her stood a scowling slab of a man—the sea captain, Mera judged by his clothes.

"Thank you for coming, mother," whispered the whore, using the traditional title of respect. "He is in here."

Mera's quick, sharp eyes took in everything at a glance: the miserable room with its lamp that smoked terribly because it burned the cheapest grade of olive oil; the sallow complexion of the girl; the captain who walked with a seaman's lurching gait; and finally the body of a man lying on a pallet.

"He was to sail with me," Naso said as he watched Mera go down to her knees at his friend's side. "He was set upon by thugs."

"Is he alive?" quaked the prostitute, whose name, Mera was soon to learn, was Zoë.

Mera gently touched the side of his neck and felt the feeble pulse.

"Yes," she said, and signaled to the linkboy who came forward with the box he had been carrying. It was made of cedar and engraved with sacred and mystical signs. Her medicine box. "Go home now, son, and thank you for coming with me," she said. "Go and get some sleep, and tell your father I shall draw out his bad tooth tomorrow in repayment."

Naso and Zoë watched in anxious silence as the slender brown hands peeled Andreas's tunic from his chest. They saw her halt suddenly, lift a chain from his neck and study it in the lamplight. At its end hung the Eye of Horus, symbol of the Egyptian god of healing. Mera looked up at the captain. "He is a physician?"

"Aye, and due to sail with my ship at dawn."

Mera shook her head. "He will not be sailing with you, captain. He has received a blow to the head."

"Dach!" Naso spat and cursed the first god that came to mind. "There's nothing I can do then," he said, and turned to go.

"Wait!" Zoë grabbed his arm. "You can't leave him here."

Naso pulled his arm free. "I've my ship to see to, girl."

"But I can't have him here!" she cried. "I bring my customers here!"

He looked down at Mera, who was opening her medicine box. "Can you take him, mother?"

"He must not be moved."

Naso shifted on tree-trunk legs. He had no idea where Andreas lived, didn't know who to send for. After a moment's deliberation, he reached inside his belt and pulled out a small leather bag. "Here," he said, thrusting it at the prostitute. "This will pay for his keep. It's what he gave me for passage on my ship."

Zoë opened the bag and stared wide-eyed at the coins inside. She looked down at the unconscious Andreas, at the expertly working hands of the healer-woman, and made her own swift calculation. "Very well," she said, "he can stay."

As Mera asked for water in a basin, and proceeded to lay out medications and linens from her box, she thought of the half-sewn *stola* waiting for her at home, the floor-length gown of womanhood Selene was going to receive at her Dressing Ceremony, and the ivory rose that needed to be taken to a jeweler to be put on a chain and the scroll of secret spells she was writing for Selene. Would she get it all done in time? Twenty days was so short, and the pain in her body was growing. Mera's hands moved swiftly over Andreas.

"I will heal him," she said to the prostitute and the sea captain. "Stranger though this man is to me, he is a physician, and therefore my brother . . .?

CHAPTER 5

Zoë sat cross-legged on the floor, counting the coins one more time.

It was not to determine their worth; she knew that already, as she had counted them when the stranger had been brought here two nights ago. The reason young Zoë spread the coins out on the floor —silver ones here, copper here—and touched the stamped face of each, lingeringly, was because they had come to represent her life, or rather, her life as it *could be,* which was altogether a different matter from her life as it was now. The coins were a doorway, an avenue of escape from this wretched existence; they were going to save her.

The problem was, the coins did not belong to her.

Naso had given them to her in payment for taking in the injured Greek, but even a dimwit could see that the total of this purse far exceeded the value of Zoë's time. Just one of these coins represented her earnings for a year. The purse totaled a lifetime—a lifetime of abuse and humiliation, of fear and loneliness. Zoë could look down the dismal tunnel of her future and see the men—hard and callous, a few gentle, many cruel—and the disease and poverty and despair, and see at its end the lonely old woman she would be, living out her last days begging beer by the docks. But these coins, with their godlike images and foreign writing, showed her a different life—one of respect and ease, in a warm climate, Sicily perhaps, where she would live in a small house and tend a little garden, maybe even have her own olive tree, and exchange gossip with the neighbors at the well. She could start anew, bury Zoë the whore and give birth perhaps to a new self, the respectable young widow who had lost her husband at sea. And she could live in the sunshine and walk with her head high and sleep respectably in a proper bed at night. The vision was so overwhelming, it seemed now so *possible,* that it took her breath away.

Zoë glanced over at the slumbering stranger. He had slept these two days, due to the pain-killing drugs the healer-woman had given him. The blow to his head had caused delirium—the few times he had wakened he had not known who or where he was—but soon, Mera had told Zoë, the veil would lift and he would regain his senses. Then he would summon his family and be taken home, where he would be tended in his own bed.

And, Zoë thought, *he will take his coins with him.*

Zoë watched him with narrowed eyes. She was thinking of his necklace. The eye of some god, Mera had said, wrought in gold and lapis lazuli and certain to be worth twice this collection of coins! With that necklace plus the purse, Zoë could change her life now, at this very hour: She could walk out of this miserable room, away from the hard life of the harbor, and join a caravan heading south, a rich and respectable widow, on her way to a life of comfort and ease.

What did it matter to her that the healer-woman had said she wasn't coming back, that Zoë was going to abandon the stranger here, unconscious and injured? Surely he would waken soon, call for help, or someone would find him eventually. His loss was her luck. Zoë smiled to herself. The decision was made—she would leave tonight.

Gathering up the coins and returning them to their leather pouch, she hurried about the room, collecting her few possessions and bundling them into her spare shawl. When she was ready to leave, there was only one thing left to do: take the stranger's gold necklace. But when she turned around, Zoë was surprised to see that the stranger was awake.

He sat up, and they stared at one another across the moonlit night; Zoë wary and clutching her possessions, the stranger frowning at her. While he had slept these past two days, Zoë had not really looked at him, but now that he was sitting up and gazing at her, she saw that the stranger was captivatingly handsome.

"Where am I?" he asked.

An emotion, new and alien to Zoë, powerful in its flood, rushed through her body, making her shudder. He was so . . . *defenseless.*

"You're in my house," she said.

"Who are you?"

"Don't you remember?" Zoë walked cautiously toward him and came to a halt in the column of moonlight pouring through the window.

"Do I know you?" he asked.

She chewed her lower lip. Had he lost his memory? The healer-woman had warned of that possibility. If so, might he not also forget about the coins? "We met," she said, "two nights ago."

His high forehead wrinkled in confusion. He brought up a hand and rubbed his head. "What happened?"

"You were set upon by thieves. In an alley in the harbor."

His frown deepened. He was confused. The dark-blue eyes studied Zoë with an intensity that made her clutch the edge of her *palla* over her breast. And as she stood there staring back at him, it occurred to Andreas that she was familiar somehow, her mouth so red . . . "The marketplace," he said slowly. "The rug merchant. There was a girl . . . "

Zoë held her breath.

"Are you she?"

She hesitated. It was a charade Zoë had played many times. Men came to her in their loneliness, drunk and sad, wishing they were back with Bythia or Deborah or Lotus, looking for something in Zoë's skinny body, something more than simple sexual gratification—they needed the fulfillment of a dream, of a wish, of a lost hope. Many nights she had lain on that pallet not as Zoë the whore but as a wife not seen in a year, as a sweetheart from long-past youth, sometimes as another man's wife, occasionally, even, as mother. So if this bewildered stranger wanted to see in her a chance-met girl in a marketplace, what harm the masquerade, if it made him happy? So she said, "Yes, I am that girl."

"You hurried away," he said vaguely. "You never told me your name." Andreas rubbed his forehead in bafflement. What day was it? Why was his head so full of pain? And why did he have the nagging feeling that there was something else, something important he should remember? Naso . . . It was all so unclear. His head throbbed, his body ached. He looked up at the girl standing in the moonlight, her skin white like milk, her hair so black it blended into the night. Was this indeed she, the girl of the marketplace?

Andreas's confusion deepened. He had been dreaming. So many dreams, swirling, mixing, difficult to sort out. What had they meant? An Egyptian healer-woman with cool, gentle hands; Naso and a platter of sausages; a basket of henbane. What did it all mean?

The pale-skinned girl came to him and knelt. She spoke in a melodious voice. "Have you been searching for me?"

It seemed to Andreas that he had. "Yes . . . "

"Then you have found me," she said with a smile.

Andreas took hold of her hand for a moment, and sank back onto the pillow with a sigh. No, this was not quite right. Something was wrong. But he could not think. His head hurt and he was abominably weak. Malachus. Where was Malachus? And this girl, claiming to be the other, he could see now that she was someone else entirely. Andreas's eyelids drooped, he sighed again and slipped into welcome sleep.

An hour later, Zoë stood by the window looking out over the rooftops and the silver ribbon of river beyond the docks; she pondered what had happened.

When she had told him she was the girl of the marketplace, the stranger had stared at her, his eyes clearly begging her to be telling the truth, and now he slept, more peacefully than before, it seemed to Zoë, and she was left alone, feeling cold and hollow, to puzzle it all out.

She was no less confused than he, because here was a man like none she had ever met. Zoë had thought she was an expert on men, wise to their every thought and wile and secret. But Andreas fit none of the neat categories into which Zoë had been sorting her men ever since the age of ten, when she had started selling her body. What struck her most was the power of his tenderness. When he had reached for her hand and taken it in his, her body had felt a jolt more stunning than if she had been struck by a fist. How was it possible that such sweetness could carry more strength than the muscular strength of men she had known? Zoë, so used to being dominated by men, to being at the mercy of their violence, could not believe the sweetly submissive way this soft-spoken stranger had trusted her. As he had laid his head back down on the pillow, his pain-filled eyes had remained fixed on her so questioningly, he had seemed so *lost,* that Zoë had had to look away.

She turned from the window and stared down at him again. As she did so, a soft warm tide washed over her; she felt protective and possessive and motherly all at once, and full of desire for him, too. The first real desire she had felt for a man after years of loathing the beasts that used her. And suddenly she yearned, not for the sunshine of Sicily or the little house with its olive tree, but for this man. In place of the vision of freedom and ease she had entertained just a short while before, Zoë now saw the gentle stranger, grateful to her, indebted to her, loving her. Zoë the whore, who had so recently learned to dream for the first time in her life, saw now, in her naïveté, the long life she and this stranger would have together.

She knew what she would do. She would give him a new memory. She would tell him his name was . . . Titus. Yes, she liked that name, Titus, it sounded strong. And she would tell him that they were betrothed, that they were planning on going away together . . .

Zoë curled her hands into fists at her sides and vowed to keep this man with her always.

CHAPTER 6

Selene looked up and down the sunny street, hopeful. But, once again, she saw no one coming.

Disappointed, she went back into the house and resumed work on her medicine box. It was like her mother's, but new, and made of ebony with inlaid ivory mosaic. The box contained many drawers and compartments to hold medicines and supplies, and had a thick leather strap so she could carry it over her shoulder. It was Mera's gift to Selene for her sixteenth birthday.

In a little while, Selene was going to go through the Dressing Ceremony, the ancient custom that had come down from before the founding of Rome. She was going to lay aside childhood, cut her hair and dedicate it to Isis, and then she and her mother were going to enjoy a celebration dinner.

Selene paused to stare at the food spread out on the table.

It was the custom, on a girl's Dressing Day, to set out plenty of food and drink for all the friends and relatives who stopped by with congratulations. Last month, at Ester's party, the crowd had been so large that the tables of food had had to be carried into the street. As Selene eyed the cakes her mother had baked and the two roast ducks purchased with money they could ill afford, she thought there was an awful lot—too much, perhaps. But Mera had wanted there to be enough for anyone who dropped by.

With another glance toward the door, hoping someone was going to come to her party, Selene sighed and went back to work.

Her medicine box was a duplicate of her mother's, with bandages and ointments, sutures and needles, and a flint for making fire. No surgical instruments, however, since Mera did not believe in cutting. The knife in the medicine box was for lancing boils, the forceps for grasping bandages, the needles for sewing lacerations. These did not compare with the fine instruments Selene had seen at the house of Andreas the physician. He had had bronze scalpels, hemostats for grasping blood vessels, forceps for crushing bladder stones and many other instruments for which she could not name a purpose.

How wonderful to own such fine things! she thought, as she filled a jar with foxglove extract and tucked it into place in the box. *To have such skill in one's hands! To have knowledge of the mysterious world beneath the flesh!* Since she had left the house of Andreas the physician, three weeks before, Selene had been able to think of little else.

Nor was she thinking only of his surgical instruments. The face of the man himself had never left her, and every night before she fell asleep, she relived that wonderful meeting.

One afternoon a week later, Selene had worked up the courage to look for his house again. But she had not been able to find it—one gate in a wall that looked like any other wall! And she had not had the nerve to ask someone.

Hearing footsteps outside her door, Selene ran and looked out. But it was only a passerby, continuing on down the street.

Turning back inside, she glanced again at the table.

Mera had had to borrow money to buy the food. Under a cloth stood a platter of flat round bread, ready to be filled as one wished, with olives and onions, with chunks of lamb, rice, even honey still on the comb. There were three large cheeses, gotten in exchange for treating the cheesemaker's son for an eye ailment, and the amphora of wine had been gotten by Mera's promising to treat the wine merchant's family for illness through the coming year. There were figs and apples, and some costly oranges— all carefully set out on the table, protected from flies and dust but growing stale in the hot day.

They will come, Selene reassured herself. *There is time yet.*

Selene returned to her medicine box. She was alone in the house. Mera had had to hurry away to the Street of Jewelers to fetch the ivory rose, which was ready at last. Mera had given it to the jeweler some days ago, to have a hole bored in its strongest petal, and a chain passed through so it could be worn as a necklace. The rose and its special contents were to be given to Selene this evening, to wear with her new *stola*. The jeweler had sent word this morning that the necklace was ready, and Mera had pulled off her apron and rushed away, reminding Selene to make their guests welcome.

Guests? Selene thought, as she glanced again at the door. If none came, then Selene would go through the Dressing Ceremony at sunset alone, with no one to witness her passage into womanhood.

She thought of the new *stola* folded carefully in its box. Mera had labored many nights on it. The cloth had come from a caravan leader Mera had treated for a cough; it was made of the softest cotton, dyed dark blue, and Mera had painstakingly embroidered pale-blue flowers around the hem and down the sleeves. It was Selene's first long dress, the gown that would proclaim her a woman, and at sunset she was going to put it on, along with the pale blue *palla*, the long shawl that women wore.

Traditionally, it was the father who officially received the girl into the family as a woman, when she emerged newly dressed before the assembled company, and it was her brothers who cut off the symbolic lock of hair to be consecrated to the household gods. But Selene, lacking father and brothers, was going to be received by her mother, and in the place of the sisters who were supposed to bind up her hair in womanly fashion, again Mera was going to perform that service.

Selene thought wistfully of Ester's Dressing Ceremony last month. What a large crowd there had been; such merrymaking! Ester's six aunts and three sisters and four female cousins had gone with her into the upper room of their house and had helped her out of her girl's dress and into a *stola* of bright, sunflower-yellow. When she had come out, the guests had all fallen silent; then Ester's father had walked to her, embraced her and welcomed her into the family as a woman.

Such cheering there had been! And then Ester's brothers had clustered about her, holding the barber's knife, teasing her, pretending they were going to cut off *all* her hair, and Ester had giggled and blushed. Then there had been the solemn ceremony of laying the lock of hair on the altar of the household gods, where it would be kept in an urn that contained the locks of her older sisters, her mother and her grandmother. Ester's hair had been beautifully bound up, symbolizing her passage from maidenhood, and then, with great formality, her dolls and short dresses had been laid away in a chest.

Selene, from her corner, by herself because Mera had been called away to deliver a baby, had smiled and applauded Ester, while filled with envy and longing. For Ester's betrothed had been at the party, a good-looking young man with shoulders as straight as arrows and eyes as green as leeks.

Now Ester was considered to be a woman and she participated in all the household duties required of women—spinning, weaving, maintaining the shrine of the household gods. And now, when she walked down the street, the hem of her *stola* hid her ankles and her head was modestly covered by her *palla*. Ester had, with dignity and grace, left girlhood behind.

A sound at the door caused Selene to turn sharply. But it had only been the wind, stirring the summer herbs in the little garden.

Selene was of course aware that her own Dressing Ceremony was more a matter of following custom than an actual delineation between her two phases of life. Living alone with her mother, having no father or brothers, Selene had in fact assumed an adult role years ago—spinning and weaving, taking care of their little shrine of Isis, and more: working in the herb garden, mixing medicines, helping her mother treat the sick. Indeed, Selene's dolls had been laid aside long ago, her childhood had been shortened because of her mother's need for her; they would skip that part of the ceremony. There were no dolls to be put away.

Nevertheless, this did not lessen the importance of the day in Selene's eyes. She had looked forward to this moment for years, ever since she had started attending these parties as a little girl, invited not because any of the neighborhood children had wanted her—they had not, having made her an outcast among themselves—but because her mother was Mera, and the neighborhood respected the Egyptian healer-woman. Selene had stood alone every time, at the edge of the company, and had watched with yearning as each young woman, over the years, had received the coveted dress, the embrace of a proud father.

"Selene, child. Day of days."

She spun around to find the doorway filled with the pudgy form of the baker's wife. "W-welcome," Selene said, closing her medicine box and going to the visitor. "P-please c-c—"

The woman stepped in out of the hot sun, fanning herself, and squinted around the single room that was Selene's house. "Where is your mother?"

"G-g—"

"Gone out?"

Selene nodded.

"On this day of days? Where did she go?"

"To fetch my n-n—"

"Necklace? It is ready then?"

Selene nodded again, and motioned to the table and to the best chair in the house, which the woman immediately occupied after taking a handful of olives from the table.

"W-where is—"

"My husband? He won't be coming. It's his kidneys again."

Selene felt a small pang of disappointment. She did not particularly care for the baker, but he would have been one more guest at her party.

"When did your mother go out?"

"This m-m—"

"Ah, this morning. Then she'll be back soon. It's midday already, you know."

Selene didn't need to be reminded of the hour. At Ester's party, by noon the guests had been spilling out into the forecourt.

Silence fell between them as Selene remained politely standing and the baker's wife sucked on olives and eyed the spread on the table. Selene felt her anxiety start to mount. What if no one else came? Surely some of the people her mother had treated for illness over the years would arrive. But she did not expect to see any girls her own age.

When she was little, Selene had been excluded from the street games because they called for quick speech and the other children had thought her slow and stupid. Later, girls shunned her because, although this was a poor neighborhood and no family could make any grand claims, the stammering Selene was always dressed a cut below everyone else. Her mother, everyone knew, spent all their money on medicines instead of on clothes for her daughter. The cliques of giggling, whispering little girls in the neighborhood had scorned Selene's clothes, which were just a bit shabbier than theirs, and her bullrush sandals, of the kind only the lowliest peasant wore. They fell silent when she came near, and snickered when she tried to talk. And then, when they passed from that cruel age and grew into adolescence, when they might at last have had the maturity to be kind to Selene, the rift was too wide to be bridged. She was a strange one, they murmured among themselves. People had seen her collecting herbs by moonlight; she never talked; and hadn't they all witnessed the way she had held her hands over old Kiko, the retired soldier who had the falling sickness, how she had closed her eyes and held out her hands and his fit had subsided?

But the final reality was that, after living on this cramped little street for nearly sixteen years, Selene was a stranger among her own people. If they did not come to her party, it would not be out of malice or dislike, but simply because it would not occur to them to do so.

However, her mother was respected and so a few more people began to appear at the door: the young tentmaker and his wife with their three-week-old son, the widow Mera treated regularly for joint pain, the crippled fuller whose leg Mera had once tried to save and who now earned his living begging in the marketplace, and old Kiko, the epileptic soldier. It was a ragtag group, but they had come to Selene's party.

Even so, there was still far too much food. Why had her mother insisted on having so much? Such extravagance only made the party look smaller, not grander. Selene could not help thinking that there was something sad about such a banquet for a handful of people. She hoped the guests could be persuaded to take some food home with them.

She was passing around a plate of saffron cakes when the sunlight was momentarily blocked in the doorway. Everyone looked up to see who the new arrival was, and, instantly, all chatter ceased.

They stared, Selene with them, at the handsome gentleman on the threshold.

Andreas.

Selene blinked, not believing her eyes. Had her fantasizing produced a vision?

But then the vision spoke: "I was told this is the house of Mera the healer-woman."

Seven pairs of eyes stared at him for a moment more, then Selene, putting down the plate, went to him. "Th-this is her house," she said. "W-welcome."

Now it was Andreas's turn to stare. "You!" he said.

They gazed at one another, unable for the moment to speak. Was he truly standing here, this man she had been dreaming about? While Andreas thought: *I have found you again, when I never thought to.*

Remembering herself, Selene said, "P-please c-c—" flustered, cursing the tongue that betrayed her.

Andreas entered and saw six dumbstruck faces, mouths hanging open, staring at him.

"Th-these are my f-friends," Selene said, fighting to make the words plain. It was suddenly the most important thing in her life, to speak perfectly for Andreas, but the harder she struggled, the more twisted her tongue became.

"I am Andreas," he said to the guests, who continued to stare. Each was searching his or her memory for the last time such a prestigious gentleman had appeared in their midst. Then they realized: never.

The old sailor quickly shot to his feet and offered his stool to the gentleman. But Andreas politely refused.

He was dressed in clothes these people only rarely glimpsed, when a knight walked through the marketplace, or when the nobility sat in their private boxes at the Circus. Not even the tax collector was ever this finely dressed! All six guests eyed the lavender tunic with its gold-bordered hem, the white toga without a smudge of dirt on it, the leather sandals laced up to the knees, the carefully clipped beard and curled hair. Who was this elegant gentleman who paid honor to Selene today?

He turned to her and said, "I am looking for Mera. Is she your mother?"

"Y-yes."

Andreas nodded, suddenly understanding, and marveling at the workings of fate. "What is your name?"

"S-Selene."

He smiled. "Now I know who you are."

In his hands was a beautifully carved alabaster jar, and as a sweet, familiar scent filled the house, everyone knew it contained myrrh, a very costly medicinal ointment. Andreas held it out to Selene and said quietly, "I came to give this to your mother. She came to my aid when I was hurt."

When she shyly took the jar, their fingers touched and Selene felt a jolt.

Quickly turning away to place the jar on a shelf where it could be seen by all, she wondered, *hoped: Had he felt the jolt also?*

Selene turned back to him, and said as slowly, as precisely as she could, "You w-were hurt?"

"Down at the harbor, three weeks ago. A blow to the head. And your mother treated me."

Selene remembered the night: Her mother had been summoned from her bed by a sea captain.

Andreas took a step closer. Being half a head taller than Selene, he looked down at her with dark-blue eyes, and said softly, "I awoke in a strange room. There was a girl there. I thought she was you."

Held by his gaze, hypnotized by his presence, Selene was unaware of the puzzled looks her guests exchanged with one another. Andreas spoke intimately to her, as if there were no one else in the room.

"And then my memory returned and I saw that she wasn't you, and I was afraid that I would never find you again." He paused, his intense eyes searching her face. "Do you remember when we met? The rug merchant?"

She nodded.

"He recovered, you know. He has gone back to Damascus. When he thanked me for saving his life, I told him that his gratitude belonged to a girl whose name I did not know."

Selene could not speak; she was lost in his eyes.

Finally, a chair scraped the floor, someone coughed. Andreas looked up with a raised eyebrow, as if surprised to find himself here, and said, "But I am intruding! You have guests." Then he saw the table, weighted with food. "I shall come back another time," he said, and started for the door.

"Wait," Selene said, reaching for him. "D-d—"

Andreas looked down at the hand on his arm, then at the beautiful mouth trying to form words.

"D-don't g-" she said, grimacing as if in pain.

Andreas waited.

"D-don't g-g-"

"She's trying to tell you not to go," the baker's wife said.

Andreas shot the woman a look. Then he said to Selene, "What is the occasion?"

Selene frowned, frustrated, angry with the gods who had handicapped her so. It was a lot to say: This is my birthday. I am sixteen years old. Today is my Dressing Ceremony. And then, to her surprise, as she looked up into his face, Selene realized that Andreas had already guessed what the occasion was. *But he wanted her to say it.*

"M-my birthday," she said. "D-Dressing . . . "

His smile broadened. "I should be honored to stay, if you wish. And I want to express my gratitude to your mother."

There was a brief flurry as the guests sought to accommodate the gentleman, offering chairs and food; at the same time another small flurry of activity was occurring down the street. Ester, the young woman whose party last month had been such a grand affair, had been in her tiny front garden when she saw Andreas walk up to Selene's house. Ester had stopped what she was doing and stared while the finely dressed gentleman went inside. Now, a few minutes later, he had not yet come out and her curiosity was too much to bear. And so, after passing the news on to her mother and sisters—"A rich man if ever I saw one, carrying something, a gift it looked like to me!"—Ester hurried up the street to the house of her best friend, Almah, a young wife pregnant with her first child.

"Her Dressing Day," Almah said, welcoming this bit of diversion into her dreary life. "He must be a guest. I wonder who he is!"

"I had not planned to go—"

"But she did attend *our* parties—"

"For Selene. It's the least we can do."

And as Ester and Almah were making their way back down the street toward Selene's house, the baker's wife was also hurrying back to her own house, to rouse her husband from a nap and tell him to come to the party, that there was a magnificent stranger attending Selene's Dressing Day.

Word spread, and by the time Mera arrived at her little street, weary from the long walk to the Street of Jewelers, the pain in her side almost unbearable, she heard the sound of many voices, talking and laughing. A celebration, she thought, and wondered whose it was. And then she saw the people in her own doorway, standing in her own courtyard, people she knew, milling about in the hot summer afternoon eating and drinking. Mera stopped short.

What had happened? Had all these people come to Selene's Dressing Ceremony? Surely there were more people here than had attended Ester's party, and that event had been the talk of the neighborhood for weeks!

When she reached her gate, friends and neighbors greeted her with smiles already loosened by wine. And by the time she could push through the doorway to find her little house jammed with people, all laughing and talking, Mera was speechless.

The food on the table, she saw, was rapidly disappearing; already some platters stood empty, and a new jar of wine, one she had never seen before, had been produced. Everyone hailed Mera and congratulated her. Baffled, she searched for her daughter, and found Selene at the center of attention, cheeks flaming, eyes bright. Standing next to her was a tall gentleman who was vaguely familiar to Mera.

As she pushed her way through, saying, "Yes, it is a day of days," Mera tried to recall where she had seen the young man before. Then, remembering the injured man in the prostitute's apartment by the river, and guessing that he must have found out the name and whereabouts of the healer-woman who had treated him, Mera also realized now why her house was so full of people.

If the young physician had come to thank her for helping him, Mera decided, then *she* was doubly grateful to *him*. Because of his novelty and the simplicity of her neighbors, the young stranger had unwittingly ensured the success of Selene's Dressing Day.

When he saw Mera, Andreas stopped in the middle of what he was saying, turned to her, and bowed formally. "I am Andreas, mother," he said. "I came to thank you for what you did for me."

Mera's eyes shone, and for an instant she forgot the terrible pain in her side. "It was my honor to help you, Andreas."

"M-mother," said Selene. "L-look!" She took the alabaster jar from the shelf and held it out.

The fragrance reached Mera before she touched the gift. Myrrh. A blessed balm she had never before been able to afford and which she could put to such valuable use. Mera was overcome.

But in the next instant, as her daughter babbled breathlessly about how she had met Andreas three weeks ago, before his accident by the harbor, and wasn't this a wonderful coincidence, Mera saw the flush heighten Selene's cheeks and noticed how she chattered unselfconsciously, the imperfect words tumbling out. Mera also remembered Selene's excitement that afternoon three weeks ago when she had met Andreas the physician, and her shortlived joy turned to alarm.

Selene had fallen in love!

Then Mera felt herself being drawn away from her daughter and the beguiling stranger, drawn away by guests anxious to congratulate her. The baker's wife had Mera by one arm, the old widow by another, both were talking rapidly, saying what a great day this was and how proud Mera must be. She nodded absently and thanked them, and saw, between the shoulders and backs that surrounded her, Selene gaze up at the physician with an unmistakable look.

The party grew more lively. People went out for more food; men hurried home to fetch wine. Musicians appeared, playing pipes and harps that were barely heard above the din. Everyone jockeyed for position near the glamorous stranger; Ester and Almah flirted with him. And finally, as the sun neared the western horizon, the time came to take Selene away from the party, to be dressed and readied.

Since there wasn't another room in the house, Mera took her daughter up on the roof, where in the summer they cooked and slept, and where an arbor of rosemary made a private screen behind which Selene could dress.

Mother and daughter stood in the golden glow of the setting sun. Cooking fires spiraled up from distant rooftops, creating a haze that settled over the city; temples rose up through the haze, giving Antioch a mystical look, and the sky blazed in breathless hues of orange, red and gold.

Selene could hardly stand still while her mother dressed her. "Isn't he w-w—" she tried to say as her threadbare dress came up over her head. "Isn't Andreas . . . " Selene washed in a basin of water, then put on a clean chemise. Mera was silent as she carefully lifted the midnight-blue *stola* out of its box; downstairs she heard the noise of the party. Everyone was waiting for Selene to appear.

Mera was torn. On the one hand she was grateful that the party had turned out so well for Selene, but on the other, the cause of that success, Andreas, was a fresh worry for her.

In eight days the first full moon would appear. On that night, Mera and Selene were going to be in the mountains nearby, in a solitary encampment, fasting and praying and communing with the Goddess. There, in that wilderness, Selene's final initiation as a healer-woman was going to take place. And there also, Mera was going to tell the girl the truth of her birth; the ivory rose was going to be opened, and Selene was going to take over from her mother the quest for her own identity.

All had been going according to plan, until tonight.

These past twenty days had been filled with final instruction. Mera had rushed to pass on to her daughter all her worldly knowledge. In eight days, the spiritual knowledge would also be imparted, and then, Mera had hoped, she could die content, having done her job. But now there was a terrible complication. At this fragile and precious moment in her life, Selene had fallen in love.

"You must think upon other things tonight, Selene," Mera said as she helped Selene into the *stola*. "You must think of the gravity of this occasion. A girl no longer, Selene. But a woman. And no ordinary woman, but a healer-woman, who cannot live an ordinary life. You must think of your future responsibilities, Selene."

"I d-don't want to th-think about anything b-b- . . . but Andreas!"

Mera pressed her lips into a thin line. Twenty days ago she had begged an audience with the Oracle at the temple. Mera needed to know what was written in her daughter's stars. She needed to know Selene's future before she died. But she had been told to come back in twenty-seven days. Although she had pleaded with the Temple Guardian, it had been to no avail. One did not choose when one saw the Oracle.

A pain shot through her body. Mera winced. But Selene had not seen, did not know her mother was dying.

When the *stola* went over her head and billowed down over her body in a caress, Selene fell silent. Never had such fine cloth touched her skin. The hem, dancing with pale-blue flowers, only just reached the ground. The sleeves, loose and flowing, open along the outer seam and gathered at intervals, felt like a breeze on her arms. A long cord of hemp dyed blue went around her waist and crisscrossed between her breasts, binding the dress to her.

Finally, Mera brought out the ivory rose.

Its whiteness, when it lay against the dark plum color of the *stola*, was striking. Every detail of the exquisite flower stood out, each delicately carved petal. It rattled slightly as it fell into place upon Selene's breast, bespeaking the mysterious contents inside. The back of the rose had been sealed long ago with ceramic; it was intended to be opened only once. Selene knew that this would be when she and her mother went up the slope of Mount Silpius, overlooking Antioch; tonight, however, she could think of nothing but Andreas.

The last thing Mera did was brush out Selene's long black hair, worn tonight for the last time in girlish waves down her back. She stood back to gaze at her daughter for a moment, and felt a pain. But it was not the pain of the lump that was killing her; this pain was not of the flesh at all, but of the spirit.

You came to me in my childlessness and my loneliness, Mera thought, as tears filled her eyes. *Our time together has been a short one, sweet daughter, but I regret not one hour, one second of those sixteen years.*

In a flash, the face of the dying Roman appeared before Mera, as vivid and lifelike as if he stood there. *She comes from the gods,* he said. *The ring will tell her everything; it will lead her to her destiny.*

Mera wanted to reach out and seize the vision. "Who are you?" she wanted to cry. But the face faded away into the smoky sunset.

The crowd downstairs fell silent when Mera appeared at last at the back door. All heads turned to await Selene's entrance. There was great expectation in the mind of every guest, for truly this had been a day of surprises. Who would have thought such a distinguished gentleman would attend Selene's party? Who would have expected so much delicious food, such a generous flow of wine? And now, surely, no ordinary girl was going to come through that door.

Their expectations were met.

Several of the guests gasped when Selene stepped into the room. From their place beside Andreas, Ester and Almah gaped at the stunning blue *stola*. Where had Selene's mother found such a garment? How had she been able to afford it? And each thought: Mine *was not embroidered with flowers* . . .

Selene entered hesitantly, smiling shyly, afraid to meet the eyes of the astonished guests. Mera saw their faces and her tears rose anew. *Now* they were seeing her daughter for what she really was, a beautiful, pure spirit. These people who had scorned Selene for her awkward speech, who had warned Mera that her daughter could never make a good marriage, would never amount to anything, these neighbors who had for years stared right through her daughter as if she weren't there—look at their faces now!

Then Mera turned to Andreas and her joy dissolved in an instant. She had known enough men in her life to read his eyes correctly, and it made her pulse quicken in fear. Andreas must not be allowed to make a claim on Selene . . .

The scene was suspended in a moment of silence, then Mera went to her daughter and embraced her in front of the gathered company. Cheers erupted, accompanied by clapping and shouts of congratulations. Squeezed in her mother's tight embrace, Selene looked over Mera's shoulder at Andreas. He neither clapped nor cheered, nor said anything at all, nor even moved. He was gazing at Selene with an intensity she remembered and that she had recalled time and again in her dreams. The smile was gone; his dark eyes brooded once more beneath scowling brows.

Mera pulled away, wiping tears from her cheeks, then she reached up to a shelf for the knife that would cut one symbolic lock of Selene's hair. But as she lifted it and was about to say the required words, Andreas stepped forward.

"It is the custom for the brothers to perform this duty," he said, holding out his hand.

Mera blinked in surprise, then laid the knife in his hand, uncertain. Andreas stepped close to Selene and said quietly, "Think of me, for this moment, as your brother."

When his hands touched her hair, Selene closed her eyes. And everyone stared, knowing that this day was going to be talked about for a long time to come.

As Mera watched the curl of black hair fall into the physician's hand, she thought: *He is taking her away from me.*

The lock was given to Selene, and everyone watched as she dedicated it on the little household shrine of Isis.

Then the music started up again and the wine flowed once more. Talk and laughter rose to the ceiling and out into the hot August night. As she turned away from the shrine, Selene could not meet Andreas's eyes. She felt as if she walked in a dream, as if she might any moment wake up to a cold dawn and bitter disappointment.

But the dream went on. Someone produced a chair and Selene sat ceremoniously in it. Then her mother brought out the combs and pins for her final rite—the dressing of Selene's hair in adult fashion.

Ester and Almah, anxious to catch the eye of the gentleman, came forward and insisted that they take the place of sisters, for it was sisters who performed this task. And so once again Mera stood back while strangers attended her daughter; and again she watched Andreas out of the corner of her eye.

He will take her away from me, she thought. *He will take her away from the Goddess and from the purpose of her life. The child was given to me for safekeeping. The gods chose me to be her guardian. She has a duty to them; she must take up the search for who she is. And nothing, no one, must be allowed to divert her from that path.*

In seven days, Mera reassured herself, the Oracle would tell her what to do . . .

When Ester and Almah were finished, everyone praised their work. It was a simple hairstyle, but the very latest, worn, they insisted, by the ladies of the Imperial Court in Rome. And now all the rituals were done and Selene was accepted by her neighbors as a woman. They shook her hand and praised her; more food was sent for, the musicians struck up again; the celebration rose to fever pitch.

Selene sat through it all like a queen on a throne, her face flushed, her eyes aglow. She felt disembodied, as if she stood apart from the young woman in the blue *stola,* the white rose shining like a star on her breast, her hair piled up in curls, and wondered if that could really be Selene. Then she looked around at all the people who ate and drank and celebrated in her honor. She felt dizzy; as if she were climbing to the stars.

The touch of a hand on her wrist brought her down, back into herself. Mera was saying, "You must say something now, Selene, and bid everyone good night."

She looked up at her mother in horror. Say something? In front of all these people?

"A few words of thanks is all," Mera said gently. "For the blessing."

"B-but—"

"Selene," Mera said, quietly but firmly. "Stand up now and just say thank you."

"I c-can't," Selene whispered.

And then Andreas was at her side. "She needs air," he said to Mera. "She needs a moment away from all this noise and excitement." He held out his hand and, Selene, gazing up at him, slipped her own into it. Only a few saw them go through the back door—Almah and Ester, who exchanged a knowing, envious look, and Mera, who was left standing where she was.

Selene and Andreas went up to the roof, an island of peace and quiet in the boisterous neighborhood; they stood beneath stars and amid the glow of the thousands of lights from all over the city.

"Selene," Andreas said, turning to her. "Don't be afraid. You can talk to them. You can say what is required."

"B-but I c-c—"

"Wait," he said. He looked down at her, at the expectant eyes, the beautiful mouth, and marveled at what he was doing. The last time he had cared about anyone or anything had been years ago; after that, he had hardened his heart. In the twelve years since, no one had been able to touch him, to find the narrow avenue into his soul; there had been those who had tried, but he had sealed himself against love and sentiment, against the things that could hurt. He was a physician, and he understood that his spirit, so terribly injured years ago, could not risk another wound.

And yet here he was, on the rooftop of a simple house, taking into his hands the fearful, timid face of a girl he barely knew, and saying to her, "I know you can talk plainly to them, Selene."

"H-how?" she said.

"You are able to heal others, now you must heal yourself. The rug merchant. Do you remember his seizure?"

She nodded.

"Then turn that power on yourself, Selene."

Her eyes widened. She had never thought to use the centering technique on herself. Could she do it?

"T-teach me h-how," she said.

"Whenever you try to speak, you always concentrate on your words; because you do, you trip over them. You try too hard and make yourself tense. The trick is this: You must not think of what you are saying, you must concentrate on something else, and that way your words will come out on their own, clearly. Look at your audience, Selene, but don't *see* them. Stand aside from yourself. What was it you saw that day with the rug merchant? A flame, did you say? Then picture that flame, concentrate on it, allow nothing else into your vision or into your mind. And then speak."

Selene gazed up into his face, mesmerized. He was teaching her as Mera had taught her years ago, when she had first been trained in the ancient touch. To conjure up the soul flame, to center her universe on it.

"Picture it now," he said softly.

A breeze blew down over the rooftop, stirring Selene's *stola*. The hem of her dress brushed against Andreas's bare leg; and the hem of his toga fluttered against her thigh, curling around it. She closed her eyes, then opened them. She saw the flame, and grew calm, at peace. The flame burned more brightly and hotly than it ever had before, as if Andreas's eyes were fueling it. Then Selene opened her mouth and said, "I shall try, Andreas. For you, I shall try."

Everyone crowded into the house for the final moment of the evening. They stood so quietly that the herald of the second watch could be heard far across the city. Selene looked directly at them and spoke without blinking, without stuttering. She thanked them, named them individually and lastly she blessed them. When she was finished, no one moved. The gathered company stood as still and silent as stone.

Then the party broke up, everyone stirring slowly as if waking from a spell. They murmured farewells, reached for cloaks and sandals, and gradually drifted out into the night. Ester said, "Selene, I'm weaving a new pattern and I should so like to know your opinion of it." And Almah said, "May I come and see you some time, Selene?" When the baker's wife said good night, she had a strange look on her face, and a handsome young man, the olive merchant's son, shyly asked Selene if he could take her out walking.

Andreas was the last to go, repeating his thanks to Mera for tending his injuries and congratulating Selene once more on her birthday. He left thinking of the long night ahead of him, knowing he was not going to sleep.

CHAPTER   7

You are dying, my daughter," the Oracle said.

Mera bowed her head and said, "Yes, mother, I am."

"And the child does not know this?"

"No."

The Oracle gazed at Mera through eyes deep with ancient wisdom. "Why have you not told the child you are dying?"

"I wanted to keep her mind and spirit free from worry and anxiety. She is preparing for the final initiation into the secrets of the Goddess."

The Oracle nodded and turned away from her visitor to gaze out of the window to the temple precincts beyond.

It was a gray, cloudy day, typical of August, with a summer storm threatening. A few supplicants were walking about the compound, bringing offerings to the Goddess. A sacred stone dominated the center of the yard, an ancient monolith rising up out of the ground that legend said had once been touched by the Goddess Herself. A well-worn path led up to it, because mothers brought their children to bang their heads against the stone in hopes of knocking sense into them.

The Oracle returned her gaze to Mera. "When will she be initiated?"

"Tomorrow. We go up into the mountains."

The Oracle nodded approval. This healer-woman was a pious and devoted daughter of the Goddess. High in the pure, thin air of the mountains that guarded Antioch, she would bring her own daughter into the covenant of the Great Mother.

"Is she ready?" the Oracle asked.

Mera raised her head and looked directly at the Oracle.

She was a woman of advanced years, small and frail looking, diminished by her black robes and the black veil that covered her white hair. Mera was humbled and awed by the persona of the Oracle, for the elderly women who tended the House of the Goddess wielded formidable power. Like the priestesses of Minerva and Sophia, the women who served Isis were in those years of life when the moon-flow has ceased, allowing all their moon-wisdom to remain within them. The entire world respected such women as the wisest of the wise.

"I don't know," Mera whispered in answer to the Oracle's question. "She should be ready. I have instructed her, prepared her. But . . . "

The Oracle waited.

"But there is now a man."

"You know that your daughter must be pure and untouched for the rite."

"I have forbidden her to see him!"

"Does she obey?"

Mera wrung her hands. *No,* she thought. *In all her sixteen years Selene has been a good and obedient daughter. But now she sneaks out and runs to his house in the upper city.*

"Does she know the danger?" the Oracle asked, as if seeing Mera's thoughts.

"I have warned her. On the night of her Dressing Day, seven days ago, when we were alone, I instructed her. But, mother, she thinks she is in love! Her thoughts have strayed from my teachings. She thinks only of him, speaks only of him—"

The Oracle held up a hand, small and brown and twisted with age. She said: "Your daughter is no ordinary child. She has a destiny to fulfill. You have told me that she came from the gods and was entrusted into your care. Do not fear, daughter, the Goddess will guide her." The Oracle paused and searched Mera's face. Then she said, "There is more. This man frightens you. Why?"

"Because he is luring my daughter away from the true teachings. He is a *surgeon,* mother. He practices an abhorrent kind of healing. And he does not call upon the Goddess for help, he uses no sacred fire, no prayers. And he is teaching my daughter these impious ways! He is dangerous, mother. He will destroy everything I have tried to instill in her." Mera lowered her voice. "It is not the virginity of her body that is threatened, mother, but of her mind."

The Oracle remained silent.

"What shall I do?" Mera asked, leaning forward. "Can you tell me what is written in her stars?"

The Oracle said, "What were the stars of her birth?"

"She was born in Leo with Venus rising in Virgo."

"And at what hour?"

"I . . . I don't know, mother. It was a hasty birth, her parents were fugitives."

"You know that we must have the true Ascendant, daughter. There can be several planets in her First House; we need to know the one closest to her cusp."

Mera already knew this. Over the years she had strived to have Selene's stars read, but to no avail. Mera's facts were scanty: three planets had been flanking Leo—Mars and Saturn rising, Jupiter about to rise. But it was an approximation only. She could be off by an hour, which would shift the focus of the Ascendant.

"There is more," the Oracle said. "Tell me what you have not yet told me."

"There was a twin, a boy, born just before Selene. The parents named him Helios."

The Oracle's eyebrows arched. "Helios and Selene? *Sun and Moon?*" The priestess thought for a moment, her eyes seeming to draw inward; then she said, "The girl must find this brother, for he is her other half. It is vital that she be reunited with him. Do you know where he is?"

Mera shook her head.

"Now give me the lock of hair."

Mera had taken it from the household shrine of Isis, the tress Andreas had cut from Selene's head, and she placed it in the hands of the Oracle.

After a long moment, sitting in the shadows and incense of the Oracle's chamber, the Servant of Isis spoke. "You have spent sixteen years nurturing this child," she said. "The time has come for you to step aside and let her follow her own road."

Mera waited. When nothing more came from the Oracle, she leaned forward anxiously and said, "Before I die, mother, can you tell me who she is?"

"I cannot. The girl will have to find that out for herself. It is the purpose of her life. But the path of her quest does not begin here in Antioch. You must take her back to where her life began, to the place of her birth, and from there the Goddess will lead."

Mera stared at the Oracle in disbelief. Take her back? To Palmyra? "But, mother," she said hesitantly. "That is a very long journey. It would be a great hardship for me."

"And so it must be, daughter. You will not live to see Palmyra, but you must take the girl to the desert there, so that she may begin at the true beginning of the road that will lead to her destiny. You will leave tonight. It is the most auspicious time, under the first full moon," the Oracle said. "From there, the moon will guide your way."

Mera suddenly felt numb. Speechless, she watched the Oracle slowly rise from her chair and make her way, bent with age, to a cupboard in the wall. From it she withdrew an object and placed it on the table before Mera. "Give this to your daughter," she said. "One day it will save her life."

It was a lump of sulphur, known as Brimo's Stone, and was burned in sickrooms to drive off evil spirits. Did this mean, Mera wondered, that some dreadful illness lay in Selene's future?

"That is all I can do for you, daughter," the Oracle said, sitting down with an effort. "You have much to do if you are to obey the Goddess and leave Antioch tonight with your daughter. Go at moonrise."

CHAPTER 8

rimum non nocere," Andreas said softly, as he rubbed the numbing salve into his patient's ear. "It means, Selene, first, do no harm. And it is the cardinal rule of all physicians."

The patient was lying on the couch in Andreas's treatment room, drowsy from the drink he had been given. His head was turned to one side, his hair shaved away from the ear. By the light of the summer sun streaming through the window, Selene could see the deformity of the earlobe.

The man was a former slave, now freed; he had brought his certificate of manumission to Andreas, to prove he had the right to have his earlobe restored.

It was the mark of slavery to have a pierced ear. The perforation was usually done with an awl at the slave market, when the slave was young, and it usually produced an unsightly, pendulous lobe from which a slave's earring hung. Andreas was one of the few men trained in the skill of restoring such ears, removing traces of former slavery. And this morning he was passing that knowledge on to Selene.

She stood close by his side, and when she picked up the scalpel and Andreas repositioned it in her fingers, her bare arm brushed his. "Cut here first," he said, guiding her hand. As soon as the incision was made, dividing the lobe, Andreas stanched the bleeding with a hot cautery stick. "Now remember what I told you, wound edges must be raw and clean or they will not knit."

Selene's hand was steady as she scraped the two posts of earlobe, steady because Andreas was there, his hand ready to help, and also because she held in her mind the image of her soul flame, which calmed her.

Andreas watched Selene as she worked, the intensity in her eyes, the way her full lips were pursed in concentration. And he felt, once again, as he had on each of these seven days since her Dressing Day, a tremor that threatened to topple his stubborn heart. And, strangely, he welcomed it. For the first time in twelve years of cynicism, of erecting walls to protect himself from love, he opened his arms to the tenderness Selene had brought back into his life.

Could it truly have been only seven days? Was it possible for a man to feel so reborn, to feel growing within him a new wisdom and suddenly to discover a purpose in life, all in the improbably short span of one week?

It must be so, he thought, *for it has happened to me.*

"Teach me what you know," Selene had said to him. Two ordinary words, *teach me,* and the doors had been unlocked and flung wide open.

"Cauterize now," Andreas said, reaching across her hands to wipe away the blood. "Now take the suture."

It was a thread of silk tied to the end of a curved fishbone and Andreas guided Selene's hand in the sewing. "The edges must be perfectly aligned," Andreas said, "or they will not knit. Our patient wishes for no one to know he was ever a slave; it is our duty to see that he has his wish."

Selene felt her excitement mount, as it had each time they neared the end of a surgical procedure. At the beginning of an operation she experienced only bafflement, unable to see in the flesh what Andreas obviously saw—a new form, a new shape, perfectly healed. And during the actual operation she concentrated too hard to think of anything but the cutting, the blood, trying to absorb the lesson. But at the end, molding the flesh—the Greeks called it *plastikós* surgery, Andreas had explained, because *plastikós* was the Greek word for "mold"—drawing the raw flesh into a proper shape and sewing it like cloth, Selene could finally see what Andreas had been able to see earlier, and the miracle of it excited her.

That, and the feel of Andreas's hand upon hers.

When he had first taught her how to handle a scalpel the morning after her Dressing Ceremony, when he had first laid the bronze knife in her hand and curled his fingers over hers, Selene had been overcome with an unexpected sense of coming home. It felt so right, holding the knife and subsequently cutting and repairing the wounded flesh. Selene believed that this was what she had been born to do.

And she knew beyond a doubt that a much larger threshold had been crossed that magical night seven days ago—more than the stepping from girlhood into womanhood. Selene felt as if she had been reborn. Andreas had opened the door and shown her a world much larger than any she had previously imagined to exist—a new world, with horizons so far away they could not be seen, only envisioned, a world of more miraculous healing than Mera was capable of, a world in which Selene would learn all there was to learn, and wed it to what she already knew. Mera's herbal healing joined with the wider scope of Andreas's medical arts. There was so much out there waiting for her. Selene wanted to embrace it all.

"Now the rust," Andreas said, handing Selene the spear.

While she carefully wrapped the freedman's head in a bandage, she listened to Andreas. "We will let him sleep and then he can go home. He will return in two days for the bandages to be changed, at which time you will examine the ear for infection. In eight days you will remove the suture and he will be healed."

Andreas walked away from the couch and went to a basin to wash his hands.

The practice of medicine had long ago ceased to hold wonder for Andreas. He healed because it was what he knew how to do. But there had been little drive in it, little sense of purpose. Each day had been like the others, each illness like the last. But in thinking of ways to teach Selene, he had felt a fire start to burn again. He had realized he was a good teacher. In the afternoons that followed, teaching Selene, instructing her, guiding her, Andreas had felt more alive than he had all his life, waking each dawn anxious to get on with things, to see Selene and teach her, perhaps to teach *others*, in fact.

He had not been aware he was staring at her until she suddenly looked up and smiled.

Something else had been reawakened in Andreas seven nights ago, something that had been killed years before, but had now come alive again. And it was something Andreas knew he must handle with extreme care. It was not to be rushed into, his sexual desire for her.

Andreas wanted to take Selene into his arms immediately and make love to her. He had opened doors to other worlds for her; now he wanted to be the key to this one. His hunger was at times a physical ache; there were moments when he wanted to forget caution and take her at once. But then he remembered her youth, her innocence and their new bond, which in many ways was so astonishingly deep and abiding. It seemed as if they had known each other for years. Still, the bond was new and must be gently nurtured.

After all, what did Selene want? Andreas was fourteen years older than she—although that was not an obstacle to marriage, for many good matches were made between young girls and mature men. But he was much older in other ways. Andreas had traveled the world; he had witnessed the range of the human condition; Selene had spent her entire life protected.

How did she regard him? When Selene gazed at him with such open affection, was it with the love of a scholar for a mentor, of a sister for brother, or even, the gods forbid, a daughter for a father? What would

result if he ventured to reveal his feelings, only to frighten her, and shatter
their delicate new union?

Andreas's thoughts were interrupted by a commotion in the street. He
went to the window and looked out.

"What is it?" Selene asked, joining him.

An unruly mob had come around the corner and was now clamoring past
Andreas's house. It was a parade of some sort: The participants were
adorned with flower garlands and crowns of acorns; musicians played pipes
and drums. It was a merry crowd, and it grew as people joined it along the
way.

Then Andreas saw the lifesize effigy carried at the rear of the procession,
and he said, "It's a birthday celebration, in honor of the God Augustus."

"Where are they going?"

"I would guess they were going to Daphne. Festivals are held there to
honor the gods. They are going to pay homage to Augustus."

"But isn't Augustus dead?" she asked, seeming to recall that another
emperor ruled in Rome, named Tiberius.

"Augustus died sixteen years ago."

"Then why do they celebrate his birthday?"

"Because he is a god."

Selene watched the statue go by, thinking that Augustus must have been
a very handsome man in life if the effigy were a faithful likeness. She said,
"But if he was a man, how can he now be a god?"

"The people made him one."

"Have they that power?"

"It is the mob that rules Rome, Selene. They have the power to make
gods, or to destroy them. The Julio-Claudian family rules only because the
mob allows them to. They made Julius Caesar a god, too. And I should
not be surprised if they made Tiberius a *living* god."

Selene was wide-eyed. What must they be like, these people who were
gods and who inhabited the Imperial Palace in far-away Rome?

"Would you like to go to the festival?" Andreas asked.

Selene looked at the water clock. Was there time? She had only been
able to come here today because her mother was out of the house. Mera
had gone to the temple of Isis and was there now, consulting with the
Oracle. Mera had forbidden Selene to visit Andreas. But how could she
stay away?

CHAPTER 9

Zoë watched them go. Standing at the window, her eyes filled with tears of jealousy and rage. She saw Andreas and the girl join the parade and watched as it wound its noisy way down the street, around the corner and off into silence.

Zoë stood there for a long time. In all her twenty-two years of poverty and abuse, of being handled by loveless hands and betrayed by callous hearts, in all her loneliness and bad luck and in her darkest nights of despairing, Zoë had never, until this moment, fully understood the injustice of life.

She should be walking with him to the festival; *she* was the one who had given up her bed and had taken him in when he was injured. She was the one who had sent for the healer-woman, and who had sat with him until he woke. And it was *she*, Zoë, who had made great plans for herself and for him.

And she had almost had him. He had wakened in her apartment and for a brief moment had looked on her with tenderness and vulnerability; for the first time in her life her heart had softened. But then he had wakened the next day and asked for someone named Malachus, and he had been taken away, out of her life, out of her great plan for the two of them, leaving her with a dream broken in pieces.

But then, a few days afterward, she had received a summons from Andreas! He had called her to this house and had offered her a reward for having taken him in. The Zoë of a month ago would have asked for money and would have sailed to Sicily in search of the little house with the olive tree. But the new Zoë, foolishly in love, had asked to be allowed to stay here, in Andreas's house, as one of his servants. And so Zoë had a small room of her own; she was dressed well and received a wage for working as a maid. She was taken care of now, and respectable.

But none of this mattered to Zoë. All she cared about was being near Andreas.

And it had been so wonderful for a while, bringing him wine, putting flowers in his rooms, seeing to his every comfort. But then that girl had appeared and now everything was spoiled.

Zoë was not stupid. She knew what the look in her master's eyes meant when that girl was around. It was a look Zoë herself gave Andreas, although he did not see it.

Well, she was not going to give up. Zoë had finally found a man worth sacrificing and fighting for—and she was going to do both in order to secure Andreas for herself. She would sacrifice her youth, what little was left of it, by staying in this house, his willing servant, and she would serve him loyally until she was bent and gray, if necessary. And then she would fight, if she had to, with that girl or with any other who tried to make Andreas her own.

But first, she decided, when the noisy parade could no longer be heard in the street, she was going to start with that girl.

As she turned to walk away, Zoë was unaware that she herself was being observed at that moment by Malachus, who watched her with hungry eyes.

It was a terrible irony, and a curse as well, for a man so late in years to fall in love at last, and with a girl so very young and so hard of heart that the love brought him more misery than joy.

Malachus knew what Zoë thought of him, she had once told the housekeeper that she thought he was like a big stupid bear, who followed his master around. Well, Malachus could not deny that he was a big man, and clumsy, and not given to smart speech. But his heart was also large, and it was loyal, and he was eternally faithful. He did not know if Zoë knew that he loved her; he suspected not, he *prayed* not, for if she knew of his love, then she treated him cruelly indeed. In his simplicity and awkwardness, Malachus harbored the hope that, once she knew how he felt about her, she would act more kindly toward him. And possibly someday return the feeling.

But not while I am a slave, Malachus thought unhappily, as he watched her disappear down the hall. *She will not love me while I have this slave's ring in my ear.*

For the first time in his life, after so many voyages and knowing so many masters, Malachus the slave cursed his lot. While he was tasting passionate yearning, he was also tasting bitterness and discontent.

He wanted his freedom. That was what would win Zoë. All the gifts he gave to her—the figs, the scarf, the bracelet that had cost so much—she accepted with a cool indifference that stabbed at his heart. But his manhood, his freedom, ownership of his self, surely she would see how precious that was; but to achieve it he must buy himself from Andreas, the master he had thought he would never leave.

In these old years it was vital to a slave to have a comfortable life, and Malachus was luckier than most. Andreas did not mistreat his people; he was kind, generous, and kept the old ones long past their usefulness, seeing that they had a bed, food, medical care. Malachus had looked forward to a secure retirement under Andreas's roof. But not any longer. Now he needed to be free. He would purchase himself out of this household that had been his family for ten years and he would try to make his way in the world as a freedman. Doing what, he had no idea.

The first thing he would ask of Andreas would be to close up the hole in his earlobe so that Zoë would not have to be reminded of her husband's former slavery.

Malachus sighed and turned away.

There was one obstacle to his plan: Zoë seemed to have her heart set on Andreas. Of course Malachus knew how hopeless that was, that no woman was ever going to snare his master's heart, not in *that* way; only Malachus, who had joined up with Andreas back in Alexandria, knew that Andreas was as untouchable as the distant stars, and only Malachus knew why. But Zoë still pined for her master. And, fruitless though that hope might be, Malachus knew that while Zoë yearned for Andreas she would never see the devotion Malachus had for her.

But there was one hope. Four days ago, Malachus had learned that Naso the sea captain was back in Antioch, having, for some reason, turned back from his voyage to Britain. Malachus knew that Andreas would not be able to resist a visit with the man; Andreas was as addicted to sailors and their sea-talk as some men were to liquor. Perhaps, Malachus hoped, since his master had missed sailing with Naso three weeks ago, he would go with him now, and this time, Malachus had heard, Naso was planning to sail farther than ever before—around the southern tip of India and eastward to distant China.

Malachus was filled with hope. Because Andreas, he knew, would never be able to resist such a journey.

CHAPTER 10

The birthday parade, having multiplied in size during its journey through the streets of Antioch, poured boisterously through the southern gate of the city and up the road that led to Daphne. This massive gate was the terminus for many caravans, and the whole area was one gigantic encampment: tents, camels, donkeys as far as the eye could see. Threading her way through it all was Mera, frantically racing against time in the hope of finding a caravan that was due to depart tonight.

Upon leaving the temple a short while before, Mera had gone straight home—and had not been surprised to find Selene absent; with Andreas again! She had gathered her few possessions of value: the alabaster jar of myrrh, her spare leather sandals, a tortoiseshell comb. The one really valuable object she owned she had given to her daughter, and Selene wore the ivory rose at all times now, hidden beneath her dress as a precaution against theft. Mera would not have sold the rose anyway; with what she had been able to gather up from around the house she had secured enough money to buy passage for the two of them for the long journey eastward. Into the desert, back to Palmyra.

There were so many caravans, some arriving, some departing. The terminus was a chaotic bustle of travelers, traders, beggars and animals. Mera worked her way among the tents and booths, clutching her side, dizzy with pain, asking along the way. In order to fulfill the Oracle's command, she had to find a caravan leaving for the east this very night.

And so she paid no attention to the merry birthday parade which passed by and turned up a wooded path. Mera did not see her daughter and Andreas walking hand in hand in the singing throng.

It was called the Grotto of Daphne because it was here, so the legend went, that Daphne turned herself into a laurel tree in order to escape the sexual embrace of Apollo. Everyone who came to this lush place searched for the specific tree that had once been the virginal goddess, and so Selene did now, her hand in Andreas's. She held on to him as the mob carried them along, and wondered why Daphne would rather have been a tree than experience the physical love of Apollo.

The parade broke up when it reached the grotto. The statue of Augustus was set on a hillock and people began to dance around it. Food and wine materialized; baskets appeared; cloaks were spread on the ground. Merrymakers cavorted on the grass without a care in the world, rattling tambourines, calling to one another. Although the sky was growing dark and the air was damp, the mood was one of sunshine and optimism.

Selene felt as if she and Andreas had stepped into a magic world. The grotto was enchanting—wooded and fragrant, sprinkled with sounds of waterfalls and running creeks. As she walked hand in hand with Andreas, forgetting all her cares, not thinking of medicines and illness, nor of the spiritual initiation she was to undergo tomorrow night, not far away, but in a more isolated spot, Selene pondered the plight of poor Daphne, who had been turned into a tree because Apollo had wanted to make love to her.

Why had she done it? Selene wondered, as she felt the warmth of Andreas's hand around hers. *Why would she run from passion? I would not. If Andreas desires me . . .*

Selene looked at him out of the corner of her eye. He was so beautiful, so strong. And she was so much in love with him, it took her breath away.

How did Andreas think of her? Was she too much a child in his eyes to think of passion? Did he see her only as a student, a protégée? "Look upon me, for this moment," he had said at her Dressing Ceremony, "as your brother." Was that all he would be?

She ached for him. She wanted to feel his arms around her, wanted to tell him how she felt. But whenever she thought she would take the chance, make some sign, she grew afraid and shied away. Their new union was too precious, and too new. She daren't threaten it with anything that might shatter the dream.

As she looked around at the celebrating crowd, at men and women embracing, Selene again searched for the tree that had once been the goddess Daphne.

When the first warm raindrops fell, Andreas and Selene looked at each other in surprise. In the next instant, the clouds opened and rain scattered the crowd. People ran for the nearest shelter, gathering up cloaks and picnics. Andreas took Selene's arm and they fled to the thick sheltering overhang of a tree.

Selene laughed as the rain fell harder; the summer day had turned suddenly turbulent, but people still called happily to one another from under trees, and a few danced about in the rain. When drops started to fall through the overhead branches, Andreas removed his toga, held it out around his shoulders like a cloak, and drew Selene against him, pulling her back from the rain so they leaned against the tree trunk.

Her laughter died. She gazed out at the rain, thinking only of his arm around her shoulders.

Andreas, too, grew quiet, and after some time, when the torrent showed no sign of letting up, Andreas drew Selene to sit on the ground with him, the tree trunk at their backs, their knees drawn up under the toga. He said, "It rains like this in Alexandria."

The tone of his voice caused Selene to turn and look at him. His face was inches from hers; he stared straight ahead.

"It brings to mind someone I once knew in Alexandria," he said quietly, still staring ahead. "I don't know why I should think of him now, after all these years. He was a boy I knew in the School of Medicine. We studied together there."

Selene felt Andreas's body expand and contract with a sigh, and his arm seemed more heavy on her shoulders.

"He was nineteen years old when I met him, and he came from my native Corinth, although I never knew him there. He was a quiet, with-

drawn boy, and people wondered about him. He used to wake up screaming in his sleep."

Selene watched Andreas's profile. She had never been this close to him
before. She could see the gentle throb of the pulse in his neck, where the
dark-brown beard thinned and met the top of his tunic. "Tell me about
him," she said.

Andreas seemed not really to have heard. He kept his eyes on the rain,
as if searching for something. Then at last he said, "One day, this boy told
me an extraordinary story."

He had lived in Corinth with his parents, the boy's story went, an only
child. His father had been a physician of modest skills, his mother one of
those round, comfortable women. The boy had been apprenticing with his
father for as long as he could remember, and had had no ambition to be
more than a village doctor. And then one day he met a woman.

"I believe he said her name was Hestia. Anyway, the boy told me that
he fell desperately in love with Hestia. He was sixteen years old and knew
nothing of life. Hestia was older and had known many men. He would
loiter around her house, hoping to catch a glimpse of her, and he sent her
such presents as he could afford—simple things. Hestia neither encouraged nor discouraged him, but tolerated his youthful infatuation as she
might the devotion of a pet. One night, he told me, he forced his way into
her house and proclaimed his undying love for her. Hestia neither scolded
him, nor laughed at him. Worse, she was kind to him.

"The fire in his blood," Andreas continued quietly, "grew hotter until
he became obsessed. He neglected his duties at home and spent his days
and nights trying to find a way to capture Hestia's heart. And one day it
came to him. He saw that such women were impressed by wealth, and that
rich men received more attention than did poor men. To the boy's innocent mind, therefore, if he were very rich, he believed she would be
content to be his.

"Working as a village physician would not please her, he knew, nor did
he believe she would wait for him to make his fortune. He needed wealth
at once. And he knew of one way to get it."

The boy had heard of the amber-hunters, men who risked their lives to
journey to the ends of the earth in search of amber. It was common
knowledge that amber was one of the most valuable commodities in the
world; one small figurine made of amber was equal to the cost of six slaves.
So the boy decided he would sign on a ship bound for the amber fields,
work for a year and return to Hestia a wealthy man. So reasoned his
sixteen-year-old mind.

Andreas paused, and when the pause stretched into a long silence,

Selene turned to look at him. The frown had faded from Andreas's fore-head. His face was smooth and blank, his eyes distant. When he finally spoke again, his voice came from far away. He told of how the boy had gone to Hestia, telling her what he was going to do. For the first time, Hestia gave him encouragement. She promised to wait for him, and said that if indeed he came back with amber, she would be his special friend. He never told his parents what he was doing, but left the house in the dark of night and went to the harbor, where he had heard of a man who was outfitting an amber ship.

The boy found the captain, and when he was told he was too young, too inexperienced, the boy swore on his gods that he would work harder than any other crew member. The captain had seen the passion in the boy's eyes and signed him on; then he explained the terms of the contract.

"There is no more greatly guarded secret in all the world," Andreas said, "than the whereabouts of amber. The few men who captain the amber-hunting ships are fiercely jealous of that secret, and so, knowing how a common sailor likes to tell tales, such captains have devised a way of swearing these men to silence so that the secret of the amber fields is never revealed.

"Every crewman is made to sign a contract. On that paper are listed the names of family or loved ones left behind. It is understood by every hand who signs on that this is the captain's guarantee against loose tongues. If the sailor ever talks, if he ever boasts, in whatever tavern in whatever harbor in the world, it will be known. And the shipping company will exact retribution from the names listed on the paper. Such a bond keeps sailors honest, and this is the way the amber fields are kept a secret. The boy told me that he wrote down the names of his parents, and the location of their house in Corinth."

The story went on, about how the boy sailed the next day without saying goodbye, because he was so full of shame. But his blood boiled for Hestia, his mind was filled with visions of his grand return. The ship set sail and disappeared between the Pillars of Hercules, out over the misty sea toward the North Star. The voyage took two years, and in that time the boy became a man.

As Selene stared into the lightly falling rain and listened to Andreas's quiet voice, she saw the ocean waves as tall as mountains and the sailors who fell to their watery deaths; she imagined terrifying sea monsters, and the foggy land of the blue-skinned savages. She felt the sickness of the sea that drove men to madness, the awful thirst when the ship's water supply ran out, with miles of water all around and crewmen dying of the gum disease, men turning upon one another for a strip of bad meat. She heard the deadly call of the beautiful sirens on the rocks, she felt the bitter cold of snowy seas and saw men lose fingers and toes to it, and she knew in her own soul the despair and loneliness of a young boy far from home.

"They found the amber," Andreas went quietly on, "and loaded the ship until the boards creaked. And then they began the long journey homeward, a small crew now, on a crippled vessel. By the time they limped into Corinth's harbor, it was a crew of strangers that stepped on the dock. But they were wealthy men, wealthy beyond counting, and well set up for the rest of their days."

The boy, by then eighteen but looking older and of a far older mind, had gone straight to Hestia's house. In the two long and nightmarish years, on those nights when he had slept with a knife in his hand, when he had wept bitterly, when his belly had collapsed against his spine in hunger, it had been the memory of Hestia that had kept him alive. So when he found her house occupied by strangers, people who had bought the house nearly two years before, but who had no idea where the previous owner had gone, something snapped inside the boy.

He spent a year searching, but never found her. And one night, in a tavern in a harbor, he drank himself senseless. He cried out all his pain and anguish, and without realizing it, he told about the amber fields, on the beaches of the North Sea where the Rhine River empties its cold waters. When he came to himself and realized what he had done, it was too late.

Andreas drew in a deep breath and let it out slowly. He brought Selene closer to him and held her so tightly his fingers dug into her arm. "An example had to be made, of course. A visit was paid to the boy's parents, late one night. Everything was stolen, the little house destroyed. And the next day stories began to circulate about the scandalous practices of a certain local physician. A young girl had died, it was rumored, in a messy abortion."

Andreas's voice broke as he said, "You know, Selene, that a physician can turn his skills to taking life as well as to saving it. And so the boy came home to find his parents laid out in the company of a single mourner. There was a note. The boy must have memorized it, because he was able to repeat it to me: 'We learned of your misfortune when it was too late for us to help you,' the note read. 'Do not grieve for us, son, for all of life is vanity and we depart it with relief. Always remember that in our last moments we loved you.'

"The boy went to Alexandria then, and enrolled in the School of Medicine, which was where I met him and where he told me his story."

When Andreas fell silent, Selene turned to him and asked, "What became of him? Of the boy?"

"He developed a fascination for ships. He would go down to the harbor and spend hours there . . . just watching. And then one day, shortly after he had recited the Hippocratic oath, the right ship must have come in, because the boy walked straight onto it without a single backward glance, and he sailed away, never to return . . . "

Selene stared at Andreas's tight profile, the handsome arching nose and the square jaw under the trim beard; she felt his heartbeat through the soft cloth of his tunic, and the slow respirations like those of a man asleep. And she wanted to say something, but had no idea what.

Finally she said, "That's a very sad story."

He turned his dark gray-blue eyes to her and she saw her own reflection in them, and something else—ocean depths and currents.

Andreas stirred like a man waking; he brought a hand up and laid it on her cheek. "You *are* different, aren't you?" he said. "What did I do to deserve you? Why have the gods smiled upon me? It makes me afraid."

Selene leaned into him, into the firm hardness of the body that electrified her. "Don't be afraid, Andreas," she whispered, pressing her mouth against his neck, his beard.

When their mouths came together it was in a gentle kiss, almost an uncertain one, as if each feared the other would suddenly flee—like Daphne, running—but when Selene lifted her arms and curled them around his neck, the kiss became harder and very sure. Andreas eased her down onto her back, onto the wet grass and the earth, and the white toga protected them from the rain.

They kissed for a long time, caressing each other, but when Selene let out a moan and arched her back, Andreas pulled back sharply.

"Not now," he said in a tight voice.

She sat up. "Andreas—"

He touched her mouth with his fingertips. "There is time, Selene. We have time. We have all the future and all the world."

"I love you, Andreas."

He smiled and stroked her hair. "We have come from far away, Selene. We have come from two great distances that are farther away than the stars in the sky. We are like two travelers on earth, just born, alone together, you and I." His eyes searched her face. "I love you, Selene," he said. "And it is more than the love of a man desiring a woman, although I desire you with all my heart. You walked into my life and awakened me. I was not living, Selene, I was only existing. But you have given me purpose. I want to teach you, Selene. First you. And then I want to teach others." He spoke with passion, his eyes burning. "We are together now, and we shall never be apart. I shall go to sea no more. All those journeys, all that searching. I don't know what I was searching for, I only knew that I must somehow punish myself through the rigors of the sea. But I feel that's all over now. I've been forgiven. I've been given you, and a second chance. Selene, you are my life, my soul."

He raised his hands to the chain around his neck. It was a gold chain and at its end hung the golden Eye of Horus he had received the day he had recited the Hippocratic oath at the School of Medicine. He lifted the chain up over his head and laid it over Selene's, settling it down around her neck. "This is my most precious possession. With this, I bind myself to you."

"And I give myself to you, Andreas," Selene said, reaching beneath the fabric of her dress and lifting over her head her own necklace—the ivory rose. When she placed it on his chest, she said, "My mother has told me that this rose contains all that I am. Therefore I give it to you, Andreas, as I would give myself."

They kissed again, then he drew her to him and held her tightly. And they watched the gentle rain.

C H A P T E R   1 1

Palmyra! Mother, you can't mean it!"

Mera did not reply. She hurried about the house, putting the last of their possessions into the one basket they were allowed to take on the caravan.

"Speak to me!" Selene cried.

She had come from Daphne to find her mother packing a large basket with clothes, food and necessities. At first Selene had thought it was for their two-day mountain retreat the next day, but when she saw the scrolls of herbal formulae, the woollen winter undergarments, bread and cheese enough for a week—things they had no need of for a short retreat—Selene had asked her mother what she was doing.

"We are leaving at once," Mera had said. "We are taking a caravan to Palmyra."

"Mother!" cried Selene, taking hold of Mera's arm and forcing her to stand still. "Why are we going to Palmyra?"

"It is the command of the Goddess. The Oracle told me so this afternoon."

"But *why*, Mother? Why Palmyra? That is hundreds of miles from here! Across a desert. We would be gone for weeks!"

I shall be gone for but a few days, Mera thought. *But you, daughter, will be gone forever.*

"I told you. It is what the Goddess bids."

Selene was stunned. She stepped back from her mother and slowly shook her head. "No. I won't go."

"You have no choice."

"I'm going to marry Andreas."

"You will *not* marry Andreas," Mera said, with such ferocity that Selene was taken aback. Mera's eyes blazed as she repeated, "You will go to Palmyra as the Goddess bids. You will obey."

"But . . . *Palmyra*, Mother! Why Palmyra?"

Mera returned to the basket, closed the lid and tied the rope. "Because your destiny lies in Palmyra."

"My destiny is with Andreas!"

Mera spun around and confronted her daughter with challenging eyes. "Listen to me, Selene," she said, evenly. "I had not thought you would come willingly. I do not cherish this journey myself. But we have no choice in this. You belong to the gods, Selene. You came from them, you must go to them. You must do as they bid."

Selene felt the room tilt. "What . . . do you mean?"

"When the time comes, I will tell you. But now get your cloak, and your spare sandals. We must leave at once."

"I have to tell Andreas."

"There is no time." Mera's hand shot out and grasped Selene's arm in a painful grip. "You will not tell Andreas."

"I must!"

"He does not figure into your destiny, Selene. You must forget him."

Shock and disbelief registered on Selene's face. She felt the pain of her mother's grip, saw the deadly earnestness in her mother's eyes and felt the world start to turn and tumble about her. "No," she said, trying to pull away.

"Selene! You owe obedience to me, and to the Goddess."

"I will not do it, Mother."

Their eyes met and locked. But Mera had anticipated this; she was prepared. "You must come," she said in a low voice. "It is my dying wish."

"What do you mean?"

"I am dying, my daughter."

Mera let go of Selene's arm and reached down for her wrist. Raising it, she placed Selene's hand against her side, where the hard lump, the size of an orange, strained against the fabric of her dress.

Selene gasped.

"I kept it a secret from you," Mera said, turning away, "because I wanted your mind free from worry. I wanted you to concentrate upon your initiation into the covenant of the Goddess. But now I have no choice. The Goddess bids that I take you into the desert near Palmyra and give you your final instruction there." She faced her daughter squarely. "Very few days are left to me, Selene. My purpose is drawing to an end, and yours will just be beginning. I promised the Goddess that I would take you to Palmyra tonight. Before I die."

Selene's mind was racing. Andreas—he must be told.

"Come, daughter. We have to hurry."

"But what will we do in Palmyra?"

"The Goddess will make Her purpose known. Here is your cloak, Selene. Get your medicine box."

Selene moved woodenly. Surely her mother had gone mad! "I shall come right back to Antioch, Mother," Selene said. "I shall come back to Andreas."

"If it is your destiny to do so. Although I think not."

"I shall make it my destiny!"

Mera stood in the open doorway. "It is not for you to decide, Selene. Come along, now. We haven't much time."

They hurried down the street toward the south of the city, with the westering sun on their right, breaking through the afternoon clouds. They did not look back at the house they were leaving; Mera knew it would stand vacant for a while, and then the city magistrate would take it over and sell it. The little house had served its purpose; neither she nor Selene, Mera was certain, would ever see it again.

The caravan terminus was still in chaos. A train of five hundred camels had just arrived from Damascus; a larger one was about to depart for Jerusalem. Selene followed her mother through the pandemonium. There were many camps: Tents and cookfires filled the space between kneeling camels and tethered donkeys; people of races and tongues from all over the Roman Empire filled the evening air with their shouts, their arguments, their raucous music.

As Selene stumbled through, clutching her new medicine box which swung from her shoulder, her mind was awhirl: What to do? Was her mother really dying? Would Mera lie about such a thing in order to get Selene away from Antioch? And why must they go to *Palmyra,* of all places?

"Here we are," Mera said breathlessly, lowering the heavy basket to the ground. "We will be sharing a donkey."

Selene looked around the smoke-filled compound, marked off by lines of snorting camels. She saw tent pegs coming up and canvases going down. People were bustling to and fro, purchasing last-minute food, filling water jugs, strapping bundles to animals. Selene was numb. This could not be happening! She was having a bad dream. Andreas!

Selene watched her mother straighten up and clutch her side. *Dying*, she had said.

Reaching out to her, Selene said, "Mother—"

"I shall be all right for a little while, daughter. But the opium no longer works."

Then Selene remembered her mother waking in the night to drink from a jar. Selene had thought she'd just been thirsty.

"Mother!" she cried. "You are not well enough to make this trip!"

"I must. Now wait here, daughter. There is more to do."

Tears pricked Selene's eyes as she watched her mother make her way toward a man who was surrounded by other people, all waving their arms and shouting something about water rights at oases. Selene saw the way her mother limped, the way she held her side, and she realized the truth: Mera really was dying.

Selene stood for an instant longer, watching, then she made her decision.

She spun about and ran back through the throng, dodging crates and chickens, sprinting around tent lines and campfires. Andreas, Andreas, thumped her heart.

By the time Selene reached his street in the upper city, out of breath, desperate, the sky had grown dark and the barest beginnings of moonlight could be seen to appear over the rooftops.

Would Mera leave without her? No. But Selene knew that if she did not get back to the terminus in time, the caravan would depart, leaving Mera behind, alone in the midst of a night camp full of travelers and thieves. And surely by now Mera had noticed her daughter's absence. *She will think I have run away. She will be terrified. Andreas and I must hurry back to her.*

He would persuade Mera against this madness. If not, then Andreas would go with them to Palmyra. Andreas.

Selene pulled on the bellrope as if to break it, and when the gate in the high wall opened, she had to lean against the gatepost and catch her breath before she could speak.

"I must see your master!" Selene blurted out. "It is most urgent!"

Zoë regarded Selene with cool eyes, taking in the traveling cloak, the beautiful ebony and ivory medicine box, the disheveled appearance. And she said, "My master is not in."

"Not in! But he must be!"

Zoë's eyes flickered. "He went out."

"*Where?*"

"To the harbor. He went to see a sea captain."

Andreas! Selene cried with her heart.

There was no time to go in search of him. The caravan was about to depart; Selene had just time enough to run back.

Abruptly, she swung the box off her shoulder, dropped to her knees and opened the lid. Zoë, standing over Selene, looked down as the girl took a piece of pottery from the box, the sort on which physicians wrote prescriptions. She spat on an ink cake and smeared the tip of a pen into it.

"Give this to your master," Selene said, as she wrote. The note read: *We are on the road to Palmyra. We are traveling with a caravan that goes under the banner of Mars. Come for us. My mother is dying.*

She paused, and then added: *Love.*

Snapping the medicine box shut and hoisting it back onto her shoulder, Selene stood and held out the shard. "You know who I am, do you not? Tell your master that I was here. And give this to him as soon as he returns. It is urgent!"

Zoë took the shard. "As soon as he returns," she said, and stepped back to close the gate.

"And tell him," Selene added, her hands gripping the leather strap of the box until her knuckles were white, "that I am on the Palmyra road with my mother. Tell him to come after me!"

Zoë nodded that the message would be passed along, then she closed the gate and listened to the slap of Selene's sandals as she ran back down the rain-damp street. When she was gone, Zoë looked at the piece of pottery with its inky scribbles, dropped it to the garden path, ground it to a powder under her heel and brushed the path clean.

———

Andreas looked up from his writing table and saw, through the open window, the beginnings of moonlight start to appear over the rooftops. He thought he had heard the gate bell. He waited, pen in hand, poised over the blank parchment on his table. If there had been someone at the gate, a patient most likely, then it would be reported to him momentarily.

He listened. The house was silent. No one came. Deciding it must have been a neighbor's gate bell, Andreas addressed the blank scroll once more.

He had purchased it that afternoon, after he and Selene had left Daphne, the first purchase of his new life. Indeed, he saw this scroll as that new life. Blank and fresh and waiting to be written upon. It would contain his medical notes, a medical textbook-to-be. It was his future, his and Selene's.

With Selene at his side to encourage him, inspire him and love him, Andreas knew he could achieve great things. The thought of it made him tremble. It was such a great step, he was almost afraid to take it. With Selene, he was learning to trust again.

He paused and closed his eyes. He felt a joy that seemed more than one man could contain. As he opened his eyes and proceeded to write the first words—*"De Medicina"*—on the blank scroll, Andreas did not hear the sound of sandaled footsteps running down the rain-damp street.

BOOK II

PALMYRA

CHAPTER 12

K azlah, the Chief Physician of the palace in Magna, had only two
ambitions in life: to be Queen Lasha's lover, and to live forever.
Of the two, he was beginning to wonder whether the latter was
going to be accomplished sooner than the former.

As the queen's personal physician, Kazlah was the only member of the
court permitted to look directly upon Lasha's face; he did so now, while
he spoke, yet all the time he was speaking, he was also wondering how he
was going to insinuate himself into the queen's bed.

"Virgins are what are needed." Lasha's sharp voice sliced through the
torchlit night. "Virgins. They will cure the king's impotence."

Kazlah doubted this. King Zabbai's failed sexual ability was beyond the
usual stimulation—virgins indeed, for a man with over a hundred wives!
But the Chief Physician dared not contradict the queen. Technically, it
was not the queen at all who was speaking, but the Goddess Herself.

The Goddess was known variously as Allat, Allah, and Alla', the Morning Star, she who devoured her lovers. Her home had originally been in
Sheba, deep in Arabia, but she had been brought centuries ago to the city
of Magna, far to the north, by nomadic Arabs who ranged the great desert
in between. In this exotic city on the Euphrates, the Goddess Allat spoke
her commandments through Lasha, queen of Magna.

"It is the Goddess's wish," Queen Lasha now repeated to Kazlah. "The king must be rejuventated. It is not his time to die."

Kazlah stroked the dark V of beard on his chin as he gazed up at the Goddess, tonight in her Devouring aspect, gobbling up night and stars in her path. Kazlah's primary responsibility as chief physician was keeping King Zabbai alive, but it was life saving of a type that did not ordinarily fall under his purview. The king, though getting on in years, was still healthy and vigorous. The untimeliness of his death would not lie in natural causes but in religious ones: An impotent king had to be killed.

The custom had its beginnings far back in time, in an age when women ruled and men were discarded when their purpose came to an end; it was an ancient belief found all over the world—the replacement of the old king restored the virility and immortality of the city and its people. In the ancient city of Magna, sixty miles east of Palmyra, King Zabbai, after a life of excess and self-indulgence, had come to that pass, and rumor now swept through the palace that the time for his replacement was at hand.

But there was a problem. No one in the palace, least of all King Zabbai himself, wanted the crown to pass on to a younger man just then. For Chief Physician Kazlah and other powerful officials, Zabbai was a puppet ruler who never got in the way of their many court intrigues; as for Queen Lasha, her weak consort allowed her to be the dominant ruler, and it would greatly inconvenience her to share the throne with an ambitious young man.

It was therefore generally agreed all around that King Zabbai's sexual potency had to be restored.

The Chief Physician turned away from his contemplation of the night sky and looked at the queen. Despite blindness in one eye, she was beautiful, in an austere, almost frightening way. Just as his love for her was. Kazlah was no ordinary man, and therefore his lust was no ordinary lust; he had been born with a heart incapable of affection and sentiment, and his was a love of possession, a primal urge to capture, subjugate and subsequently *own* that which was supremely unattainable: Queen Lasha, Goddess-incarnate on earth.

"Does the Goddess say how this is to be achieved?" he asked.

Lasha's eye turned hard and cold. "That is your worry, physician."

Kazlah, tall and lean, a man whose face was all profile, studied the queen's expression, then turned away. He had to be careful now. Everything he had worked for, plotted for, even murdered for, was hanging in a delicate balance. For the first time in their years together, Queen Lasha was placing all her hope and trust in *him*. This could at last be the way to that sublime goal beyond her bedchamber door.

Kazlah's sandaled footsteps whispered on the polished floor as he paced in thought while Lasha watched him, half hating, half admiring this physician whom she had come, against her will, to rely on too heavily. He was an ambitious man, and ambitious men could not be trusted. Lasha recalled the day when Kazlah, new to the court, had groveled before her in fear and humility, not daring to look upon her face: even now, seeing it meant instant death to anyone else. Those days were now long gone; years of plotting had lifted the son of nomad Arabs up to imponderable heights. On his way, Kazlah had learned the priceless and secret healing arts, collecting them, hoarding them like treasure. Eventually, over the years, he had cleverly instilled among the royal family and courtiers who lived in the palace an unshakable dependency upon him. For life, or death, there was no one to turn to except Kazlah. Hate him though she did, Queen Lasha needed her chief physician.

"Very well. Virgins," Kazlah said at last, inclining his reed-thin body toward the queen. "Perhaps white, with pure, unblemished skin. Perhaps that will stimulate the king."

Lasha's glacial face shifted into a frown. Where, in this land of harsh sun and desert winds, were they going to find milk-skinned girls? "Send to Palmyra," she said at last. "There is a man there, a slaver, who keeps an eye on the roads."

"But, my lady, the roads are policed by Romans."

"They cannot be everywhere at all times."

"And the Palmyrene desert police! Those oasis merchants guard their caravan roads as jealously as a man his daughters, for without guaranteed safety along them, the city of Palmyra would lose its position as Crossroads of the World. It would return to the scorpions and the sand. Sooner cut off their water supply than threaten those who travel their roads!"

Lasha narrowed her one eye at her adversary-advisor. "I have heard that this man in Palmyra is discreet. He strikes quickly and vanishes into the desert like a *jinn*. More, he knows which fingers to caress with gold. It must be done, physician."

The tone in which the last words were spoken counseled the physician to silence. Lasha was in no mood to be crossed by him, and Kazlah knew why. It had nothing to do with King Zabbai's impotence. Queen Lasha was furious with Kazlah over his failure to cure her son of a summer fever.

There were moments when Kazlah rued his post of Chief Physician. Having to ease the many ailments of the gouty, overindulged court, being called out of bed at all hours of the night for real and imagined ills, expected to work miracles, to see through human flesh, to have instant answers, to know everything! Look at him these days: black hair streaked with gray, deep lines etched in hollow cheeks, thin lips curving more downward with each passing year. Lasha's only son had burned for three days with a mysterious fever and, thus far, none of Kazlah's remedies had worked.

The palace was starting to buzz with speculations as to Kazlah's fate. What, everyone wondered, would happen to the mighty and indomitable Chief Physician if the young prince died?

Kazlah shivered in the warm August night. He hated to think! Queen Lasha was not known for compassion and mercy. Her punishment for him would be unique, Kazlah was certain of that.

"Very well, lady," the physician relented at last. "Tell me the Palmyrene's name."

C H A P T E R   1 3

There," said the elderly Roman, pleased with himself. "What do you think of that?"

Selene stared at the flame that had blossomed suddenly and as if by magic from the kindling of the campfire. But she said nothing.

Ignatius looked at the transparent stone in his hand and shrugged. Most people were impressed with his trick of lighting fires with it. But then, this girl was not like his usual audience. For one thing, there was the dying mother she was responsible for; for another, she seemed to be obsessed with the idea that she was being followed. Ever since they had left Antioch two weeks ago, Ignatius had often seen the girl look back over her shoulder, as if watching for someone on the road behind them. He felt sorry for her, and was moved to give her a gift. "Take this stone, child," he said kindly. "It is yours."

Selene took it. "Thank you," she said, and reached for the ebony-and-ivory box she always kept near at hand. She lifted the lid, put the stone inside, closed the box and returned to staring into the fire with big, solemn eyes.

Ignatius had made friends with the girl and her ailing mother as the caravan had wound its way down the Lebanon Mountains; and when their meager supply of bread and cheese had run out a week from Antioch, Ignatius, an old retired Roman lawyer on his way to live with his son and daughter-in-law ("who is as tough as a boiled owl," he had told Selene), had started providing food and cooking fires for the girl and her mother. Every sundown, when the caravan camped on the road, Ignatius produced juniper-root charcoal and ignited it with the transparent stone that, when held over the charcoal and angled to catch the sun's rays, miraculously brought forth flame.

Cook fires were now springing up throughout the massive encampment of the thousand-camel caravan as the sun drew low to the western horizon. It was a bleak and desolate region that surrounded them; after coming down through the green mountains, the caravan had crossed miles of flat steppe, a scrubby land of hard earth, thorny shrubs and a nomadic people known as Bedouins. Palmyra stood at the eastern edge of this desolation, and beyond the oasis, far to the east and southward into Arabia, stretched the formidable Syrian desert that melted into flat nothingness. And beyond that stood the ancient city of Magna, ruled by Queen Lasha.

There were other caravans along the road, trains of people from unheard-of lands who had come up in ships through the Lower Sea, up the Euphrates, through Magna and westward across the desert—caravans from China carrying silk and jade and spices, caravans from the Mediterranean transporting purple-dyed wool and Syrian glass. And Arab caravans up from the south moved along this busy road, from Mecca, where the Goddess Allat was symbolized by a crescent moon, and where the women were entirely covered by a single black garment, with only a slit for the eyes.

"I bought some fish for us," Ignatius said. "Some very nice pieces," he added, hoping to tempt Selene to eat. He smiled apologetically as he said, "I am an old man and set in my ways. Today is Venus's Day, the last day of the week, and in Rome, to honor the Goddess, we eat only fish on this day. It is a very old custom and I fear I am much governed by old customs."

Selene did not respond. Her heart was too heavy for speech.

Andreas.

Where was he? Why had he not yet caught up with the caravan? It had been two weeks, two long weeks of yearning and aching for him, of suffering and worry, of watching constantly, of expecting him to ride up at any moment. *Where was he?*

Selene felt sick at heart, but it was a sickness beyond the cures found in her medicine box. She felt as if her soul had received a fatal wound, and there were no balms for it, no salves to make her well. Only Andreas could do that, with his touch, his smile, his love. Selene saw his face in the flames of the campfire—he would come soon and find her. He *had* to.

Things were going very poorly. She had no money. Her mother had paid an initial fee to join the caravan, which entitled them to one donkey and water rights at all oases along the way, but when their bit of food was exhausted a few days after departure, Selene had found herself buying something to eat from fellow-travelers at unheard-of prices. At times she had been able to barter with her healing skills: A young Syrian mother had begun premature labor, and Selene had prescribed a constant state of drunkenness to prevent the birth from occurring on the road. A goblet full of wine each hour was, to everyone's amazement, working—the contractions had stopped. The grateful husband had given Selene bread and fish for three days. But even that had run out.

Selene turned away from the fire and looked at the sleeping form of Mera. Her mother was getting worse.

That afternoon, when the caravan had halted for the night, Selene had gathered desert plants known as "rolling things," over which she had draped her *palla* to form a little tent to provide shade for Mera against the desert sun. She slept beneath it now, curled on her side, her breathing labored. Mera had not eaten in two days.

Selene felt the cold grip of fear in her stomach, as she thought, *I shall lose her! My mother will die here in this terrible desert!*

Andreas, Andreas! Have I lost you, too?

Selene looked behind her. The desert road was growing dark with nightfall. Her eyes strained to see the image of a solitary rider galloping toward her at high speed. Where was Andreas? Why didn't he come?

Selene felt a hand on her arm; she turned to look into the kind eyes of old Ignatius. He thought he knew what was troubling her. He, too, had observed her mother's declining health.

Ignatius was a thoughtful and generous man; he had taken Selene and Mera into his own small traveling group of eight camels and twelve slaves, and had appointed himself their protector. Ignatius knew all too well, after his years of traveling, what vulnerable creatures women were who dared to journey alone.

"I'm frightened, Ignatius," Selene finally said in a tight voice. "The moon is on the wane. It is the time when ill and aged people are most likely to die. I'm afraid she won't make it to Palmyra. I don't think she's well enough to travel tomorrow. We have to stop and rest."

Ignatius nodded solemnly. The same thought had occurred to him. "Very well," he said, laying aside his wine and fish. "I believe it is time to have a talk with the caravan driver. I'll see that he spares you a camel, an escort and water."

"Will he agree, do you think?"

Ignatius stood and smiled. "The man's as predictable as a tree."

As she watched Ignatius thread his way among the tents and campfires, Selene felt doubtful. The few times she had glimpsed the leader of the caravan he had not struck her as a generous man.

Before she knew it, Ignatius was back. He dropped himself down on the stool and picked up his wooden traveling goblet (on journeys, one hid one's wealth and displayed only meager possessions). "I curse this age and the men who made it," he grumbled, first spilling some wine to the desert gods, then gulping down the rest.

"Ignatius, what—"

"All I asked was a chit from him so you could get water rights when you arrived at the oasis. After all, you've paid for them. The contract made with the caravan was sealed upon the goddess Bona Fides, so it is binding."

"Won't he honor it?"

"I'm afraid it's as hopeless as finding a core in an onion, child. The man is mean through and through."

"Oh dear!" Selene wrung her hands. "What am I going to do? My mother can't be moved! She needs to rest before we go on!"

"Now, now," said Ignatius, patting her arm and feeling guilty for having scared her. "It's not as bad as all that. You're only two days out of the city. This road is well traveled; you'll never be alone."

"It frightens me!"

"Nothing to be afraid of. These roads are the safest in the world. The mounted archers of the Palmyrene desert police are a force no bandits wish to reckon with!" Ignatius sat back and regarded Selene, her pale face illuminated by the fire's glow.

"Don't worry, child," he said softly, laying his hand over hers. "I'll stay with you. I'll take care of you and your mother."

CHAPTER 14

Even though she was the Bath-Sheba (meaning "Daughter of the Goddess") and therefore supposedly limitless in her power, at this moment Queen Lasha felt utterly powerless.

She was kneeling at the side of the bed that held the feverish, body of her son.

The physicians and attendants hovered nervously around the chamber, shifting their feet. They had tried every possible remedy to reduce the boy's fever, but none had worked. Now the queen's fury was multiplying in direct proportion to the rising heat of the prince's skin. She lifted her head and fixed a single basilisk-like eye on the physicians. "Where is Kazlah?" she finally demanded.

They looked at each other. "He is in the temple, lady."

Her eyebrow lifted. "Does he pray to the Goddess for the life of my child?"

Again, a nervous exchange of glances. Fear ran through their veins like the icy waters of the Euphrates. "It is, ah, on the king's business, gracious lady."

"Send for him. If my son dies, he will not die alone." She rose wearily. "Now get out, all of you."

After a brief flurry in which the courtiers, exiting too quickly, collided with one another, Queen Lasha finally relaxed her guard. It was not easy, the constant need to maintain control, to show bravery and aloofness in front of her subjects. Especially now, with her son so ill.

She turned from the bedside, a tall woman with broad shoulders and regal grace. Her black hair was arranged in a thousand braids, layers of silk whispered against her body, and her forehead, neck and wrists were heavily adorned, even at this hour, with precious jewels.

She walked away from the bed and out on to the balcony, from which she could see the river, resplendent under the moon, follow its eternal course. Gazing down at the groves of weeping willows, Queen Lasha felt humble. After years of commanding death, it seemed now to be commanding her. She loved her son more than anything else in the world.

Queen Lasha raised her face to the silver Goddess in the sky and spoke a simple prayer: "Mother-of-All, do not let my son die . . . "

CHAPTER 15

Selene raised her eyes to the crescent moon in the black sky and whispered, "Mother-of-All, please let my mother live . . . "

She was on her knees, cradling Mera's head in her lap. A while ago, Selene had given her mother some sips of water which had brought about an alarming fit of coughing; Selene feared to move her again. Shortly after midnight, Mera opened her eyes and looked up at her daughter. "It is time," she said softly. "My hour is at hand."

"No, Mother—"

"It's no use, child," Mera whispered between labored breaths. "There is no time for anything but the truth, now. So please, listen to me. Listen carefully. I have important things to say to you and it is a great effort for me to speak."

Mera tried to change her position slightly; she shifted and her face twisted in pain. When she drew in a deep breath, in order to say what she had to say, there was a rattle in her throat. "I was not meant to reach Palmyra, daughter. I have served my purpose. My work is at an end. I have brought you back . . . "

"Mother," Selene murmured, stroking Mera's hair. "I don't understand what you're saying. What do you mean, you brought me back?"

"Sixteen years ago . . . You are especially chosen . . . "

Selene frowned. She studied her mother's bluish lips and tried to fathom the meaning behind the words, tried to help her mother by understanding before she had to speak.

Chosen? Selene thought. *Chosen for what?*

"Your father . . . " Mera breathed. "He said you came from the gods. He said you belong to them."

Selene stared at Mera. Years ago, Mera had told her of the fisherman who had died in a boating accident before she was born. After that, her mother would never speak of the man who had left her a widow. But why would a simple fisherman claim that his child came from the gods?

Tears welled up in Mera's eyes, and she cursed the body that betrayed her, that had become her enemy. *I should have told her days ago, when I still had the strength. Why? Why, oh why did I wait until now to tell her the truth?*

Mera closed her eyes and knew the answer: *It is because I was afraid. I wanted to keep her for just a while longer; I wanted her to be my daughter for just a few more days. I could not bear to see her, once I had denied my motherhood of her, knowing that she thought of another woman, that poor young woman, dragged from childbed by red-cloaked soldiers. I would not have been able to look at my daughter's face knowing that she was no longer mine.*

"Selene. You were the one sweet thing in my life. You came to me when I was alone. I was selfish. I wanted to make you completely mine. But I always knew that someday the gods must claim you, for it is their right. They marked you at birth, and you carry that mark with you still. Whenever you curse your own tongue, Selene, as I know you do, remember that it was the gods who made you so, that it is their mark of favor upon you . . . "

Mera's voice died. Selene gazed down at her mother, baffled, and waited.

From his place by the campfire, Ignatius watched the two silhouettes in the makeshift tent. It was their second day on their own, two days since the caravan had left them on the Palmyra road, a tiny band of eight camels, fifteen people and one tired donkey. With the departure of the immense caravan and a settling of the dust, the scrubby Syrian desert seemed larger and more menacing than it had before. Ignatius was keeping a keen watch through the night; he now wore a dagger at his belt and had told his slaves to arm themselves.

Although the girl had insisted that a friend was following her on the road and that he would arrive at any moment, Ignatius much doubted it. If the friend were coming, he would surely have arrived by now.

"You were born for a purpose, Selene," Mera's breathy voice lifted into the night. "You are special. A unique destiny awaits you, the destiny for which you were born, for which I have spent sixteen years preparing you, and which you must now seek. I don't have the answers for you, Selene. You must find them yourself. You must make it your life's work."

Selene shook her head in puzzlement. "What are you talking about, Mother?"

"Listen to me, daughter, listen. You must know the truth now . . . "

As she knelt with bowed head, watching her mother's parched lips form the words, Selene listened, and heard the vast desert silence slowly give way to another sound, the sound of a howling wind, a wind that moaned through the night, rattling doors and windows, and which brought with it the clatter of horses' hooves and the commands of Roman soldiers.

Mera brought back that night of sixteen years ago, and painted the picture so vividly that her daughter thought she was seeing it as it happened: the handsome Roman patrician and his young wife; Mera's little house on the outskirts of the city; the birth of the first baby—a boy named Helios; then the risky delivery of the second—a girl named Selene; the bursting in of the Roman soldiers; Mera hiding in the corncrib; and then, finally, the Roman noble lying in too much blood and instructing Mera to lift a ring from his hand.

"He said . . . you came from the gods, Selene. He said you were special. The Goddess brought you to me in my loneliness and childlessness, and in return I have kept my covenant with Her. I brought you back to Palmyra, as the Oracle commanded, in order to set you on the path to your destiny."

Selene stared down at her mother, stunned. She tried to embrace it all —the incredible story of her birth, the parents with faces she could not see, the prophetic words spoken with the Roman's dying breath—but she might have tried to take the sky and the stars into her arms, it was all so fantastic.

Mera lifted a trembling hand. "It is time now, Selene. Give me the rose."

"The rose?"

"The necklace. Which I placed upon your breast at your Dressing Ceremony. It is time now for you to see what it contains, and for me to explain its contents to you."

"But . . . I no longer have the ivory rose, Mother. I gave it away."

Mera's eyes flew open. "You . . . *gave it away*? Selene, what are you saying?"

Selene pressed her hand to her chest, where she could feel, beneath the fabric of her dress, the eye-shaped outline of Andreas's necklace. "I . . . gave it to Andreas. We pledged to one another. He gave me his Eye of Horus, and I—"

A wail came from Mera's throat that rose up to the stars and filled the desert night. The camels stirred and grunted; Ignatius and his slaves looked up, startled.

"What have I done?" Mera cried, beating her breast with a weak fist. *"What have I done?* In my fear and foolishness I kept you ignorant! I should have told you long ago! What have I done?"

"Mother, calm yourself. *Please!"*

Sobbing, Mera told Selene of the gold ring which the dying Roman had said would tell the child everything. There had been something stamped on it—a face, and some foreign writing which Mera had not been able to read. "Give it to her when she is older," he had said. "It will lead her to her destiny."

"But how will you be led now?" cried Mera, "without that ring? And there was a lock of his hair, your father's hair, and a piece of the blanket that had received your brother—powerful ties, Selene, and all that there is in this world to bind you to them. *Gone!* You have been cut away from them! What have I done?"

Spellbound, Selene pictured the ivory rose as it had lain upon Andreas's chest. She had given more to him than just herself, she realized now; she had placed in his hands her destiny.

"Child, listen to me. You must go back to Antioch. You must go back to Andreas and take the necklace back. Open it, daughter. Look at the ring . . . "

Selene stared at her mother. *Go back to Antioch, to Andreas . . .*

"Selene, promise me!" Mera reached up and seized Selene's wrist with unexpected strength. "Daughter, Isis is your goddess. She has chosen you for a special purpose. You must find out what that purpose is. It is your duty. You must find out who you are; you must find your brother and be united with him again . . . "

Mera's voice died a second time, and when she closed her eyes, she appeared to sleep. Selene stared for a long time, cradling her mother's head. At last, it all started to settle down over her, like a night mist; she shivered, hot tears blurred her vision. *You are not my real mother?* she silently asked the sleeping woman in her arms. *Then who . . .*

Selene raised her head and looked out over the desert, far out toward the distant horizon that lifted in bleak hills. Behind those hills lay the city of her birth, Palmyra.

Is she still there, my real mother? And my twin brother, Helios?

And will Andreas find me there, in that city? Will he follow this road and search for me? Or should I turn back now, back toward Antioch, turn my back on a mother and brother who might be in that foreign city . . .

Selene started to weep.

How could this gentle woman not be her real mother? This sweet woman had wiped away Selene's childhood tears and calmed her childhood fears; had patched her scraped knees and explained the movements of the moon and the planets to her. This woman had taught her the secrets of healing—of plants and magic. It was Mera who had guided a young Selene down the shadowy roadway into her soul and had taught her how to capture her soul flame.

And it had been this simple, loving woman who had labored so many nights stitching a beautiful blue *stola* so that her daughter could shine in her most important hour.

No, Selene decided. Her destiny could not possibly lie in that distant, unknown city. It lay in Antioch, with medicine, with her beloved Andreas.

When her mother tried to speak again, Selene stroked Mera's hot forehead and said in a tight voice, "Don't trouble yourself now, Mother. Sleep."

"There is nothing but sleep ahead of me, daughter. I want you to promise me that you will take up my mantle, that you will walk in the ways I taught you, that you will revere the ancient healing arts, and that you will always remember the Goddess. You must take responsibility for yourself now, Selene, and for your specialness. Promise me, daughter . . . "

Crying, Selene took her mother's hand and promised.

Then Mera, relieved, said, "Now . . . prepare a grave for me."

"No!"

"Corpses decay faster in moonlight than in sunlight, I have taught you that. Make haste. There isn't much time."

Still weeping, Selene removed herself from beneath her mother's head and shoulders and positioned Mera comfortably on the *palla*. As she was about to hurry away, Selene was stayed one last time by her mother's hand. "It is a foolish thing to fear dying, daughter," Mera said tenderly. "It is like falling asleep. When I awake I shall be reunited with the Mother-of-All. And you and I shall be together again, my dear child, in the Resurrection. The Goddess promises us this. I shall wait for you . . . "

As Mera lay beneath the tent created by Selene's *palla* and the "rolling things," listening to the sounds of a grave being dug in the hard sand, she was filled with regret. If only she could have lived long enough to learn who her daughter was, and to see at last the greatness for which Selene had been born. For the first time in her life, Mera did not want to do as the Goddess willed.

In her last moments, Mera experienced a sudden flash of insight, and she received a vision. Rolling her head to the side, she gazed lovingly at the weeping girl and thought: *You will return someday to Antioch and you will search for your beloved Andreas. But it will not be as you expected, it will not be in circumstances you can ever imagine . . .*

Just before dawn, Mera's final words to her daughter were, "Remember to keep friendship with Isis," and then she died.

CHAPTER 16

When the raid struck, they were packing the last camel and Ignatius was saying, "I have no doubt that you will find a caravan bound for Antioch the very hour we arrive in Palmyra. And I shall see that you are comfortably placed for the journey, and are not cheated."

In the dawn-bright moments between laying the last stone on Mera's grave and breaking camp to continue on to Palmyra, Selene had decided her best plan would be to go to that city and try to find a caravan back to Antioch. She was thinking of Andreas's surprise should she meet him on the road. And then the first arrow hit.

They seemed to come from nowhere, as if suddenly materializing out of the sand, giants on horseback thundering down upon the little encampment. Ignatius's slaves broke rank and ran in circles, screaming; an elderly woman had taken the first arrow in her back, next an old man fell. For an instant Selene stood and stared, then she whispered, *"Jinn!"* and started to run. The attackers formed a circle and bore down with great curved swords flashing high overhead in the morning sun. Their faces were concealed by black turbans and black veils, but fearsome eyes blazed under heavy brows; and from their throats came an eerie, inhuman cry.

Selene searched frantically for Ignatius. The camels started to stampede; in moments Selene knew she was going to be trampled in the forest of animal legs. All around her the Roman slaves fell before the scimitars like wheat before scythes. Sand and grit was churned up in a blinding cloud, and the cries and shouts of the victims were deafening.

Then a hand seized Selene's arm and she found herself being dragged away. It was Ignatius, desperately pulling her from the center of the fight, where the monstrous feet of the camels were crushing the bodies of the fallen slaves. "Cut their horses down!" he shouted, slapping a knife into her hand. Selene stared in shock at the heavy blade and in the next instant saw Ignatius whirl to slash the forequarters of an onrushing horse. He missed, and the attacker's sword made a deep slice in his arm.

"Ignatius!" Selene cried, trying to reach out for him. And then another horse was galloping toward her, its rider's eyes boring into Selene. She stood frozen, hypnotized. When the charger was almost upon her, with the deadly scimitar raised high and about to fall, she felt herself lunge forward, sinking her knife up to the hilt into horseflesh. The animal screamed and reared, unseating its rider. Ignatius, recovering, fell upon the man and slit his throat.

Selene was no longer thinking, no longer feeling. Her body acted on its own even as her mind recoiled from the horror. She sobbed as she lashed out, blindly, spinning in circles, cutting and jabbing, surrounded by blood and screams and flying sand.

And then it ended.

Suddenly, there was silence, except for the heavy breathing of horses and the jangle of harness. She found herself pressed against the body of a slain camel, her bloody knife beside her. Ignatius lay dead a short distance away, his blood running darkly into the sand.

An order was barked in a language she did not understand, and the next instant Selene was being bound and gagged. She struggled feebly as she was lifted off her feet by one of the attackers and thrown over the neck of his horse like a sack of grain. At once they were off at a gallop and Selene, jolted up and down on her stomach, her arms bound painfully behind her back, felt an awful sickness rise up within her.

Six of Ignatius's slaves had been spared along with Selene, all of them young women; the males and the elderly women were left behind for the desert scavengers. The captives were carried across the desert at a furious speed, away from the Antioch road, high up into the craggy hills to the north of Palmyra. There the raiders were joined by another group who likewise carried a captured human cargo; without stopping to rest, they struck off eastward into the great desert, away from roads, away from Palmyra.

As a welcome darkness rose to engulf her, Selene's last thought was of Andreas, and what he would think when he came upon the campsite, which was now a scene of carnage.

CHAPTER 17

Kazlah hefted the bag of gold in his hand and gave the visitor a calculating look. "You will receive the rest of this if any are found to be virgins."

The visitor, dusty from his long ride, eyed the purse with greed. "Four are very young, master. They can only be virgin. As for the others . . . " He shrugged.

"I will find out when I examine them. In the meantime"—Kazlah tossed the bag to the floor—"this is your preliminary payment. After I have examined the girls, I will send a slave with the rest of your money. Do not come back to the palace."

The man narrowed his eyes in suspicion. Dare he trust Kazlah not to say that none of the girls was virgin? He was glad now he had had the presence of mind to collect some booty along with the girls, as insurance against such an event. His orders had been to strike quickly and get away with the women before the police knew of it. But he had not been able to resist bringing along what appeared to be an unusual treasure.

"Master," he said as he picked the bag of gold off the floor, "perhaps I can interest you in merchandise of another kind?"

Kazlah regarded the man with disdain. The pirating of defenseless women was not the worst of the Palmyrene's activities; he was known to trade in children, boys in particular. Kazlah hated dealing with him, but Queen Lasha had insisted he handle the distasteful matter personally. But this was going too far. "We made a bargain. Get out."

"If I may show you something unusual—of the utmost interest?"

"If you do not leave at once, I shall have you thrown out and then you will never see the rest of your money."

The visitor turned, pulled the door open, and signaled to a cohort waiting outside. Then he turned back to Kazlah, dragging behind him a large rawhide sack.

The Chief Physician was irritated. "What is this?"

"If you will take a look?" The sack was placed in the center of the room; the Palmyrene untied the cord that sealed it, carefully reached inside, and brought out a square chest built of ebony and inlaid with ivory.

Kazlah's curiosity was aroused, despite himself.

Placing the chest on a table, the man lifted the lid and watched the physician's face. "It is a medical box," the Palmyrene said carefully. "See? Clearly it belonged to a wealthy and knowledgeable physician."

Kazlah's eyes took in the rows of little jars, the rolls of fresh papyrus, the pestle and mortar, the tiny drawers neatly labeled in Egyptian hieroglyphs; the spool of suturing thread, the bone needles. This was not only the box of a wealthy and knowledgeable physician, but the box of an extremely *learned* physician.

"Where did you get this?" he finally asked.

"It came from the raid on the Antioch road. There was an old Roman and a retinue of slaves. He was no doubt a physician planning to set up practice in Palmyra."

Kazlah nodded. Palmyra had more physicians per capita than any other city in the world, more even than Rome. This elderly Roman would have been just another fish in a big and crowded pond, but he would have been a very knowledgeable fish.

Kazlah stretched out a long, tapered finger and touched the contents of the box one by one, as if mesmerized by their potential: a transparent stone, a lump of sulphur, a small statuette of Isis. This medical box was the culmination, Kazlah could see, of years of work and learning.

He picked up one of the little jars, pulled out its stopper and sniffed the contents. Whatever the substance was, it was unknown to Kazlah. He replaced the jar with great delicacy and stared thoughtfully at the box. Clearly it had belonged to a physician trained in Egypt; in all the world no physicians surpassed those trained in Alexandria.

He felt a stab of envy, an emotion his withered heart had not felt in many years—envy for the man who had owned this box, for his formal training, perhaps indeed at the great School of Medicine in Alexandria. Kazlah himself had never had the benefit of formal education; his medical knowledge had been fought for, stolen, connived after: when he was young and new to the palace, Kazlah had seen the power the Chief Physician held there, power even over the king and queen, who were as subject as the lowliest peasant to aches and pains. And so he had ingratiated himself with Malal, who was then the Chief Physician; it had been a demeaning campaign, and one that had cost Kazlah a great deal of pride. The foundation of his medical knowledge had come from old Malal; after that, Kazlah had learned by trial and error, practicing on members of the court. This medical box told of a man who had had all the advantages Kazlah had not. He resented it.

After a moment's deliberation, the Chief Physician turned away, strode across the room, reached behind a curtain and withdrew a second, smaller bag of gold. "I'll buy it," he said, throwing the bag onto the table.

CHAPTER 1 8

When Selene awoke she had no idea where she was.

Her first awareness was of pain, an intense, burning pain in her wrists, her back, her ankles. As consciousness slowly returned, she became aware of other things: the straw pallet beneath her, a great dryness in her mouth and throat and finally the stone wall an arm's length from her nose.

Groaning, she sat up. The floor seemed to tilt; she fell back on the pallet, where she lay for a long time staring up at the ceiling, trying to catch hold of her muddled thoughts.

Where was she? What had happened? And then it all came back to her: Mera's death, the ambush, the nightmarish ride.

Hearing the sound of soft sobbing, she rolled her head to one side, and was greatly surprised as she took in her surroundings.

It was a large chamber, and clean, with sunlight streaming through a high window. There was a carpet on the floor, basins of water, towels and in the center a low table holding what appeared to be bowls of food. But it was not these that caught Selene's attention. Across the room, lying on a pallet, was a young girl, crying.

Then Selene saw the others: all around the room, lying or sitting, one even standing up and leaning against the wall with dazed eyes—young women in various forms of undress and disarray, weeping, groaning, ill.

Selene had difficulty focusing, her head throbbed so, and when she moved a sharp pain shot through her chest.

She blinked in confusion as she saw one of the young women, dressed in a costume Selene had never seen before—leggings and a blouse—stand up and cross over to one of those who was weeping. She knelt and spoke foreign words, and at the same time laid gentle hands on the girl. The one who had been weeping cried out in pain and the strangely dressed girl pulled her hand away. It was covered with blood.

Selene tried again to sit up, and this time she was successful. She managed, with one arm held tightly about her rib cage, to cross the room.

After inspecting the slash in the weeping girl's arm, Selene said, "She's badly hurt. We must . . . " Dizzy, Selene brought a hand up to her forehead. When the vertigo subsided, she said, "We must do something to stop the bleeding. And we must wash the wound."

The girl in the strange costume stared quizzically at Selene. Then, as if comprehending, she jumped up and went to fetch one of the bowls of water. It was perfumed, Selene noticed, and the towels were of the best linen. Strange treatment for prisoners, she thought, and then she set about taking care of the wounded women.

———

By the time the stranger came, all the young women were awake and talking, trying to piece together what had happened, where they were, and what the purpose was of this curious cell. Selene could talk to the ones who had been Ignatius's slaves, but the rest spoke a variety of foreign dialects. The petite girl in the pantaloons, the one with eyes too large for her head, managed to convey the fact that her home lay far to the east, beyond the Indus, and that her name was Samia.

When the tall man in dark robes entered, the girls all fell silent. Behind him stood two mute guards holding swords. The man paused in the doorway and surveyed twenty frightened faces. He studied them with an eye, Selene thought, that might have been assessing horses or camels. She trembled in her torn dress and closed her eyes, praying to Isis.

The man went methodically about his work, uttering terse commands. At first the guards were needed to hold the girls down, but when the others saw that submission meant it would be easier for them, they stopped fighting. He spoke the universal Greek of the East, and when Selene understood the orders he barked at the guards, her trembling increased.

"These two are not virgins," he said. "Take them to the main barracks. A slave dealer will come for them tonight. This one is a virgin. Turn her over to the Chief Eunuch of the king's harem."

He was still on the other side of the room, but already Selene had drawn her knees up protectively to her chest and was hugging them. She was a virgin; she would be taken to the king's harem with the others.

"What is this?" the man said suddenly, holding the weeping girl's arm and frowning at the linen bandage. He looked around the room. "Who did this?" he asked sharply.

No one made a sound.

Then the sobbing girl inadvertently glanced at Selene, and the stranger turned to her. "You did this?" he asked.

Selene opened her mouth but no sound came out.

He gestured to one of the guards who took one step toward Selene. "Yes," she said suddenly. "I did it!"

"Why?"

"It . . . It was—"

"Speak up, girl!"

Selene struggled to get the words out. "It was bleeding."

"There is honey on this bandage," the man said, his eyes flickering to the bowls of porridge and figs and honey on the table—food meant to strengthen the captives. "Why did you put honey on the wound?"

Selene swallowed hard and prayed to Isis to give her command of her tongue. "It . . . it keeps out the evil spirits of infection."

His eyes, so cold they made Selene shiver, held her with an almost physical power. Then he let go of the bandaged arm and strode over to Selene. The other girls all stared in terror. "How do you know this?" he demanded, towering over her.

Selene shrank back. A sob escaped her throat. "My . . . "

"Tell me!"

"My mother was a healer-woman," she said. "She taught me."

Behind his eyes a quick calculation was going on. Then he asked, more quietly, "Your mother was a healer-woman? Was she with you on the caravan?"

Selene nodded.

"You were with a Roman on the Antioch road. Was he a physician?"

"No."

Kazlah's thin mouth twitched at one corner. He thought of the beautiful medicine box back in his quarters, and the myriad contents inside which were a mystery to him. "Prove to me that your mother taught you healing skills. Tell me, for instance, how you would reduce a fever in a child."

"There are many ways: bathing the child in very cold water, rubbing his body with barley alcohol—"

"And if those fail?"

Selene swallowed again. The pain in her ribs stabbed with each breath. She felt faint, weak, and feared she was going to pass out. "There is Hecate's Cure," she said in a whisper.

"And what is that?"

"A tea. My mother makes it. My mother—" Another sob choked her.

"Tell me!"

Selene started to cry. Her thin body shuddered. "My mother is dead," she said softly. Then she buried her face in her hands and wept.

Kazlah stared down at her with a faint smile on his lips. Hecate's Cure, she had said.

CHAPTER 19

K azlah searched in the medicine box and found a blue jar with the toad-symbol of Hecate on it.

He experimented first on a condemned criminal awaiting execution. When the man suffered no apparent harm from drinking a few drops of the bitter tea from the blue jar, Kazlah next gave it to a slave burning with common summer fever. When his fever went away, the Chief Physician decided to administer the cure to the royal prince.

The hour was late and the prince's bedchamber was crowded with silent onlookers. Allat's priests were arranged around the room, swinging censers that gave off pungent smoke, rattling tambourines, and invoking the many names of the Goddess; the Chief Chamberlain stood ready with his retinue of attendants; the Chief Scribe sat cross-legged on the floor with his ink and papyrus; and Queen Lasha sat at the bedside, her one eye fixed on Kazlah's every movement.

He wore a leopardskin over his shoulders; his black hair was slicked back over his narrow skull; he sat motionless over the sleeping prince as if he were in a trance, his eyes unblinking, his lean body barely seeming to breathe.

From beyond diaphanous hangings came the cries of night birds. The polished floor was bathed in starglow. Just over the crowns of palm trees could be seen the last sliver of Allat's crescent. And on the night air, which ebbed and flowed like an invisible tide, wafted the marshy, fertile odor of the Euphrates.

The first dose of the mysterious medicine had been given at dusk, administered in tiny spoonfuls; the prince's young throat had risen feebly in instinctive swallows as all those gathered around him looked on anxiously. Kazlah had no idea how much to give the boy, but he daren't interrogate the captive girl further in case she became suspicious and decided to withold information. Torture might get it from her, but he would never be certain she was telling the truth. She could make Kazlah the unwitting assassin of the prince. Far better to keep her locked up and cultivate her dependence on him. In time, if he was careful, she would impart to him everything she knew, at the end of which he would have her put to death, so that all traces of her existence and all knowledge of the hidden medicine box would remain Kazlah's secret.

Lasha sat stiffly in the cloud of incense. Kazlah knew that if he failed now, he would die a thousand deaths before dawn. But if the boy should miraculously recover . . .

A sigh whispered through the room, fresh and new, as if the river itself had breathed. The prince's deep sleep seemed to be lifting.

Kazlah leaned forward and placed a long hand on the royal forehead. Then he reached for the little blue jar again. No one knew where it had come from, no one knew about the medicine box. Nor about the girl he kept his secret prisoner.

Kazlah replaced the jar on the night table and sat back. All eyes in the room were riveted on the young face. The tambourines and chanting ceased; the censers stopped swinging. Courtiers stood stiffly around the room like statues. There was fear in their eyes—if the boy died, the queen's fury would touch them all.

Suddenly, the frail form stirred beneath the silk coverlet, the eyelashes fluttered; then the eyes opened, and the prince gazed up at his mother the queen.

"Mama . . . " he said.

C H A P T E R   2 0

Selene was drawn to Andreas's eyes. There was a strange power in them, a power she could not have resisted even if she wanted to. Their color was the dark gray-blue of a stormy sky, shadowed by angry brows with a furrow between them; but, paradoxically, they were kind eyes, and compassionate—windows into a tender and loving soul.

Andreas pulled Selene to him. His body was hard; he held her tightly against him. She felt her pulse quicken and the breath catch in her throat. She lifted her mouth to his, hungry for him, aching for him. Then Andreas kissed her, his arms, his body tight against her. *Take me,* she whispered. *Take me now.*

A loud crash startled her awake; she sat bolt upright, blinking. She was confused, and then she realized: It had only been a dream.

Turning to the window set high in the wall, Selene saw it was raining and realized that it had been thunder that had awakened her. Shivering, she drew the thin blanket around her and stood up.

This cell had had many occupants before Selene had been put into it; someone had dug toeholds into the wall below the window so that one could hoist oneself up and look out through the bars.

Selene pulled herself up now and saw a city obscured by torrential November rain. She pressed her forehead against the cold iron bars and murmured, "Andreas, my love. We kiss only in dreams."

Her eyes were soulful as she gazed down from her stony tower.

Every day for ninety days Selene had pressed her face to these iron bars, watching the city gate below, the busy road winding away into the desert, her eyes searching obsessively for a familiar form on horseback. *He will come,* she had told herself every day, gripping the bars until her hands hurt and her shoulders ached. Andreas, Selene was certain, would travel the Antioch road and hear of the raid upon a camp; and then, not finding her in Palmyra, he would search the wide desert for her. It had been three months; but there were many miles to cover between that road and this place. Eventually, Selene knew, he would come to this city and so she must watch for him, and be ready.

But today the rain poured down, and it was difficult to make anything out; only a few shadowy figures were abroad. Selene looked across at the streets she had memorized, and sent her mind along the escape route she had chosen.

It was not a physical escape, for her body was locked within impregnable stone walls; it was an escape of the spirit, her thoughts racing through narrow, twisting lanes, leaping over walls, running away across the desert to Andreas. It brought her some small comfort in this terrible captivity.

Where was Andreas now, at this very moment? she wondered. Was he warming his hands over a fire that was perhaps down there, in that street with the colorful awnings?

Selene felt the rain start to invade her soul and dampen her spirit; but she pushed it away. She conjured up her soul flame, centered her energies into fueling it, to keep it burning brightly. Selene knew she must not let despair claim her, for then she would be lost. She must keep herself alive for Andreas and for Mera, whose dying legacy had filled Selene with a passion to survive.

You are chosen . . .

She watched the date palms bend under the force of the storm, but she was not seeing them; visions filled her eyes: the ivory rose, a gold ring, a twin brother named Helios. Andreas.

Selene let go of the iron bars and slipped down to the floor. She paced the width and breadth of the tiny room to keep warm.

She was alone. One by one the captured girls had been taken away, to the public slave block or, like Samia, the Hindu girl who had briefly been her friend in their shared captivity, to the king's harem. And then, finally, Selene herself had been taken from that comfortable chamber and put into this miserable cell, the iron door clanging shut behind her, the key turning the lock, the footsteps of the guard receding into silence.

It had been three months of a desperate existence in this stone box, not knowing who her captors were, or where she was, or what fate lay in store for her, knowing only that she must not give way to despair, that she must survive, she must escape, and find her way back to Andreas and her destiny.

Her one solace in this nightmare was her golden Eye of Horus, which she wore beneath her dress and which no one had detected. Her medicine box was gone; she pictured it lying in the sand, being slowly buried over time, until it became one of the many sand dunes of the desert. Her medicine box—her only ties with the past, with her mother, with her sacred medical healing. Without it she felt naked, stripped of identity and purpose; but when grief threatened to overcome her, Selene had only to clasp the Eye of Horus and feel its healing power. Andreas's spirit lived in that necklace.

The sound of footsteps beyond her door brought Selene to a standstill. She stood shaking with cold, her arms wrapped about herself, and listened. She was filled with dread.

Was it he again?

Her persecutor, the man who tortured her. Selene never knew when he was going to come, sometimes it was morning, sometimes it was the middle of the night, and always it was with questions. "What is the meaning of this symbol?" he might ask, thrusting a piece of papyrus at her. Or, "Tell me what this powder is." Selene knew what he was after—her healing knowledge. And she knew it was what kept her alive, what kept her safe from his terrible threats.

"If you do not answer me to my satisfaction," he had warned her on her first day in this cell, "I will send you to the harem where you will be used by the king, and then when he is tired of you, by whoever wishes. You will answer all my questions or I will send you to the soldiers' barracks for their amusement."

It had filled her with a greater terror than she had ever known, and a sickness in her soul that she had fought to dispel. To be used thus by men! To be passed around, brutalized, discarded. How was it possible, her confused mind asked, that the same act—a man and a woman coming together—could serve two opposing purposes? How could the same thing fulfill love on the one hand, and yet also be used as an instrument of terror?

Selene wanted to lie with Andreas; she dreamed of it; she thought of little else. To take his body into hers, to feel his force and passion. But this other! With the old king! With soldiers!

Selene gripped her stomach. The footsteps had halted outside her door; keys were rattling in the lock.

She belonged to Andreas. He was the only man who would ever possess her. How could she go back to him soiled?

The door opened and the stranger strode into the cell. Over one arm he carried a thick blanket, in his other hand he held a cup.

Selene stepped back.

"Are you cold?" he asked.

She nodded.

"Would you like this blanket?"

She looked at it. It was woven of rich wool and was the red-gold color of a blazing fire. Oh, to wrap herself in it; to feel warm again! She nodded a second time.

He held out the cup. "Tell me what these are."

Staying with her back to the wall, Selene leaned forward and peered in. There were some leaves in the cup, and they gave off a lemony fragrance. She wondered where he had gotten them from, and why, if he did not know what they were, he should think them significant enough to ask her about. "They are lemon balm," she said.

"What are they used for?"

His questions always puzzled her. Because, if he did not know what they were or their purpose, how then did he know they were medicinal? "Lemon balm is a 'gladdening' herb," she said. "It quiets the heart when drunk as a tea."

"Is that all?"

She shivered and eyed the blanket. Her fingers were so cold they had gone numb; even her bones ached from the cold.

This was the other side of the stranger: he not only had the power to harm her, but he was her provider as well. Just to let her know the extent of his power over her, he had starved her the first few days she had been in this cell. Then he had come with food and questions. And when she had not been able to tell him what to do for the king's impotence, he had had her pallet removed so that she slept on the cold stone floor. He could dispense comfort, or he could deliver pain.

Selene glanced at the two guards who stood behind him, blocking the doorway that led to the corridor and, in her mind, eventually to freedom. If she could but run . . .

"As a lotion," she said at last, "lemon balm eases joint pains and bruises."

He stood looking down at her, his harsh face masked as if carved in stone; but when she met his eyes, Selene saw in their cold depths an awful loneliness that surely the man himself did not know others could see.

She pitied him; she also feared him. The day would come, she knew, when he would have no more questions, and then, being useless to him, she would be handed over to a terrible fate. Selene must go far away from here before that day; she must somehow get a message to Andreas.

"Tell me, please, where I am. What city is this?"

Kazlah turned away, strode out of the cell and signaled to the guards to lock the door. When all was silent in the corridor again and Selene was left alone in the dark, listening to the rain, she realized he had taken the blanket with him.

CHAPTER   21

Queen Lasha intended to be immortal. More specifically, she intended to reign in Heaven as queen of the gods.

Lasha's belief in the afterlife was as solid and unshakable as the walls of her mighty palace. She believed in the Seven Spheres of Heaven, in a Judgment of Souls, in eternal punishment or reward, and in the pantheon of the gods. The gods dwelt on the topmost level of Heaven, high above the celestial canopy of the cosmos, and they dwelt in eternal luxury and bliss. Queen Lasha knew that, as a royal person, she would automatically gain entrance to one of the sublime levels of Heaven when she died, but that was not enough for her. Lasha's ambition was aimed at the highest apex of Elysian splendor: not for her a lesser eternity; the gods themselves were going to receive her.

Like her mother before her, and *her* mother before her, all the way back to when Magna was a mud village on the Euphrates, Lasha had spent this earthly life in preparation for the next. She had begun work on her tomb the day she had been crowned, a girl of twelve, and since then not a day had gone by in which she did not visit her final resting place.

It was going to be a more splendid tomb than Queen Cleopatra's, which stood in Alexandria and which was rumored to be a tomb surpassing those of the greatest pharaohs. Lasha's was going to be more than just a house of eternity—it would be a *palace*, complete with throne room, extensive baths, many chambers, and a hundred slaves to serve her in the afterlife, sealed alive into the tomb when her body was laid in the sarcophagus. And not only was Lasha's tomb going to be more magnificent than her mother's or the tombs of the fabled Persian kings, outlasting the great Alexander's; her house of everlasting was going to surpass them all in one very important aspect: its treasure.

Queen Lasha was in her private apartment, having spent the afternoon at the tomb, overseeing the stonecutters and talking with the architects. She sat deep in troubled thought. She had returned to the palace to learn that the news from the harem was bad: The virgins captured and brought to Magna three months ago had not cured her husband's impotence.

Her hands curled over the arms of her chair and gripped them hard. She must not take a new husband!

There was only one way Lasha's ambition to reign in Heaven could succeed—by being the richest woman among the gods; and there was only one way for her to keep the treasure she had secretly amassed in her tomb —by keeping old Zabbai as her consort.

Lasha's husband cared nothing about the afterlife or about gods; he was an impious libertine who lived only for his food, his wine and his sexual distractions. Lasha had begun the slow and deliberate process of putting away her fortune as a loveless girl of twelve, who had lain unresponsive in her new husband's arms, driving him to his concubines and his pleasures in a separate part of the palace. Whenever her army marched against other kingdoms and brought back magnificent booty, Zabbai was interested only in the girls who had been captured; when vassal kings paid tribute to Magna, he did not bother with the gold and jewels, but looked for gifts of flesh; and when the taxes were collected, filling Magna's treasure house, Zabbai did not look at the accounting books but demanded only enough money with which to purchase diversions. As a result, it all went to Queen Lasha, who was now one of the richest women in the world.

But the world did not know it. She had purposely kept it a secret. Where other sovereigns outfitted their palaces in splendor, displaying before all the world their wealth and worth, Lasha horded her riches in preparation for the next life. She kept the palace in sufficient magnificence to awe her enemies, subjugate her friends and keep Zabbai happy, but the rest of the wealth that poured into Magna went straight into that tomb, where mute guards watched it day and night against the time when Lasha would step up to the seventh of the heavens and blind the gods with her affluence.

Only in that way could she ensure her place among them, for they were the greediest of beings and were great respecters of money. They would accept her into their ranks and set her up on a throne, a ruler in Heaven, outshining even Isis and Ishtar.

But now . . .

Zabbai's impotence meant that he must be put out of the way, for an impotent king signified disaster for the city. His spiritual fertility was linked with his people's; when the king failed, so did Magna. And Zabbai out of the way meant that a new royal consort must be brought in to rule with Lasha, a young prince, virile, most likely ambitious, and one who, Lasha did not doubt, would set his eye upon her tomb and take the treasure for his own uses.

She made a fist and struck the arm of her chair.

Foolish woman! she scolded herself. She had allowed distaste of her husband to keep her from her royal duties. Zabbai could have gotten her with child years ago, and by now that prince-heir would have been able to take his father's place—under his mother's guidance. But she had allowed it to be left until too late, performing her duty finally because the High Priest had said the Goddess had spoken; that one union with her husband had borne fruit, her son, who was yet too young and years away from the manhood and virility the city needed.

Lasha struck the chair again. Why, after all these years of unfailing sexual power, was her husband suddenly afflicted with impotence?

"Hail, my lady."

Lasha looked up to see the high priest of Allat enter her chamber. "Why do you trouble me tonight?" she asked wearily.

The priest took care not to step around to the front. Whenever she granted an audience, Queen Lasha always sat in profile so that only her good eye showed. Were anyone to be caught staring at her face, in particular at the giant emerald that concealed the blind eye, that person would be put to death, so great was the queen's vanity. The priest looked around the large bedchamber, which had many lamps burning to stave off the gloom of the rain. There was a nervous uncertainty on the faces of the handmaidens and courtiers who stood in attendance upon the queen.

"I have come to ask what plans have been made for the royal husband. The people of Magna grow restless. They read his impotence as a bad omen."

Lasha made no reply. She sat on her high throne, draped in silks and jewels, her feet on a cushion, staring into the dark shadows that seemed to mock her.

"I have come to ask if you plan to make use of the last of the virgins."

The queen stirred. "What are you talking about?" she asked.

"I refer to the last girl—she is obviously being held for some special purpose."

Now Lasha looked directly at the priest, who discreetly lowered his gaze. "In the tower," he said smoothly. "There is a young girl, beautiful, who is being given special treatment. No one may see her."

"How do you know about this?"

The priest shrugged self-deprecatingly. "I have many friends, my lady. Those who prepare the girl's food, who guard her door night and day." *And I have enemies,* he thought, *whom I will see destroyed.* The priest was jealous of Kazlah's power, and this secret information, gotten at high cost, might be just the weapon he had been looking for.

"Who keeps her there?" the Queen demanded.

"Kazlah, my lady."

A stir rippled through the courtiers gathered in the room. Queen Lasha said softly, "Bring her to me."

=====

"You will not speak, no matter what," the priest said, as he prodded Selene with his staff. "And you will not look at her. If you look upon the queen's face it will mean instant death. Keep your eyes to the floor."

Selene walked past the many attendants of the queen's court who were in the corridor. They stared at the thin, unnaturally pale girl who walked with the High Priest. Her dress was plain and she was barefoot; her long black hair swung free and unadorned—a prisoner, surely—but there was an undefinable air about her, a presence, a kind of quiet dignity.

When they came to the queen's chamber, Selene stared; never before had she seen a ceiling so high, columns so large. She was pushed to her knees before a throne.

"Who are you?" came a sharp voice speaking perfect Greek.

Selene looked down at the marble floor and tried to command her tongue. She couldn't speak.

"Speak, girl!"

"Selene," she said.

The priest struck her. "Say 'my lady.' "

"Selene, my lady."

"Who is it that is keeping you prisoner in the tower?" asked Lasha, leaning forward on her throne.

"I do—" Selene bit her lower lip. Her tongue would not obey.

"What's wrong with her?" Lasha asked.

The priest struck her again. "Speak!"

Please, Isis, Selene prayed. *Free my tongue. If it is the mark of the gods upon me, then let it not imperil me.*

"You dare to disobey?" came Lasha's voice.

Selene tried again. "I—"

"Do you play games? Speak! Or I'll have that tongue of yours ripped from your head."

Selene screwed her eyes shut tight. She tried to bring up her soul flame, but she was too frightened. Behind her eyes there was only darkness. Then she raised her hand to her breast and felt, beneath the cloth of her dress, the Eye of Horus.

Suddenly she heard Andreas's gentle voice: "You must not think of what you are saying, Selene. That is the trick. You must concentrate on something else and then your words will come more easily on their own."

Staring down at the marble floor, Selene saw Andreas's handsome face in the swirls of the marble. She fixed her eyes on him; she saw him there; she made him *be* there, with her, smiling at her, encouraging her, protecting her with love.

"I-I do not know who k-keeps me in the tower, my lady."

"Are you there alone?"

"Yes, my lady."

"Does anyone visit you?"

"A man, my lady."

"And what does he do when he visits you?"

"He asks me questions, my lady."

The queen fell silent, as if surprised by Selene's answer. Selene shivered as the cold of the marble floor went up her legs; her knees were in pain. She wondered what was expected of her; what this woman wanted to hear. *Have I said something wrong?*

Then: "What sort of questions does he ask you?"

"About healing."

"Healing?"

"He asks me about ailments and their cures."

"Why should he ask *you* such questions?"

Selene hesitated, afraid that at any moment she would say the wrong thing and be punished for it. Her head began to swim. "Because I am a healer-woman," she said at last.

The queen fell silent again and Selene braced herself. "When did you come to this place?" the queen asked.

"I was brought here in August, my lady."

"Were you brought here alone or with other girls?"

"With other girls."

Lasha fell silent a third time and Selene, kneeling and in pain, began to shake. What was happening? Why had she been brought before this strange woman? The man had kept her a secret prisoner. Why? Was he now going to be punished for it, and Selene herself as well? There seemed to be anger in the voice of the woman who was questioning her. Was Selene now going to be given over to the soldiers? Her body used before Andreas could find her?

She concentrated on the vision of Andreas, reached out to it in love, drew comfort from it.

The woman spoke again: "You say you came in August. The man who comes and asks you questions, did he ever ask you about fevers?"

"Yes, my lady."

"A *child's* fever?"

"Yes, my lady."

"What did you tell him to do for the fever?"

"I told him that Hecate's Cure would bring it down."

"And how is the cure administered?"

"It is given in a drink."

Then the queen's voice grew sharp: "Fetch Kazlah at once!"

Selene remained kneeling as she heard sandaled feet hastily exiting. The priest stayed behind her while the woman on the throne continued to sit in silence. Selene was growing weak; she tried to take her mind far away, to a safer place.

The doors of the chamber opened and the next voice Selene heard made her blood run cold. It was *his.*

"Yes, my lady," Selene heard the voice of her nightmares say. "I have kept the girl in the tower. When I learned that she had some knowledge of healing, I thought it wise to keep her for a while."

"And keep her from the king for whom she was originally intended?"

Selene's heart thumped. So that was it! She was to have gone to the king in the first place; and now this woman would see to it that she was taken to him at once.

"I thought that the king had virgins enough, my lady. I was thinking of the prince."

"Then the cure was not yours?"

"I never said it was, my lady."

"Where did you get the medicine from? Did she tell you how to make it?"

Now Kazlah hesitated slightly and when he spoke again there was an edge to his voice. "The medicine was part of a medicine box which came with the captured girls."

Selene snapped her head up. "My medicine box! Then it was not lost in the desert! *You* have it!"

"Silence!"

"It's mine! That box is mine!" She jumped to her feet. "That's why you have been asking me all those questions!"

"On your knees," Kazlah growled, reaching for her arm. But Selene twisted away.

"You must give it back to me," she cried. "It's all I have in the world."

Queen Lasha said, "Control her!"

Selene spun around, twisting away from hands that grasped at her. "My lady," she said, looking directly at Queen Lasha. "You must listen to me. That medicine box—" She stopped short, stunned.

The queen was sitting like a goddess upon her golden throne. A thousand black braids descended from her head, ending in gold beads; her arms

were not to be seen, so heavily laden were they with bracelets and arm-
bands; her shoulders seemed to slope beneath the weight of so many
jeweled necklaces and collars; on her head was a dazzling crown of pink
sapphires. And she wore silk! Selene could not believe it. Back in Antioch,
where a pound of silk was worth a pound of gold, because it came from
far-distant China, no one used silk as a *garment.*

But what arrested Selene most was the queen's face.

It was not a human face.

It was painted the whitest possible white, with lips as scarlet as blood;
the cheekbones were sprinkled with gold dust and the hollows beneath
them had been blackened. But what mesmerized Selene even more were
the eyes. The right one was heavily lined with kohl and painted above and
below with brilliant green shadow. But the other eye! There was no eye
there at all, but rather an enormous emerald, encased in a frame of spun
gold and fastened to the face with delicate gold bands. Selene stared,
transfixed.

A rough hand pulled her to her knees and a voice whispered in her ear,
"You've done it now! Your throat will be cut for having looked upon the
queen."

"Why are you staring?" Queen Lasha demanded.

"Your eye, my lady," Selene said. A collective gasp circled the room.

"By the gods," someone muttered, and an awful hush fell over the room.
Even Kazlah seemed afraid to move.

"What about my eye?" The queen's voice was hard-edged; she sat as
still as stone upon her ornate chair, her face like a marble mask, her
white-knuckled hands grasping the arms of the throne.

"My mother was an Egyptian healer-woman, my lady, trained in very
ancient secrets. Egypt is a land greatly troubled with eye diseases, as
everyone knows. My mother knew many treatments."

The stiff body of the queen leaned forward ever so slightly and her
thousands of jewels cast reflections on the walls and ceiling. "What sort
of treatments?" she asked.

"Treatments for blindness. There are ways, in some cases, to cure it."

"How is it done?"

"With a needle."

Queen Lasha continued to sit like a statue on her throne while everyone
waited. Beyond the palace walls, the November rain fell harder, churning
the gray river and whipping the fragile branches of the royal willows on
its banks.

Selene held her head up, looking at the queen. What had she done? She had merely spoken the truth. And Mera had always taught her that honest words spoken honestly would never bring harm.

Finally the queen spoke four clipped words, to which her hosts of attendants reacted as if struck by lightning. "You will heal me."

Selene felt herself go weak. "My lady. Yours might not be that form of blindness! Some afflictions are beyond the healing arts!"

But the queen had made up her mind. "It was you who saved my son's life, and now you will restore my sight. Send for the astrologer!" she called sharply. "He will read the omens."

"But, my lady," Selene pressed, "even if the needle works, it does not always restore full vision."

"Vision I already have," the queen said. "In my good eye. The other eye is disfigured. That is what you will treat. You will make it so that I will no longer have to hide the eye. Now go and prepare yourself."

As Selene left, Kazlah whispered into her ear, "And so, now you will see. You were safe with me, but your arrogance will be your executioner!"

CHAPTER 22

I shall need fire from the temple of Isis," Selene said to the slave who had been assigned to her.

The slave, a mute, gestured that Isis did not dwell in Magna and pointed to the crescent-moon symbol of Allat that hung about her neck.

"Fire from your god, then."

Selene had to force herself to be calm as she went through the preparations; she was so nervous that her hands shook.

Surely this was a sign from the gods! Surely they were going to deliver her from this terrible imprisonment and show her a way out. It was the answer to her prayers. To restore someone's sight was a great and wonderful thing; Selene had no doubt that the queen would reward her handsomely. *I shall ask only for my freedom,* Selene thought, as she washed her hands and set out the needles and medicines for the operation. *I shall ask to be put on the road to Antioch, and I shall find my way back to Andreas.*

Selene was so full of joy, so eager to be away from this place, away from the man who had tormented her for three months, that she could barely concentrate on her work. But concentrate she must, for, in order to be rewarded with that freedom, the operation must be a success.

And Selene had never done such an operation.

She fingered the contents of her medicine box lovingly; each was like an old friend come home: the jar of honey thyme, the little bag of dandelion roots, the precious lavender flowers, dried and preserved in a wooden box.

Selene now saw that these had all been brought to her at one time or another by Kazlah; she had not recognized them as her own carefully harvested and preserved herbs. Comfrey leaves are alike the world over: when Kazlah had asked her what their purpose was, she had said, "Make a poultice of them to apply to cuts and burns," not knowing that she was speaking of leaves she had cultivated and gathered with her own hands.

The slave returned with holy fire from the temple, and over it Selene set a cup of water to boil. When the water was ready, she carefully put into it a measure of fennel seeds, saying as she did so, "Holy spirit of the fennel, awaken your healing life in this tea," and then set the cup aside to cool. The fennel infusion would be used when the operation was over as an eyewash to keep out the evil spirits of infection.

Selene turned at last to the couching needle.

She had never used it before, but had watched her mother perform several couchings. Selene stared at the long, delicate needle that lay in the palm of her hand, as weightless as a butterfly's wing, but also as heavy as the walls of this palace, because in its fragile length of bronze lay the power that would either restore sight, or would kill.

Selene placed the needle next to the flame in which, in a few minutes, she would purify it, and considered what she was about to do. If her hand was sure and steady and the operation a success, then Selene would soon be on the road heading for home. But if she made a mistake—then she was doomed.

Lifting her hand to her chest, she felt the Eye of Horus, and thought: *Let it be true, that I came from the gods, for they will guide my hand tonight. They cannot have brought me to this place to die; I was born for a purpose. I must find out who I am. I must be with Andreas again. And so I must be set upon the road to freedom.*

Picking up the needle and holding it in the fire, she murmured, "Holy spirit of the flame, purify this needle and drive away the evil spirits that bring disease and death."

Selene closed her eyes and called upon all her powers, centering them in her hands. In a strange way she felt as if she were being reborn, that the interlude of captivity had been but a dream, a period of preparation.

Suddenly, Selene saw that these three months had been her spiritual initiation, the one which she and her mother were to have completed in the mountains; she understood now that the gods had placed her here in the palace in order for her to be made ready for the final rite: She was about to perform her first act of healing entirely on her own—no one was with her now, not Mera, nor Andreas. With her own medicine box and the knowledge she had been taught, Selene was ready to step over the threshold into independence. A healer-woman in her own right at last.

"It is called a cataract," the smooth, nasal voice of Kazlah was saying when Selene came into the bedchamber. "It is a film covering the pupil of the eye. It blocks the vision and renders the eye useless."

The queen silenced him with an impatient hand. She didn't care about vision; her other eye was sufficient for sight. What plagued Lasha was the ugly cloud which, years ago, had slowly grown over her eye, making it look grotesque, an object of revulsion. That was when she had begun wearing the emerald, and no one, not even King Zabbai, had seen the eye since. But it was exposed now, wide open and staring blindly up at the ceiling.

Selene came forward and placed her medicine box on the table next to the queen's couch. Behind her, a slave followed with the sacred fire. Selene said, "I need soap and water."

"What for?" barked Kazlah.

"To wash my hands."

He eyed her suspiciously.

"It's an Egyptian practice," Selene said.

"Fetch what she wants!" the queen snapped.

Selene set her medicine box down and lifted the lid. "Will someone please bring a goblet of wine for the queen to drink?"

She took a small clay jar from the row of jars in her box and turned it to the light in order to see its inscription. The symbol for the deadly nightshade plant was engraved, and below it was stamped the Egyptian hieroglyph for evil, which was a warning that the jar's contents were lethal.

When the wine was brought, Selene poured some of the drug into a small copper funnel that was plugged with cotton, and this she held over the goblet. All the courtiers and attendants watched in silence as Selene held the funnel over the wine, appearing to be doing nothing at all. After a moment, a drop appeared at the tip of the funnel's tube, and it fell into the wine. Selene stood very still, holding the funnel over the goblet, her eyes fixed on it. Another drop formed and fell. Finally, a third.

Quickly removing the funnel and setting it into the mouth of the jar of deadly nightshade in order to collect the unused portion of the costly narcotic, Selene then picked up the goblet and moved it gently in circles in order to mix the drug with the wine. The safe handling of deadly nightshade had been one of the first lessons her mother had taught her; used in correct amounts, it brought sleep and relief from pain; one drop too many, and it was poisonous.

Selene held out the goblet to one of the queen's ladies-in-waiting and said, "Give this to the queen to drink."

But Kazlah took it and said, "What is it?"

Selene looked at this man who had terrorized her in the tower cell; he would terrorize her no longer. "It is a secret," she said, and saw him stiffen.

"Give it to me," the queen said, impatient to get on with the operation. This tongue-tied girl had saved the life of her son; Lasha trusted her.

But as she watched the queen drink, Selene felt an unexpected chill creep into her arms and legs. The enormity of what she was about to do suddenly struck her, and the possible consequences afterward. During her preparations she had seen only the road back to Antioch and Andreas, but now, watching the queen's eyelids grow heavy and her head fall back onto the pillow, Selene realized that she was about to pierce this woman's eye with a potentially deadly needle.

If I fail, Selene thought, suddenly afraid, *what will happen to me?*

She looked at Kazlah whose thin lips were pressed in an angry white line, and thought: *What if I am handed over to him for punishment?*

"The queen is asleep," the lady-in-waiting said, and Selene closed her eyes. She tried to conjure up the image of her right hand, of the needle it would hold, of the path into the eye. She tried to visualize how her mother had done the operation. If it went in wrong, the needle could do more damage than good: It could puncture the orb so that its fluid leaked out, hideously collapsing the eye; it could trigger a bleeding that might never be stanched; and worse, it could slip in too heavily and accidentally touch the vulnerable root at the back of the eye, bringing instant death to the queen.

Selene trembled. She clenched her fists, fighting for control. For the operation to be successful she needed steady hands. But the more she tried to calm herself, the more she seemed to shake.

"What are you waiting for?" Kazlah asked from behind her.

Taking a deep breath and thinking of her mother, Selene picked up the couching needle and approached the slumbering queen. Close up, Selene could see the years etched in the powdered face, the harsh lines and wrinkles that Lasha, in her extreme vanity, was adept at hiding. Selene placed her left hand over the queen's cool forehead and very gently, with thumb and forefinger, separated the lids of the afflicted eye. It stared up at her, unseeing, an eye once beautiful but fogged now with an unsightly blotch.

The procedure for removing the blotch was simple—pressing the lens of the eye with the tip of a needle until the lens became detached and floated back into the vitreous fluid. Selene had watched her mother do it many times, and had even seen complete sight restored to some. It was not the procedure that was tricky, but the skill of the hand that guided the needle. Mera had had years of experience and practice; Selene had never touched a couching needle, not even to wash it.

She held it first in Allat's purifying flame to drive off the evil spirits, then, drawing in her breath, she brought the needle down to Lasha's eye.

Suddenly Selene stopped. Surely this was not the correct angle! Drawing back, she surveyed the contour of the orb, trying to determine the correct point of entry. *Here,* she decided. *Just to the side of the iris.* But she drew back again. That was wrong, too. Did the needle go in through the top, or must it come up from the bottom? *I cannot remember! Mother!*

"Why are you hesitating?" Kazlah pressed her.

Selene was determined to ignore him. She brought the tip of the needle down again and touched the glassy surface of the eye. *Here,* she told herself. *Press the tip ever so lightly. Now!*

A tremor shook her hand, and she quickly pulled it away again. Forty pairs of eyes watched her from all around the room; the rain outside whipped the palms and willows and drove the river in a frenzy.

I cannot do it, she thought in panic. *I cannot do it!*

And then, unexpectedly, she remembered another lesson taught to her long ago by Mera. Selene had been nine years old and her mother had said, "Picture the world within you, daughter. Imagine a pathway from the outer world going into you, a road for traveling. It turns corners, it goes over hills, and makes its way through the darkness. There is something at the end of that road, Selene. Something deep in your soul. You must reach out for it. Reach . . . "

And she had seen it. A little blue-white flame, no more than a teardrop of fire, trembling in the darkness. Selene had fainted then, her nine-year-old body had not been able to stand the strain of the inner journey. But she was able to withstand it now; she conjured up the flame and it burned brightly in an imagined darkness, its warmth and light dispelling all fear.

Selene looked back down at the queen's eye. Keeping her body perfectly still, she held on to the image of the flame. As she kept it in her mind's eye, she heard her mother's voice speak from the past in yet another lesson: "The needle must go in through the top," Mera had said during a couching, while Selene looked on. "Enter at the edge of the color of the iris. Hold the needle exactly perpendicular to the surface of the eye."

Concentrating on the flame, superimposing its image over the queen's face, Selene carefully touched the tip of the couching needle to the edge of the iris and exerted a gentle pressure. Slowly, almost imperceptibly, the lump of cloud started to move.

Selene continued a steady pressure, her mind watching the flame, seeing the queen's face through it.

There wasn't a sound in the room; even the fierce rain seemed to abate, as if the gods were holding everything back. The light of a hundred lamps danced over the walls, casting flickering shadows. Anyone entering the room would see a frozen tableau: the royal attendants in their long robes, the soothsayers in their cone-shaped hats, the mute slaves and guards— no one moving, all watching the seemingly motionless hand of the girl who had been a prisoner.

Slowly, the clouded lens broke away from the wall of the eye, and as the needle probed deeper, the lens gave way, and with a barely felt snap, it floated harmlessly back into the fluid of the eye.

Selene withdrew the needle, lifted her head and said, "It is done."

C H A P T E R   2 3

When Queen Lasha awoke, still groggy from the sleeping potion she had been given, she felt over her face with tentative fingers and found that the emerald was once again fixed over her eye. Then she felt a strong, familiar hand take hold of hers. It was Kazlah. "What happened?" Lasha asked.

"It is over."

"Was it successful?"

"You must tell *us* that, my lady."

After Lasha was revived with a strong tea, and was sitting up flanked by her personal attendants, she called for a mirror.

From her place in the corner, Selene watched, tense, as the emerald was removed from the queen's face. Lasha took the polished copper mirror in her right hand, and with her left picked up a small oil lamp, the kind that burned linen wicks in a slow and steady flame. When the light was close to her face, she opened her eyes.

Lasha dropped the mirror and flung an arm across her face.

A nervous buzz stirred the crowd.

"The pain!" she cried, cupping her left eye with her hand. "Such pain!"

Selene stiffened. *There should be no pain,* she thought in alarm. The operation had been bloodless, the eye was intact. At least when she last saw it it had been; but that had been an hour ago and in that time, while they had all waited for the queen to waken, Selene had observed Kazlah bend over the queen's face several times, ostensibly to examine the eye.

"Give me the mirror," said the queen, when she had recovered.

"My lady. Clearly the operation was not successful."

Lasha's hand remained outstretched and the mirror was placed into it. This time she opened her eyes in the natural light of the chamber and, though she winced, she held on to the mirror. When she opened her eyes a third time, Lasha said, "The pain is gone. It was but the brightness of the lamp that hurt." Then she said, "It is a miracle. I can see."

The room erupted in excited murmurs that were silenced by the queen. "For what you have done," she said to Selene, "the gods will bless you. Come forward now, child, for I will reward you greatly."

Selene's heart leapt. *Tomorrow!* she thought, joyfully. *I shall ask to leave tomorrow, at first light.*

"Because Allat is merciful," Queen Lasha said, "and in gratitude for what you did for me, you shall have a painless death."

Selene stared at her, not understanding. With a scowl, Kazlah gestured to the guards at the door, and in the next instant, Selene was seized.

While one of the guards bound her ankles with a rope and tied her hands behind her back, the other produced a short knife and hacked off Selene's long hair. It all happened so quickly that Selene didn't have time to think or react; she was pushed to her knees before the queen and a goblet of drugged wine was pressed to her lips.

"You are fortunate. Very fortunate, indeed," the queen said, while Selene stared up at her, incredulous. From his place at Lasha's side Kazlah gave Selene a look that explained everything: *It is death for one such as you to lay hands upon the royal person.*

"Wait," said Selene, suddenly understanding.

But the queen was not listening. Raising her arms to the ceiling, Lasha recited a prayer to the Goddess while at the same time two mute guards took their positions by Selene. She saw one of them raise his sword.

"No . . . " Selene whispered as a heavy hand forced her head forward. Selene saw, out of the corner of her eye, a fall of short black hair over her cheek, *her* hair, cut ridiculously short and baring her neck to a cold draft. *She was going to be beheaded!*

"Please," she whispered again and saw a giant shadow on the shining floor as the monstrous sword came down. When she felt the sharp blade lightly kiss the back of her neck, Selene swayed from the impact of a blow that never came.

Then she heard Queen Lasha say, "Rise, Fortuna." And the guards were releasing Selene from her bonds.

She stared dumbfounded at the queen as the guards helped her to her feet; they continued to hold her up as Selene's legs would not support her.

"Selene of Antioch is dead," Queen Lasha declared in a commanding voice. "Let it be written." She waved a hand to the court scribe. "On this day, Fortuna of Magna has been born. Come forward, child."

Selene stumbled toward the throne, assisted by the guards, and continued to stare in a daze as the queen stepped down and regarded her newly born subject with two clear, perfectly seeing eyes. "I have named you Fortuna, for you are my good fortune. From now on that is your name. Selene has died; you are born anew." Something glittered in the queen's hands. It was a gold-link necklace dripping with rubies. She fastened it around Selene's neck, and proclaimed it a symbol of the "beheading" she had just suffered.

The queen stepped back, held out her arms and, as Selene looked on in horror, declared: "I will keep you by me always. Fortuna of Magna, today begins your new life in my house."

BOOK III
MAGNA

CHAPTER 24

E scape.
   All that Selene thought about was escape.
   Getting away from Magna, getting back to Andreas, getting back to the search for her destiny.

It was a great risk. First there was the danger of being caught while trying to escape from the palace. Lasha meted out terrible punishment to people who dared to defy her: Selene recalled the poor handmaiden who had been trying to elope with the officer of the guard—the man had been castrated; the girl, buried alive. And then, once outside the palace walls, there was the desert, hostile and formidable, and inhabited by bandits and scorpions. Yet Selene would risk it all. The queen and her army of mute guards were not going to be allowed to keep Selene from her destiny. The gods had marked her, Mera had said so; a dying Roman had promised that Selene was born to a purpose.

How shall I ever fulfill my purpose in this insane prison? she asked herself as she hurried down the hall toward the harem. Catering to the imagined ills of overindulged royalty was not *healing.* Selene believed she had been born to do great good, that a sacred calling awaited her in the world—she had realized this when Andreas had opened new doorways for her. But she would never achieve that dream if she did not find her way back to him, and to the gold ring Mera had said would tell her everything.

Lasha was with one of her lovers, a boy brought in from the city, and she would spend the afternoon with him, in private. Selene always seized these occasions to make her way to the king's harem, where she would visit her only friend, Samia, the Hindu girl who had been captured with Selene two years before. And there, in the privacy and solitude of the harem's lotus pool—Selene's slaves were not allowed to enter that part of the harem —while the other women slept through the heat of the afternoon, the two would talk of escape.

In the month following her "execution" two years before, while the palace was busy with preparations to celebrate the winter solstice, Selene had been reunited with Samia. Samia had failed, as had all the other women captured to restore the king's potency, and consequently had been consigned to the harem, there to be ignored and forgotten. Almost at once the two had begun plotting their escape; for the ensuing months they had talked of little else.

Selene glanced behind her. There were spies and enemies everywhere. Being in the queen's protection was no guarantee of safety, especially when one's primary enemy was a man almost as powerful as Lasha herself, a man with eyes and ears in all corners of the palace, a man who lived for revenge against the girl who had humiliated him and who could destroy her with one crook of his finger: the Chief Physician, Kazlah.

As Selene hurried past a doorway opening onto a garden, she saw the summer sunshine and was suddenly engulfed in grief. It reminded her of the day she had met Andreas, two years ago. She had been about to turn sixteen, and all her life had seemed to be before her. And then—what had happened? Suddenly her dream had been denied her, and a strange fate had brought her to this present state.

And what of my beloved? she thought. *What did he do when he could not find me? Does he search still? Has he forgotten me? But he will not forget me; we are bound to one another, forever.*

People nodded to Selene as they passed her in the corridor, in recognition of her status as the queen's personal healer-woman. Outwardly Selene was a typical resident of this luxurious court. Like all the women, she wore a veil over the lower half of her face, evidence of the strong Arabian influence in Magna. Her black hair, now grown past her shoulders, was worked into tight braids and bound up under a lavender veil. Across her forehead lay a row of gold coins; her dress was voluminous and sweeping, bound at the waist by a belt crusted with gems; at the queen's bidding, Selene now wore cosmetics for the first time in her life.

As she neared the harem, Selene slowed her pace, and the three slaves behind her bumped into one another. Slaves accompanied her everywhere;

they were at her side every minute of the day, spying on her, watching her, reporting her movements to the queen. One of the slaves—Selene did not know which one—had found the letter she was preparing to smuggle out of the palace, to be given to a traveler bound for Antioch, a letter to Andreas. And the slave had taken it to Lasha. Since then, even in her bath, asleep in bed, or treating the ailments of the court, Selene had never, for a single moment, been alone.

Two guards now opened the huge double doors for her, and then inner doors guarded by eunuchs were opened. Selene, alone at last, leaving her slaves to wait for her, entered a splendid room splashed with afternoon sunlight.

She lowered her veil and smiled at the young man who greeted her, a delicately handsome eunuch with soulful eyes. He was Darius, a recent addition to the eunuch staff that watched over the women of Zabbai's harem. In only a few weeks he had become the object of many love-hungry hearts.

Darius had been sold into slavery at an age too early for him to remember: there remained only the faint memory of a courtyard, of a woman singing, of a green river beyond a wall. His sleep was often visited by a dream, of hands seizing him, of a sack being tied over his head, of a long ride away from the green river. Then the company of other boys, and finally the recurring nightmare of blood, of pain too sublime to have been real; a healing period and lastly the bewildering discovery of his body's mutilation. It was all so long ago that Darius was now not sure what was dream, what was truth; all that was left was today's reality: after years of being passed from master to master, he had come to Magna's harem, a young, sensitive man who saw a dark tunnel of lonely years ahead of him.

Selene could not but feel sorry for the eunuch, who, she had predicted rightly, was suffering through no fault of his own. He could no more help his gentle nature and melting beauty than the unfortunate women whom he served could help their passions and frustrations.

The harem both fascinated and repelled Selene. It was an unnatural existence, she thought, to be kept caged so. Many of these women had not seen the corridor beyond the heavily bolted door since they were brought here as children; indeed, some had been born inside the harem and had grown up knowing only the patch of sky above the inner garden—young and old women, beautiful and homely, dull and sharp witted, with nothing more taxing on their minds than deciding which veil to wear. They lived out their days in the perfumed baths, gossiping, rearing small children, languishing. It was no wonder, then, that the harem was a hotbed of plots and intrigues, of cliques and factions; there were amorous liaisons among the women, and jealousies, and the occasional handsome eunuch, like Darius, who sparked hatred and war.

Such a young man, if he wished, could turn these circumstances to his own advantage. Many a court eunuch had used his sexual favors for his own advancement; some of the women in the harem were rich and powerful in their own right, being daughters and sisters of Eastern rulers. Darius was fortunate to be one of those castrates who could still function sexually, since Zabbai's was a harem in which the king did not care if the women had male lovers, only that they should not be impregnated. Darius was fortunate that he was not the other sort of court eunuch, like the guards who stood at all doorways—men who had been deprived of their sexual organs entirely so that they were of no use whatsoever to women.

But Darius was not interested in becoming involved with palace intrigue, with joining plots, with using his sex for special favors, because the night he had been brought to the palace, branded and shamed, he had fallen in love for the first time in his life.

Now he greeted Selene with the firm handshake of genuine friendship. "Is it safe?" Selene asked, looking anxiously around. He nodded, then indicated that Samia was by the lotus pool, waiting.

Darius was a little in awe of Selene, as were most people at the court. He had not been a resident of the palace at the time of Queen Lasha's eye operation, or, later, when King Zabbai's potency had been restored. But Darius had heard all about it—how this young woman from Antioch had restored the royal health in several afflicted areas. It was whispered among the halls of the palace that Fortuna had the blood of an ancient Egyptian sorceress in her.

Selene waved across the courtyard at Samia. It was Samia who had helped Selene bandage the wounds of the other girls on their first terrifying night in the palace; and Samia had shared Selene's misery and grief as, one by one, the girls were taken away to the king. Samia had been among the last to go and they had clung to one another, weeping. Those days of shared imprisonment had woven a strong bond; Samia was the first real female friend, other than Mera, that Selene had ever had.

They embraced, and then Selene sat down at the pool's edge, anxious to impart her news. She did not at first see the look on her friend's face.

"They will be here in two weeks," Selene said hurriedly, looking over her shoulder. Darius stood in the archway, on guard. "A delegation from Rome. There will be a large retinue. A whole new wing of the palace is being opened for them! Think of it, Samia! The palace will be turned upside down. We shall surely find an opportunity to escape then!"

When Samia lifted her eyes, Selene saw that she had been weeping. "I already know about the Romans," the girl said, her voice bleak. She glanced past Selene and looked yearningly at Darius. "They are going to take my beloved Darius away."

Stunned, Selene turned around and noticed for the first time the unhappy expression on Darius's face. "How?" she asked, leaning close to Samia, whispering. "How can they?"

Tears welled up in the girl's eyes. "The king is going to make a gift of twenty of his women to the Emperor Tiberius. Darius is being sent to accompany them."

Selene sat back in shock. "To *Rome*? Darius is going to be taken to *Rome*?"

She stared down at the surface of the lotus pool, which rippled with sunlight and flashed gold when fish neared the surface. She was recalling the night she had met Darius, four months ago. There had been the secretive summons from Samia, sent to her along a grapevine from eunuch to guard to servant; then Selene's furtive flight down dark corridors, hoping the queen would not waken and demand to know where Fortuna was. Selene had found her friend at the back of this very garden, huddled beneath a willow tree, damp with the light rain and cradling the unconscious body of the young eunuch who had arrived in the harem the day before. He had tried to hang himself with a silk veil, and Samia, finding him, had cut him down. Selene had helped her to nurse him back to health.

She cared deeply for these two young lovers who shared her captivity. Samia and Darius were the only ones who knew Selene's story—of Andreas, of her quest. They were the only ones who called her Selene instead of Fortuna, a name she loathed: their knowing her secrets and speaking her name gave Selene a feeling of having kept the identity and past of which Lasha had tried to rob her.

"There must be a way you can go with him," Selene said, feeling again the pain of her own wound—her own separation from the man she loved.

But Samia shook her head. "There is no way. The gods have abandoned me."

"Join the group of women!" Selene whispered. "Go to Rome with them!"

"Only twenty are to go. The guards will count and will know if there is one extra."

"Then take the place of one. Bribe her!"

Samia shook her head more strongly. "Selene, I have already thought of these things! I have asked around, and they all want to go! I could not pay one enough for her to let me take her place. They all want to see Rome!"

Selene turned and looked again at Darius.

On the day he had been brought to the palace, his body had been bruised purple from the lewd pinches of the guards. The women had clustered around him, hungry for anything new in their lives, examining him, commenting among themselves, heightening his shame with their remarks and speculations. He had believed he had come to the end of his miserable life and had crept that night to the tree with his silken noose. But in the four months since, Samia and Selene had taught Darius to love and to trust again, to find joy where he could, and to look into the future, such as it was, and draw hope from it. Now, if Darius was taken to Rome, there would be no future for either of them.

"I have an idea," Selene said suddenly. "Since you cannot join the group because the guards will notice one extra woman, and since you have not been able to bribe any of the women to let you take her place, then you will have to stay behind. And then you will be separated from Darius."

"I know all this, Selene."

"Then listen. If Darius stays behind, too, you will not be separated from him."

"But . . . he *must* go. He has been ordered to go."

"He will stay and *I* will take his place."

Samia stared. "It cannot be done!"

"Why not? He and I are the same height and of similar build. In the dark of night, at the center of a group of women, with soldiers hurrying the women down to the boat waiting on the river . . . "

"Selene, you are mad," she said quietly, but her tone betrayed interest.

Selene spoke in a whisper, urgently. It would be simple, she explained. It would not be noticed if the eunuch escorting the women should draw his traveling cloak over his head. It was no doubt going to be a hasty transfer—transfers from the harem always were. And it would be in darkness, since they were to leave at midnight. And she and Darius *were* of similar height and build.

"But Selene," Samia whispered, her eyes betraying hope, "how can you expect to make it all the way to Rome in that disguise? You will be found out!"

She sat back and said, "Because I have no intention of going all the way to Rome. I shall leave the boat at first opportunity. I shall jump into the river if I have to. Escape from the palace is all that matters to me."

Finally, Samia and Darius agreed to the plan. On the night of the departure, Selene was going to be called back to the harem on a pretext, some medical emergency. She would see to it that a powerful powder was put into Lasha's nightly goblet of wine so that Selene's absence would not be noticed until dawn. And while the traveling group assembled with all their slaves and coffers and guards, Selene and Darius would make the switch. He would hide in the palace after that—it was large enough for one slave to get lost in—and then work on a plan to get himself and Samia away from Magna together.

CHAPTER 25

W here have you been?" Queen Lasha said. "I have been calling for you!"
"Forgive me, my lady," Selene said as she placed her medicine box on a table. "I needed some exercise."
Lasha stirred on the couch where she reclined, her body draped in great waves of scarlet silk, her face sprinkled with gold dust. "You get exercise enough. Now then, my monthly trouble has come upon me unexpectedly again and I have cramps. Fix me the medicine."

Glad to have something to do, to hide her excitement—the escape plan *had* to work!—Selene lifted the lid of her medicine box.

Queen Lasha was entering the time of life when her moon-flow would soon cease, and her cycle was becoming irregular. While she worked, Selene looked around the luxurious bedchamber for signs of the youth who had been brought here earlier. She never knew where the young men went afterward; Lasha used a boy only once and then sent him away. Certainly they could never return to their homes, where they might tell tales of the royal bedchamber.

As Selene poured drops of Hecate's Cure into a cup of wine, she raised her eyes to the balcony that stretched beyond rainbow-colored hangings. Only once had she been out into the city, when Lasha had gone to visit a tribe of Bedouins summering at a nearby oasis.

Word of special dancing girls had reached Lasha's ears: dancers who could lie on their backs and pour wine from one goblet to another using only their stomach muscles. And whenever these whims came over Lasha —to visit strange sights, to look upon oddities—her retinue never numbered less than two hundred: attendants, priests, slaves, scribes, archers and horsemen. On that particular day Selene had traveled in a curtained litter behind the majestic palanquin that carried the queen, and when she had dared, Selene had peeked through the curtains as the procession wound through the streets of Magna.

And what she had seen had appalled her.

After months of living amid splendor and riches, Selene was shocked to see squalor, deprivation. She recalled one vision in particular now, as she handed the cup to the queen: the great throng of people clustered at the gates of the palace—cripples and beggars, little girls with skinny babies in their arms, men without arms or legs, with diseased eyes, with faces bloated in sickness; all gathered in the useless hope that proximity to royalty, to the Goddess Incarnate, might cure them.

It was then that Selene had learned there was no place for those people to go. There was no healing temple of Aesculapius in Magna where a person might go and spend the night inside the sanctuary, in the hope that the god would come and heal him in his dreams. Only the rich could afford to keep a doctor in their homes; the rest—middle-class people as well as the poor—had nowhere to go when they fell ill.

"Dreaming?" came Lasha's voice.

Selene shook her head, in reply to the queen and to dispel the awful vision. In Antioch she had worried about those same people, but at least in Antioch there had been somewhere to go for help—the temple of Aesculapius, the little house of Mera, the villa of Andreas the physician.

I would be able to help here, Selene thought now, as she took the cup from the queen and rinsed it. *If I were out there, I could be a real healer, instead of being locked up here, working my "miracles."*

Curing King Zabbai's impotency had been no miracle, but Selene was the only one who knew that. Not even Kazlah, the Chief Physician, had seen that the King's problem lay, quite simply, in his obesity.

Mera had taught Selene about the disease the Greeks called *diabetes mellitus: diabetes* meaning "running through" because of the frequent urination it caused, and *mellitus* meaning "honey" because of the sweetness of the urine. Onset in childhood meant certain death, but onset in late maturity could often be alleviated simply by weight loss. Obesity, Mera had explained, for some reason sometimes brought on diabetes in adulthood; therefore a shedding of the fat could sometimes reverse the disease. When she had first looked at Zabbai, with seventy attendants in the room watching, Selene had had no idea what was wrong with him. But once the symptoms were described—abnormal thirst, constant hunger, frequent urination—Selene had remembered what Mera had told her. So she had tested the King's urine and had found it was as sweet as honey. Zabbai did indeed have diabetes, and as diabetes can cause impotence,

Selene reasoned that a reversal of the illness might also reverse the impotence.

Zabbai was placed on a strict diet; the fat melted from his body and six months later he engaged in his first successful sex act in two years.

There were other "miracles" which Selene had worked: The queen's aged vizier had suffered for months with a terrible itching of the scalp and Selene had cured it with a shampoo of sulphur and cedar oil; the chief eunuch's swollen joints had been treated successfully with Hecate's Cure; the prince's alarming summer diarrhea had been arrested with feedings of boiled rice.

There had been a few legitimate ailments in the palace that Selene had been glad to treat, but the majority were imagined, the products of boredom and lethargy. In Queen Lasha's domain, she saw herself cast more in the role of magician than healer, but out there, in the city, where so many needed her skills, Selene knew she could do much good.

Queen Lasha's gaze was fixed upon Selene. Because she was vain about her eyes, ever since the operation Lasha enhanced their beauty with drops of belladonna from Selene's medicine box; the drug dilated her pupils and the result was a strange kind of look—as though Lasha's eyes could see more than normal ones could.

The queen was watching Selene in a mixture of envy and resentment. This common girl had great power, a power Lasha wanted for herself. Not the power of life and death—Lasha already commanded that—but the power over pain, which the queen saw as something more vital. Lasha wielded half of that power already—the power to *inflict* pain. But this slum-born girl held the power to *relieve* pain, which was something altogether more wonderful.

As she watched Selene, Lasha thought: *The child does not yet know the power she holds over me—the power to grant or deny me relief from pain. She is not yet aware of what a prisoner I am, of what hurts there are in my body. Nothing, not even death, is as fearful to me as interminable pain. This gutter-girl, both ignorant and wise, has no idea of the heights she could reach with her power. But she will someday. When she is older, she will see what a slave I am to the weaknesses of the flesh, and when that day arrives, our roles will be reversed: She will be the sovereign, and I the subject. Will she, I wonder, someday try to use that power against me?*

"Fortuna," came Lasha's smooth voice. "The Romans arrive in two weeks. Surely you have already heard, for these walls have lips as well as ears. And when they come, the palace will be in chaos. You won't do something foolish, will you, Fortuna? Like attempting to escape?"

The Queen, from her couch, saw the sudden stiffening of Selene's body and thought: *So, I am right.*

"I worry for you, child," Lasha said, as she rose from the couch like a scarlet and gold column. "I sometimes fear that loneliness troubles you. I see restlessness in your eyes. You are, after all, nearly eighteen years old. And still a virgin, are you not?"

In two years Selene had come to recognize every deadly shade of Lasha's tone. Deceit was in the royal heart at this moment, Selene knew. And something else . . .

I saved the life of her son, Selene thought. *I restored sight to her eye. I cured her husband's impotence so that she need not take another consort. And she hates me. She hates me because she must be grateful to me. The Queen is in my debt, but it is I who will pay!*

"It has occurred to me, Fortuna, that you need companionship. You are too much alone."

Selene said cautiously: "I am never alone, my lady. I have many slaves."

"I mean *real* companionship, Fortuna. Someone you can truly be with and share with. You need a husband."

Selene whirled around. "No!" she blurted out; and she instantly regretted it.

Lasha smiled. Like a dentist probing for a bad tooth, the queen had found what she had been looking for—Selene's vulnerable spot.

Lasha turned away. "You are young, Fortuna. You may hold the incredible knowledge of healing your mother taught you—and do not think me ungrateful for it, or that I take it for granted. But in other ways you are still a baby. It is my duty, my . . . *obligation* to see that your life is a normal one. After all"—she turned to Selene—"you lead an abnormal existence. Eighteen years old and untouched by a man!"

I have been touched by a man, Selene thought defiantly. *I have been touched by the only man I want—Andreas.*

"As it turns out," Lasha continued, "someone in the palace has spoken for you."

Selene stared at her.

"A gentleman of my court has approached me on your behalf. He wishes to marry you, Fortuna."

Silence filled the chamber as Lasha paused for effect. Then she said: "And you are indeed fortunate, as my name for you indicates. For no ordinary man has asked for you, Fortuna. It is the Chief Physician himself who has. The noble Kazlah."

Selene groped for the table to steady herself.

"The Chief Physician would be a good husband for you, my child,"

Lasha went on. "You both have interests in common. He understands your powers. You could learn from each other, share each other's knowledge. He is much older and wiser. Think of the advantages."

Selene turned away, toward the rainbow hangings, and there, in front of her, stood the balcony wall that separated her from freedom. On the other side of it, the Euphrates flowed past.

And then her eyes no longer saw the wall but rather Kazlah, a tall and narrow specter dressed in midnight blue. He was punishing a slave for having accidentally spilled wine on Kazlah's hem. The slave had been a musician, a gentle harpist whose ears were his life and soul; Kazlah had taken a long needle from among his medical tools and pierced the slave's eardrums.

Selene stared at the wall. *I can run now, jump over it, try to swim to freedom.*

She checked her impulse—it was an insane idea. *If I should get caught and be brought back, then I shall lose forever any chance of seeing my beloved Andreas again. I will be cautious. In two weeks, the twenty women from the harem will be taken to a boat at midnight. And I will be among them . . .*

Selene knew why Kazlah had asked for her.

She thought of the hundreds of willow trees that lined the river banks outside the palace. The Chief Physician had no idea that the one thing in all the world he most wanted—the secret of Hecate's Cure—lay in the bark of those very trees.

Keeping the secret of Hecate's Cure had allowed Selene to keep her life; perilous as that was in this palace, she had managed these past two years to keep the secret safe. Over the months she had had to refill the blue bottle, and suspecting that Kazlah had spies among her slaves and that her mixing of the Cure would be reported to him, Selene always requisitioned a long list of ingredients, some necessary, most not; and then she worked in the garden, making a complex and baffling ritual of what was nothing more than a simple steeping of tea. No one, watching her, could have unraveled the intricate and meaningless ceremony, nor remembered how much of each ingredient went into each step. As a result, Kazlah still did not know the secret of Hecate's Cure and Selene lived.

She was determined that he never learn the secret.

"You tremble," Lasha said, coming up behind Selene. "Does it thrill you, Fortuna, to think of yourself as Kazlah's wife? It is rumored that he is an ingenious lover, well practiced in the more exquisite pleasures of the marriage bed. Imagine this if you will: I have heard that Kazlah likes to use a—"

"My lady," Selene said, turning around. "I am not ready for marriage. I am not . . . worthy to be the Chief Physician's wife."

Lasha smiled. "Well, perhaps you are right," she said with a satisfied sigh. "At least for now. Perhaps it is best that you be left on your own. But you do understand, Fortuna, that if you should get some foolish idea into your head, such as trying to run away—it will be found out, I assure you, before you have taken even the first step. And then I shall have no choice but to agree to Kazlah's request. For he would keep you in line, you know. Kazlah would see to it that not another thought of escape would ever enter your head. He would teach you obedience, Fortuna. I promise you that."

Selene looked at the queen and felt as if she were wading through arctic waters. Then she remembered Samia and Darius and thought: I must get away!

CHAPTER 26

Selene could not sleep, but had to pretend to do so, so that when the summons came to her door, she would appear to have been wakened. Dressing hastily and picking up her medicine box, Selene followed the mute guard down the deserted hall.

It was some minutes before she realized something was wrong. "This isn't the way to the harem," she said to the guard.

He gave her a blank look and kept on walking. Of course, the man had not said where he was taking her; Selene never knew, since the palace guards were all mutes. A knock upon her door and a gesture to follow were all that had ever been used.

Puzzled, she followed him down empty corridors, through drafty archways, past silent chambers and eventually down flights of stone steps into a section of the palace where she had never been before. With increasing alarm she wondered where he was leading her, because the air grew dank and the walls and floors became rough. When the guard finally came to a halt, Selene knew that she was far away from the center of the palace —far away from the harem.

A crude wooden door slid open and Selene's eyes widened upon a strange scene.

It was a small chamber, brightly lit with torches set in the walls, and furnished only with one table and one chair. The floor was covered with sand and the air was damp, which meant they must be very near the river. But what seized her attention as she stepped inside and heard the door being bolted behind her was the grouping in the center of the room: a young man was slouched in a chair, wrists and ankles strapped to it, his head resting back and his mouth wide open in a snore; behind him stood a squat old man whom Selene recognized as one of the lesser court physicians; standing in front of the chair, leaning over the unconscious youth, was Kazlah.

He did not acknowledge Selene's arrival but concentrated on his work. Selene had no idea what the Chief Physician was doing; he was bent over the sleeping boy's neck.

Selene watched as the tall, lean figure of Kazlah, hardly seeming to move, stood in the flickering torchlight, in a silence so great that Selene guessed the walls here must be very thick. Two guards stood across the room on either side of a second door, but otherwise there was no one else. Why had she been brought here?

Then she thought of Darius—he would have sent for her by now and would be expecting her to arrive any moment at the harem.

Selene's eyes widened. As she watched the Chief Physician straighten up and step away from the sleeping boy, Selene thought in alarm: *Kazlah knows about our plan, that is why he had me brought here!*

But then she thought: *Or does he know about it? Is this perhaps just a coincidence?*

When Kazlah finally turned to her, he said in a silky tone, "You have been wondering, Fortuna, about our palace mutes. And you have no doubt been desiring to be admitted into the secret."

Selene felt a cold presentiment start to creep up her body, as if the icy waters of the river had somehow seeped up through the floor and she now stood in them. What was he saying? She, wondering about the mutes? She had never voiced an interest.

Her eyes moved to the sleeping youth and saw that the assistant physician was wrapping a thick bandage around the boy's neck. Her heart gave a leap. There were bloodstains on the cloth.

Kazlah gestured to the guards and the boy was unstrapped from the chair and dragged unconscious from the room.

"Step closer, Fortuna," said Kazlah with an edge of command in his tone.

Selene held back, suddenly afraid.

He raised a questioning eyebrow.

"My lord, Queen Lasha would be angry if she awoke and found me gone."

"The queen is deeply asleep, Fortuna. You know that."

Selene drew in a breath. The room suddenly felt smaller; shadows seemed to menace from all sides.

"Come forward, Fortuna," said Kazlah. "It is time you were initiated into some of the finer secrets of Magna."

As she moved toward him, Selene saw the door opposite open and two guards enter with a woman between them. She was as black as Selene's ebony medicine box, with huge frightened eyes. While the guards strapped her into the chair, Kazlah said, "This slave is from Africa. We don't know her name, as she speaks a primitive tongue. She will soon speak it no longer."

Selene's eyes met those of the terrified woman and for one instant the two shared a common terror. Then the slave was forced to drink from the cup held by the other physician; soon her head flopped forward onto her chest.

"The victim must be completely unconscious, Fortuna," Kazlah said, nodding to the other man, who drew the woman's head back and held it. "The throat must be completely relaxed. If there is the slightest tension, it is possible to accidentally cut one of the major blood vessels that lie inside the neck and then a slave is wasted." His thin mouth lifted in a quick smile. "One cannot afford to be clumsy in this."

Stunned, Selene watched him work. From somewhere out in the corridor behind her, the voice of the nigthwatch came through the door calling the midnight hour. She thought of Darius, anxiously looking for her as the harem ladies assembled for departure, and felt a terrible foreboding steal over her.

"Watch carefully now, Fortuna," said Kazlah softly, and her eyes moved, against her will, to his long, slender hands. They held a small silver arrow, thin but strong looking. As her pulse quickened, Selene watched Kazlah first study the woman's neck, then bring the tip of the arrow to one side of her throat.

The scene seemed to freeze for a suspended moment, and then Kazlah's hand jabbed down and up, sharply, expertly, and Selene saw a drop of blood emerge from the tiny cut. "This is where the skill comes in, Fortuna," Kazlah said as he targeted the other side of the throat and stabbed there also. "There is a nerve in the neck which produces speech. How it does so is not known. But when it is severed—and I have just severed it —speech is no longer possible. However, one must be careful of the large blood vessels that lie on either side of the nerve."

Selene stared in horror as the woman, her neck bandaged, was released from her bonds and dragged from the room.

"Examine this instrument well, Fortuna," Kazlah instructed as he held out his hand. "See how beautifully crafted the arrowhead is, such sharpness, such delicacy. In no city other than Magna is the secret of making mutes known. Barbaric nations silence their slaves by cutting out the tongue, but how unsightly that is! And what clumsy noises they made afterward. This way, Fortuna, our slaves are not offensive to the eye or ear."

Again that dry smile, and his voice grew softer. "Now, Fortuna, you are fortunate indeed, for I am going to instruct you in this rare art."

She watched in disbelief as the door opened again and the guards entered with another slave, this time a blond man, a giant who looked as if he could fight the two guards off with ease, but who instead walked submissively between them.

"This is an unusual one," the Chief Physician said as the slave was bound hand and foot to the chair. "He comes from the Rhine valley in Germany, a prisoner of recent fighting and brought back by Roman legions. His name is Wulf."

Wulf was tall and muscled, his hair the color of wheat, falling past his shoulders. His clothes were the strangest Selene had ever seen, boots and leggings made of fur, and he wore no shirt, nothing above the waist except for a crude necklace lying on his bare chest. But it was his face that held her: heavily bearded and mapped with scars, and beneath dark blond brows stared two startlingly blue eyes. He was young and, Selene could tell from his posture, fiercely proud.

"We had anticipated trouble with this one," Kazlah said as he waited for his assistant to mix the sleeping drops into the wine. "But he has been most cooperative. You see, Fortuna, he is living in disgrace because he survived the battle while his comrades did not. I am told he is a prince of his people, and he was brought up to believe that he should have died with a sword in his hand. As far as this brute is concerned, he died when the Romans captured him alive."

Selene tried to look away but she felt the chill blue eyes fasten on her. When Kazlah forced the silver arrow into her hands, there was the barest flicker in that arctic gaze. Selene thought: *He knows what is going to happen to him!*

"I cannot," she managed to whisper.

"But you must," Kazlah said smoothly. "Come, I will show you."

When she stepped close to the barbarian she could smell the sweat and dirt on him, and the months of humiliation; she could see his muscles

tighten beneath the scarred skin. But there seemed to be no fear in him
at all. "Surely you cannot expect me to do this, my lord!"

"You must learn, Fortuna, and we have slaves in plenty for you to
practice on, if you make a few mistakes." Kazlah was standing close, almost
touching her, and his voice took on a slippery quality. "We must help each
other in our noble profession, Fortuna. I will teach you *my* secrets. And
in return, you will teach me yours. Why do you hesitate, Fortuna?"

"He—" She was nearly breathless. "He should be allowed to pray first
to his god."

Kazlah made a sound. "His god! Another useless barbaric brute! This
is his symbol." He pointed to the strip of leather around the German's
neck, and the wooden T-cross at its end. "Odin," said Kazlah contemptu-
ously.

Selene gazed into the blue eyes that never left her face. She saw now,
from this proximity, the currents of emotion in them. *He is afraid after
all,* she thought.

Suddenly she wanted to say something to the barbarian, words of comfort, to ease some of his anguish. *I was mute once,* she thought. *My tongue
was frozen and I could not speak. And after my tongue was loosened, I was
afraid to speak. Andreas set me free.* Now, the thought of what Kazlah was
expecting her to do, to condemn another human being to that silent,
helpless world, filled Selene with horror.

Kazlah leaned close and the assistant thrust the bowl of drugged wine
to the German's lips. Surprisingly, he did not drink.

"Very well," Kazlah said scornfully. "If that is the way he wishes it. He
will stay awake. Now do it, Fortuna, as I showed you."

She placed herself before the barbarian and held his eyes with hers. *I
am as terrified as you,* she said with her mind. *Listen to me if you can!*

Lifting the arrow up so that the slave named Wulf could see it, she then
raised a finger to her lips, a universal gesture, she hoped, that indicated
silence. The ice-blue eyes stared up at her; Selene brought her eyebrows
together in an effort to communicate. She pressed her lips tightly closed
and sealed them with a finger. But there was no flicker of comprehension
in the man's eyes.

"Find the windpipe," came the Chief Physician's voice. "Now feel for
the neck pulse. There, in between. It is a small space. Go carefully now."

Selene bent over the barbarian as closely as she could, bringing her face
near to his, letting the veil on her head fall forward over his shoulder as
a shield. With the blond head held firmly in the grip of the assistant's
hands, Selene palpated Wulf's neck with the fingers of her left hand while

she brought the arrowhead up with her right. She stared at the dirty pale skin and felt her heart rise in her throat.

Dare she risk it?

She had no choice. Steadying herself, moving slightly so that Kazlah's view was blocked, Selene very carefully pricked the skin surface with the arrowhead. The barbarian's body flinched. When a drop of blood appeared, she drew away.

Kazlah glanced down and said, "Good. Now do the other side. Both nerves must be severed for total muteness."

As the assistant tilted the barbarian's head the other way, exposing the neck beneath the bearded jaw, Selene repositioned herself, bent close, cut into the skin and then straightened up.

Kazlah's eyes registered brief surprise, a grudging admiration of her skill, then Selene snatched up the bandage and hastily wrapped it around the barbarian's neck. Now, she could only pray that he had understood the meaning of her gestured warning and not give them both away by suddenly speaking.

"I have done what you asked of me," she said, turning to Kazlah as Wulf was taken from the room. "May I retire now? We shall both earn the queen's wrath should she waken and find me gone."

Kazlah smiled. "And we both know that is not going to happen, don't we? Just one more lesson, Fortuna, and then you may go." He gestured to the guards. "You see, you have performed one operation excellently, but I think you are still not aware of the dangers involved. I shall show you, therefore, what can happen when the thing is done incorrectly."

Selene's panicked thoughts tumbled over one another. What was the hour? Was there still time to get to the harem and change places with Darius? How did Kazlah know about the sleeping draught in the queen's wine?

Mother Isis, she prayed in desperation. *Spare me from this nightmare!*

But when the next victim was brought in, all prayers and thoughts and even breath died in Selene's body. She stood rooted to the floor as if she had sprouted up from the sand. When the poor man was thrust into the chair, she realized with chilling understanding that this was no nightmare after all, but reality; there was to be no escape, no rescue from this horror.

The man was Darius.

"Watch closely, Fortuna," Kazlah said as Darius was being strapped down. "For this will be a most valuable lesson to you."

The eunuch stared at Selene as the assistant physician took hold of his head in a viselike grip. "There is no need to waste good wine on this one," Kazlah said, as he stepped close to the chair and picked up the silver arrow.

Paralyzed, Selene watched the tapered fingers of the Chief Physician feel Darius's throat delicately, then come to rest and spread the skin taut between thumb and index finger. "You see, Fortuna," Kazlah said quietly, "the speech nerve lies here, dangerously close to the big blood vessels. Years of practice enable me to perform this task a thousand times without making a fatal error. But since you are new to this and must be made aware of what can go wrong, I shall purposely make a mistake."

"No!" screamed Selene. But as she lunged for the arrow, one of the giant guards dashed from his place by the door and seized her in a strong grip.

"I told you, Fortuna," said Kazlah. "This is going to be a valuable lesson for you."

"No!" she screamed again, fighting against the guard's hold. "Don't do it. I beg of you. I'll do anything, Kazlah, *anything*. Just don't do it!"

But the arrow plunged.

Kazlah stepped back and said, "There are some men, Fortuna, who claim that arteries carry air. But as you can see, this artery, which leads from the heart to the brain, carries blood."

"Please . . . " she whispered, struggling.

When he saw her go limp in the guard's arms, Kazlah nodded to the man to release her. But as soon as she was free Selene shot forward and clamped her hand over Darius's bleeding neck. As she groped frantically for the bandage, Kazlah grabbed her and pulled her back. Selene lost her balance and fell against him; he held her, pressing his hard body into her. She struggled. She felt sick. Close to her ear Kazlah said, "You will be mine, I promise you. And when you are, you will obey me. There will be no secret from me that you can keep, for as my wife I will have the right to punish you and no one will interfere. And I assure you I can punish you in ways you cannot yet imagine."

Selene watched in horror as Darius's head moved feebly in the assistant's hands; but soon his eyelids were drooping, and then he was unconscious and then he was dead.

With his lips against her ear, Kazlah murmured, "You didn't think I would let you get away, did you? Your silly plan would never have succeeded. Shall I tell the queen what you did? How you drugged her and plotted to run away? Then we can have a grand wedding, tomorrow. And then you will know the real meaning of imprisonment. Or . . . we can strike a bargain."

Selene stared at Darius's lifeless body and felt the life go out of her own. Tears streamed down her face as she said in a tight voice, "You have made a mistake, my lord. One that you should not have made. You should not have killed my friend. Because now I shall never tell you what you want to know. You may tell the queen, you may do to me what you wish. But I will always carry the memory of this night. And I promise you it will give me strength to keep from ever giving in to you."

CHAPTER 27

King Zabbai died suddenly and unexpectedly, in his sleep.

The palace was thrown into chaos. The Seeress of Allat fasted and communed with the Goddess, while the priests burned sacrifices and the people in the city prayed.

Finally, they had their answer; the Goddess spoke: there was a ritual, ancient and holy, that was practiced throughout the East; a ritual older than time, invented in a distant age when matriarchs ruled. A queen suddenly left without a consort and with no immediate resource to replace him could choose from among the ranking families a proxy husband, a young man of good blood and handsome looks, known for his strength and bravery, and he would be the queen's consort for one night. And the next morning his blood would ritualistically enrich and fertilize the land.

A candidate was found, and preparations began.

For three days, the priests and priestesses of Allat invoked the mystery of Madam Moon, calling upon the compassionate shelterer of the dead and the unborn to bless the union of Lasha and her sacrifice-husband. They made fruit and honey sacrifice to the Cup of the Fluid of Life as she shone radiantly from her starry kingdom, to ask that Queen Lasha and Magna, sacred city of the moon, receive Her blessings. Every person in the palace, from noble to slave, took part: lunar amulets were distributed and worn by all, moon-prayers were upon everyone's lips, and ancient superstitions were revived and carefully observed (such as the taboo of *khaibut*, the making certain that one's shadow did not fall upon a sacred object). The festival spread to the city beyond the palace walls: street hawkers sold effigies of the moon goddess; newly married women purchased jars of "guaranteed" moon-dew in which to bathe and thereby make themselves fertile; and pregnant women close to term drank herbal infusions to induce premature labor so that their infants would be born in the lucky light of the full moon.

The precincts of Allat's temples, from small shrines in the city to the massive pillared House of Allat adjacent to the palace, were congested night and day with supplicants; the air was filled with cadenced chanting and the smoke of continual sacrifice. And deep inside the palace, in a suite of rooms used only for the purpose of sacred ritual, the queen underwent the miraculous transformation from human woman to the personification of Goddess-on-Earth.

In another part of the palace a different preparation was going on.

Selene inspected the contents of her medicine box one last time.

She had not slept well these past nights, nor had she been able to eat. Since that terrible hour in the muting chamber, Selene had been kept a prisoner in her own room. She was watched day and night, her door kept locked, her every move monitored. But there was one glimmer of hope in this dark nightmare: only one other person was to be in the sacrificial chamber with Lasha and her prince-husband, the person who must slay the man after consummating his "marriage" to the queen. And Lasha had chosen Selene to be that person.

Selene closed her medicine box and went to stand at the edge of her garden. It was a hot night, thick with humidity and the smells of overripe fruit. Selene's garden was sprinkled with the supernatural light of the full moon, a light that etched black shadows against stark white walls, that made everything look eerie, altered from its daytime aspect; tonight, the garden looked ghostly, magical.

She curled her fingers around the golden Eye of Horus and said in her heart: *I swear by our love for one another, Andreas, and upon the spirit of my father whom I never knew, and the ancestors I hope someday to find, that I shall make good my escape tonight. It is my last hope.*

Selene had a plan.

Two days ago, priests had come to escort her to the connubial chamber far beneath Allat's temple, the place where the rite would be performed. It was an ancient room, built hundreds of years ago, a room not used in a long time but opened now and being ritualistically purified and furnished with the sacred bed. Selene had been taken there blindfolded, led from her own room through the palace, across an open space, into musty corridors, down steps, and ultimately into the sacred chamber, where she had received instructions from Kazlah.

"You will stand there, Fortuna," he had said, showing her. "When the 'husband' is brought in you will purify him with the symbols of the Goddess. The queen will then dance for him, after which you will help Lasha onto the bed and prepare her. When she signals that the act is done, you will slay the false king with this dagger." Kazlah had given Selene a long golden knife, which now lay in her medicine box, an instrument of murder among her tools of healing.

On her return to the palace, again blindfolded, an inspiration had come to Selene.

She knew she was being led a circuitous route so that she might not memorize the way, back and forth, up and down the same corridors, and then finally to the secret door which led to the open space that was, she suspected, a walkway between the palace and the temple. In the past, when she had attended ceremonies at the temple, Selene had noticed many doors, all of which no doubt opened upon different corridors and different mazes. Going through the wrong door, she knew, would mean getting lost in the labyrinth beneath the temple, lost and wandering in the darkness for days, perhaps never finding her way out. However, if there was some way the right door could be marked . . .

This time her escape *must* work. Selene could not shake from her mind the vision of poor Darius's death. She still felt the shock of learning the next day that Samia had hanged herself from the tree in the harem garden.

There was a knock at her door. The priests had come for her, in their white robes and gleaming with holy oil, and again Selene was blindfolded. She already knew the route through the palace, but that was useless information as she had no intention of returning to her room. What Selene took note of as she was led through the open space beyond the palace was that it was unsheltered—she thought she felt a breeze from the river. She counted her paces: exactly one hundred, and then she was being guided through a door.

As the door swung closed behind her Selene stumbled and dropped her medicine box. It hit the stone floor with a loud crack and the lid flew open, spilling the contents. There was alarmed murmuring among her escort— surely this was a bad omen?—but before they could come to a decision Selene was down on her knees frantically trying to gather everything up. When the priests stopped to assist her, Selene created more confusion by carelessly knocking things away; jars rolled along the floor, a string of beads broke and scattered, and in the confusion, as she babbled that everything must be found, and as the priests' anxiety grew, Selene turned slightly away from them, and plucked from her belt what she had earlier hidden there.

As the priests searched the floor for the fallen medicines and tried to reassemble the jumbled medicine box, their hands colliding, their voices rising in aggitation, Selene struck a spark against the lump of Brimo's Stone. Then she spun around, and gestured that they must go on.

Once again being led by the priests, Selene hurried away from the Brimo's Stone, not knowing that she was fulfilling the prophecy of the Oracle of Isis in Antioch, spoken two years before.

The ancient chamber symbolized both the womb and the underworld, a reminder of the Goddess's dual role of mistress over life and death. The Goddess, Lasha, was there now, waiting, swathed from head to foot in veils that covered her completely, seven veils to signify the seven levels of the Underworld and the seven Spheres of Heaven above the earth, veils wound so intricately about her body that only her eyes showed.

When Selene was brought in and her blindfold removed, she blinked through the haze of incense and torchlight, at first thinking she looked upon a statue on a throne; and then she realized she was seeing Lasha, the Bath-Sheba.

Selene wasted no time, once the priests withdrew and the door was closed. She set her medicine box in order, because after the sacred dance Lasha was to be revived with a potion, and the proxy-husband was to be given a drink that was believed would increase his potency: oil of spearmint for the queen, and powdered silkworm moth for the man. Ready also were the white cloth and bowl of water with which Selene must wash the bloody dagger, the victim's blood being sacred and therefore to be kept for ceremonious burial.

The sound of sistra beyond the closed door alerted her to the arrival of the sacrificial consort. Once the ritual was underway, Kazlah had explained, the priests would withdraw to the temple, where they would hold vigil until the rite was completed, at which time Selene was to signal them. But if her plan went as she hoped, Selene would be signaling no priests; by the time they started wondering when she would call, Selene should be far out in the desert, on her way to freedom.

Straightening her robe, she turned to the door. Her pulse raced; her palms were wet. The atmosphere in the chamber was uncomfortably stuffy. The door swung silently open and two priests led the blindfolded victim into the chamber. When the cloth came away from his face, two confused blue eyes fixed on Selene in the gloom.

She was stunned. It was Wulf, the barbarian prince, standing wrist-bound and cleanshaven, his pale, scarred body washed and perfumed, but still dressed in his leather and furs.

Selene had seen the German slave around the palace in the last two weeks, when she had been taken back and forth, under heavy guard, to the queen's chambers. Wulf had been silent each time. Selene feared now that Kazlah had found out about her deception—that she had only pretended to make him mute—and had brought the barbarian back to that terrible dungeon, to do the job again, properly.

As she untied his hands and proceded to draw, in oil, the sacred signs of the Goddess on his body, Selene tried to avoid his gaze; but at last she could not keep from meeting his eyes. And when she did, she was taken aback.

There was no bitterness in them, no anger or hatred against those who abused him. There was only sorrow, defeat and acceptance. *He knows he is going to die,* Selene thought, as she traced the moon-sign of Allat on his forehead. She wanted to whisper words of assurance, to tell him of her escape plan, but dared not. The priests had departed, but might there not be one still at the door, listening?

So instead, as she traced the last holy sign on his chest, Selene rested her fingers on the wooden T-cross that lay in the hollow of his throat and she looked into his eyes. *Your god will not forsake you,* she said with her mind, and Wulf blinked.

A faint tinking caused Selene to turn around. She saw that the queen now stood, a pillar of silk veils the colors of spring's brightest garden. It was the signal that the dance was to begin. Selene withdrew to her place by the wall while Wulf remained where he was, staring at the queen.

Lasha's dance was a very old one, older than the memory of any race, and so old that no one race could claim its invention. It was a dance shared by all nations and cultures in that it was basic and primeval and spoke a universal message. In the East it was called the Dance of Shalomé, *shalomé* meaning "welcome" in the Semitic languages, and it was called this because it harkened back to when Ishtar, most ancient of the Goddess's manifestations, went down into the Underworld and then returned, bringing with her a welcome spring and a rebirth of the earth. The seven veils, which Lasha now removed as she danced, represented the seven gates through which Ishtar had passed, and it was a seductive, erotic dance, centering in the hips and belly, with an aim to release sexual energy which enabled the dancer to unite with the Divine Force.

Lasha moved and swayed with fluid rhythm, her veils drifting away from her body one by one and floating to the floor. She accompanied herself with finger cymbals and the gentle slap of her bare feet on the stone floor; her body glistened, her muscles rippled beneath the smooth skin. She danced for Wulf. She danced around him, on her knees before him, mesmerizing him with arms that looked like snakes twining and fluttering; she seduced him with hips and thighs that moved as they would in love-making, her belly undulated in an imitation of labor and childbirth, her naked breasts shivered with the promise of life.

Lasha's eyes were open but unseeing because the priests had given her a drink made of sacred mushrooms. The visions she followed were not of this world, the passions that burned in her soul transcended desires of the flesh and lust for the blond barbarian. Lasha was one with the Goddess; she danced for the moon, as her ancestresses had danced down through the ages. She danced for Life.

When it came to an end, Selene did not at first move. Then, remembering, she moved quickly, helping the Queen onto the bed, massaging her arms and legs with the oils of Allat, tracing sacred signs on her breasts, belly and thighs. Selene kept her thoughts in a disciplined order. She must be very careful now.

Her mother had taught her the trick long ago, when Mera had been called to treat patients who could not be rendered unconscious by the usual drinks and potions. Men whose strong bodies defied the most potent sedative could be put to sleep by a simple but risky application of anatomical knowledge.

Mera had shown Selene where the great vessels of the neck lay, the same vital vessels Kazlah had shown her in the muting chamber; Mera had shown her how to feel for their throbbing life with her fingertips, and how to put even the biggest of men into a deep sleep merely by pressing on both vessels at the same time. Too long a pressure, Mera had warned, and death resulted; too short, and the sleep lasted only minutes. As she massaged the queen and wiped away the sweat from her body, Selene slowly drew her hands up to Lasha's neck. They rested there for a moment, feeling for the carotid pulse, then, certain she touched both arteries, she pressed gently down.

The queen's eyes widened in brief surprise, her lips parted in silent protest; and then, almost instantly, without struggle or fight, her body relaxed and her eyes rolled back under their lids. Selene pressed down a moment longer, trying to remember her mother's words, suddenly afraid she had held the pressure too long, and then not long enough, and finally sat back. She made the sacred signs of Allat and Isis over the sleeping queen, then jumped up.

She swung the strap of her medicine box over her shoulder and stole to the door. As she paused to listen with her ear pressed against the cold stone, Wulf suddenly came to life. He ran to the door, pulled her back and pressed his ear to the stone. After a moment, he pushed the door until it swung silently open, looked right and left in the dark hallway, then signaled to Selene to follow.

As she had hoped, the corridor was empty. She stepped cautiously out, peering this way and that into the darkness, close behind Wulf who stood hunched over, his muscles tightly coiled and ready to spring. They briefly explored the silence, satisfied themselves that they were alone, and then

Wulf turned around, seized the strap of Selene's medicine box, hefted it over his own shoulder, and gestured for her to go ahead.

Selene watched Wulf pull the heavy door closed behind him, plunging them both into deep darkness, and wondered: *How long?* How long would the priests wait before they realized the signal had not been sounded? How long before Lasha came groggily to her senses and sent her soldiers in search of them?

The two delivered themselves into the unknown, moving silently down the dark tunnels, walking in blindness because there was no light, not a crack of it, not a flicker, just an awesome, swallowing blackness that Selene had anticipated. She had known days ago that it would be too dangerous to carry a torch from the sacred chamber, that its light could alert priests and guards, and then, knowing that the darkness would be an obstacle as well as her protection, had realized it would have been useless to mark her way with string or pebbles or chalk, even if she *could* have, because there would be no light to see such signs by. And then she had thought of the Brimo's Stone—the sulphur. In this night within night that was devoid of all sensation—there was no sight, no sound, no feel in these smooth blind tunnels—she had known that smell could be her only beacon—the smell of burning sulphur, a smell like rotten eggs.

If the sulphur had continued to burn.

They groped along the walls as if they walked a ledge over a precipice, backs and hands pressed to the cold smooth stone, inching along until they came to an end; then Selene would stop and sniff the air for the barest trace of sulphur. Each intersection was like tumbling into another void, because the wall would end and Selene would have to step away and feel for offshooting paths. She would seize Wulf's callused hand and walk out as far as their two outstretched arms would allow, then she would sniff the air again and feel for the wall opposite.

As the minutes passed, then what felt like an hour and then another, Selene began to panic. Surely they had already been in this tunnel! They were going around and around in circles! They were heading back to the sacred chamber! Just around the next corner they would find priests and a raging Lasha . . .

They paused with increasing frequency, Selene to sniff the air, Wulf to shift the burden of the medicine box. Words never passed between them; they struggled on through the darkness in a peculiar communication that ran along threads of fear and anxiousness, Wulf's body close to Selene's.

They both felt, far above, the monstrous weight of the temple bearing down on them. In just such a labyrinth, this maze that symbolized the Underworld, a Greek of long ago—Theseus—had fought a bullheaded monster. What monsters, Selene wondered, lurked in *this* terrible darkness?

The darkness went on and on. It seemed endless, eternal. It was indeed the Underworld, and these two trespassers had stumbled into it before their time. Yet after a while a curious phenomenon visited them both: they started to *see*.

A strange light materialized from nowhere and visions appeared and dissolved around them. Selene saw the little house in Antioch's poor quarter, the boats in the harbor, Andreas standing under the laurel tree. Wulf saw a familiar forest, blankets of snow, and his wife lighting the winter Yule log. At first the visions were alarming; after a while they ignored them, and soon the illusions disappeared. Their world started to shrink, growing small, smaller, down to the size of the palace, and then down to the labyrinth, and then to just the corridor they walked; they became aware only of each other's touch, of the heat of each other's presence, of the fear they shared.

The air smelled the same at each turning, an endless, empty sameness that held nothing in it, no salt of earth nor sweetness of sky nor breath of summer, just a blank, bodiless air that mocked them in its nothingness. And no sulphur. No sulphur.

We shall die here, Selene thought in a strangely detached way.

She felt a yank on her hand. Wulf was signaling to her. She turned, and then she froze.

A smell! An awful smell, of eggs gone bad. It was the sulphur!

Selene sniffed, trying to determine where it came from, and when she started down one tunnel and found the smell to be weaker, she turned in the other direction, where it became stronger. They had stumbled finally into the first corridor that held a trace of the sulphuric fumes. They followed it carefully, turning back from tunnels where the air became bland and plunging into darkness thick with the odor.

As the smell became stronger, their excitement grew. On and on they forged, hurrying now, Selene drawing Wulf along and conveying to him that the source of the smell would be the end of their search. He stayed close behind her. He didn't know why she was trying to escape—she who had seemed so high ranking in the court—but he trusted her, and hoped she knew what awaited them at the end.

What awaited them at the end, Selene and Wulf found as they turned the last corner, was Kazlah.

They came to an abrupt halt. The Chief Physician was standing with a torch in one hand, the Brimo's Stone in the other. His face was expressionless. Kazlah neither smiled nor frowned, nor evidenced surprise that Selene and the German should suddenly appear. His narrow face was half in shadow, half in light; his tall slender body seemed to fill the small corridor.

Selene stood with Wulf right behind her. She could feel the rise and fall of his chest against her back. Wulf was a large man, and strong. Was he swift as well? Would he be cunning enough to catch Kazlah off guard? And who else stood on the other side of that door? The door which opened onto escape and freedom . . .

The two adversaries measured each other across the short passage that flickered in the torchlight. And still Kazlah made no move. He did not speak or blink, but continued to gaze at Selene while the sulphur smoked in his hand.

And then she knew. He was not going to make the first move. He never would, if they stood here for eternity. Selene knew what Kazlah wanted. And now the gamble was: What would be his price?

She felt Wulf shift uneasily behind her. Should she let him try to overpower the physician? Would he succeed? Or would she and Wulf both end up dead?

The hard eyes of Kazlah stayed fixed on her. Selene had to make a decision. Now. With a brief mental prayer to Isis, she said quietly, "Hecate's Cure is made from the bark of willow trees. Steep it in hot water until it is the color of strong tea and store it in a cool place. Ten drops in wine for monthly discomfort, twenty for joint swelling and fever. A drop directly on a bad tooth will take away the pain."

The Chief Physician's eyes flickered slightly. Selene held her breath. Then, to her astonishment, he stepped back, turned, and walked smoothly away down the corridor until his torchlight was just a fading glow around the corner.

Selene stared after him for an instant, then rushed to the door. Stopping first to listen, and hearing nothing on the other side, she gave it a push. It didn't move. Wulf came up behind her and pressed his weight against it. With a whisper that sounded like a prayer, the granite door swung on silent hinges and cool night air rushed in.

CHAPTER 28

They had run for miles—how many, they could not guess—until they were near to dropping.

The palace had been surprisingly easy to get away from— all attention was focused on the temple. But the city had been less easy. Selene and Wulf had hurried through Magna's dark streets just as they had the corridors of the maze, stopping at corners, listening for the night patrol, then darting down alleyways. The city gates were closed for the night, but Wulf had been able to scale the wall with a stolen rope and had pulled Selene up with him. Then the vast desert and all its dangers had spread before them.

They had hurried from dune to dune, knowing how brightly the full moon shone on them, marking them against the sand. And when at last they reached the naked hills some distance from the city, they heard far away the bleat of trumpets as the alarm went out. Selene and Wulf were now hunted criminals and there would be no rest in Magna, they both knew, until they were found.

The rocky ridge to the southeast of Magna was an ugly spine of barren hills and forsaken canyons, spattered with boulders and riddled with caves. Exhausted, they forced themselves to press on, high up to a craggy plateau and then deep into a ravine, where a tiny opening in the rock revealed a moderate-sized cave on the other side. They did not stop to debate, but squeezed in through the opening and tumbled to the sandy floor, their muscles screaming with pain, their breath coming in gasps. Selene lay where she fell, wanting nothing more than to sleep, but Wulf collected her in his arms and staggered with her to the back of the cave where they were unlikely to be seen. He laid her down and covered her with his body. They fell asleep immediately.

The medicine box lay forgotten and exposed near the opening of the cave.

When they awoke to the sound of horses' hooves and the low murmuring of soldiers, both were blinded by the morning sunlight that flooded the cave.

Wulf sat up at once, turning to the cave entrance. When Selene started to say something he put a hand over her mouth.

They sat unmoving, cramped and aching, and listened to the movements of Lasha's soldiers. There were many of them, all on horseback, calling quietly to one another as each cave and boulder was inspected. As the irregular tread of hooves drew nearer and nearer, Selene widened her eyes, now accustomed to the light, and stared in amazement at the entrance of the cave.

Covering it completely, from top to bottom and all around, was a newly spun spider's web.

Wulf stared, too, not believing his eyes. The veil of delicate filaments had been woven in the few hours they had slept, and it moved slightly now in the early morning breeze.

Finally the soldiers were at the cave. Through the gauzy covering Selene and Wulf saw the outline of horses' legs; they heard the low rumble of soldiers' speech. And then, incredulously, they heard one voice say, "Not in here. Look at this web. Nothing's gotten into this cave in months."

Selene and Wulf held their breath as they watched the horses, inches from the cave entrance, move on, and listened to the voices draw farther away. Then they sat still for a long time, disbelieving; finally, Wulf slowly unfolded himself and crawled to the cave entrance. He cocked his head this way and that, searching the ravine with his acute warrior's hearing, then gestured to Selene that the soldiers were gone.

She came to join him at the cave's entrance, where they marveled at the spider's web. When Selene murmured, "The Goddess is watching over us," Wulf brought up a hand and clasped his Cross of Odin. She smiled and nodded. "Yes, perhaps it was your god who saved us."

Selene sat back on her heels and regarded her strange companion. He seemed like a wild animal only barely tamed. She wondered what he would be like out in the open once again, in the free air, away from chains and guards. Perhaps he would revert to his barbarism; perhaps run away and abandon her in the desert.

He was not what Selene would call handsome, his features were too rough and alien, but there was a compelling attractiveness to him all the same. Especially now that the wild beard was gone and his angular jaw was smoothly shaven. What sort of man was he, what manner of strange people did he come from, where men wore their hair so and dressed in wolf skins? He sat watching her, his legs crossed, his arms lying casually on his knees. The blond hair, still braided in places, fell over his shoulders and brushed his thighs. And Selene could see now, in the morning light that bathed him, the myriad scars covering his naked chest and arms. A warrior. A man who lived by fighting.

Selene looked away and stared at the bleak world on the other side of the spider's web. With a sigh she said quietly, "Well, I suppose we must move along."

To her great surprise, Wulf opened his mouth and said something in a language Selene did not understand.

"You can talk!" she cried. "You understood what I was trying to tell you back in that awful dungeon! I had been so worried. I thought Kazlah might have brought you back there a second time—that you were *really* mute."

Wulf spoke again in a guttural, incomprehensible language Selene realized must be German.

"I'm afraid I only speak Greek and Aramaic," she said with an apologetic smile. "And I suppose you only speak German. Ah well. At least we got away. I wonder why Kazlah let us go . . . "

Wulf interrupted with a single word and then gestured to the cave entrance.

Selene nodded. "You want to know where we go from here. There is only one direction that I must follow. West. To Antioch. To Andreas . . . " Selene's voice died. The enormity of what she had done— successfully escaping from the palace—was beginning to dawn on her. Free at last! After two years, I am free to go home!

She saw her road again, and her destiny at its end. To be with Andreas, to begin my new life with him! To learn, to give our healing gifts to those who need it so badly. And to find out who I am, why I was born.

Wulf rose, brushed the sand off himself, and picked up the medicine box. As he hoisted it over his shoulder, he held out a hand to Selene. She took it and was pulled to her feet.

"We can start on our way home now," she said. "And I am sure we shall find it. I hid some food in my medicine box; it will last us for a few days. And there are some strengthening herbs among my medicines, to fortify us in the desert. And I have this." She touched the strand of pigeon's-blood rubies around her neck, which Lasha had given her two years ago. "With this necklace we can buy food and shelter, and perhaps join a caravan."

As Wulf brushed aside the web and stepped out into the sun, Selene thought: *I shall be home by autumn . . .*

BOOK IV
BABYLON

Fatma was growing concerned. The party had begun at sunset, and Umma the healer-woman had not yet arrived.

Fatma knew that Umma was anxious to learn the secret of extracting wool-fat from fleece, which the women of Fatma's tribe were now engaged in doing and which was the reason for the party. And in exchange for learning that skill, Umma would share with Fatma more secrets from her wonderful medicine box.

Why, then, wasn't Umma here?

Excusing herself from the company of her sisters and female cousins, who were laughing and singing as they kneaded the fleece in water, Fatma went to the doorway of her tent and looked out. She scanned the desert camp. It was unlike Umma to be late or forgetful.

Umma was a marvel to Fatma: never before had the Bedouin woman seen a person with such a thirst for knowledge! To Umma, it seemed, learning was like eating; she had an insatiable appetite for knowledge and insisted upon tasting everything. A few days ago, when the tribe had arrived at last at this summer encampment and the sheepshearing had begun, Umma had expressed an interest in learning the process of removing the wax from fleece, and the mixing of that wax with animal fat to make a base for medicinal creams and ointments. As the extraction of wool-wax was women's work and came around only once a year, the women of Fatma's tribe always made a special occasion of it—gathering in one tent with their raw fleeces and scouring tubs, and sharing wine and gossip as they scrubbed the wool clean. Umma had been invited to join in, to help with the scouring and later with the tricky process of drawing the fat from the water.

But the hour was getting late; the women had been a long time at their labors and merrymaking. Where was Umma?

In the eighteen months that Umma and her strange blond companion had lived with Fatma's tribe, since the day the two had been found homeless and wandering in the desert, parched with thirst, exhausted with hunger and running from soldiers, in that year and a half Umma had never missed an occasion to learn the ancient secrets of the Bedouins. Why, then, was she not here now?

Fatma scanned the encampment again.

They were camped at a large oasis not far from the city of Babylon; several Bedouin families had pitched their tents here; and there were caravans and solitary travelers as well, all sharing the water and dates that grew in abundance. Nearly a thousand people, Fatma estimated, and twice as many animals. Tents standing in the smoke of a hundred campfires; voices rising to the stars in song and laughter. Had Umma seen soldiers in the crowd, perhaps? Had she sensed danger and gone into hiding again? Or, Fatma wondered in hope, had Umma found at last the way of escape she had been searching for?

Fatma knew her young friend was a driven woman, a woman obsessed —with a dream, with destiny, with love for a man from whom she had been cruelly separated. When Umma had told her story to Fatma, late one night while everyone else slept, Fatma had seen visions burning in Umma's eyes. "I have seen so many helpless people," she had said. "People who need care and treatment and who have no one to help, nowhere to go. That is my calling, Fatma, to bring my gifts of healing to those people. To work with Andreas . . . "

Fatma shook her head. The poor young couple. Umma and her foreign companion never knew a moment of peace. They were forever looking over their shoulders, fearful, restless, living under the constant threat of danger, searching for a way to escape. And always yearning for something else, living only for a dream, desperate to get back to families and loved ones. What sort of a life was it for the poor girl? Nearly twenty years old and not yet married!

The irony of this last thought filled Fatma with sadness, because the tribe had given the girl the name Umma, which was the Arab word for "mother," when she had saved the life of Fatma's baby.

An eruption of laughter came from inside the tent. Fatma frowned over the camp again. *Pray Allat that nothing has happened to my young friend!*

What a terrible curse followed the shadows of Umma and Wulf! Fatma's husband had told the tribe of the royal decree, when he had brought his sheep into the night enclosure eighteen months ago. Soldiers had ridden by, he said, and had told him of two fugitives who had escaped from the palace at Magna, far to the north. There was a large reward for their capture; but severe reprisal, too, for anyone giving them sanctuary. And then later, when the Bedouins had found the two, sunburnt, hungry and exhausted, and had taken them in, the tribe had heard the most incredible tale.

Poor Umma! thought Fatma. To have incurred the wrath of an awful queen, and worse, to be without a family, a home. To the Bedouins, for whom the family was everything, Umma's greatest tragedy lay in not knowing who her parents were. And worse—to have a twin brother somewhere! There was a saying among Arab women that a husband can always be found, a son can always be born, but nothing can replace a brother.

Fatma wished there were something more she could do for Umma. Fatma was, after all, the *shaykha*, the wise-woman of the clan, and therefore she wielded great power. She could never repay Umma for saving the life of the baby eighteen months ago, when Fatma, exhausted from the labor of her late-in-life baby—for she was old by Bedouin standards, in her fortieth year—had turned away from it when the midwife had tried to give it to her to be suckled. And then Umma had intervened. She had taken the baby, which had been born premature and weak, and had bound it to Fatma's chest with a long length of cloth, literally wrapping it to her in an enormous bandage while Fatma slept. And when Fatma awoke the next morning, to find herself bound, she could feel the tiny body pressed against her breast. Fatma had discovered that she loved this child more than all her others.

Voices called to Fatma from inside the tent: it was time to harvest the wool-fat from the scouring tubs. Fatma's sister began to sing a song, and the others joined in, clapping their hands, their bracelets jangling. A beautiful fragrance suddenly filled the air: almond oil, being heated in preparation for mixing into the wool-fat to make a healing salve.

Fatma gave one last look for Umma and went back into the tent.

======

Selene kept herself hidden, afraid of being seen.

She knew the hour was late and that she had missed the wool-scouring in Fatma's tent, but Selene had to hear the end of this conversation. It could mean escape and survival for her and Wulf.

The men didn't notice her, hiding behind the date palm, and if they had, they would have seen just another Bedouin woman: a figure robed entirely in black, with only her hands showing, and a slit in her black veil for the eyes. The travelers from Jerusalem were unaware of her.

But Selene was very much aware of them. Earlier, she had watched them from a distance as they had performed their snake tricks around the campfire. Desert camps were never without visiting tricksters and magicians, performing for a meal, for a few coins. These two had turned sticks into snakes, and snakes back into sticks, and they were no different from countless other traveling entertainers in this wilderness, with one exception: Selene had overheard them say that they were not idle wanderers, but were on their way to the city of Babylon for a very definite purpose.

She stood behind the tree, tense and anxious, listening to their conversation. And as their voices drifted over to her, she felt her heart begin to race.

They were speaking of joining circus ships bound for Armenia.

Selene clutched herself in fear and excitement. Armenia! Which lay far to the north. Was it possible? Had she found their escape route at last? She wasted no time. When she had heard what she needed to know, she hurried away from her hiding place and made her way across the camp toward the tent she shared with Wulf. If what she had heard was true, then they would be leaving this desert at dawn's first light, and be on the road homeward again.

Selene was full of anxiety. They had come so far east! There stood Babylon on the horizon—she was farther away from Antioch than ever!

And yet she and Wulf had no choice in the matter. From the day they had emerged from the cave that had saved them from Lasha's soldiers, they had found the way to the west blocked. It was as if an invisible wall stretched across the desert from the Euphrates to Arabia. Lasha had at first deployed special patrols to search for the runaways; but then, a few months later, after her wedding to a young and ambitious prince, she had dispatched nearly her entire army into the desert.

All routes were watched; all travelers were stopped and questioned; all caravans were searched. Once, Fatma's tribe had been approached, and the male members of the tribe—fierce fighters when aroused—had driven the soldiers off. Selene and Wulf had soon seen that safety and survival lay with the nomads, but they were ranging *eastward*, taking Selene and Wulf farther and farther away from home. *We must go west!* Selene's panicked mind had cried each time the tents were unstaked and the tribe headed into the rising sun. But Fatma's tribe followed ancestral routes and could not be persuaded to turn back.

Now they had stopped near Babylon, at an oasis where they would remain during the lambing and shearing season. It was time for Selene and Wulf to make their bid for freedom; they must search for a hole in Lasha's net, get safely away—and then circle back by a safer route.

Circus ships, the men from Jerusalem had said, carrying a large troupe of entertainers up the Euphrates to Armenia, which lay far from Lasha's power. *We must try it!*

As she hurried across the camp, Selene glanced up at the stars. There, as Fatma had taught her, Selene could pick out the body of the great Bear-Goddess, worshiped by the Bedouins because the world, on its pole, revolved around Her. Tonight the heavenly She-Bear's tail was pointing to the east, which meant that spring had arrived.

Fatma had taught Selene many things. A proud and wise woman, Fatma was the "mother" of the tribe; noble blood flowed in her veins because she was descended from the Koreshites, the people who guarded the sacred shrine of the goddess Kore in Mecca. Fatma's ancestors were the priestesses and "great mothers" who had written the Arabs' sacred scriptures, called the Koran after the goddess Kore. From Fatma, Selene had learned the practical wisdom of the Bedouin women, which had been handed down from mother to daughter through the ages. Fatma could read omens and cast spells and predict weather; she had taught Selene that a mackerel sky meant rain within a day, and that low-flying bats meant a storm was coming. Selene had learned a date cure for headaches and how to make tampons out of papyrus to use during her monthly moon-flow. Because of Fatma, Selene had added much to her medicine box and to the skill in her hands; and she was going to take it all back to Andreas and share it with him.

As she neared her tent, Selene reflexively pressed her hand to her chest and felt there Andreas's comforting Eye of Horus. *Though the distance between us be great, my love,* she thought solemnly, *we are bound together still.*

Selene and Wulf's tent was a typical Bedouin dwelling: it was long and low and made of woven goat hair, and was divided into male and female compartments. The male side was away from the wind and open, as custom demanded, to show hospitality, and a small fire was always kept going in case visitors should stop by. In the hidden women's half Selene and Wulf kept their few possessions, and they slept there also, in separate bedrolls.

Their clothing was also that of the Bedouin. Wulf wore a long robe, an outer cloak, and a large headcloth he secured on his head with a rawhide band. When they traveled from watering hole to watering hole, as the Bedouin did in the winter months, Wulf pulled a corner of his headcloth up to cover most of his face so that, except for the blue eyes, he looked like all the other men in the tribe.

It was a harsh life, being at the mercy of the desert wind and sand and scorpions, and eating the Bedouin food, which consisted of curds, cheese and dried fruit. But there was security in this extended family: at night the black tents of Fatma's brothers and cousins and nephews clustered close together, and there was sharing and companionship. Though they were foreigners, pale-skinned and very tall next to the small, dark and malnourished Arabs, and though they did not worship the same gods and their customs were different—the Arabs had been shocked to be told that neither Wulf nor Selene was circumcised—they had been accepted into the clan.

"I have news!" Selene said as she entered the tent, removing her veil.

Wulf looked up from the camel saddle he was repairing and saw how flushed her face was, the brightness in her eyes. Selene was breathless as she spoke; and she stuttered at times, which she only did when excited or frightened.

"The king of Armenia, I heard these men say, lives in a palace that is like a fortress, and although he is very rich, he is lonely, because his kingdom is isolated high in the mountains. Once a year, the men said, the king sends out agents to gather up entertainment and bring it to his palace. There are seven ships docked right now at Babylon, Wulf! And they are taking on people who can entertain the Armenian king. The ships are heavily guarded and will travel under royal protection, which means they cannot be searched by Lasha's soldiers! And they depart tomorrow at midday! Perhaps we can get on board, Wulf. You can show them your wonderful boar-hunt dance, and I shall amaze them by starting a fire with my transparent stone!"

Wulf was thoughtful. "Do the ships sail past Magna?" he asked.

Yes, the ships were going to sail past Magna, Selene said, because it lay on the river in the direction of Armenia, two hundred miles from here. The Euphrates ran right through Magna, in fact; the circus boats would pass under the very shadow of Lasha's palace. But it would be a circus of many people, Selene assured Wulf. A crowd of performers of all types, and such a stew of strange and exotic persons that surely two would go unnoticed.

"North of Magna lies the boundary of Cilicia," she explained excitedly.

"Lasha's soldiers cannot go there, for it is a rival kingdom. Beyond Cilicia lies Armenia. And from Armenia, a safe route home!"

Selene came to sit before him and took his hands into hers. "Wulf," she said quietly. "We must try it. Perhaps this is a sign from the gods. A doorway to the west, which will open only for a moment and then close again."

Wulf watched her mouth as she spoke. Her mouth fascinated him; it was full and sensuous, and the lips looked bruised. Months ago, when Selene had painstakingly taught him, for his own survival, to speak a little of the Greek of the East, he had watched her mouth as if hypnotized. And then suddenly, one night during a lesson, as he was concentrating on the way her lips formed the foreign words, Wulf found himself imagining what it would be like to kiss her.

He looked down at the hands that held his and wondered again, as he often did, if there truly was magic in her touch, or if it was only his imagination. His imagination, and his growing, painful love for her.

"Yes," he said finally, looking up into her eyes. She mystified him. Selene was at times so childlike, at other times she seemed so full of wisdom. "I think we can do it."

"Yes," she whispered, squeezing his hands.

They sat for a few moments, gazing at each other, sharing this sudden windfall of hope: *Tomorrow!* they both thought, and their hearts raced in unison.

Then, abruptly releasing his hands and turning away, Selene thought: *In Armenia I will say goodbye to you forever . . .*

She felt a lump gather in her throat. It was not going to be easy to say farewell to this man who had shared her eighteen months of exile, this man who had trudged at her side through hostile territory, who had carried her when she was weak, who had made the cold nights under the stars bearable. Wulf had listened to her talk about her past, about Antioch and Andreas, and about the destiny that called to her, and he had in turn told her about his home on the Rhine, about the wife and son he had left behind and to whom he was desperate to return.

Selene felt great tenderness toward Wulf, she felt protected by him, but at the same time protective of him. His looks were deceiving—the warrior's body, the scars, the fighting instinct. Behind the barbaric façade she had found a gentle soul, a man who would sit at the campfire and make straw dolls for Fatma's daughters. And when she had taught him to speak Greek, Wulf had seemed to Selene like a young boy, trusting, trying earnestly to please. And suddenly she had seen him as he really must be:

gentle father and husband, loving protector and provider for his family in the far-away forests of the Rhine.

Selene knew what drove Wulf; he had told her of the burning revenge that was the thing he lived for.

Stamped upon Wulf's memory was the face of a man, a Roman officer, narrow-faced and cruel-eyed, the man who had led an army into the forests to cut down Wulf's people. It was a face he would never forget; it had kept him alive these eighteen months in the desert, feeding his spirit whenever it threatened to lag. And whenever he spoke the name of that Roman officer, a lethal glow burned in Wulf's eyes: *Gaius Vatinius.*

He had heard the name spoken, had watched the man high up on his white stallion, the red plume of his helmet dusted with snow. Gaius Vatinius, who had raped and tortured Freda, Wulf's wife, who had destroyed the forest, razed the village, and carted the men away in chains, leaving the women and children behind, violated and defenseless. To get back to Germany, to find Gaius Vatinius—that was what Wulf lived for.

As Selene moved away from him, she recalled a night eighteen months ago: They had been sleeping in the desert, close together against the freezing night wind, and Wulf had suddenly tossed and turned in a violent dream. He had cried out and thrashed his arms, and Selene, alarmed, had held him and soothed him until he came to full waking and the name Gaius Vatinius died on his lips. Wulf had turned his face away and sobbed.

She was not surprised to find that she loved Wulf, for he was a good and gentle man. She knew that her love for Wulf was not a betrayal of her love for Andreas, for she loved Wulf in a different way. For Andreas she felt a singular passion that she could never feel for another man; he had awakened her soul, her sexuality. She was bound to him in spirit, and she did not doubt that soon she would be bound to him in the flesh. But, for Wulf she felt a sweet and tender love, a friendship-love; they had been through so much together—he had taken care of her, and she of him. Selene wanted to hold him and to be held by him, and kiss him, too, softly, not in the soul-giving way she wanted to kiss Andreas, but as a way of showing how dear he was to her, and as a balm for his pain, for his unhappy soul.

But Selene knew that Wulf was fiercely devoted to Freda, his wife, who he believed, *hoped* was still alive. He kept Freda with him at all times, spoke often of her and of the day of his return to her, and so Selene knew that Wulf would not want to share his love and his body with another woman. Selene respected this, and long though she did to make love with him, she kept her desire a secret.

As Wulf lit the charcoal brazier to stave off the chill of the spring night, he was filled with sadness.

It was spring now in the Rhineland, and his people would be making the yearly sacrifice in the sacred groves. There would be much singing and horns of mead passed around, and the sagas would tell the old tribal stories.

He had been away so long! He was trapped in this wretched land of people who knew nothing of Odin and Thor and Balder, who were ignorant of the World Tree and the winter Yule log; these strange desert dwellers did not know of frost-giants or the wolflike monster Fenrir, who lay chained in the Underworld. These people did not know that the clouds in the sky were the hairs of the slain giant Ymir, or that gold was the tears of the goddess Freya. It was a puzzlement to Wulf how these people managed to survive without the sacred trees or dead-women to protect them, and no holy mistletoe to be found anywhere.

Home . . . Wulf's heart was heavy with homesickness. He missed the trees and the snow, the boar hunt, the fellowship of his brothers and cousins. And the solid, wise love of Freda, his wife.

There were times when Wulf was overcome with despair. Then he would build an altar of stones and pray to Odin and resurrect the memory of the invasion of his homeland. He would conjure up the face of Gaius Vatinius, he would relive the nightmare of that final night: the flames, the cries, the passive look on the Roman general's face. And he would feel his blood surge with renewed determination. *Revenge against Gaius Vatinius.* And then for a while Wulf would realize that his exile was his *wyrd,* what the Bedouins called *qis-mah,* his fate; that this was Odin's forge upon which his soul was being hammered in readiness for the day of reckoning. And Wulf would harness his rage.

But then the night would come and he would sit by Selene at the campfire and watch the flames dance in her eyes. Or lie wakeful on his bedroll and listen to her gentle breathing as she slept nearby. And he would long to cover the short distance between them and take her in his arms and make love to her.

It seemed to Wulf that he had lived a lifetime with Selene—hiding in caves, fleeing from desert police, protecting each other during the desert storms, when Thor's chariot thundered across the sky. How sweet it would be, just for one night, to express his love. Not the deep love he felt for Freda, but a tender affection that rose up in him every time Selene smiled at him, or touched him in order to calm his anguished soul. But Wulf knew about the Greek physician back in Antioch to whom Selene was pledged, and the destiny that bound her to Andreas, body and soul. Wulf knew that she would not want to make love with him, and he feared that, if he made the gesture, she would be hurt and disappointed in him.

Selene put on her veil again, the black shroud that covered her youthful beauty and turned her into an anonymous desert woman. Umma, the Arabs called her. Wulf knew that she liked it when he called her Selene.

"I must go and talk to Fatma now," she said. "I will tell her of our plan to leave in the morning."

When Selene left, Wulf retreated into thought.

Tomorrow they would find the ships bound for Armenia, and once there, Wulf would have no trouble making his way back to the northern forests. He would be with Freda again—if she was still alive—and with his son, Einar, who must be growing into manhood now. And he would make his sword drink the blood of Gaius Vatinius.

Finally, Selene returned to the tent and it was time for sleep. They agreed that they would rise at dawn, say their farewells to Fatma and the tribe, and, disguised as Bedouins, they would follow the road into Babylon.

Selene extinguished the flame in the lamp that hung from the ceiling of their tent and climbed under her covers fully dressed, as did Wulf under his. Between their bedrolls was a space of a few feet, and each knew it would take only a short reaching-out to touch the other. But neither moved, each believing the other would not want it so; they lay together in the darkness, fully awake, thinking far into the night of that day in Armenia when they would finally go their separate ways.

CHAPTER 30

They kept their eyes and ears alert, and stayed close to each other as they joined the multitude passing under the great Ishtar Gate, its tiles blazing bright blue in the morning sun.

To Selene, who knew only the sprawl of Antioch and had but glimpsed Magna from a tower, Babylon seemed formidable; and Wulf, whose exposure to large cities had been from slave ships and slave caravans, could not believe his eyes. When the Romans had come to the Rhine forests and had built their impressive stockades, the barbarians had thought they must be gods. But *these* walls! he marveled, looking at the massive stone, crenellated and buttressed, rising majestically out of the Euphrates, these walls looked as if they must have been built by giants. When his eyes reached the tops of them, Wulf squinted. He could make out the silhouettes of archers in the watchtowers.

Selene kept her eyes on the streets. Babylon was far from Magna, but she knew the extent of Lasha's wrath. The queen of Magna had no doubt cast her net from horizon to horizon in her mad pursuit of the two people who had defiled the ritual in the temple, forcing her to take a new husband. Selene and Wulf had heard of the new king's extravagant lifestyle, and that he had had pleasure lakes and barges built for himself out of the riches taken from Lasha's tomb. Her ambition to rule in Heaven had been crushed; Selene knew that Lasha would not rest, would spare no effort in her determination to find the runaways.

There were no soldiers in Babylon's streets with the crescent-moon insignia of Magna on their shields, nor were there any red-cloaked Romans; the soldiers of Babylon wore the peculiar costume of Parthia—a conical hat that flopped forward, baggy tunic and leggings—because Babylon stood within the western boundary of that mighty empire of the East. The ancient city of Hammurabi was a buffer between the two frontiers of Parthia and Rome, and it seemed strange to Selene to walk where Roman influence was not in evidence.

Nonetheless, there was danger here. Selene and Wulf, in their Bedouin disguise, carrying packs on their backs, Selene's distinctive medicine box concealed in a goatskin wrap, kept to the busiest streets as they made their way toward the river, where, the travelers from Jerusalem had said, seven Armenian boats were moored at the base of Marduk's temple. Whenever they saw soldiers, Selene and Wulf discreetly stepped into an archway or sidetracked down an alley. Although hidden beneath Bedouin veils and robes, Wulf's height could not be disguised; he rose head and shoulders above the short people of the East.

Selene stayed close to him, looking this way and that, praying they would get to the river without mishap. Lasha had placed a generous bounty on their heads. Anyone bringing Selene and Wulf back to Magna would be wealthy for the rest of his life. Instinctively her hand went up to the Eye of Horus beneath her robe, and she clutched it. She felt also, hanging next to it on a leather thong, the magic charm Fatma had pressed upon her that morning when they had said farewell to each other. The Arabs called it a shamrakh, a three-lobed clover leaf that symbolized the three phases of the Moon Goddess, and it was said to bring good luck.

Eventually, Selene and Wulf passed under an archway and they found themselves entering an enormous square. They both stopped short.

"What *is* this?" Selene whispered.

Wulf shook his head, baffled.

The square stood at the base of a heaven-mountain that was dun brown beneath the bone-colored sky. The tower was called Ba-Bel, which means "god's gate," and there were hundreds of people in the square at its base.

They crowded along the walls, clustered around the fountain in the center, and lay about the vast space on mats, on straw, on the bare ground. The noise was monstrous. It was the unified chorus of human suffering.

Selene and Wulf entered the square slowly, looking all around—at men propped up against walls, at children crying on blankets, at young women veiled in shame. There was hardly space to walk, there were so many lying end to end and side by side on the mud-brick floor of the square: people of all types and ages, in all forms and stages of illness and invalidism. Those who were able to, reached out to tug Wulf's and Selene's hems; others called feebly for help. Many were attended by one or more persons who seemed to be providing care. But many were completely alone.

Selene's eyes grew wider.

The people all had labels on them, bearing the person's name and nature of affliction, and either hung about the neck or tied to the afflicted limb. They read: "Nebo, from Uruk. Gangrene." And: "Shimax of Babylon, a carpenter with one hand growing numb." The less literate wore badges of paper with pictures drawn on them—of the heart, of a rash, of a swelling. The poorest simply had tags of cloth bound around the forehead or an arm or ankle.

When Wulf and Selene arrived at the fountain, which was beyond reach at the center of the crowd, Selene said to Wulf in a voice loud enough to be heard over the noise, "Oh, what *is* this place?"

And a voice behind her said, "You are strangers to Babylon if you do not know Gilgamesh Square. It is famous the world over."

Selene turned to see a middle-aged man, portly and well dressed, rise up from a stool. He had been offering a cup of something to a woman lying on blankets at his side. "My wife," he said. "Can you help her?"

Selene looked down at the skin-and-bone woman stretched out under the spring sky, with little space between herself and a man next to her who was digging at a festering ulcer on his leg. "Why have you brought your wife here?" Selene asked. "Why are these people here?"

He looked at her blankly. "She's ill! Where else would I take her?"

"But why bring her to this terrible place? Why not take her to a physician?"

"To seek a physician is blasphemy, and we Babylonians are a pious people. To go to a physician is to defy the judgment of the gods, so we bring our sick to the Square of Gilgamesh and pray that the gods send a cure. You see the tags they wear"—he pointed to his wife, whose swollen belly bore a clay tablet that read: "I am Nanna and my baby has died inside me." "We come here in the hope," the man said, "that the gods will send a passerby who once suffered the same affliction and will know of a cure."

Selene scanned the square again and saw now what she had not noticed before: people standing or kneeling over the sick, talking and gesturing and offering medicine. But not everyone was receiving attention.

"Is this not the same as seeking a physician's help?" she asked.

"There is a difference," the man replied in mild annoyance. "In that case it would be defying the gods, to go in search of human intervention against their divine judgment. This way, it is the gods who deliver a pardon from their punishments."

"Punishment for what?"

"For sins, of course."

Selene looked down at the unconscious woman. "And your wife? What was her sin?"

The man's face darkened. "The child must not have been mine for the gods to kill it."

Selene stared at him. "You are saying that her sin is adultery?"

"She denies it. But what else can the death of the baby mean?"

Selene knelt next to the woman and gently laid a hand on the swollen abdomen. She knew at once there was no life there. The woman's forehead was curiously cool and dry; her pulse was rapid and her respiration labored. Selene wanted to examine her further but could not, lacking the privacy to do so. She stood up, glancing at Wulf who was looking nervous, and said, "I wish I could help. There might be a way."

The man eyed her suspiciously. "How?"

Selene hesitated. The baby would have to be crushed and brought out. Selene had never done it before; she had only once seen her mother do it, years ago.

"Can you help my wife or not?" barked the man.

Before Selene could reply she felt Wulf's hand on her arm; he gave her a cautioning look.

"I do not think the gods sent you," the man said brusquely, taking in with a contemptuous look their Bedouin robes and traveling bundles. "I do not want you touching my wife. Move away. Be off."

Starting to protest, Selene was pulled away by Wulf. They must get to the river, he said; the hour was growing late.

But Selene would not be led out of the square. She held back, looking around: She saw a man with a recently injured foot trying to manage with a crutch, a woman bent over a sickly child, a teenaged boy with his back against the fountain, his legs stretched before him, dead, a corpse. She whispered, "Wulf, this is monstrous . . ."

He looked up at the sun. It was nearing the end of its climb; it would soon be midday. "We must go," he said, taking her arm again.

"Please—" came a small voice from nearby. Selene looked down to see a little girl tugging at her robe. "Help my mama."

Selene followed her and knelt beside a young woman who lay curled on her side on a blanket; she clutched her abdomen and moaned. "When did this happen?" Selene asked, as she felt the feverish forehead.

"In the middle of the night," said the little girl. "All of a sudden. Poppa brought us here but he had to go to work. Please help my mama."

Selene tried to get the young woman to straighten out long enough to permit an examination of her abdomen. "Do you have bleeding?" she asked, gently pressing a spot above the groin, causing the woman to cry out. Yes, there was bleeding, the woman said, and her moon-flow had ceased two months past. Selene settled back on her heels in thought. Then, asking Wulf for the medicine box, which he reluctantly passed down to her as he kept his eye on the guards at the ends of the streets branching off the square, she poured some opium wine into a cup and held it to the young woman's lips.

Then she stood and said quietly so that only Wulf heard: "It is nothing I can treat. A baby is growing outside her womb. She will die soon, but the opium will at least ease some of her pain."

A man a few feet away, who had watched Selene with the young woman, hauled himself up on a crutch and hobbled over to her. The placard around his neck read, "Gout." As Selene was sprinkling some powdered autumn crocus into his drinking cup—an old gout cure—Selene was assailed by another man, from whose ear hung a clay tablet that read, "Going deaf." And before she could examine him, an obese woman grabbed Selene's arm and demanded help for her arthritis.

Wulf, seeing what was happening, that Selene, with her medicine box, was about to be overwhelmed, took hold of her arm and drew her away. He was about to point out the Parthian soldiers patrolling the perimeter of the square when Selene was stopped by a man in very expensive clothes.

"Please see my wife," he said, pointing with a ringed finger to where a matronly woman sat on a chair surrounded by what could only have been the gathering of a large family. "She has pains in her head," he said anxiously, "and she sees stars out of the corner of her left eye."

Selene knew what that meant: A devil had laid its egg in the woman's brain. It was an ailment beyond Selene's skill; Andreas was needed here. Andreas!

Wulf said, "Selene," quietly and sternly, and when she looked at him she saw that his look was fixed across the square, upon two guards who now seemed to have taken an interest in them.

Moving quickly, Wulf rewrapped the medicine box in its goatskin, hauled it up on his shoulder, and took Selene by the hand.

They had gone only a short distance when Selene overheard a passerby recommend oleander tea to a man whose placard read: "Ulcer." "No!" she said instinctively, turning. "Oleander is a poison!"

But a beautiful young woman in the gown and cape of a temple prostitute stepped in front of Selene and said hurriedly, "My sister has been in labor for four days. Come, she is over there, under that archway."

"No," said Wulf, seeing that the two guards had now started to move slowly across the square, their eyes on the two strangers. As he pulled Selene away, he said close to her ear, "It might be nothing. But they saw the medicine box. And they saw you treating the child's mother."

Selene looked past Wulf's shoulder and saw the pair of Parthian soldiers now cutting a purposeful path in her direction. They had reached the pious Babylonian in his fine clothes who knelt over his wife, his face pressed to her swollen, lifeless belly.

"He will tell them that we are strangers to Babylon," Wulf said to Selene. "He will tell them you had considered helping his wife. They will have our description, Selene, and a description of the medicine box."

Knowing that Wulf was right, Selene quickened her pace, clutching her bundle while people reached out to her from all around. Wulf looked back once and saw that the guards, having questioned the Babylonian, were now crossing the square at a determined rate.

He looked around. Several narrow streets branched off the eastern side of the square: dark, twisting alleyways overshadowed by awnings and balconies. If they could reach this maze and run as fast as they could, they might lose the guards and make it to the boats in time to find safety on board.

As they hastily picked their way among the seated and reclining bodies, Selene harbored the slim hope that they were mistaken about the guards, that they had looked at Wulf and Selene only out of idle curiosity and now crossed the square with another purpose in mind.

But the Babylonian might have told them that the Bedouin man had spoken with a strange accent and that his eyes were the color of the sky . . .

"Halt!" a voice behind them shouted.

Wulf and Selene looked back over their shoulders.

"You two! Stop!" shouted the guards, and one drew an arrow out of the quiver on his back.

"This way!" hissed Wulf, and together they dashed into the shadows of the nearest street.

More angry shouts behind them made Selene and Wulf break into a run. They dodged in and out of market stalls, around fountains and under ancient archways. Behind them they heard the thump of hobnailed sandals as the guards also broke into a run. People jumped to the side as the Bedouins sprinted through the crowd. Some shouted obscenities after them; others cheered. Chickens and children flew out of their path; a table of dates crashed onto its side. As they turned one corner, Selene lost her grip on her bundle and it fell to the ground. She started to turn back for it, but Wulf pulled her along.

Selene's robes got in her way; she gathered them up in her arms and ran bare-legged. Wulf's black head-covering slipped back so that his blond hair danced around his head like a halo. The guards shouted at them to stop but Wulf and Selene continued running; they zigzagged and dodged, they climbed walls and threw barrels and baskets out behind them. But the guards closed in, more familiar with this city than the two fugitives were, more used to the chase, better trained.

Selene followed Wulf through a doorway just an instant ahead of an arrow that whizzed past her head and lodged in the wooden door jamb. They ran across a private garden, startling a family sitting down to their noon meal, up over a wall, across another private garden, and down another winding street. Wulf still clutched the medicine box, but he had lost their second bundle of possessions. The Bedouin robes flapped around his legs and caused him to stumble several times. Once, Selene fell, and he dragged her up without breaking his stride.

A second arrow barely missed Wulf's shoulder. A third caught Selene's veil. When at last they came to the river, Wulf paused long enough to look up and down the busy dockside; then, seeing the last of the Armenian ships starting to pull away from the dock, he seized Selene's arm and ran.

They were at the foot of the gangplank when the arrow struck her.

Crying out, Selene fell at Wulf's feet, clutching her thigh. "Help!" she gasped. "Don't let them take me! I must . . . get away . . . "

Wulf snapped the arrow in half, leaving the tip buried in her thigh, then he gathered her up around the waist and ran with her.

When they reached the top of the gangplank the guards were close behind. The boat was about to depart, and in all the confusion no one on board at first saw what was happening. Wulf threw the medicine box in its goatskin on the deck, then lifted Selene over the railing. As he climbed up behind her, an arrow grazed his calf.

The gangplank swung away and the boat moved out.

"Halt!" shouted the guards. "Stop for the emperor's police!"

The captain, seeing the uniforms and drawn arrows, quickly shouted orders to throw the lines to the quay, and dockhands raced forward to draw the boat back in.

Wulf and Selene, temporarily concealed by the crowd on the deck, watched in horror as the gangplank was brought back.

Wulf made a quick decision, and ripped off his black robes, then roughly pulled Selene free of hers. When the cloth snagged the shaft sticking from her thigh, Selene cried out, and everyone on the deck turned. They gaped at the arrow; they watched Wulf take the goatskin from around the medicine box and toss it, with the black robes, down an open hatchway. Then he picked Selene up in his arms and carried her to the river-side of the ship.

Suddenly aware of the plight of the two newcomers, and no strangers themselves to running from the law, the circus crowd closed in behind them and presented a chaotic, impeding block to the guards. A pair of dwarfs helped Wulf lower Selene over the side into the water, and a juggler passed down the medicine box. Then an enormously fat lady with a monkey on her shoulder managed to wedge herself in the way of the guards, obstructing their view.

Selene and Wulf, in the water, clung to the side of the ship and trod the current, while the ebony medicine box bobbed on the tide between them.

A pair of acrobats, seeing the desperate situation of the two in the water, leaned over the side of the ship, one holding on to the other, and cut free a small round raft that had been lashed to the boat's side. It splashed into the water and Wulf, with a wave of thanks to the acrobats, seized it, hoisting Selene and the medicine box on board. A second later, a bright red robe flew down from the boat and landed on the raft in a crumpled ball. Wulf got behind the raft and started kicking his legs in the water to propel it away from the ship.

An Armenian sailor, up in the ship's rigging, gave a signal to Wulf: The circus people had sent it, they were going to see that the guards were kept distracted for as long as possible.

Wulf propelled the raft as rapidly as he could, keeping the Armenian ship in sight, until they were safely behind reeds. He paused long enough to look at Selene, who lay clutching her thigh, and to spread the red robe over her; then he resumed swimming—away from Babylon.

Just before he guided the raft around a bend in the river, Wulf looked back and saw the crowd on the boat all pointing northward. Knowing they were telling the guards that he and Selene had been seen escaping to the north, he pulled himself up on the raft and lay there, exhausted, while the river's current carried them along, southward and to the east.

CHAPTER 31

It was dusk when Wulf thought it safe enough to stop the raft and anchor in a brake of tall reeds; up and down the river, other craft, illuminated by lanterns, were likewise mooring for the coming night. He gathered stones and clay from the bank to make a small brazier, and in it he burned twigs. He also found a small ceramic lamp, no bigger than the palm of his hand, tucked inside the medicine box; it had a linen wick and was full of olive oil. This, too, he lit with the flint and steel.

Selene was awake, and lay moaning softly. Earlier, when Wulf had tried to stop the raft and see to her, Selene had insisted they keep going, to get as far away as they could by nightfall. Babylon was miles behind them now, after hours of riding the swift current, but the river banks might be patrolled by soldiers. If there was to be any temporary safety, it would be among the reeds and night darkness.

Wulf knelt to examine Selene's thigh.

The piece of arrow shaft rising out of the white skin looked harmless, but Wulf knew that it must be taken out, and soon. He was somewhat relieved to see that the blood trickling from the wound was bright red; "black blood" would have meant the arrow had been poisoned. Now Wulf had to determine which way to remove it.

Had he been home he would first have located the direction of the arrowhead with a magnet, but he could find no magnet in the medicine box. And then, to draw the arrowhead swiftly out, he would have tied the shaft to a horse's bridle and startled the horse so that its head jerked up, or tied the shaft to a tree branch that was strained down and then let go. But there were neither horses nor trees on this marshy river bank; Wulf knew he had no choice but to extract the arrowhead with his own hands.

Selene opened her eyes and saw the worry on Wulf's face; she knew what he was thinking. There was only one way it could be done: "Push it through . . . " she whispered. "Hammer the shaft through, and pull it out the other side. It's the only way . . . "

Wulf laid a hand on her forehead and told her to be still. He had to think. There were terrible risks involved in such a method, and Wulf knew what they were: the arrowhead could cut through a nerve and paralyze her leg forever, or it could sever a large blood vessel and she would quickly bleed to death.

Wulf went to the medicine box. In his own forests he would have used a sturdy pine needle to locate the barbs of the arrowhead; now he chose a long silver probe with a worm's-head tip. Before proceeding, he lifted Selene's head into the crook of his arm and gave her opium to drink; when she could swallow no more, he settled her as comfortably as he could on her side, with the red robe keeping her warm, and pressed the small statuette of Isis into her fist.

Mentally calling upon Odin for wisdom and strength, Wulf bent over Selene's thigh and began to search for the arrow barbs. As soon as the probe touched her flesh, she cried out. Wulf tried to give her more opium, but she could not swallow. She breathed in gasps; her face contorted in pain. "Quickly!" she whispered. "Hammer it through!"

Wulf gripped the probe in a trembling hand. As the raft bobbed gently on the river and night fell all around, he reconsidered his actions. Then, deciding that Selene's way was too dangerous and too painful, Wulf removed a roll of bandage from the medicine box and slipped it between Selene's teeth. Now when she cried out the sound would be muffled.

He commenced his probing. Wulf had seen this done many times, and once on himself. But at home there had been the tribal wise-woman with her herbs and incense, and the log-built longhouse with its warm fires and beds of furs. There, too, had been the priestesses of the Great Mother to keep evil spirits away, and an endless supply of mead to dull the victim's pain. Here, Wulf was alone in a rapidly descending night, kneeling on an unstable raft, working by the light of a small lamp, and praying that soldiers were not patrolling within hearing distance of Selene's cries.

Four probings located the barbs of the arrowhead; Wulf marked their positions with spots of blood on Selene's white skin. Then he sat back on his heels and studied the wound.

There was only one way to extract a barbed arrowhead without further tearing the flesh—by using the quills of eagle feathers.

As if his wish could produce the bird, Wulf looked up at the sky. When had the stars come out? He had been concentrating so hard he had not been aware of the dramatic transition from spring day to blackest night. The silence was disturbed only by the creaking of the boards, the kiss of water against the raft. Up and down the river other boats sat in the protection of reeds, and occasionally a laugh, a spoken word, the tinkle of a harp reached his ears.

He looked at Selene's face. Her eyes were closed. She was panting through the bandage in her mouth.

Wulf went to the medicine box again and searched through its contents. He had watched Selene use many of these things, when taking care of someone in the Bedouin tribe, when exchanging information with Fatma, but to Wulf most of them were a mystery.

He searched again. He picked up objects and replaced them—a piece of transparent stone, jars of oils and ointments, fishbone sewing needles, bags of dried herbs. His search grew urgent. Plucking a reed from the river bank, Wulf tried to split it down the middle, but it was too green and shredded. He searched for something round, long and hollow, to sheath the barbs of the arrowhead, and finally returned to the medicine box for one last look.

Then he saw it, the scribe's palette box strapped to the underside of the lid. He slid the box open and saw, to his relief, the writing pens inside. Choosing one that he guessed to be a goose quill, Wulf slit it lengthwise with the scalpel so that he held two long half tubes. Now he prayed they were strong enough.

Before returning to the wound, he soaked the bandage roll in the opium and replaced it between Selene's lips. She looked up at him with frightened eyes.

"I shall extract it now," he said softly.

She feebly shook her head.

"I will not do as you ask, Selene," he said firmly. "I will not hammer it through, but will do as my father taught me. There will be pain, but it will be quick and clean."

Her eyes met his; they held for a moment; then she nodded.

Wulf knelt over her thigh and brought the little lamp closer. The arrow shaft was sticking out by barely a fingerbreadth. If he should somehow push it farther in, he would have to cut Selene's leg open to retrieve it.

Wulf worked cautiously, as if coming up behind a butterfly on a leaf. The end of one quill-groove went into the wound and slowly sank beneath the skin. Selene groaned and started to move. Wulf held her leg down as he inserted the second quill groove, feeling it, as with the first one, barely touch the buried arrow barb and slide over it like a sheath.

He paused to run the back of his hand across his sweating forehead. The night was growing cold but Wulf, dressed only in a loincloth, was perspiring. He looked at Selene. Her eyes were closed again and her face was pale and damp. She shivered beneath the red robe, even though only her wounded thigh was exposed.

He now surveyed the three shafts rising up from Selene's skin: the broken arrow, the two quill halves. If he had not lost his skill, if the quill halves were well placed, and if his hand held steady during the extraction, Selene should suffer only brief pain and no additional injury.

Calling upon Odin and his sacred bird the raven, Wulf gently placed his hands on the cold flesh, drew in several steadying breaths, then, anchoring the two quills with his left hand, carefully grasped the arrow shaft with his right.

Selene's head rolled back and the bandage fell out of her mouth.

In one quick jerk Wulf yanked the arrowhead out. Selene screamed.

He had his hand over her mouth in an instant and gathered her into his arms, where she whimpered against his chest. While he rocked her and stroked her hair and murmured that it was all over, Wulf listened to the night and searched the darkness with his warrior's eyes.

———

There was fresh green grass on the riverbank; Wulf collected some, crushed it and laid it over Selene's wound as he wrapped a tight bandage around her thigh. Green leaves, he knew from experience, prevented flesh decay. Then he dipped the corner of a cloth into the river and squeezed the water over Selene's lips. She had fainted after she had collapsed in his arms, and now she slept deeply.

The arrowhead had come out cleanly, there had been little bleeding, but complications could still arise—Wulf knew this from experience. Arrow wounds were the worst for infection, because of their depth; they corrupted the flesh from beneath, unseen. Fever could follow, a fever that could kill, and then there could be the dreaded creeping blackness from the toes that meant the leg would have to be amputated. So he sat up for a long time, frequently touching Selene's forehead, watching her respiration, examining the dressing until, as the moon began its descent, he finally lay down behind her, on his side, and pulled her to him so that she slept in the warmth of his embrace.

———

When Wulf awoke a little later it was not yet dawn. He blinked a few times; he was stiff with pain. Then he felt Selene in his arms. He explored her body with a tentative hand and found, with relief, that the bandage was dry. Selene slept deeply, breathing in regular rhythm, but her skin was unnaturally cold and clammy, as if death had begun its insidious claim on her; knowing new fear, Wulf rubbed her arms vigorously, and tried to warm her with his breath. Selene did not stir. Her sleep was deeper than he had thought—too deep. It terrified him.

Had he given her too much opium? Had he, in his fear and haste and inexperience, given her a lethal dose? Killed her with his own hand?

You cannot die! his mind cried, as he gathered her into his arms and rocked her. *We have not come this far to be separated by death!* A tear fell and splashed onto her face, which was marble-white and alarmingly still. *Don't go!* he called to her departing spirit. *Don't leave me!*

Finally, desperately, Wulf bent his head and pressed his mouth to Selene's. Her lips were cold and unresponsive, but she still breathed. And while there was breath in her body, Wulf knew there was a chance.

Odin, cried his mind. *Isis, help us . . .*

Wulf raised his face to the predawn wind and there, on the paling horizon, over the tops of the reeds, he saw Venus rising in the east. In his anguish he took it as a sign of hope.

BOOK V

PERSIA

CHAPTER 32

B y all the gods!" cried the midwives, stepping back from the royal birth-bed. "Her womb has come out with the baby! See, the child is still inside it!"

Dr. Chandra, standing in the corner, thoughtfully stroked his great beard. He did not normally attend childbirth; he was here because the king had requested it, this young princess being one of the favorite wives. Recalling this, and seeing how the midwives buzzed in confusion about the canopied bed like bees from a disturbed hive, Dr. Chandra stepped forward.

His black almond-shaped eyes flickered over the newly born baby lying on the sheets in its transparent casing, and he reached out a brown finger and poked the membrane. It broke and water spilled out. Not the princess's womb after all, everyone saw, but the baby's amnion, which indicated an auspicious birth.

The midwives cheered and descended upon the bed to resume their functions. Dr. Chandra, having restored order to the royal birthing chamber, nodded a wordless good evening to the women and hurried out. He had promised the king he would report the birth immediately to the Astrologer, so that the stars might be read.

A short, plump man in lemon-colored silks and a turban, Dr. Chandra made his way along the palace corridors deep in thought. What could it mean? he wondered. Never in all his years as a physician had he observed such a phenomenon. There it had lain upon the sheets, like a pink shrimp encased in a transparent pearl, the newborn baby still in its amniotic sac. It was a sight he would never forget.

Sunset was past and night had fallen, but Dr. Chandra saw, as he crossed one of the royal parklands, the tips of the palace spires blazing golden with the light of a sun long gone behind the horizon. The domes and minarets stood majestically black against a sky beginning to glitter with stars, and yet up there, cloud-high, those delicate towers still gleamed with daylight.

If a man could but climb those awesome pinnacles, Dr. Chandra thought, what sights might he see? How many miles might his eyes travel? How far would he be able to send his soul? It was another humbling miracle, in this day that seemed to have been full of miracles.

The caul-birth of the princeling had not been the first. The day had in fact begun with a miracle, with the staggering pronouncement of the Astrologer just after sunrise, and its effects, even after a full day in the surgery and in the pavilion, and then in the birthing chamber, even after the breaks in between to work on his manuscript on the management of wounds, even after all that, the effect those words at dawn had had upon Dr. Chandra was not diminished.

He came to the celestial observatory and found the Astrologer's Chinese servant already waiting for him. Dr. Chandra had never gotten used to Nimrod's nerve-racking invention. Because the Astrologer loathed interruption while he worked, he had restricted access to his jealously guarded tower to the wooden box that now rose up off the ground as the Chinese cranked the handle. They rose high in the air, swinging perilously in the breeze, while Dr. Chandra clung with white knuckles and tightly shut eyes. Then, securing the lift so that no one on the ground far below could bring it down and use it (and what lunatic would? the doctor wondered) the servant led Dr. Chandra across an equally perilous suspension bridge, which gave a view of the sprawling palace and mountains all around, until they came to a pair of massive doors marked with mystical symbols.

The Chinese servant brought Dr. Chandra into a round chamber, then bowed and departed on silent, slippered feet.

This was the Astrologer's domain, where he had lived these past uncountable years. And this large, round stone room was not the summit of Nimrod's tower; the tip extended upward another fifty-two steps that ended, high on the domed roof, in an ancient observatory. It was here Nimrod was at this moment, among his stars, listening to their silent song.

Impatiently the Hindu doctor lifted his eyes to the domed ceiling, which was plated with gold and inlaid with precious stones to represent the stars, and he tried by mental will to bring Nimrod down. The Astrologer could be up there for *hours:* The heavens were all Nimrod knew, and he knew them as none other did, for he was the Daniel of all Persia, last of the line of holy Danites descended from the time of Nebuchadnezzar, when the Daniels (from Dan-El, an ancient Phoenician god) were prophets. Nimrod was not a prophet, but he nonetheless could tell future events because they were written in the stars. No move was made in the palace without a consultation first with Nimrod, no business was conducted, no step taken, indeed not even any wine jars were opened without first finding out from Nimrod if the stars were favorable. And the Astrologer was rarely wrong, rarely did his predictions go awry. Which was why Dr. Chandra now paced the circular chamber nervously: He was anxious to hear more about the incredible prediction that Nimrod had made that morning.

That I, after thirty-six years of living within these walls, shall go away at last, on a long journey, never to return!

Meanwhile, Nimrod, up in his tower, held his face to the sky and moved his lips in an oft-spoken, voiceless chant. He had spent the entire day from early morning measuring and calculating, locating aspects and ascendants, pinpointing polarities and conjunctions. He had written and sketched until he had worn down three pens, and the sheets of vellum now lay scattered about his feet like October leaves. They were charts of trines and sextiles, columns of mathematics, symbols of stars and planets; and he had read them over and over up here in the dark of night, first silently, then in a whisper and then out loud as if to convince himself through his ears what his eyes refused to believe. For the message was too distressing.

So now he was praying. He was praying for reassurance, for some sign from the gods that his findings were wrong. But the problem was, lip service never got the attention of the gods; it was the heart that spoke to them, and Nimrod's heart remained stubbornly mute.

He was trying hard to believe. He wanted desperately to believe, as he had once done, so many summers ago that he had lost count, when he had been virile in soul as well as in body, when he had revered the gods to the point of fanaticism. But then, somewhere along the way, after autumns and winters spent up here among his cosmos while the busy human hive that was the palace went about its vagaries below him, Nimrod's belief in the gods had trembled and flickered and died like a flame. And so he had done what a lot of once-faithful do (and who are afraid of discounting the gods altogether): He had turned religion into a scholarly study and had started collecting and studying the gods as one would butterflies or stones.

But he discovered a terrible thing: The more he studied the gods, the emptier his faith became. Until the day arrived—when? in his fiftieth year? his seventieth?—Nimrod had made one more bone-creaking climb of these fifty-two steps and his aged body had shouted through its every pore: *They do not exist.*

His chant stopped. His lips stopped moving. Nimrod lowered his trembling hands and gaped at the stars like primitive man seeing his first fire. *These* were all that mattered—the stars; they were all that existed, these slowly swirling ice-lights that had been tossed across the black sky eons ago before even the earth was formed. These stars governed men's destinies, Nimrod firmly believed, not the invented gods; stars and constellations directed the tides and eddies of mortal beings. Not little stone statues that broke when dropped. *These* were divinity; and now these were what Nimrod the Astrologer worshiped.

When he reached the bottom of the spiral staircase some time later, he leaned against the stone wall to catch his breath. His scrolls and charts were clutched to his chest like children. He closed his eyes and sighed. It was Nimrod's curse to be able to read the future, and what he had read just now caused him great suffering. He swore now that he would not tell his old friend what he had seen in the stars; he had said too much already that morning. Dr. Chandra would be down there now, in the round chamber, waiting to hear more. Ostensibly he will have come to report the princeling's birth, but Nimrod knew his old companion too well. Chandra was going to want to know, and Nimrod was not going to tell him.

With another sigh he pushed away from the wall and thought unhappily that the stars must be playing games on an old man who had somehow missed his appointment with the tomb.

The two bowed politely to one another, physician and astrologer, even though they had been friends for thirty years. The pair were as unalike as midnight and noon. The pudgy physician, with his olive skin and bushy beard, contrasted oddly with Nimrod's unusual height. It was as though his constant yearning for the stars had lengthened him. His long white hair was twisted into a knot on top of his head and held in place with ivory combs, and his snowy beard reached to his waist and was tucked into his belt. Unalike on the surface but kindred in spirit; from the day when Dr. Chandra had first arrived from India as a young man three decades ago, they had spent many an evening in intellectual talks, chess games, religious debate and the general agreement that they were the mental and spiritual superiors of everyone on earth.

Dr. Chandra reported the astonishing birth of the princeling and Nimrod at once set about drawing the child's star chart. After a few moments of watching the Daniel labor over the work bench, Dr. Chandra realized that his old friend would be too distracted now to elaborate further on the ominous prediction he had made that morning, when he had said, "My friend, the stars say that a four-eyed person is coming to Persia who will put an end to your long residence here!"

And what else, Dr. Chandra asked himself for the thousandth time, could that mean but that he was to go away on a long journey?

Seeing that no illumination would be thrown on the cryptic prophecy tonight, Dr. Chandra made a silent exit and could be heard, a short while later, making the rickety descent in Nimrod's box-lift.

After visiting his patients in the pavilion and inquiring into the state of the newly born princeling, Dr. Chandra finally made his way to an annex of the palace where few people went, and there he knocked on a door. He was admitted to the secluded apartments of a patient who lived as a recluse, the princess known as the Pitied One, and the one patient whom Dr. Chandra could not cure, and would not cure were it ever in his power to do so.

CHAPTER 33

Selene opened her eyes and blinked up at the ceiling. She rolled her head to the side and saw that Wulf's pallet was empty. Then she remembered: He had gone out into the city again, in search of someone who would take them to Persepolis.

Selene moved slightly and winced. These first few moments upon waking were always bad, when her leg was especially stiff. She had to force herself to get up; if she did not, the pain would linger. In fact, it was upon this issue she and Wulf had had their first argument: As soon as they had landed on this Persian shore, after crossing the Lower Sea, he had found an inn and settled Selene there, forbidding her to go outside. The leg was still healing, he argued. She needed rest. But Selene hated being confined and had insisted the leg needed exercise. Wulf had won. He had seen with his own eyes how close she had come to death. Now he treated her as if she might break.

Selene washed and dressed, and ate the breakfast Wulf had set out for her, then went onto the balcony where hyssop blossoms were spread out to dry in the summer sun. She paused to lean against the door frame and massage her thigh. Wulf was right. She was still not well. And she *had* come very close to death.

I glimpsed the other side but was snatched back before I could step over.

What force had brought her back?

Selene shook her head and sat in the sun to work on the hyssop for her medicine box. She carefully separated the flowers and shoots from the leaves. The blue buds would be infused in water with the tender shoots, and be used as an expectorant for winter-lung. The narrow, aromatic leaves would be distilled into perfumed oils and flavoring to be traded in the marketplace for goods. Just as Wulf was at this moment bartering for pack donkeys and a guide, with the transparent fire-stone from her medicine box. Except for the medicines and other medical supplies, it was all they had left of any value.

There was still the golden Eye of Horus Andreas had given her four summers ago, and which Selene always wore under her dress. If it should come to it, Selene would sell the necklace, but only when they were really desperate.

So far, Wulf had made some good bargains, starting with the marsh-dwellers at the mouth of the Euphrates: He had exchanged the labor of his strong body (being much larger than the small, malnourished natives) in trade for their care of Selene during her convalescence. And then later, when she could hobble with a crutch and insisted that they go on, that they get as far away from Babylon as possible, now that their trail was hot again, Wulf had traded a tooth-and-gum ointment for passage across the Lower Sea, the captain of the boat suffering, like all sailors, from mouth disease. And then here, in this port town on Persia's western coastline, Wulf had been able to get food and lodgings, and was now looking for a way to reach Persepolis, the city in the mountains where, the sea captain had assured them, they would find a safe route back to their homelands in the west.

Selene lifted her face to the hot sun. An eastern sun, she reflected, a sun that shone on lands and people as alien to her as if they lived on the moon. What an ironic destiny it was that drew her ever more eastward despite her frantic attempts to go west! Four months ago they had fled Babylon on the southeastward current of the Euphrates, which had carried them to the Lower Sea, which they had then crossed over to Persia. And now they were *still* going eastward. "Persepolis is a great and mighty city," the sea captain had declared. "It is said that there is nothing that cannot be obtained there. In Persepolis you will be able to earn money, and find a safe route home."

And so to Persepolis they were going, eastward yet again, and northward into hazardous mountains in this alien land of the Persians. Putting yet more miles between Selene and Antioch.

The summer heat eased Selene into a thoughtful state. The sea captain had been so pleased with the relief brought by the tooth-and-gum ointment that he had offered any favor in return. So Selene had used the last of the papyrus in her medicine box to write a letter to Andreas, and the captain had promised to deliver it, on his return voyage to the Euphrates, to any boatman or caravan driver heading for Antioch. It was a small chance, a slender, fishbone-thin chance, but upon it Selene hung her hope.

Andreas must not forget me. I must let him know that I am alive. To wait for me.

When she heard the door open behind her, Selene turned to see Wulf come into the room, and she wondered again: Was it *he* who had brought her back from the threshold of death? Was it *his* voice she had heard calling to her?

She had been so close to departing this life—a breath away, a heartbeat away—but a strength other than her own had pulled her back, and it was during that painful, stormy return journey that Selene had experienced the visions.

The visions that had shown her clearly, finally, her purpose in life.

I understand it all now, she thought, as she rose to greet Wulf. *I know now that it is not by chance but by design that I am in Persia.*

For four years Selene had lived for the dream of creating a healing art that was a combination of her mother's teachings and the teachings of Andreas. But in her feverish delirium on the river, Selene had seen a much larger vision, one that had astonished her, dazzled her. There was so much *more* to learn; the world was such a great, wide place. Suddenly, Selene saw the purpose of her exile; suddenly she understood why she was being led thus. She saw that she had been born to gather from the corners of the earth all the knowledge and healing skills of others—in Magna, among the Bedouins, from her glimpse of the terrible Gilgamesh Square—and put them together to share with the world.

Selene had awakened on the river and had seen the direction the current was carrying them—still eastward—and had known that it was no accident. She saw the hands of the gods guiding her way.

I am being prepared for the great work that awaits me. When I am reunited with Andreas, I will come to him rich in the healing wisdom that the world has taught me. And together we shall take it to where it is needed.

And so Selene knew that Persia must be one more step in her initiation, the step she must take before the gods, seeing that she was ready, allowed her to go home.

Selene watched Wulf pull his tunic over his head and wash the summer heat and sweat from his arms and chest. As always, she marveled at his beautiful body, which was so perfect, like the Adonis statue in Antioch's marketplace.

After putting his tunic back on and tying the rope-belt, Wulf turned to Selene standing in the balcony doorway, and asked, "How is it this morning?"

"I improve each day. Did you have any luck?"

Wulf hesitated. How to answer that question! He hoped to make his way homeward through the northwest before the heavy snows, and if he was to do so, then he must begin at once, and delay no longer. He would have to leave Selene. Today he had found a guide, a man with three donkeys who would take them to Persepolis. But then . . .

"You found someone?" Selene pressed.

He was worried about her. Despite her assurances, Wulf still was not sure Selene could make such a journey. Perhaps they should remain a while in this town, until she was stronger. "Yes," he said at last. "He knows the road well and can have us in Persepolis in ten days."

"Then we must leave at once!"

Wulf watched her limp across the room and pick up the bundles he had brought—supplies for the two-hundred-mile journey into the Zagros Mountains: hard-cooked eggs and summer apples, bags of rice, rounds of unleavened bread and salt fish. They were to travel at night because "No one crosses this land during the day in the summer except madmen and Greeks," the guide had told Wulf, referring to the great Alexander who had done just that three hundred years before and had conquered Persia while he was at it. Wulf had also purchased sturdy pairs of sandals, broad-brimmed hats to keep off the merciless sun, and leather capes with hoods to protect them as they traveled through the high mountain passes.

As he watched Selene examine the supplies and exclaim delightedly over everything, Wulf was overcome with sadness. He was recalling the desperate journey downriver, when he had steered the little raft on the current, watchful for patrols on the banks, all the while keeping an anxious eye on Selene, who had burned with fever.

Sunsets had found him anchoring in the reeds. He would spear some fish, smoke them in the brazier, and try to coax a few morsels between Selene's lips. But all she could do was drink. She had wasted away before his eyes as if melting beneath the terrible fever that had gripped her. At times her body had thrashed so violently in delirium that he had tied her down to prevent her from flinging herself into the river.

Wulf had hardly slept during those terrifying days and nights; he had held her in his arms, calling to her, helpless to break the fever that was stealing her away from him. There had been moments when he had cursed Odin and nearly thrown his wooden cross into the river; and moments when he had prayed so hard his knees had bled.

And then, just when he had come to the limit of his despair and Selene's life seemed to him no stronger than a spider's thread, when he had started bleakly searching the river banks for a place to dig a grave, the raft had finally come to where the Tigris and Euphrates empty into the Lower Sea, and there, where the terrain dissolves into a broad marshland of swamps and lagoons, Wulf had found the ancient and simple people known as the marsh-dwellers.

Selene suddenly straightened up from the spread of supplies and looked at Wulf in puzzlement. "How did you pay for all this?" she asked, holding up the new linen for bandages, the packet of elder bark, the bag of dried basil leaves. "Surely the fire-stone was not enough!"

He turned away and walked out onto the balcony.

The marsh-dwellers had nursed Selene back to life. In their peculiar, tunnel-shaped huts the women had tended Selene with their ancient remedies, while Wulf had joined the small men in their canoes and snared duck and heron in the canebrakes. Until the day had come when he had returned to their hut to find Selene sitting up and eating rice with her fingers; her face, when she saw him, had broken into a smile.

"How were you able to buy all these things, Wulf?" she asked again.

The dun rooftops of the harbor town shimmered in the Persian heat. At sunset, the guide had said, they would depart. In ten days they would reach Persepolis.

Ten days . . .

Wulf reached out and gripped the balcony rail. His powerful hands nearly splintered the dry wood. He had to put those memories behind him now—of their months in the desert, of Babylon, of their short time among the marsh-dwellers. The future was all that mattered, all that he must live for. To get back home. Back to his wife, to his son; to his people, who would need a leader to pick up the pieces of the shattered tribe and raise a force to fight the Romans.

Back to the Rhineland, where he would find Gaius Vatinius and carry out the vengeance he had sworn.

"Wulf?" Selene said again, from behind him. "How did you pay for these things?"

Let me hold her just once more, before we part forever. Let me taste her lips, feel her against me . . .

He turned impulsively and pulled the headcloth from his head.

Selene stared. Wulf's blond hair, which had nearly reached his waist, was cropped short.

"I sold it," he said. "There is a wig-maker in the marketplace. He saw me and offered me a lot of money. Yellow hair is very fashionable and in high demand, he said." Wulf reached into his belt and drew out a leather purse. "There is some money left over. Enough for Persepolis, to find someone there who can show us the rest of the way home."

Selene started to lift a hand to his hair but he stepped away, saying, "It will grow back."

She watched him move around the room, gathering their supplies and packing them into bundles and pouches, and she wanted to say something more. But there was nothing to say. In Persepolis their paths would part forever. Their journey together as Wulf and Selene must end, as she had always known it would.

And now she had the strength and conviction to face that ending. Because she had wakened from her delirium to find a strange new courage inside her. It was as if her spirit had fed upon her body during those days of fever; as if, while her flesh had wasted away, her soul had grown in power and conviction.

She had had dreams during her battle with death, and those dreams had instructed her, had shown her the larger vision, and had infused her spirit with new drive. She had wakened anxious to be going, but had been held back by the frailty of her body. Now, however, after weeks with the marsh-dwellers and days on the ship crossing the Lower Sea, Selene was strong enough to push on, and in a hurry to do so. A calling awaited her in the west.

CHAPTER 3 4

Help!" screamed the girl as she ran. "Somebody help me!"

She ran through one of the many private parklands of the pleasure-palace, across a lawn so green and smooth and bordered by thousands of summer flowers that it resembled one of the carpets for which Persia was famous. The girl ran as if for her life, frequently looking back with terrified eyes.

A man was in pursuit. When she saw him emerge from a copse of oak trees and head toward her across the lawn, she screamed again and ran faster. But she was a petite girl who ran on short legs, while her pursuer was a tall man with long legs, and he was rapidly gaining on her.

From the privacy of her terrace, unseen, Princess Rani, the Pitied One, watched.

The girl ran a frantic course, trying to elude the man by dodging around hedges, sprinting down serpentine paths, leaping over flower beds. Her bright orange pantaloons, billowing like pennants, were damp from the spray of fountains. Her long, jacket-like tunic, also orange, had lost a button and the tops of her breasts showed.

"Help!" she cried again. But to no avail: The park was enclosed on all sides by walls, and there was no exit; and there were no people about, only Princess Rani, hidden behind a vine-covered trellis, silently watching.

Finally, out of desperation, the girl plunged into a cluster of flowering myrtle bushes and dropped down to the earth, breathing heavily.

The man drew up short and looked around. He stood with his hands on his hips, searching, and when he turned in her direction, briefly, Princess Rani saw that he was darkly handsome.

A noble, she deduced, from the size of the emerald on his turban. A handsome young noble, with broad shoulders and a straight back that strained at the dove-gray silk of his jacket. Even from where she sat, Rani could guess his intentions. Was the girl aware, Rani wondered, of the irony of her having chosen the myrtle bush for protection? Myrtle was sacred to Venus, the Roman goddess of love.

The man waited. Presently, unable to keep still any longer, the girl darted rabbit-like from the shrubbery. With an easy reach, the man grabbed for her. But he only caught her veil. Throwing her hands up to her face, the girl cried out and raced across the lawn. The man took off after her, serious intent on his face now.

Prince Rani felt Miko, her old handmaiden, come and stand next to her. Miko said nothing, but also watched the two on the lawn.

At last the man reached the girl. Seizing her, he pulled her around, pinned down her struggling arms, and kissed her hard on the mouth.

Miko made a sound of disapproval.

Then the two, laughing, collapsed together onto the grass, the girl wrapping her arms about his neck, the man laying his body over hers. As the girl's excited shrieks filled the summer air, Princess Rani finally looked away.

Discreetly, Miko pulled a screen down over the vine trellis and said, "Why do you always watch? It brings you pain and sadness, and yet you always watch."

"It brings me some small joy," Rani said in an unconvincing tone, "to see others enjoying what I can never have."

Miko gave her mistress a significant look. Princess Rani knew what her old handmaiden was thinking—that it did not have to be like this.

But it does, Rani argued in her mind. *I do it for Dr. Chandra.*

As the squeals of the happy couple finally died down and the park was quiet again, Princess Rani rested her head back and looked up at the sky. She thought of what the two young people were doing down there, what she had never experienced and never would, and it filled her with melancholy.

Sex. What was it like? All the world engaged in it, it seemed to Princess Rani. Everyone made love, even old Miko had once had a husband; and in this pleasure-palace, love and the pursuit of love were the main pastimes.

I made my decision long ago, Rani thought stoically. *I shall stand by it and I shall continue to pay the price.*

She guided her thoughts away from such nonproductive thinking and settled once again upon the mysterious prophecy the Astrologer had made that morning.

Dr. Chandra's existence within these walls was soon coming to an end, Nimrod had declared, to everyone's great astonishment (after thirty years of service in the palace, no one, least of all the doctor himself, had ever thought he would leave) and a four-eyed person was going to be the instrument of his departure.

But leave *how*? Princess Rani wondered. There was more than one way a person could depart an existence: by walking away from it, by dying.

Which is it to be for Dr. Chandra? And who, or what is a four-eyed person?

The princess closed her eyes. Her garden terrace was quiet, peaceful. This far corner of the pleasure-palace, high in Persia's mountains, was beyond the reach of the music and laughter that hung continually over the domes and spires like an invisible tent. By her own design, Rani had had herself installed well out of the mainstream of palace life, so that she would not have to be reminded of her tragedy, nor spoil the happiness of others by reminding them of herself. Rani knew they called her the Pitied One. Nearly thirty years ago they had started whispering it, when all the doctors of the palace had declared they could not cure her.

And so, lonely as this life was, with her few slaves and pets, the occasional diversion of young lovers meeting in the park, Rani preferred this life to living with normal people. Here, she was safe; here, her *secrets* were safe.

Or . . . had been. Until now. Until the shocking and dismaying pronouncement of the Astrologer that Dr. Chandra would soon leave the palace.

Can it be true? the princess wondered with a racing heart. *After all these years—how many? Thirty—ever since the day Dr. Chandra suddenly appeared within these walls, on my eighteenth birthday. He is to go away?*

What, then, will become of me?

Princess Rani, normally of a calm and tranquil nature, a soft-spoken, gentle woman who lived out her days confined to a couch, her body being lifeless from the waist down, started to feel, for the first time in years, fear.

===

Nimrod, in his high tower, was worrying about Dr. Chandra, too.

The stars told the future and they never lied, but they did not always tell all the facts. Nimrod banged an angry fist on his work table, where star charts and measuring instruments lay in a clutter. When and how would Dr. Chandra be leaving the mountain palace? And who was this four-eyed person that the stars said was coming?

Throwing down his pen and pushing aside his astrolabe, the old astrologer glowered at his charts.

So, the day had finally come, had it? The day he must leave his tower. For it was clear to Nimrod that no further answers were going to be found here; the stars had revealed all they were going to. The rest of the answers would have to be found elsewhere. Outside, beyond this tower, which Nimrod, like the princess in her apartments, had not left in many years.

He needed a lamb. A perfect, unblemished lamb, of just the right age and coloring. And he could not trust anyone in the palace to bring him the perfect one. This was too important. Nimrod was going to have to go out and find one for himself. And then examine it and read in its liver Dr. Chandra's future.

CHAPTER 35

They departed at dusk with the setting sun in their eyes, and they followed an ancient royal road built hundreds of years before by Cyrus, first king of the Persians.

The flatland rose gradually from the coast into gently rolling hills, which in turn lifted the travelers up into the steep slopes of the

Zagros Mountains. As the road climbed, the air grew thinner and cooler. Ten days after their departure from the coast they reached the famous Persian Gates, where, three hundred years before, the great "Sikander" had fought a valiant battle, and the guide explained to Wulf and Selene that they were now a mile and a half up from the level of the sea.

Rather than being weakened by the strenuous trek, Selene felt a new vigor surge through her. Up here the stars seemed brighter, closer to the earth; the moon was big and fat and round, washing the oak groves in silver light. The air was so clear and pure that it was intoxicating. Selene grew lightheaded. As she and Wulf followed the guide and his donkeys over the crest of the moonlit mountain pass, Selene felt electrified with excitement and hope. Their journey would soon be at an end; just over this rise they would see ancient Persepolis, from where, in a few days, she was certain, they could begin their way westward and homeward.

She knew just what Persepolis would be like—the captain of the boat had described it to her during their voyage over the Lower Sea: "A broad plain sits within a ring of mountains," he had said, "and the entire plain is a garden of trees and flowers and grass. There are canals and water-courses, there are game birds and tame gazelles. It is a Garden of Heden where the pavilions of the nobility shimmer in the sun. It will take your breath away!"

When they finally crested the path and the three stopped to look down on the plain below, even though they were too high up to see very well and the plain stretched into darkness, Selene nonetheless could visualize the great stone and cedar palace brilliantly painted and hung with a million gold tassels.

Persepolis, Selene thought giddily. This city was one more step on the road to her destiny; the gods had brought her here.

They were soon down the eastern side of the mountain and following the road onto the plain. It was midnight and the moon was high; their way was lighted as if by a ghostly torch. And as they followed the royal road, Selene felt a queer, inexplicable chill start to creep into the pores of her skin.

A silence that seemed unnatural lay over the valley like a weight, as if the invisible hand of some god were cupped down from mountain rim to mountain rim, cutting this place off from the rest of the world. The clop-clop of the donkeys' hooves echoed on the pavement. Selene and Wulf began to look around, first in bewilderment, then in dismay. And when they crossed the old wooden bridge over the River Pulvar, the guide talked as if there were nothing wrong. He spoke of "Sikander," the great Alexander who had conquered this land long ago, and how he had, to show his might and power to the Persians, set a torch to this city and stood by while Persepolis blazed like a bonfire that surely must have been seen at the ends of the earth.

Selene stared in shock at the piles of stones and broken walls and toppled pillars that had once been the palace of Darius the Great. There were no gardens here, no trees or flowers, not even any grass—just a flat, barren plain shorn to its crust, like an accursed ground the gods had damned.

They reached the Gateway of Xerxes, and the guide continued to talk while his companions walked in silence. No golden tassels hung here, they realized; no brightly painted columns or walls of cedar—the sea captain had been reciting something he had read in a book! He had never been to Persepolis!

"Oh, Wulf," Selene whispered in the icy night air. "It's a dead city. There is no one here."

Wulf lifted his eyes to the tops of the few pillars still standing, seeming to hold up the starry canopy of sky, and he wondered what gods had built this place and why they had let it tumble into disgrace.

"Wulf," said Selene, disappointed, "we have come to a dead place. There is nothing here. Why did the gods bring me to this graveyard? Now we shall have to journey on, to another city. And I am so very weary of traveling . . ."

When Selene leaned against Wulf, he put his arms around her and gave the guide a look. The man retreated with the donkeys, pointing to the place in the ruins where he was going to set up camp. He left his tourists to themselves—that was what he thought they were—tourists. The only people who ever came to Persepolis were tourists.

Selene and Wulf stood together like one of the stone statues found throughout the ruins, holding each other, drawing warmth from each other against the cold night. They were so tired, they had come so far and so full of hope, only to discover that they must go on, to another city, another road.

Their embrace was motionless at first, a mutual supporting in their exhaustion, but then Wulf started to stroke her hair, and Selene's hands moved over his back.

Selene sought Wulf's mouth at the same time he sought hers. They came together gently, in a kiss that was tender and sweet. There was no urgency, no great passion; they held each other in a loving affection that was like balm to their weary souls. Home was so far away; they sought a home in each other.

The ground seemed to reach up and draw the lovers down onto it, and the stars revolved overhead on the tops of the pillars. Selene and Wulf made love slowly, far into the night, dispelling for this one brief time their loneliness and yearning and despair.

Sunlight broke over the eastern peaks and in an instant the plain was washed in bright light. A breeze, cool now but which would soon turn hot and dry, stirred their hair as they walked through the ruins.

They saw charred columns and a layer of powdery dust everywhere—cedarwood ash from the enormous rafters that had crashed down during the terrible inferno set by Alexander's torch. Walls of dark limestone that had been laboriously engraved by skilled stonemasons depicted stiff parades of people long forgotten, now the only inhabitants of this desolate place.

When the guide came up he was leading the donkeys. They must find shelter for the day, he said, because soon the heat would be unbearable. He eyed Selene. There was sand in her hair and her lips were swollen. The Persian shrugged. These were not the first tourists to come to Persepolis for carnal purposes. There was something about ruins that excited men and women to lust. Who could explain it?

When the guide headed in the direction of the road they had just come, intending to take his tourists back to the coast, Wulf and Selene insisted they go another way. The way home was not back the way they had come, because of the danger from Lasha's soldiers. Could they not travel north? they asked. Could they not reach Armenia by taking a road that led west from northern Persia? The guide scratched his head and said, "That road over there leads to an ancient pleasure-palace in the north. And from there is a road going westward, all the way to Europe, I am told."

Wulf and Selene had heard of that pleasure-palace, and knew that it stood at the terminus of a safe and swift road. Better to take their chances going that way, they decided, than to risk encountering Lasha's soldiers.

The guide would not take them to that mountain palace, nor would he sell them his donkeys, so Wulf and Selene bade him farewell and struck off across the ruined plains alone.

CHAPTER 36

One day away from the mountain pleasure-palace, the incident occurred.

The sun was starting to climb and they went off the road in search of a shady place to sleep through the day. The road was behind them and out of sight, and they were heading for an oak thicket when they saw the white-haired man come running from behind a cluster of boulders.

Selene and Wulf stopped and stared as he ran in their direction; he did not seem to see them, but kept his eyes fixed upon a lamb that scampered some distance in front of him. Because his hat flew off and his long white hair streamed out behind his head, Selene started to laugh. But then Wulf seized her arm and pointed to a shadow on the ground, moving swiftly and closing in on the old man.

Selene looked up in horror, to see the bird swoop down from the sky and attack the man's head. She and Wulf stared for an instant in shock, then, hearing the old man's screams, broke into a run.

He was on his knees and shrieking as monstrous wings flapped about his face and shoulders, and as fierce talons dug firmly into his skull. Scarlet trickles started to run down his head, and then he fell onto his back, arms and legs flailing. Wulf was upon the man in an instant, his large hands seizing the hawk and grappling with it. The bird let go, fluttered for a moment then lifted its great wings and took off into the sky.

Selene was at the man's side immediately. His scalp was bleeding terribly.

Wulf was already opening the medicine box. Selene worked quickly to stop the blood flow, wash the wound, and then stitch it and bind it with cotton. When she was done and about to ask Wulf what they should do with the unconscious man, she saw the most amazing sight materialize from the base of the hills.

Wulf saw it at the same time, and slowly rose to his feet.

There must have been over a hundred people in a fantastic caravan, all dressed like kings and all riding elephants painted with colorful designs. They moved in a slow, stately procession, tinkling with hundreds of bells, wending their way toward Wulf and Selene where they came finally to a halt.

Without a word, one member flung himself down from his horse and came running. He fell to one knee, examined the unconscious man, then turned and shouted something in a language Selene did not understand.

Now four more men came out of the parade, bearing a litter on their shoulders. Selene watched as the old man was gently lifted onto it and carried back to the crowd, where he was hoisted onto an elephant draped in blue and gold velvet.

The leader at the head of the train, tall, swarthy and handsome, atop an elephant painted bright yellow, gazed down at Wulf and Selene with an unreadable expression. Selene stared in amazement at his arm; it was outstretched, and upon it sat the very hawk that had attacked the old man. Its feathers and talons were touched with blood, and it wore a little leather hood.

Six soldiers now came out of the train and ran toward Wulf and Selene. They were told to mount a horse, with Selene riding behind Wulf.

———

The mountain pleasure-palace of the Parthian emperor was so grand it would have made the palace in Magna seem a mere stable. It contained so many rooms that it was said a man could visit one room a day for ten years and still not see half the palace. The procession reached the palace by crossing a bridge over a dry riverbed; the heat was so intense that lizards and snakes were seen frying in the streets. And when Selene saw the palace, she thought: *Was* this *the place I saw in my visions?* Alabaster walls shining whitely in the sun. *Had that vision been a message from the gods telling me that I would be brought to this place for a purpose? And will I find something here that will bring me one step closer to my destiny?*

The procession passed through seven towering gates, and finally entered a spacious square that baked in the summer heat. Hundreds of attendants appeared and swarmed to the procession with ladders and footstools. It was chaos, and Wulf and Selene wondered if they were going to be overlooked in the confusion. But a cohort of Parthian guards quickly surrounded them while they dismounted. They were marched across the courtyard and through a door studded with gold.

They followed what seemed miles of corridors surprisingly cool in the killing heat of the Persian summer day, and passed people in the halls wearing colorful coats and trousers, turbans on their heads adorned with plumes and large jewels. Wulf stared as he passed them, and they likewise turned curious eyes on the blond giant who strode by in leather leggings. And when the guards led them across an outdoor garden with a small lake at its center, Wulf stopped altogether, amazement on his face. For there were swans on the water, the first he had seen since being taken prisoner on the Rhine, and they produced an ache in his soul. Swans were the incarnations of the Valkyries, Odin's daughters.

Finally Wulf and Selene were ceremoniously delivered into a room that was comfortably furnished and led into a private garden. The guards departed and the doors were locked.

CHAPTER 37

A man came to see them. He wore brown silk and a gold turban, and introduced himself as Dr. Singh.

"Why do you keep us prisoner?" Wulf demanded. "We have done nothing wrong."

Dr. Singh, intimidated by the barbarian who towered over him, retreated a step. "I assure you that you are not a prisoner here! You are our honored guest!"

"You keep the doors locked."

"For your own protection."

"How is the old man?" Selene asked.

The doctor glanced at her, as if surprised she should speak, then addressed Wulf: "You must understand that this is a delicate situation, and a highly unusual one. It is a crime for anyone but a Brahman to lay hands upon the Daniel of All Persia; yet you saved his life. As we were in a dilemma about what to do with you, we decided to wait and see the outcome of the Daniel's injury. He has regained consciousness and he is asking to see you."

"Then he's all right?" Selene said.

Again Dr. Singh's eyes flickered to her and again he dismissed her, addressing only Wulf: "The *old man* you saved is our Astrologer. His untimely death would have been a national calamity. But now"—Dr. Singh stepped aside and held out an arm—"you will please come with me."

"Where are you taking us?" asked Wulf.

"I am taking you to see the Astrologer. He has asked to meet the man who saved his life."

When Selene fell into step beside Wulf, Dr. Singh said, "Not your woman. She stays here."

"But she is the one who saved the old man. Not I."

Dr. Singh's eyebrows shot up. "What? Surely you cannot mean that!"
"She is a healer."

The doctor gasped. "And she . . . *touched* the Astrologer?"

"I had to, in order to—" began Selene.

But the doctor silenced her with a hand. Annoyed, he said, "This is most unexpected. Most irregular. I shall have to find out what to do." And he hurried out the door.

Dr. Singh returned a short time later and said, "The woman may come."

Wulf and Selene were led through a maze of corridors and finally to a place Dr. Singh called simply the pavilion.

Selene stared in astonishment. The pavilion was a large, airy room with a row of beds along one wall; the opposite wall opened onto a broad terrace that admitted breezes. Each of the beds was occupied, and each occupant, Selene saw as she walked slowly by, suffered from some form of ailment or injury. Garlands of flowers festooned the walls and ceiling; a formidable sword stood by each bedside; the air was full of the smoke of mustard incense.

Selene was amazed. The patients were lying on white sheets, their heads rested on white pillows, and white covers draped their bodies. Basins and cloths and sticks of incense stood on small tables between the beds; attendants were bent over the patients—washing them, changing bandages, feeding them—and all the while they laughed and joked. In fact, the room was clamorous with laughter. Some of the attendants were even singing; one man stood on a pedestal in the center of the room reciting what Selene guessed was a humorous tale, since he frequently caused explosions of laughter and applause.

When they came to the last bed, Selene recognized the old man with the bandaged head, whom Dr. Singh identified as Nimrod, the court Astrologer. Three beautiful women sat at his bedside singing and clapping their hands in a cheerful rhythm. When Nimrod's eyes started to close, one reached forward and slapped his cheek, and his eyes snapped open.

"What are they doing?" Selene asked when they reached the foot of the bed.

Dr. Singh sniffed in distaste. "They are keeping him awake. If you are a healer, you should know that it is bad for a patient to sleep during the day."

Ignoring the contempt in his tone and the fact that she had never heard such a preposterous notion, Selene asked, "What do you call this place?"

"The pavilion."

"But . . . what *is* it?"

Dr. Singh frowned. He and Selene had been conversing in Greek, but he could not think of any word in that language which described this place, so he gave her the Sanskrit word, which was *chikisaka.* "It is the place where we take care of our sick. What word do you call it where you come from?"

Selene also frowned. She, too, could think of no Greek equivalent. And then she realized it might be because there was no such phenomenon, to her knowledge, as a sick-tending place, beyond the temples of Aesculapius, in the western world. "We have no such thing," she admitted.

A look of disdain came over his face. *Foreigners,* he thought. *What must the Astrologer be thinking of, to wish to speak with them?*

He turned away and approached the bedside where the three women kept up their singing. While Dr. Singh bent over the Astrologer and conversed with him in Parsi, Selene looked around the amazing pavilion once again and this time saw, standing in the shadow of a corner, a short, plump man watching her. He wore peach-colored silks and a turquoise turban, and a pair of suspicious eyes stared out over a bushy black beard.

"You may approach the Daniel now," Dr. Singh said dryly, "but make it brief."

Selene stepped up to the bed and looked down at the gray face. *He should be allowed to sleep,* she thought in concern, wishing the three singers would go away. "Hello," she said gently. "I am Selene."

The milky eyes searched the air for a moment, then focused on her face. "*You* saved my life?" Nimrod asked in a croaky voice.

"I and my friend," she said, gesturing to Wulf. "He fought the hawk away from your head. I tended your wounds."

Nimrod sighed and said, "The blasted bird mistook my head for a hare. It was my mistake. I should never have joined Mudra's hawking party."

He was having difficulty speaking, and Selene saw how exhausted he was. When she started to reach down and feel his forehead Dr. Singh cried, "Stop!"

She looked up at him.

"You may not touch the Daniel," he said.

"But I must find out how he is. His skin does not look right. Let me examine the wound."

"You may not touch him."

"But I've *already* touched him!"

"Your presence is a disturbance in this room. You are upsetting the cheerfulness. Go away now."

Stunned, Selene stared at the physician. When her eyes flickered above his shoulders, she saw in the corner, the black-bearded man still watching her. "But this is ridic—"

"Go!" snapped Dr. Singh, and he signaled for the guards.

As she and Wulf were taken from the pavilion, Selene looked back over her shoulder and saw Dr. Singh conferring with the man who had watched her from the corner.

CHAPTER 3 8

Princess Rani, half reclining on her couch, silk cushions at her back, studied the two visitors in frank curiosity. The girl's coloring was unusual—such white skin, contrasting with all that black hair—and she was tall. If Rani could stand, she guessed she would barely reach the girl's shoulders. And her companion! Was it possible for a human scalp to sprout hair the color of cornsilk? Rani had heard tales of such men, but she had never thought she would meet one.

"I am told you saved the life of our court Astrologer," she said in a kindly voice. "For that you have the gratitude of myself, everyone in the palace, and no doubt of the gods as well. Please sit down."

Selene was reminded of Lasha's apartments in Magna, but only in a general sense. The rooms of this princess were far more lavish than anything found in Magna. There were gold tiles inlaid in the marble floor; strange birds strutted about, giant turquoise birds with great tails of colorful feathers dragging behind them. When one, all white, lifted and spread its tail in a magnificent white fan, Selene gasped.

"You have come from far away," said Rani with a smile. "What brought you to Persia?"

Selene took her gaze away from the peacocks and studied the princess. She was small and plump and brown, like many of the inhabitants of this pleasure-palace, but she did not seem possessed of the arrogance the others wore like badges. Selene wondered about the legs hidden beneath the satin cover; she had yet to see them move.

"We came here seeking a way home. Fate has brought us far from our road."

Rani nodded, understanding such things. She would never forget how fate had twisted her own road thirty-six years ago; a cruel trick that she would never forgive.

"Dr. Chandra told me about your visit to the pavilion this morning. He said you wished to touch the Astrologer. Do you not know that, as a woman, you may not do so? Nimrod is of the Brahman caste."

Selene thought back to the morning: Who was Dr. Chandra? Then she remembered the short, bearded man in the corner who had watched her with a critical eye. "I cannot be faulted for my ignorance, your highness," Selene said. "We have no such taboos in my world. I apologize for any offenses we have given; my friend and I wish only to be moving on. We understand that there is a route from here, westward—"

"Dr. Chandra told me that your repair of Nimrod's scalp was a professional one, and that you claim to be a healer. Is this true?"

"I know some healing."

The princess gave her a long, considering look, then said, "Are women allowed to be healers where you come from?"

Slightly surprised by the question, Selene said, "Of course."

Rani shook her head in amazement. "You see, I know so little of the world beyond these walls. And I never receive visitors. All the news I receive is reported to me by Dr. Chandra, who is my only friend as well as my personal physician."

When Selene's eyes automatically went to the satin cover over the lifeless legs, Rani said, "I have been paralyzed for thirty-six years."

"I'm sorry."

Rani's eyes, which were almond shaped and fringed with thick black lashes, met Selene's gaze and held it. For a brief moment there seemed to be communication in the look, or possibly, Selene thought, the princess was contemplating sharing an intimacy. But then the moment passed and Rani looked away. "I am curious about you," she said. "In this part of the world women are not permitted to learn medicine. We are also not taught reading and writing. Can you read and write?"

"I can."

Rani sighed. "What a marvelous world you come from that allows women such freedom!" She clapped her hands and the gold bracelets on her arms jangled. Almost instantly a slave appeared with a tray, which she set before the visitors, and as she did so she stared blatantly at Wulf.

"You are an oddity!" Rani said after the slave had gone, gesturing that they pour the wine and help themselves to the sweetmeats. "Before the day is out people will be clustering about you to get a look. That was how it was when the Romans came."

"Romans?" said Selene. "This far east?"

"Oh, we are in the Parthian Empire and Parthia is very strong, but the Roman eagle is greedy and is trying to spread its lethal wings into Persia. There was a Roman delegation to this palace not three months ago. A peaceful mission they called it! A mission of diplomacy! And yet they sent one of their generals, a *military* man! And a hard man at that—Gaius Vatinius."

Wulf suddenly sat up. "Gaius Vatinius?"

Rani looked at him. "You have heard of him?"

"Gaius Vatinius was *here*?" Selene asked. She turned to Wulf. "Can it be the same man?"

"He commands the Rhine army," Rani said.

Wulf shot to his feet. "When did he leave? Which direction did he go?"

"Calm yourself, my friend. There are men in this court who can tell you what you wish to know. I myself never saw the Romans; Dr. Chandra reported their visit to me. But I do know that the general left three months ago and that he was returning to the Rhine."

Selene looked up at Wulf, at his clenched fists and the fire in his blue eyes, and she felt her own heart race.

"I can see now," said the princess slowly, studying the faces of her visitors, appraising them with a new eye, "that it was no accident that you have come to Persia. The gods brought you here for a reason." Then she narrowed her eyes and thought: *Is it possible that one of you is the one heralded in the stars, the one who will be responsible for the end of Dr. Chandra's existence here?*

"I should like you to visit me again before you leave Persia," the princess said to Selene. "I should like to hear how women become healers in your world."

But Selene was still looking up at Wulf. "We are in a hurry, your highness. We cannot linger here."

"Are you on your way to the Rhineland as well?"

Now Selene met Rani's gaze and she spoke with emotion in her voice: "I must return to my home in Syria, where a calling awaits me."

"A calling?"

Selene told briefly of her brush with death on the Euphrates River, and of the visions she had seen in her delirium. It was not a simple thing to make another person understand how she had relived in those visions events from her past, events either forgotten or thought insignificant but which now, blazing before her feverish eyes in new light and passion, took on new meanings: the rug merchant from Damascus who almost died in the street, the clusters of afflicted and crippled gathered around Magna's palace gate, the terrible Gilgamesh Square in Babylon. Selene had relived each episode in sharp detail, but this time she lived them differently, with new eyes.

"I did not *understand* before," she said, leaning forward, speaking urgently to the princess. "Then, I was simply using the skills my mother had taught me. But when I relived those moments in my dreams, I saw myself as a different person, altered somehow.

"You see, the woman who raised me was not my real mother. My father died the night I was born and he told the healer-woman that I had a destiny which I must seek. When the visions came to me in my delirium, I experienced an astonishing revelation: I suddenly realized that my calling as a healer and my quest to find out who I am are not two separate things, but are somehow tied together! I saw that healing and my identity are in some way inextricably bound, that one does not exist separately from the other. The gods revealed to me, in a way words cannot express, that my calling as a healer and who I am are linked, and that the two will eventually combine to create the great purpose for which I was born."

Rani gazed at Selene with veiled eyes and a faraway look on her face. "It is as if," she said quietly, "the healing comes not from what you have been taught, but from within, from your soul. As though you were born a healer."

"Yes," Selene said.

"As though healing were not something you merely do, but that *is* you. As though in healing lies the very definition that is you, and that without it you would not *be.*"

Selene stared at the princess.

Rani smiled. "And do you know what the great purpose is that the gods are preparing you for?"

"I believe," Selene said quietly, "that it was put upon me to gather from the far corners of the earth all that is good in healing, and to take it to where it can do the most good for the most people."

"And where will that be?"

"I do not know."

"Then you must go back to your homeland and do what you have to do. I envy you."

These last words contained a trace of sadness; they made Selene look around the room again, at the silk hangings and gold lamps and peacocks. Her eyes finally came to rest on the small woman confined to the couch. "Would you like me to examine your legs?" Selene asked. "I know that others have before me, but perhaps . . . "

"You may. But I am beyond help."

Wulf strode away, to stand at the edge of the princess's garden, to look out over the trees and grass but to see only the face that was stamped upon his heart, the face of Gaius Vatinius. Selene rolled back the satin coverlet to expose Rani's small brown feet.

"I was born into one of the noblest families of India," Rani said, as she watched Selene manipulate her feet, "and when I was twelve my father betrothed me to a prince of Persia. I was brought up here from the Ganges Valley to marry a man I had never seen, to be one of his many wives, to live the rest of my life among strangers in a foreign court. On the eve of the wedding I came down with a fever. It burned for days, and when I recovered I found that my legs no longer had life in them."

"Can you feel this?" Selene asked, pinching slightly.

"No, I cannot. The prince refused to marry me and my father would not take me back, so I was put here and forgotten. For six years I was terribly lonely—my only friend was Nimrod, who taught me to read and write so that I at least would have some diversion. And then, when I was eighteen, Dr. Chandra appeared. He came from my own Ganges valley."

Selene lifted Rani's right foot and ran her thumbnail over the bare sole. The toes curled. She picked up the left and did the same thing, and again the toes curled. Selene frowned, perplexed.

When the cover was back in place, Rani said, "You see? It is a spinal ailment, an incurable one. But I thank you for wanting to help. Will you come again and visit me before you leave Persia?"

Out in the corridor, as they were being led back to their room, Selene said quietly to Wulf, "There is something strange going on here. There is nothing wrong with Princess Rani's legs. She should be able to walk."

Then Selene thought of Dr. Chandra and wondered what mysterious hold he had on the princess.

CHAPTER 39

To her delight, Selene was allowed to return to the pavilion. Not only allowed, but encouraged. And Selene was eager to do so, since there was so much to learn there.

While Wulf spent his hours poring over maps and conferring with men in the court who knew northern routes to the west, Selene passed many days in the *chikisaka,* the place where the ill were brought and taken care of. She learned that this was not a phenomenon peculiar to the pleasure-palace, but was found all over Persia and India. They had been established, she was told, by the benevolent Buddha, who instructed his followers to take care of the sick and the infirm.

Selene learned that the beds were set to face the east so that the patients could make obeisance to the celestial spirits which inhabited that part of the sky; she also learned that the sword placed at the bedside was meant to impress evil spirits with the patient's determination to get well. The flower garlands were to give evidence of the patient's lightheartedness and refusal to be conquered by disease; finally, all the laughter and singing was to discourage evil spirits from attempting to take the patient's life.

Much of what Selene learned she disagreed with, but much impressed her, too: the use of beds instead of pallets on the floor, having specially trained attendants nurse the sick, collecting patients all in one place so that the doctors could make more efficient use of their skills—none of which was practiced in the western world, not even in the healing temples of Aesculapius.

Selene also learned exotic new medical practices, some quite startling.

One afternoon she observed Dr. Chandra closing skin wounds with large ants and beetles. He allowed Selene to watch, and he even spoke, saying, "When the mandible of the beetle pinches the wound edges together, quickly twist off the body of the beetle and you see that the head and jaws remain clamped. They are removed when the wound has healed."

Dr. Chandra had a strange voice, and as he spoke he never looked directly at Selene but cast unreadable sideways glances at her. It was difficult to guess what he might be thinking. His enormous beard hid much of his face and even covered his chest. But she often caught him staring at her, and when she did, before he quickly turned away, Selene tried to read what had been in his eyes. Was it mistrust? Curiosity? Jealousy?

Dr. Chandra was Princess Rani's only friend, her only visitor. Selene began to wonder what they did together in the evenings, and why he never came when Selene was there. Were he and the princess lovers? Did he resent Selene's intrusion into their private life? And had he noticed, as Selene had, that, physically, there was nothing wrong with Rani's legs?

Was he, in fact, the cause of her inability to walk?

Whatever it was, Selene recognized that he was an excellent physician, and tried to learn from him all she could.

CHAPTER 40

In the Gilgamesh Square in Babylon," Selene told Rani one evening as they sat drinking mint tea, "all the sick and injured are brought together, much like in your *chikisakas*. But there the similarity ends. There is no organization, help is haphazard and often harmful. Many people are not even helped at all, and die where they lie. And in our temples of Aesculapius in Syria, the person who comes pays a penny to the priest and is allowed to spend the night in the sanctuary. If the god comes to the person while he sleeps, he will be cured. If not, he must leave. The god can come in the person of a physician or a priest, but it is random at best, depending upon the mood or abilities of the physician, and the patients always take a great chance. Sometimes they leave in worse shape."

"You approve of our methods then?"

"Of the *chikisaka*, yes. Back in Antioch, my mother walked all over the city to visit her patients. Many of them lived alone and had no one to care for them; even those who had money were cared for by ill-equipped people. We do not have such a thing as healing attendants, as you have in the pavilion. In my delirium, I received a vision of a large place, like a temple or a palace. A voice spoke in my mind—or possibly I was hearing my own feverish thoughts—and it said: *Alabaster walls shining whitely in the sun.*"

"What does it mean?"

"I thought at first that I had glimpsed the future, that I had looked upon a place I would one day visit. When I was brought to this palace after helping Nimrod, I thought that this was what the vision was. But now I think not. I think perhaps that it was not the vision of a real place, but of a concept. And when I saw the pavilion, and learned of your *chikisakas*, it came to me: I shall someday build a *chikisaka* of my own, in Antioch, where the ill and injured can go for rest and care. Like a hospice, I think, a hospice for the sick and infirm, travelers on the journey back to health."

Rani sighed. What ambition this young woman had! And how lucky she was to have the freedom to pursue it! *What a different turn my own life would have taken,* she thought in envy, *had I been born into her world instead of into mine.*

A clap of thunder made both women turn their faces to the terrace. A light October rain started to fall.

Setting aside her teacup, Selene rose and walked to the silk hangings. Behind her, the princess asked, "When do you leave?"

"Tomorrow."

"Then you have found a good route?"

Selene did not turn around but spoke as if addressing the rain. "Wulf and I are joining the caravan of a man named Gupta. He is very familiar with the road through Armenia, and he has paid protection to the mountain bandits. He promises we shall reach the Black Sea in safety."

"And then?"

Selene stared a moment longer at the rain, then turned to the princess. "On the Cappodocian coast Wulf will take a ship across the sea to the Danube River. But I shall turn southward on the road through Cilicia. I shall be in Antioch before spring."

The two women stared at one another across the room. "I shall miss you," Rani said.

"And I, you . . ."

The princess had to look away. It had crossed her mind to try to persuade Selene to stay in Persia for a while, but she knew all about Andreas, about the ivory rose that held the key to Selene's identity, about Selene's vow to a dying woman to seek her destiny. A full and promising future stretched before Selene, a future Rani had no right to deny her. Rani did not really understand about futures: she did not have one now, nor had she ever had one. From the hour of her birth as a girl child, Rani's course had been set for her—to marry, to have babies, to be kept ignorant and uneducated.

Once, long ago, Rani had cursed her fate. But the years had tempered her bitterness and she had learned to be thankful for what she had. Although husbandless and childless, a useless creature in this part of the world, contemptible even, she was alive nonetheless, able to read books and converse with learned men. Selene's arrival, however, had unburied the old anger and resentment; restricted to a couch and these few rooms, Rani cursed anew the society that had spawned her.

She also thought: *I was wrong. Selene is not the one prophesied in the stars. The one who is going to take Dr. Chandra away . . .*

The two women retreated into silence, the princess on her couch, Selene standing looking out at the rain, together in the physical sense but spiritually miles apart. While Rani was already mourning the departure of her newly found friend, Selene was struggling with the terrible decision she was going to have to make.

For I can no longer leave with Wulf, she thought forlornly. *Yesterday I could have gone to Armenia with him; but today everything is different.*

Selene turned and regarded Rani, wondering if she should confess her secret to the princess, ask her advice. In these few weeks Selene had come to appreciate Rani's quiet strength and wisdom. To be a prisoner of that body and to live alone in this room for so many years! Only a woman of great internal strength, Selene suspected, could survive with her dignity and integrity.

What must it have been like? Selene wondered, as she stood by the terrace staring at Rani's bowed head, a small round head with graying black hair knotted at the neck. *What has it been like to live in these rooms for thirty years, visited by only one person, Dr. Chandra?*

Dr. Chandra . . .

Once again that enigmatic little man insinuated himself into her thoughts. Quiet and unobtrusive though he was, Dr. Chandra plagued Selene's mind like a moth circling a flame.

What was it about him that seemed to prickle her so? In these past weeks he had spoken but few words to Selene. She suspected it was because it was beneath him to address a woman like herself: foreign, lowborn. And yet, Selene knew, he was curious about her. Whenever she visited the pavilion, Dr. Chandra was there, standing apart, watching her. And almost every evening when Selene came to visit the princess, Rani asked questions about something Selene had done that day with a patient, something Dr. Chandra had observed and reported to the princess.

Like the morning Selene had used the "touch" on Nimrod.

Although the scalp wound had healed well, his days of lying in bed had caused a pooling of fluid in his lungs. None of the efforts of the doctors and attendants had helped; the old Astrologer had coughed and rattled and wheezed in an alarming way. Since medicine and mist-tents seemed to be of no help, Selene had suggested she might try her "touch," adding that while it did not always work, it also never caused harm.

So she had stood over the Astrologer's bed, stretched out her arms, conjured up the image of the flame, and had moved her hands up and down his body. The "touch" had had a calming effect on Nimrod. He began to wheeze less and ceased to struggle for breath; after a few days his lungs dried up and he was on the road to recovery.

Dr. Chandra had watched Selene perform her "touch," and that evening Rani had asked her about it.

Selene had discovered Rani was very interested in healing. She was also surprisingly knowledgeable on the subject. One afternoon, Selene had observed a sheep being brought into the pavilion. It had been led to a bedside where the patient had breathed into its nostrils, and then the sheep had been led away. That evening Selene had asked the princess about it, and Rani had said, "It is a way of making a difficult diagnosis. The sheep was taken afterward to the temple and slaughtered, and its liver was examined to see what the patient's ailment was."

"You know a lot about medicine," Selene had said that evening, and the princess, looking away, had replied vaguely, "My only friend is a physician."

Now, as Selene walked away from the rain and came to join her, Rani said, "You and Wulf will leave in this wet weather?"

"We must, if we are to miss the worst snows." Selene picked up her teacup, held it to her lips for a moment, then put it down on the table and said, "Rani, I have a problem."

"What is it?"

Selene said softly, "I'm going to have a baby."

Rani looked at her in surprise, then reached out to clasp Selene's hand. "The gods have blessed you, my dear! It is not an occasion for sadness!"

"But it is. Don't you see? I can't go with Wulf! I can't travel now!"

Rani's smile faded into a frown. "I see. Of course. What does Wulf say? Will he delay the trip?"

"I haven't told Wulf yet."

"Why not?"

"Because if I tell him I'm pregnant, he'll stay here. He won't go with Gupta."

"Then you can both leave after the baby is born."

Selene shook her head. "It will be a strenuous journey. A baby would hamper us. We would have to wait until it was old enough to withstand the rigors of travel before we could leave Persia. And then what, after that? Where would we go? What sort of a family would we be? Wulf has his family in Germany, a wife and son he must return to. And I must return to Antioch, and Andreas. How would we live, the two of us with a baby? This was not meant to happen, Rani. Wulf and I were not meant to be together forever."

Seeing the tears in her friend's eyes caused a pain in Rani's heart. "Then you must not tell him," she said gently. "For both your sakes. You must give him an excuse for your staying here. You must insist that he go on alone."

"How can I keep it from him?" Selene whispered. "How can I keep such a secret? He has a right to know!"

A dark look came over Rani's face as she thought: *Secrets. I have borne my awful secret for thirty-six years, and only one person knows of it. Nimrod. Nimrod knows . . .*

Selene said, "It would be selfish of me to tell Wulf about the baby. Because then I know he would stay with me. I know that if he knew about the baby, he would not leave Persia. But he must go *now,* back to his people, who need him. And I must return to Syria and find Andreas. I love

Wulf, Rani, but it is Andreas I am pledged to body and soul. They are two different men and I love them in two different ways. Wulf was with me in my exile; I saved his life, and he saved mine. The bond we created between us is unique and special. But we follow different destinies. Oh, Rani," Selene sighed. "What am I to do?"

But the princess did not immediately reply. She was staring at Selene with a shocked expression, having just realized something. When she finally did speak, it was to whisper, "By the gods, it *is* you after all . . ."

Selene looked at her.

"*You* will be the end of Dr. Chandra," Rani said in a rush. "Selene, what will you do after the baby is born? Where will you go?"

"To Antioch. When the baby is strong enough, and by a southern route. Lasha's soldiers will not be looking for a woman alone with an infant—"

"Take me with you!"

"Take you—?"

"Let me go with you to the West, Selene! Let me escape from this prison! I want to see the world. I want to see *your* world! Selene, listen." Rani spoke hurriedly, her face flushing with excitement. "Nimrod told me that a four-eyed person would come to this palace and end Dr. Chandra's life here. You are that person, Selene. You and the child within you together have four eyes."

Selene was confused. "But what have *I* to do with Dr. Chandra?"

"You are planning to go away from here, are you not? If I go with you, then Dr. Chandra's existence will end and the prophecy will be fulfilled."

"I don't understand."

Rani clapped her hands and Miko, the old handmaiden, appeared. The princess spoke a few words to her in Parsi, bringing a look of surprise to Miko's face, then Rani said to Selene, "I am going to tell you a secret that no one knows, except for my personal slaves and Nimrod."

Puzzled, Selene watched as old Miko returned with a bundle in her arms. After placing it near the princess, she retreated, a dubious look on her face; then Rani startled Selene by suddenly throwing off the covers and swinging her legs over the side of the couch.

"Here," Rani said, reaching for the cloth that covered the bundle, "is Dr. Chandra."

To Selene's further astonishment, Rani whipped the cloth away and revealed, on top of folded garments Selene recognized from the pavilion —the lemon-colored jacket and turban—an enormous bushy black beard.

"Look," Rani said as she held the beard up to her face. "Do you understand now?"

Selene's eyes grew wide. "You?" she said. *"You're* Dr. Chandra?"

Rani stood up from the couch, dropped the false beard onto it, and walked to the draperies.

"I have wanted to be a healer for as long as I can remember," the princess said as she watched the gently falling rain. "Even as a small child, I was always taking care of injured animals. I could not accept the injustice of the world into which I had been born, a world that believes a woman is beneath the dignity of the healing profession.

"I was a willful child. My father and I had some terrible fights. I wanted to go to one of the big schools of medicine in Madras or Peshawar. I might as well have been asking for the moon! When he told me I was being sent to Persia to marry a prince, I locked myself in my room and tried to starve myself. I was twelve years old and I knew what I wanted to do with my life."

Rani turned and smiled at Selene. "Marrying a fat prince and having his babies was not in my plan."

Selene listened in fascination. As Rani confessed to her deception—that she had these past thirty years lived two identities, one as Dr. Chandra—many pieces of the puzzle began to fall into place: why Rani knew so much about medicine, why she had seemed to know the smallest detail of Selene's activities in the pavilion, why Selene had never encountered Dr. Chandra in the princess's apartment, and why Dr. Chandra had rarely spoken to her.

"I made sure that no one saw me in both guises," Rani explained. "Those who work with Dr. Chandra have never met the princess. Aside from Nimrod, you and Wulf were the first people in thirty years to see me as both the princess and the man."

Selene then revealed to the princess her puzzlement over Rani's "paralysis"; she told her of the test on the sole of the foot Andreas had taught her. "In a healthy leg, when the sole of the foot is stroked, the toes curl downward reflexively. In a paralyzed leg they do not. *Your* toes curled downward. I found that mystifying."

Selene rose from the couch and joined Rani at the edge of the rainswept terrace. "What happened when you were first brought here?" she asked.

"I tried to run away at first," the princess said, her small brown hand resting on the drapery. "I thought I could disguise myself as a boy and travel the world. I had a very restless spirit . . . " She sighed. "But I was confined to my room until the eve of the wedding. As a desperate measure, I invented a 'fever' and pretended afterward that I could not walk. I knew that no man would want me then."

She turned to Selene. "We do not know of your foot reflex here in

Persia. If we had, perhaps my deception would have been found out long ago. I suffered the pinchings and prickings of the doctors until I was left alone and finally forgotten. The prince married someone else and I became the Pitied One."

Rani's soft voice joined the whisper of the rain on the leaves and grass of the terrace. She spoke of her first six years of solitude, of making friends with the Astrologer when he came to cast her horoscope, of learning to read and write, and finally, when she was eighteen, of the plan she devised in order to give her freedom about the palace.

"Nimrod helped me. He brought me man's clothing and a false beard and introduced me in the pavilion as Dr. Chandra. I stayed in the background, watching, saying little and learning. It was my plan to leave the palace as Dr. Chandra and travel to the great cities of learning. But . . . somehow, that never came to pass."

Rani explained how she had gradually come to enjoy her dual existence in the palace—a respected physician by day and enjoying men's privileges, a pampered princess by night. "My slaves kept visitors away, telling them that I slept in the daytime. But really, I was forgotten. Few people tried to see me. It was an ideal situation. I was free to study whatever I wished. All the things forbidden to women: books, the patients in the pavilion, the stars above Nimrod's celestial observatory. The only price I had to pay for all this . . . was the normal life of a woman. I knew long ago that once I embarked upon this dual road, I would forever deny myself the chance to fall in love, to be loved and taken care of by a man, to have children. I would have been punished, put to death, if it had been discovered that I had been disguising myself as a man. So . . . "

She sighed wistfully. "When I did think I was going to fall in love, when a doctor in the pavilion began to find his way into my heart, I would turn myself against him. No one knew of this, of course. Least of all the handsome young doctor I fell in love with years ago. He left the palace some time past . . . "

"Why did you never leave?" Selene asked gently.

Rani turned away from the rain to face Selene. "Why should I have left? After a while, it seemed such an ideal life, with the exception of the sacrifice I spoke of, that I no longer felt the draw of the outside world. But now I do, Selene, because of you! I realize that I have learned everything I can here, and that the time has come for me to see the world. When Nimrod told me that my stars predicted a departure from this existence, I was gripped with dread. Was I to leave? I wondered. And if so, to what place? Or was I to die? And then *you* came to me." She reached out and touched Selene's arm. "You reminded me of my long-forgotten childhood ambition. To see the world."

Her brown eyes grew moist. "Selene," Rani whispered urgently, "there is so much I want to see, so much I want to do. I can learn so much, I can *offer* so much. I am forty-eight years old, it is time for my life to begin. Selene, *take me with you.*"

C H A P T E R 4 1

S elene and Wulf had argued all through the night and now they were saying farewell.

In the end Wulf had relented. Selene wanted to stay in Persia, she had said, and then travel southward in the spring. But he must go on; Gaius Vatinius was back in the Rhineland, and Wulf had been away too long. "You must ride the winds that blow through your soul," Selene had said to him, "and I must follow where my destiny leads." They had argued and then they had wept and now they were embracing for the last time as dawn broke in orange hues on the eastern horizon.

As she clung to him, Selene thought: *This is not just the beginning of a new day, but of a new life.* "Write a letter to Andreas," Rani had urged, "and we will send it by royal courier. I shall give instructions that the carrier is to search Antioch for him. By spring, Selene, you will have your reply."

So Selene held on to Wulf and cried into his neck. Already she could feel their two years together starting to slide away from her; clutching him, feeling his physical presence, she felt him already beginning to dissolve into the memory he would become.

Sweet friend of my exile, whispered her mind, *you will be with me always, in my heart, and in the child I carry . . .*

BOOK VI

JERUSALEM

CHAPTER 42

The girl was being led through the streets on a rope, her hands tied behind her. An angry mob followed, gathering rocks and stones along the way.

Suddenly realizing what was about to happen, Selene stopped and turned around. Where *were* they?

With growing anxiousness she searched the crowded street for the two familiar heads, Rani's small gray one moving alongside Ulrika's teak-colored curls. Already they had been separated from Selene several times since they entered Jerusalem, and Selene was growing alarmed. She did not like this noisy, congested city, and the volatile mood of its population frightened her.

"Rani!" she cried, spotting them at last. "Ulrika! I'm over here!"

But the mob that was following the tethered girl separated them. Selene gestured for her two companions to stay where they were, to try to duck into a doorway, but she saw to her horror that they were being pulled along by the human tide. *No!* Selene thought. *Ulrika must not see this!*

Selene and Rani and Ulrika were part of the multitude pouring in from the Damascus Gate. Jerusalem was overcrowded because of the spring rites. Outside the city walls a beautiful springtime painted Judea in rich colors. The countryside was wild with tulips and yellow crocuses and blood-red anemones; farmers were in the orchards pruning trees; vines were in flower and green fruit was hanging from the fig trees. But inside the city walls pilgrims crammed the streets and taverns and hostels, and passions were running high; tempers were short and explosive.

What had the girl done, Selene wondered, to be dragged through the streets this way?

Selene tried to push against the mob toward Rani and her daughter, but the angry tide was too strong. Then, to Selene's shock, someone thrust a rock into her hand.

"Rani!" she called again, but the crowd, having reached the end of the street, surged into a small square, nearly carrying Selene off her feet. She saw Rani's head disappear, and then Ulrika's.

The mob, faces distorted in fury, spilled into the little sunlit square as the girl on the rope was dragged to a far wall.

"No," whispered Selene as she tried to fight her way through the press of bodies. When her medicine box was nearly yanked from her shoulder she swung it around and clutched it to her chest. Faces and shoulders and flailing arms blocked her view; she could not see Rani, and Ulrika, too, had vanished.

At the edge of the mob, in the space cleared around the tethered girl, someone was addressing the crowd. He was using words like "whore," "sinner," and "traitor." And the people shouted in response. In sudden fear, Selene redoubled her efforts to break through, to get her daughter away from the scene that was about to happen. But the bodies were packed in so tightly, men and women and even children, that Selene was immobilized.

In spite of herself, she turned in the direction of the cleared space and could see, between heads, the girl standing with her head bowed.

She's just a child, Selene thought.

The man who was addressing the crowd finally shouted words of damnation, which Selene could only barely hear—something about "the law," "scriptures." And then, to her horror, she saw him leave the space and join the crowd.

When the first stone flew, Selene stared with wide eyes, unable to move, buffeted by the mob. It missed the girl, who stood with head bent, hands tied behind her back. The second stone hit her shoulder; she made no move to try to defend herself.

As more rocks were thrown, many just missing the girl or grazing her, Selene felt the warmth of the spring day turn to a dreadful chill. She saw a frail-looking old woman on the edge of the mob, white hair peeking out from under her veil, throw a stone that landed squarely on the girl's face.

There was fire in the old woman's eyes, and she wore a grimace that could have been read as pain or joy.

The rain of stones grew heavier, and the girl sank to her knees. A trickle of blood appeared on her forehead.

"Whore!" the mob shouted. "Traitor!"

And then, just when Selene thought the worst was about to happen, that the fatal rock was going to hit, two Roman soldiers appeared suddenly from a side street, their red cloaks flying, their swords flashing in the sun. They ran into the shower of stones, and protecting themselves with their shields, shouted at the crowd to stop. Their appearance seemed only to incite the mob all the more. The crowd ebbed forward as if to grab the two soldiers, then flowed back when the swords were leveled.

Selene looked around frantically for Rani and Ulrika. She felt the hatred of the crowd boil up like a tangible thing.

One of the soldiers dropped back and shielded the girl with his body. There was a gash on his arm, Selene saw, where a sharp stone had struck. His comrade was fighting the crowd alone, and losing.

And then, suddenly, there were red cloaks everywhere, and swords and shields, and people started to scream and run in panic. Selene, knocked this way and that, tried to hold her ground, searching for Rani and Ulrika; she was shoved back against a wall, pinned there as men and women stampeded like wild animals.

The Roman soldiers hacked their way through as if cutting a jungle trail until soon the small square was cleared and an unearthly silence fell.

"Ulrika!" Selene cried, seeing Rani and the child step out from a doorway.

"Mama!" The girl, tan curls flying, came running and flung her arms around Selene's waist. Rani was slow in coming, and she limped.

"Are you all right?" Selene asked, holding her daughter away from her.

"Yes, Mama!" Ulrika's cheeks were bright red and her pale blue eyes were wide with excitement. Selene breathed a sigh of relief; the child had not seen much, had not understood.

When Selene turned to Rani, she saw that her friend was not coming to join her but had gone across the square to where the girl who was crying hysterically, was being cut loose from her bonds. When her hands were free she flung herself upon a soldier lying unconscious on the cobblestones. He was the soldier who had shielded her with his body, Selene realized when she came up, her hand holding Ulrika's tightly. And his helmet had come off, revealing a bad cut on his head.

"There, there, missy," one of the newly arrived soldiers said, a gray-haired veteran who was trying to pry the girl off his fallen comrade.

"He's dead!" she cried. "Cornelius is dead!"

Rani was there at once, on her knees and examining the fallen soldier. "No, he is not dead," she said in heavily accented Aramaic. "But he needs immediate attention."

"We'll take care o' that," the veteran said amiably, signaling to two other soldiers to come and get their friend.

"We can help," Selene said, as she knelt by the hysterical girl and tried to calm her.

"No, 's all right. No need to bother. We'll set Cornelius straight. Come on then, you two."

When the weeping girl tried to follow the soldiers out of the square, the veteran gently pushed her back, and Selene and Rani took her by the arms and led her to a small fountain at the end of a side street. They washed her wounds and put ointment on them; once her crying finally subsided, they learned that her name was Elizabeth and that the fallen soldier, Cornelius, was the boy she loved.

"But they found out," she said unhappily, fingering the bloodstains on her dress. "They had no right to do that to me. They judged me wrongly. It is *not* written in the Law; I have done nothing wrong. But they hate Romans and so they think that makes me a traitor."

They walked her home, which was a short distance from the square, and when they reached her door she asked them to come inside. "You've been kind to me. And you tried to help Cornelius."

But Selene observed the position of the sun and said, "We thank you, but we have to find lodgings for the night. We have only just arrived in Jerusalem."

"Oh, but you will never find a room now!" Elizabeth said. "There is never room during Passover. And certainly not for *three* of you. Please stay with me, I have plenty of room in my house. And I would be honored."

Selene could not refuse: the afternoon was on the wane, Ulrika was getting sleepy and Rani's foot was hurting because someone in the mob had stepped on it.

Arriving that morning at the Damascus Gate, Selene and Rani had left their traveling packs with the caravan, which was resting before continuing on to Caesarea. Elizabeth paid two neighbor boys to go and fetch them.

While Selene put together a simple supper of bread and olives and cheese, Rani examined Elizabeth's wounds and dressed them with bread mold and fresh bandages. She also had Elizabeth drink a tranquilizing tea made of red clover blossoms. Ulrika, used to being taken in by strangers and spending the night under an unfamiliar roof, retreated to a corner, where she sat next to a large loom and played with a doll in her lap.

Halfway through supper Elizabeth started to weep. Rani put an arm around her shoulders, and Selene said, "Is there a friend we can send for?"

Elizabeth startled them with a vehement reply: "Oh yes, I have friends! I live here alone, you know, ever since my mother died, but I own this house and I earn a good living from my weaving, and I have *many* friends. There is Rebecca across the street, and Rachel who lives down the way, and the Rabbi's wife—" Elizabeth's face grew red with rage. "But one of them *told* on me! One of them told about Cornelius!"

She burst into tears again, cried for a few moments, then said quietly, "We are *not* lovers. Whoever told my secret lied. I met Cornelius in the marketplace. I thought he was so handsome. I started watching for him, and he for me. Soon we started going for walks outside the city. We were always careful about not being seen. But one of my so-called friends saw us because soon they were all warning me to stop seeing him. We aren't lovers! We have never even kissed! But they have ugly minds. My friends turned against me. Romans are our enemies, they say. Our conquerors. By befriending Cornelius, they say, I am a traitor to my own people."

Elizabeth dried her eyes and said, "Why is love so painful?"

Suddenly unable to swallow, Selene put down her bread and stared at the rough surface of the table.

Why is love so painful?

She felt a tightness in her chest again as she thought of Andreas.

She had gone back to Antioch at last . . .

Elizabeth was curious about her guests. She looked at Ulrika, a beautiful little girl with eyes the color of long summer days, and thought her a strangely quiet and melancholy child.

"Your daughter is lovely," Elizabeth said to Selene, and her face exhibited a question Selene had seen many times in the seven years they had traveled since leaving Persia.

"Ulrika's father died before she was born."

She had said it so often that sometimes she almost believed it. The truth —that Wulf had left Persia over nine years ago without knowing of Selene's pregnancy—she had told no one, not even Ulrika.

Speaking the rote-words now triggered a memory. They had stopped a while in Petra before coming up to Jerusalem, and one day Ulrika had run in crying because a neighborhood bully had called her a bastard.

"He says a bastard doesn't have a father," Ulrika had cried, "and because *I* don't have a father, he says that makes me a bastard."

Selene had gathered the child into her arms and said, "You mustn't listen to what others say, Ulrika, because they speak out of ignorance. You *do* have a father, but he died and now he's with the Goddess."

Rani, sitting at a table rolling pills, had given Selene a dubious look. When are you going to tell her the truth? the look had said.

When Ulrika was very little and had started asking questions, Selene had taught her what she knew of Wulf's people. Ulrika knew about the World Tree, and the Land of the Frost Giants, and Middle Earth where Odin dwelt. And she knew she was named for her German grandmother, the *saga* of the tribe, whose name was Ulrika, which means "wolf-power." The child also knew her father had been a prince of his people.

But that was the only truth Selene had told her daughter. "How can I make a small child understand why her father is not here?" she had said to Rani that night in Petra. "How do I tell her that he went away, to another place? That he has another family? How do I make her see why I could not tell him about her? She would hate me for having let him go away, and she wouldn't understand why I had to. It's better to tell her that he's dead. For now. When she's older I'll tell her the truth."

"When will that be?" Rani had asked, not entirely sure Selene was doing the right thing.

When will that be? Selene asked herself now as she helped Elizabeth gather up their plates and clear the table. Certainly not yet. Ulrika is only nine years old. On her Dressing Day, when she turns sixteen, I will tell her the truth.

But Ulrika was always asking questions about her father; lately, to an almost obsessive degree. So that Selene was beginning to wonder if she should have told her daughter the truth, long ago, on that night in Petra, or even tonight, now, in Elizabeth's house. Because Ulrika had come to deify her father; in her child's mind, Selene knew, Wulf was some sort of hero-god; Ulrika couldn't get enough of hearing about his adventures. Perhaps, Selene thought, if Ulrika knew the truth, Wulf would seem more human to her, and she would worship him less.

And despise me for having let him go . . .

As Selene listened to the silent Jerusalem night beyond the walls, she wondered if Wulf had reached his forests, if he had found his wife and family, if he had finally come face to face with Gaius Vatinius and exacted his revenge.

"Where have you come from?" Elizabeth asked, as she brought goblets of wine.

"We have come lately from Palmyra," Selene said, thankful for the wine and for the tranquillity of Elizabeth's little house after their long journey through the desert. "But before that . . . Persia."

"Persia!" Elizabeth said. "But that is on the other side of the world!"

Yes it is, Selene thought. *Miles from here, and a lifetime away.* It had been almost a decade since she first set foot on Persian soil, after escaping down the river from Babylon.

Two years ago, after yearning and dreaming of it, of setting all her hopes and plans on it, Selene had at last gone back to Antioch . . .

"Have you come to Jerusalem for the Holy Week?" Elizabeth asked.

"No," Selene said quietly. "Jerusalem is but a temporary stopping place along our journey. We have been traveling for seven years."

"Where are you going?"

"To Egypt."

"And what is in Egypt?"

Selene's face took on a faraway expression. What indeed was in Egypt? "I am searching for my family," she said in a distant voice. "I was born in Palmyra, but my parents came from Alexandria. I hope to find some trace of them there." *And,* she added to herself, *to find Andreas.*

Seven months before, in August, Selene and Rani had gone to Palmyra, thirteen years almost to the day since the attack on the caravan and Selene's abduction to the palace of Magna. She had made inquiries in Palmyra, and had, by great good fortune, found a man who recalled the Roman and his pregnant wife, and that fateful windy night twenty-seven years before.

He remembered it because it had been to his father's inn that the caravan from Alexandria had come, bringing the aristocratic Roman and his wife, who was in labor. The innkeeper had directed the couple to the house of a healer-woman on the outskirts of the city and he had given them two donkeys from his stable. When Selene and Rani remarked it was strange that the Palmyrene should remember such a small event after all these years, he went on to say: "Soon after the Roman and his wife departed, soldiers came to the inn, demanding to know where the two had gone. My father told them of the healer-woman, and one of the soldiers grabbed me, saying that I would lead them to the house. I was a boy at the time, and terrified. I led them to the healer-woman's house and then I hid by a window and watched what they did. They killed the Roman in cold blood and dragged the young mother from childbed. *That* is why I remember that night."

The soldiers had taken the young woman and the baby alive, the Palmyrene said. He did not know what became of the healer-woman.

"I think I shall not rest," Selene said to Elizabeth, who sat spellbound in the lamplight, "until I find out what happened to them—to my mother and my twin brother. I must know if they are alive, or even if they are dead. And who my family is, what my bloodline is. They were possibly of noble blood . . ."

"And you have no clue?" Elizabeth asked. "Nothing at all to link you with your family?"

"I had something once," Selene said softly. "But I gave it to someone . . ."

Selene and Rani had been delayed in Persia for two years after Ulrika was born: first because there had been an epidemic which had restricted travel out of the region, and then because they had been awaiting word from Andreas through the royal courier.

The letter carrier had returned to Persia in the spring to report that he had searched the city of Antioch and had been unable to find a physician named Andreas, or anyone who knew of him. He had given Selene her letter back, unopened.

Elizabeth was intrigued by her guests. From their appearance, one would guess that they were ordinary travelers. Both were garbed in long linen dresses with hooded cloaks that could cover their heads and conceal their faces. Like all travelers, each had a dried gourd tied to her belt, empty but for a heavy stone inside that would sink it whenever water needed to be drawn up from a well. Each also had a small dagger at her waist, and Elizabeth suspected they must be concealing bags of coins. But here their similarity to ordinary women ended.

Elizabeth could not curb her curiosity. "How is it that you are able to travel so freely?" she asked.

"We are healers," Rani explained. "We are able to earn our way." That she was very rich Rani kept to herself. When she had left the pleasure-palace, Rani had taken her wealth with her, and they carried it with them now, sewn into the hems of their clothing and inside goatskins disguised to look like waterbags.

"Healers!" said Elizabeth. "That is why you were able to help me, why you carry such wonderful medicines." Her eyes were envious. "You can travel wherever you want to, and you know that you will always be welcome wherever you go."

Yes, Selene thought. *Wherever we go . . .* For there would be no rest, no place she would call home, until she found Andreas.

After Antioch, Selene and Rani had gone to Palmyra on the thin hope that Andreas had remained there, after searching for Selene thirteen years ago. And then, not finding him, Selene had known where she must go next: to Alexandria, to the great School of Medicine Andreas had attended years ago. His sea travels had begun from Alexandria, Selene reasoned; perhaps he would be drawn back there.

Again Selene saw the hands of the gods guiding her. It could be no accident that the answers to her two quests—finding her identity and being reunited with Andreas—should lie in the same city. With each day that dawned, each mile she covered, Selene grew increasingly more certain that the visions of her delirium of ten years before had foretold the truth: that, in some as yet unknown way, her identity and her calling as a healer were linked.

But surely that road must end soon! Surely the gods must see the wealth of knowledge Selene now brought with her, gathered along the way during her strange odyssey!

When they left Persia, Selene and Rani had intended to go directly to Antioch, but there had been obstacles and delays along the way—a drought in one city, a quarantine in another, a border war sealing off all roads, Ulrika's pneumonia—so that their westward trek had been stretched into seven long years. But during that time Selene and Rani had not been idle. In each town or city or oasis they had talked with healers, with medical men, with tribal shamans, learning new ways, keeping the good and discarding the useless. They had visited the Gilgamesh Square in Babylon and learned from physicians who passed through; in Palmyra they had conversed with the priests of Aesculapius; and finally, only days ago, as they had come up from Petra and passed along the western shore of the Dead Sea, they had spent a night at a monastery and had visited the clean little *infirmaria* where the monks tended their sick brothers.

Selene thought that surely she was ready now. Surely the gods would see that she must soon begin her life and her work with Andreas.

Rani broke the silence. "You must rest now," she said to Elizabeth. "Your body has suffered a shock. You must sleep, you must allow yourself to heal."

CHAPTER 43

Selene limped as she climbed the stairs to the upper room of Elizabeth's little house. Her thigh ached—the old arrow wound of long ago; it frequently troubled her after a strenuous day.

The room was thick with lamb-smell from the bags of fleece stored here, as Elizabeth spun her own wool for the cloth she wove. Ulrika was already asleep among the fleeces, curled on her side on a mat, a blanket over her.

Selene removed her sandals and settled down next to the child, thinking:

Soon, my little one, our wandering will be over, and you will live in a house and have a proper life like any other little girl. Soon, soon . . .

Not that Ulrika ever complained. As if born to the wandering life, the nine-year-old accepted the temporary residences and months on the road as a matter of course. Neither did she question their unusual way of life; it was simply what her mother and Aunt Rani did. Ulrika never envied other little girls, children she encountered in foreign cities who lived in houses and who had the same friends year after year. Indeed, Ulrika could consider herself lucky, because her Aunt Rani was like having two mothers.

It was a wonderful life for a little girl; there was always something new, something exciting happening. And people were always giving Ulrika treats, especially after Selene or Rani cured someone, and Ulrika could never complain of being neglected because her mother and Rani were always teaching her how to do things, how to harvest herbs and what they were used for. And whenever she was frightened, such as during thunderstorms, Selene and Rani were there to take her into bed between them.

A perfect life, really, for a child, and full of love and security and adventure. But Ulrika cried herself to sleep every night, and Selene and Rani were unaware of it.

Selene reached out in the darkness, and out of habit, felt the child's forehead. Children were so vulnerable, such easy victims to illness. The terrible cough that had stricken Ulrika in Antioch, which had turned into pneumonia, had put such a fear into Selene that she was now overly cautious, constantly watching her little girl for the slightest sign or symptom, even though the nightmarish episode had happened two years ago.

Ulrika's forehead was warm and dry. Selene sighed and laid her arm over her daughter's strong, sturdy body. At nine, Ulrika was already as tall as Rani; in adulthood she would no doubt be taller than Selene, who was herself a tall woman. It was the Wulf-part of her that made her so, just as Selene knew the eyes were his, and the strong cheekbones which were just beginning to form. People tended to stare at Ulrika; her hair was an unusual color, not blond, but the ocher of the desert at sunset, and her eyes were a blue so pale they were almost colorless. Selene suspected that Ulrika was going to be a handsome woman someday, maybe even beautiful.

Was ever a mother so lucky? Selene often asked herself. *To be blessed with such a quiet, contented child?*

I think not, she told herself now, hugging the girl, unaware that Ulrika's contentment was in fact a façade, a happy show to cover up a secret pain. What Selene and Rani did not see, in their increasingly growing involvement with healing, was that the smiling little girl in their midst was slowly withdrawing from them, and that the childish joy they thought burned in

her heart had for a long time now been replaced by a strange melancholy.
Ulrika was turning into a sad, serious, lost little girl.

After folding her clothes and placing them neatly at the foot of her mat,
Rani took her small statue of Dhanvantari, the Hindu god of healing, and
placed it on the floor by her pillow. Dhanvantari had come all these miles
from Persia with her, and his healing power was still strong.

Seeing that Selene had lain down beside Ulrika and had closed her eyes,
Rani snuffed out the one lamp still burning and crept under her blanket.
Sleep, she knew, would not come for a long time, not because she was not
tired—she was, in fact, exhausted—but because it had been Rani's habit
for over twenty years to meditate before falling asleep.

She meditated now, focusing her mind on the beacon that glowed on
her horizon—shining, beckoning. She was going to see it at last, the great
School of Medicine in Alexandria!

Rani was completely gray now, and she walked a little more slowly. But,
at fifty-seven—an impressively advanced age—her eyes were still good and
her mind sharp, and her hands as nimble as ever. It was the vision of that
school in Alexandria, she knew, that kept her young; the thought of the
great learning and research that went on there. A greater school even than
those of Madras and Peshawar, to which she had so long ago begged her
father to send her.

Since the day she had taken her first step outside the pleasure-palace,
seven years before, Princess Rani had not looked back. But she looked back
now because it was safe to do so, and because it was appropriate—it was
seven years ago to this very day that she and Selene and two-year-old Ulrika
had passed through the palace gates on the road to freedom.

Rani recalled with fondness her farewell to Nimrod, her only friend for
thirty-six years. He had cried—and he had kissed her for the first time, the
only kiss from a man Rani had ever known. And then he had given her
as a parting gift his most treasured possession, a magic stone.

It was a turquoise the size of a lemon slice, and had the power to grant
good fortune to whoever possessed it. Its color changed mysteriously from
green to robin's-egg blue when the luck was used. There was a rusty veining
on one side that at first resembled two snakes twining up a tree—symbol
of physicians and healers everywhere. But on closer look, it appeared to
be a woman standing with her arms outstretched.

And has it not brought me luck? Rani asked herself in the dark and silent
night of Jerusalem. *Freed from my prison and seeing the world at last? All
of my dreams coming true? Now if only . . .*

Yes. If only her friend's dreams could also come true, then life would be perfect indeed. But Selene pursued an elusive dream, Rani believed, quite possibly one she would never attain.

Rani wished Selene would abandon her search for Andreas, that her restless spirit could find peace. For, as long as the memory of Andreas beckoned, Selene would never achieve total contentment in this life. Also, there was the obsessive quest for her identity which, by an ironic twist, was tied up with Andreas: He possessed the ivory rose that contained Selene's birth legacy.

As Rani drifted off to sleep, she thought: *Perhaps Selene will find an ending at last in Alexandria. And Alexandria lies just over the next horizon, in Egypt.*

━━━

Selene was still lying awake in the darkness, listening to the silence of Jerusalem's holiest night. She was thinking again of Antioch, and what a terrible shock she had received there.

What hope the sight of Antioch had awakened in her! How her heart had raced, as she walked those familiar streets, and then to the upper city, to the spot where the rug merchant had fallen. How she had hurried to the nearby street where Andreas's villa had stood. And then!

To stand before a strange house and be told incredible news: that the villa had burned down years ago, that nothing was known about any previous occupants.

It had nearly devastated her. Selene had subsisted on the hope that the royal courier had been wrong, or lazy, that he had *not* searched for the addressee of her letter, that it was some terrible mistake and that Andreas still lived here, in this house, waiting for Selene to come back to him.

With a heavy heart, Selene had taken Rani and her daughter down into the poor quarter of Antioch, to the house where Selene had grown up. She wanted Ulrika to see it. Standing in front of the little courtyard, Selene could almost see two ghosts working in the sunshine—Mera and a young Selene. She was amazed to discover how small the house was.

Selene had left Antioch sad and depressed. What had she been hoping to find? Her youth? A dream? Had she expected to find the past, preserved as it was in her mind, when so much had changed in her own life? *The past, once past, can never be brought back,* she thought, wondering how Ulrika would someday look back on *her* childhood, peculiar odyssey that it was.

She thought back to the night Ulrika was born, a cold and rainy March night, nine years ago. According to Persian custom, a Zoroastrian priest had presided over the birth, himself delivering the baby from the womb. As he did so, Selene had had a strange experience.

At the peak of her contractions, when her body felt as if it were overripe and bursting, she had seen more visions. Suddenly she was no longer lying on a bed in a Persian pleasure-palace but upon a pallet in a simple house. The mud-brick walls shuddered in the howling wind; she felt the gentle touch of Mera; she saw the shadowy face of the handsome Roman as he looked on with love and worry. It had been as if Selene were experiencing her own birth, were her own mother, in that little house on the outskirts of Palmyra.

But how could that be? Selene had pondered it many times. Had it been her imagination, sparked by the drama of childbirth? Or was there truly some link, some spiritual connection that existed beyond this plane, and was passed down through the generations, an ancestral memory buried in the unconscious that was brought out at times such as this? Had Selene's mother, while giving birth to the twins, seen her own mother's labor? And if so, in what house, in what city, in what year?

Selene often studied Ulrika, certain that she saw a shadow of Mera in that still-forming face, even though she knew it was not possible, that there was not a drop of that good woman's blood flowing in Ulrika's veins. But the blood of another grandmother—who was she? Was she Roman? Egyptian? And what was her name?

A noise, jarring in that peaceful night, disturbed Selene's thoughts. She lifted her head and listened. A woman was weeping. Downstairs. It sounded like Elizabeth.

Glancing over at Rani, and then down at Ulrika, both of whom slept the deep, impenetrable sleep of the elderly and the young, Selene crept out from under the blankets and stole downstairs.

She found Elizabeth sitting in the middle of the room, weeping as if her heart were going to break. The bandage on her arm, Selene saw, was starting to spot with fresh blood.

Selene picked up her medicine box which stood on the table, and went to sit with Elizabeth on the carpet. "You've hurt yourself," she said gently. "Let me take care of this."

But Elizabeth continued to cry, each sob racking her thin body. It was such an anguished crying that Selene's eyes misted in sympathy. "Let me help you," she said, drawing Elizabeth's hands away from her face.

"I don't want to lose him!" Elizabeth cried. "I love him!"

Selene untied the bandage, examined the wound, then reached for a jar in her medicine box. It contained oil of wintergreen, a soothing balm for cuts Selene had extracted from birch bark. As she rebandaged the wound, adding a sprinkle of green bread mold directly onto the cut to prevent infection, Selene listened to Elizabeth pour out her pain and sorrow.

"They will send him away," the girl cried. "He disobeyed orders. Roman soldiers are forbidden to interfere with the customs of the local people."

"But the people were doing a terrible thing, Elizabeth."

"Our Law permits it. And the Romans will not interfere when the people deal out their own justice among their own people. I shall never see him again! They'll punish him by reassigning him to an unpopular outpost, like Germany." Elizabeth covered her face with her hands and wept anew.

Selene reached out and touched the girl's arm, her own tears falling for the two lovers, separated by a cruel and unfair fate. *Just as I am separated from Andreas,* she thought as she put her other hand on the Eye of Horus, which she had not removed in thirteen years. And she thought of the ivory rose as it had lain on Andreas's breast. *Do you carry me there still?*

"Elizabeth," Selene said softly. "The greatest thing in the world is love. It is the strongest power there is, and it can work miracles. Love creates life, Elizabeth. It also heals wounds and gives courage and brings succor. If you love Cornelius enough, then you will never lose him. But *do* love him, Elizabeth. Love him with all your heart and being. Pledge yourself completely to him, and in return receive him completely to yourself, for there is nothing more beautiful and eternal than love."

Elizabeth's bitter sobbing began to subside. Soon she was crying softly; and then she was drawing in deep breaths and wiping her eyes. "He wasn't meant to be a soldier," she said quietly. "Cornelius is a gentle person. He's a dreamer, a poet. I've never met anyone like him before. And when we first met, it was almost as if . . . we had always loved one another. Does that make sense to you, Selene?"

"Yes."

"We cannot help it that our races are enemies, that his people oppress mine. We want only to live together in peace and happiness. We ask for nothing more."

Selene got up and went to the goatskin waterbag that hung in the corner. Filling a cup with water, she stirred in a few drops of oil of pennyroyal, then came back to sit on the carpet, saying, "Drink this. It will help you to sleep."

"You're very kind," Elizabeth said, after she had drunk the water. "I don't know what I would have done if you and your friend hadn't stopped to help. How can I repay you?"

Selene smiled. "I would like to have some of your fleece."

"My fleece?"

"I use it as a treatment for skin ailments. I shall need only a little. And I think," she added in a reassuring tone, "that you should not worry about Cornelius. The army will take care of him."

"Yes . . . they will have taken him to the *valetudinarium.*"

"*Valetudinarium?* What's that?"

Elizabeth chewed her lip, searching for a translation in Aramaic. There was none. "It's what the Romans call it. It's where they take sick and wounded. I know a little Latin, from Cornelius. *Vale* means health."

"And where is this health-making place?"

"In the Antonia Fortress."

Selene grew thoughtful; she had never heard of a *valetudinarium.* As far as she knew, the only healing institutions the Romans had were the temples of Aesculapius. But then Elizabeth explained: "The *valetudinarium* is owned by the army. Only soldiers go there," she said. "Cornelius told me about it when his friend Flavius was laid up with a wound. Every frontier fortress has one, he told me. Even as far away as Germany."

"Can you not go and visit Cornelius?" Selene asked, trying to visualize a house designed to care for the sick and injured, run by military physicians.

"No. Civilians are not allowed into the Antonia fortress."

"What about his friend, the other soldier who came to your aid?"

"Flavius."

"Won't he get word to you of Cornelius's condition?"

"Flavius doesn't know where I live. But . . . Selene, he patrols the street by the Temple. I can look for him!" Elizabeth took hold of Selene's hand. "Will you go with me? I'm afraid to go out alone."

"I'll go with you."

Elizabeth brightened with hope. "Tomorrow? Early?"

"As early as you wish. Now, you must get some sleep."

———

When Selene was back on her own mat next to Ulrika, she fell asleep almost immediately and so was unaware that her daughter stirred uneasily.

Ulrika's hand came up in her sleep and clutched the wooden T-cross around her neck, the Cross of Odin Wulf had given to Selene nearly ten years ago. Asleep but deeply troubled, the little girl rolled her head and her body jerked.

And in her dream she whispered, "Daddy!"

CHAPTER 44

They came upon a *trivia*, an intersection of three streets, a convergence known throughout the Roman Empire as a popular spot for people to meet and pass the time in insignificant conversation. They met Flavius here, in the shadow of the fortress.

He was very young, with down on his cheeks and ill-fitting armor on his slim body. The crowd on the street, milling through the gates leading into Herod's magnificent new Temple, paid no attention to the three women and the little girl who stood in the company of a Roman soldier.

The first thing Flavius reported was that Cornelius was still unconscious from the head wound. Elizabeth began to cry.

"Is there no way we can see him?" Selene asked, squinting up at the massive walls that loomed over the narrow street.

"You have to be a sick or wounded soldier to get into the infirmary," Flavius said. He pointed to where the *valetudinarium* was, along the eastern wall. "The infirmary itself is not guarded," he explained, "but the fortress is. These are uneasy times, you see. We've had some bad outbreaks of rebellion. Especially in there." He jerked his head toward the Temple precincts, where the moneychangers were. "We have to watch the crowds in there like hawks. There are quite a few hotheads in Jerusalem who would like nothing more than to score a strike against us."

Selene scanned the entire wall, monstrous and forbidding, like the walls of Babylon, which had intimidated her ten years ago. "What is that gate?" she asked, pointing.

"That's the civilians' entry. But you have to have an appointment with an official to get in. And it's only open in daylight hours."

Selene looked at Elizabeth, who was weeping into her veil, and said, "Surely there is another way inside." She gave Flavius a significant look. He was very young and earnest, and, she suspected, recalling how valiantly he had fought to save Elizabeth from the stone throwers, gallant. "If only we could get in to see him for a few moments. We would be so grateful."

Selene had read him rightly. Nothing could stop Flavius, feeling important in his armor, from coming to the aid of these ladies. "There *is* one possibility," he said quietly, glancing over his shoulder. "But it's risky . . ."

Rani was thankful she was to stay home with Ulrika while Elizabeth and Selene went on their risky escapade. Her sense of adventure stopped at the border of folly, which she thought this was. But nothing was going to keep young Elizabeth from her first passionate love, and Selene was stubbornly determined to see the inside of the Roman infirmary.

What more could the Romans possibly teach us? Rani asked herself, as the two women got into their outrageous disguises. *We have enough now for our* chikisaka. *I doubt the Romans can contribute anything of significance.*

But she kept these thoughts to herself, she knew the two would not be dissuaded, and she wished them luck and the protection of the gods when they left the house in the darkest night.

They arrived at the northernmost wall of the city at midnight and waited, shivering in their cloaks. For all its population and size, Jerusalem was oddly quiet beneath the stars; in fact, Selene was thinking this very strange when she remembered that it was their holiest week and that everyone, locals and pilgrims alike, was being respectfully solemn.

Holding themselves against the wall and out of the biting March wind, Selene and Elizabeth kept a watch on the dark street, anxious for the others to come.

It seemed as if hours must have passed before the first woman arrived, and when a few more came and huddled around the civilians' gate, talking softly among themselves, Selene and Elizabeth joined them.

No one paid heed to the newcomers. Selene and Elizabeth had done a good job of making themselves look like prostitutes, with cosmetics and jewelry and colorful clothes from Elizabeth's stock. Flavius had told them of this nightly practice of allowing prostitutes into the fortress at midnight; they visited the barracks and prison cells, and left before daybreak. It was against the rules, of course, but it was one of those things everyone discreetly overlooked. One tall woman with striking blond hair was destined for the very watchtower that guarded this gate.

A legionary came to the gate on the other side, unlocked it and admitted the women. "I shall be waiting for you," Flavius had said that morning. "As soon as you enter I'll claim you and take you to the infirmary."

Elizabeth's teeth chattered as she followed the women through the gate, which was locked behind them, and into Solomon's Porch. Beyond the pillars of the cloister stood the Court of the Gentiles, deserted and ghostly in the moonlight, and on the balustrade were signs in four languages warning the uncircumcised to go no further under penalty of death.

Selene looked up and down the torchlit cloister. Flavius was nowhere to be seen.

The legionary led the group of women up a flight of stairs on the left, and for a moment Selene and Elizabeth hesitated, uncertain what to do.

"Where *is* he?" Elizabeth whispered, her eyes wide with fear and excitement.

Selene thought for a moment, then took her friend's arm and hurriedly followed the group going upstairs. At the top they stepped out into a vast courtyard, deserted and silent, its paving stones worn smooth from the tramping of many sandaled feet. On the far side of the square Selene could make out a high platform with a throne-like chair on it, and she realized this must be where prisoners were brought to be tried and condemned.

Her pulse raced as she searched for Flavius. Where *was* he? Why had he not come?

The legionary, Selene realized in alarm, was leading them toward the barracks, which were brightly lit and filled with the laughter of soldiers.

She and Elizabeth tried to hang back. By now a few men had come out of the barracks and were standing in the doorway, gesturing. The women laughed and waved back, and hurried their pace. Four of them separated from the group and disappeared under an archway.

As she lagged behind the group heading for the barracks, Selene tried to search the vast courtyard for the *valetudinarium.* Flavius had said it stood along the eastern wall. But they were now following the eastern wall, and nothing here looked like an infirmary.

"Selene," Elizabeth began, as they drew near the barracks. A few impatient soldiers had left the doorway and come forward to pick and choose. The group of women was rapidly beginning to dissolve.

When one giant of a man started toward Selene, she said, "This way!" and pulled Elizabeth into the darkness of a nearby arch. They stumbled blindly into a narrow passage, and hearing shouts behind them, plunged forward into a formidable blackness.

After they had made their way some distance along the tunnel, Selene and Elizabeth stopped, pressed themselves against the wall and listened with held breath. Silence hung all about them. There was suddenly no more sound coming from the courtyard.

"Selene!" whispered Elizabeth, shaking so hard that her coin-necklace clinked. "I'm frightened!"

"Shhh. Listen. They've gone to the barracks. They've forgotten us."

"What if they're still out there, waiting?"

"They aren't. Now listen to me. We can't be far from the infirmary. We'll find it."

"*How?*"

Selene tried to think. She took her mind back to that morning, when they had stood at the *trivia*. Flavius had pointed upward. *Here* was where he had said the infirmary was. How could that be?

"Where are we?" whispered Elizabeth.

"I don't know . . . " Haltingly, Selene stepped away from the wall and raised her arms. She took a few steps, then a few more, until she felt the opposite wall. She was surprised. The corridor had widened. She explored the stone, patting it with her palms until she found something.

"Elizabeth," she called softly, "did you bring the tinderbox?"

Selene lifted the torch out of its sconce while Elizabeth struck the flint and steel. In a moment, they had light.

When Selene saw their surroundings she was further surprised. The hallways had widened considerably and the stone paving had given way to floorboards. She also saw, down at the far end, wooden benches flanking a large double door.

Elizabeth followed closely behind as Selene walked cautiously down the corridor, and when they reached the doors, they both stared. Incised into the wood were two snakes twining up a staff, and at the top of the staff two wings were outstretched. It was the symbol of Aesculapius, god of healing.

Selene sighed. "We've found it."

The orderly, yawning and stretching as he opened the door, was not surprised to see two prostitutes on the other side. But he was annoyed that he had not been told beforehand and therefore had not received his bribe, which he demanded now and which Selene paid in silver coin. After a brief examination of the stamp on the coin, he said in a bored tone, "Just see yer out before the surgeons come," and ambled back to his dice game.

Selene and Elizabeth stood by the door for a moment, hesitant.

Before them stretched a long, brightly lit hall, with doors opening off each side all the way down to the end. Curious sounds spilled through the doorways—subdued laughter, some quiet conversation, the solitary song of a panpipe and, incongruously, moaning. At the end of the hall stood two marble figures: the healing god Aesculapius, holding the winged serpent-staff, and the Roman Emperor, Claudius.

Selene stepped away from the door and Elizabeth followed close on her heels. They walked slowly down the hall, looking right and left through the open doors.

Each one, they saw, gave onto a small ward, each ward holding four beds, and all the beds were occupied. Most of the patients slept, but a few were sitting up, talking, throwing knucklebones, men with bandaged arms and legs, in short nightshirts, hobbling on crutches, cursing and laughing.

Elizabeth shrank into her cloak and instinctively pulled her veil over her face. But Selene peered boldly into each ward, intrigued, making mental notes. *Those four men,* she thought, *all have leg wounds; these four have splints on their arms.* The patients, she realized with mounting interest, were segregated according to their ailments, a practice she had never seen before but the value of which she immediately grasped.

"Hey!" came a deep voice. Elizabeth and Selene turned around to see a gray-haired veteran hobble out of his ward. He held on to the doorframe and hopped on one foot; his other leg ended below the knee. "Who're you looking for?" he asked.

Elizabeth tried to speak but had no voice. So Selene said, "Cornelius. We were told—"

"That way," the soldier barked with a jerk of his thumb. "In with the bashed heads." And a burst of laughter erupted in the ward behind him.

They passed by three more open doors until they finally came upon a small room where four men, asleep on cots, lay with bandaged heads. Forgetting her fear and shyness, Elizabeth cried, "Cornelius!" and ran to his bedside.

As Selene came into the room, she made note of everything she saw: the distance between each bed, the wax tablet nailed to the wall above each head, the table against the opposite wall and the basins of water, bandages and instruments laid out on it.

Efficient was the word that came to Selene's mind. The *valetudinarium* of the Fifth Legion was austere, practical and army-efficient. And she saw at once how some of this could be integrated into her and Rani's plan.

When she reached Cornelius's bed, Selene knelt at his side, gently pulled the sobbing Elizabeth off him and leaned forward to feel his skin, take his pulse, examine his pupils.

"Is this what they pay you girls to do these days?"

Elizabeth gasped, and Selene spun around. A man stood in the doorway, tall and lean with closely cropped hair, and wearing a long white robe. *He is like the infirmary,* Selene thought as she slowly came to her feet, *spare and reserved.* He was also, she realized as he walked toward her, very handsome.

"Who are you?" he asked. "What are you doing with this man?"

The look on his face reminded Selene of how she and Elizabeth must appear: the rouge on their lips and cheeks, the blue shadow over their eyes, the gaudy earrings and red dresses. She felt an unaccustomed embarrassment beneath his gaze.

She explained why they were there and how they had gotten in, taking care not to mention Flavius's name, and while she spoke the stranger watched her with shrewd eyes. He soon saw how different she was from the usual female late-night visitors, how confidently she spoke, the way she carried herself. Finally he believed her, and told her so. "I am Magnus, the night surgeon," he said. "How may I help you?"

———

"Whenever a pulse is counted," Selene told Rani the next day at breakfast, "it is recorded on a wax tablet that hangs over the bed. And then, as the pulse is counted at some later time, the figure can be compared with the earlier one to see if there has been a change. The Romans believe that a change in the pulse indicates a change in the patient's condition."

"Ingenious!" declared Rani, wishing now she had gone to see the *valetudinarium* for herself.

They were sitting at the table with a square of papyrus between them, and on it Selene had sketched the floor plan of the infirmary. "They perform surgery only in the morning," she explained, "when it is cool and the light is best. Those who have just been operated on are kept in a room near the surgery, rather than being taken back to their ward."

"Why?" asked Rani.

"In case of wound-break, or some other complication. They can be taken right back in."

Ulrika was sitting in the corner with her doll in her lap, regarding her mother and aunt in watchful silence. The two women sat with their heads together over the table, drawing pictures. They seemed to be very happy and excited about something.

Then Ulrika heard singing out in the garden; she turned her head to listen.

Elizabeth was out there gathering spring flowers for Cornelius.

Last night, when Elizabeth had found Cornelius deeply asleep, his beautiful curls matted beneath a bandage, his face pale, she had wept. And then—wonder of wonders!—the night surgeon had appeared and explained that Cornelius had regained consciousness that afternoon and had eaten supper and was now sound asleep because of a medicine he had been given. And even more wonderful, the doctor had reported that when Cornelius had come to, after being brought in from the square where the stoning had taken place, he had asked for someone named Elizabeth.

She could not believe her luck. Selene must be a sorceress, Elizabeth thought, to have enchanted the Roman physician so. Not only had he permitted them to stay, not only had he shown Selene around the infirmary and answered her questions, he had also granted special permission to Elizabeth to visit Cornelius every day at noon. Which was where she was shortly to go, after the flowers were bundled and a basket of food gotten together, and a brand-new cloak for Cornelius was purchased in the marketplace.

Ulrika watched Elizabeth with big, contemplative eyes, wondering why everyone was so happy all of a sudden and why they weren't sharing it with her. Well, she thought, getting up from the floor and holding her doll to her chest, they must have just forgotten again, the way they did sometimes. So Ulrika walked over to the table and tugged at her mother's sleeve.

"What is it, darling?" Selene said, not turning to her but continuing to draw on the papyrus.

"Mama," said the girl.

"Your mother's busy now," Rani said. "Why don't you go and play in the garden?"

"Mama," Ulrika said again.

"Just a minute, darling. You can see here, Rani," she said, pointing to a place on the diagram. "There is a central cupboard for bandages and medicines. Rather than storing them at each bedside table . . . "

Ulrika backed away. She recognized the look on her mother's face. It was intense and singular, and Ulrika knew it was like an invisible barrier that could not be gotten through. So she turned around and went out to the garden, which she preferred anyway.

"Magnus also gave me some advice about money," Selene said, laying aside her pen. "When I told him we were taking a ship to Alexandria, he suggested we might want to deposit our money with a banker here in Jerusalem. Ships' crews are notorious thieves, he said. No matter how well we hid our money, we would be lucky to arrive in Egypt with it. There are bankers here who have connections with banking houses in Alexandria, he said, and with a letter of credit . . . "

It was decided that Rani would go into the city that afternoon and place their money and jewels in the safekeeping of one of Jerusalem's many reputable bankers. Then, in two days, when the Holy Week was over, they would journey westward to the port of Joppa, and from there buy passage on a ship bound for Alexandria.

Selene and Rani smiled at each other. The future seemed so close now.

CHAPTER 45

Wooden spoons from Elizabeth's kitchen made nice pine trees, and a trench dug in the dirt and filled with water was a perfect river. The Rhine River. Ulrika had never seen snow, but her mother had described it so she thought the white fleece, sneaked from the bags upstairs, spread all around made good snow for her "forest."

It was late afternoon, and Ulrika was in the garden playing her favorite game, "Germany."

"Here is the river," she said out loud, firming down the banks and adding a bit more water. "And here are the trees." She straightened the spoons, which were stuck in the earth like posts. "And here is Ulrika," she said finally, placing her doll in the middle of her miniature landscape. "Ulrika is the princess and she is warning everyone that the Frost Giants are coming. Who will save the people?" cried her little girl's voice.

"Oh!" she said. "Look! It's Wulf, the handsome prince."

Ulrika had no doll to represent the hero, but her vivid mind conjured him up all the same. As she moved doll and invisible prince through her fantasy, Ulrika chatted and laughed and was more animated than she ever was in the real world.

"And everyone lived happily ever after," she said finally, sighing deeply and lying back on the ground to look up at the sky.

Once again, Wulf had saved the day. There was nothing he could not do, and it made Ulrika proud to know that he was her father. She knew that he loved her very much because he was always with her. And this was Ulrika's special secret. Her mother had told her that Wulf was with the Goddess, but Ulrika knew better. He had come to her in dreams years ago and he had told her that he would stay by her for as long as she needed him.

And Ulrika needed her father often. Aunt Rani and her mother were always so busy; they frequently left her in the care of strangers—as they had left her today with Elizabeth. At such times the awful loneliness would steal up on her and make her sad; but in the next instant the spirit of Wulf would be there, talking to her, comforting her.

He was here now, in this little garden in Jerusalem.

Ulrika was starting to doze in the afternoon sun when she was startled awake by a shadow passing over her face. She opened her eyes, said "Oh!" and sat up.

Sitting on the garden wall was a raven, and for an instant it seemed to fix its golden eye on her.

Ulrika sat transfixed. The raven was the sacred bird of her father's people; but more especially, her mother had told her, it was the personal totem of her father.

"Hello," she said tentatively. "Hello, raven."

The bird cocked its head, peered at her with its other eye, then lifted its wings and took flight.

"Wait," said Ulrika, scrambling to her feet. "Wait, don't go."

A climbing vine hugged the garden wall and it was strong enough to take the weight of a nine-year-old girl. Ulrika was up and over the wall in a wink, running down the alley, following the black bird silhouetted against the blue sky.

———

Alexandria!

It was only days away now. Selene hurried down the street as if she could make the hours speed by. In her belt she carried the three passenger tickets she had purchased from a shipping agent. She also carried a receipt for payment of passage on a caravan, leaving, not in two days, but tonight! Tonight they were going to take the road to Joppa, and from there, a ship bound for Alexandria. Within a week, Selene would be setting foot in the city her parents had come from, the city Andreas had known in his youth.

As she turned down Elizabeth's street, Selene hoped Rani had returned from the banking house. They must waste no time in joining the silk caravan that was going to depart from the Joppa Gate tonight, headed for the coast. They must pack their belongings quickly, and say farewell to Elizabeth.

Alexandria! Selene thought she could almost reach out and touch it.

She found Elizabeth at her loom, weaving one of the beautiful shawls she was known for. But, after a moment's search, Selene could not find Ulrika.

"She was in the garden," Elizabeth said, jumping up. "She didn't come through here. I would have seen her. And there is no other door."

"She must have climbed the wall, then."

"Why would she do that?"

Selene suddenly felt cold. "The alley behind the house, Elizabeth. Where does it lead?"

"That way, in a dead end. But that way"—she pointed—"it goes all the way into the Upper City."

Selene hurried to the door. "I am going to look for her. Will you stay here, please, in case she comes back?"

━━━━━

The raven was playing a game with Ulrika. It would fly a short distance, then alight on an archway or an awning, cock its head at her, and when she neared it, suddenly fly off again. Ulrika didn't know where it was leading her, but she wasn't afraid. Her father was with her, at her side.

The raven finally flew down a short alley, perched for a moment on an jutting eave, then, when Ulrika was standing below him, took off and disappeared over the rooftops.

She watched him go, disappointed. She turned to her father, who let Ulrika and no one else see him, to ask him what she should do now, and discovered that she was not alone in the alley. She had been followed.

Ulrika smiled and said, "Hello, doggie."

The dog stopped and stared at her. It was walking low to the ground, and the fur on its back was standing up.

Ulrika said, "Hello, doggie," again and held out her hand.

The animal crept closer. And then she saw that there was something wrong with the dog's mouth. It was foaming.

━━━━━

Rani was pleased with her afternoon's work. She had gone to the Street of Bankers near the Hasmonean Palace and there had found a man of excellent reputation. He had weighed her gold and silver on honest scales, and had appraised her jewels at a fair market price. The total was then deposited into safe storage and Rani was given a letter of credit in exchange.

As Magnus the night surgeon had suggested, it *was* a good idea, because Rani now walked with a light step and felt a freedom she had not known in seven years of traveling. After all that daily worrying about their gold and silver and jewels, always fearful of bandits, constantly aware of the weight in their hems, Rani's wealth was now safe and secure. It would be invested by the banker and earn interest, and it would be available for her and Selene to draw upon any time they wished at a corresponding banking house in Alexandria.

It was indeed a wise way to handle one's money. The letter of credit was stamped at the bottom with a seal the banker had given to Rani, and that seal now hung about her neck on a string—a lump of agate incised with an intricate design. No two seals in the Empire were alike; whenever she or Selene wanted to withdraw money, she must produce the letter of credit and then impress the seal into clay. The two impressions would be examined by an expert for exact likeness, and thus protect her from theft and forgery.

"Just be careful that you keep the letter and seal separately," the banker had warned. "Each is worthless without the other, so that should a thief take either the letter or the seal, he would still not be able to take your money from the bank."

As soon as she got home, Rani was going to give the seal to Selene, and keep the letter of credit, which she now carried rolled up in a wooden tube tucked inside her belt.

Rani's mind marched ahead of her hurried steps. There was so much to do. They would need provisions for the journey—food, mats for sleeping on the deck, sturdy cloaks as protection against the cold sea. Rani had a few coins left; Selene, she knew, also carried a small amount. Enough, Rani calculated, to make the purchases and then to settle them in an inn in Alexandria. Once there, they could begin drawing upon their large reserves in the bank.

She arrived at Elizabeth's house to find the young woman standing on the threshold, wringing her hands. "Ulrika is missing," she said. "Selene is looking for her."

Rani frowned. This was not like the child. She looked up at the rooftops and saw that sunlight no longer touched them. The afternoon was rapidly waning; soon the Temple *shofar* would sound and the Passover Sabbath would begin. Already, Jerusalem was growing quiet and deserted in observance of the coming holy night.

"I shall search, too," she said to Elizabeth. "You wait here. Ulrika might find her way home."

Rani struck off in the opposite direction from the one Selene had taken, and delivered herself into the warren of narrow streets and alleys in the quarter behind Elizabeth's house.

She had not gone far when she came upon a block of small warehouses, locked up for the coming night. The streets were growing dark; Rani walked alone past lightless archways and silent doors. Presently, she heard a sound. From far away, over the rooftops, she heard the hum of the city as it closed up like a flower in the dying day. But, nearer, there was a more distinct sound. And, she realized in sudden alarm, a very familiar sound.

It was the low, menacing growl of a dog.

Rani moved cautiously. She followed the stone walls and paused frequently to turn her head this way and that. As she drew nearer, Rani felt a chill run through her. An intuition, sharp as glass, told her what she was going to find.

When she reached the opening of an alley, the light was so poor it was difficult to see; nonetheless, she could make out the figure of the dog, halfway down the alley, its mouth silver with foam. And then, at the end of the alley, up against the wall, Ulrika, standing as still as a statue and staring at the dog.

Rani lifted a hand to her breast as if to stifle the thumping of her heart, and she opened her mouth to speak, but her throat was dry. Biting her lips to moisten them, Rani swallowed and finally said as calmly as she could, "Ulrika, it's me, Rani. Don't be afraid."

The child's voice came back: "I'm not afraid."

"Ulrika, I want you to do as I say. Don't make any sudden moves. I want you to look around slowly and see if there is any way out for you."

"There isn't."

Rani closed her eyes. It was a blind alley. The only exit, therefore, was past the dog.

"Ulrika," she said as steadily as she could. "The dog is sick. He doesn't know what he's doing. We have to be very careful with him. Do you understand?"

"Yes."

"You must stand absolutely still, Ulrika. And don't look into his eyes. He won't like that. Look away."

Rani tried to think. If she went for help it might be too late. If she called out, hoping to signal a passerby, it might trigger the dog's attack. What to do? *What to do?*

In terror, she saw the dog slowly begin to advance upon Ulrika. It slunk low to the ground, growling, its body quivering with the pain of its disease. Rani had seen rabid dogs before, she knew the viciousness that came over them in the final stages of the illness. It would have one cold thought in its head now, she knew: to attack and tear to pieces anyone who stood in its path.

Great Shiva, Rani prayed. *Help me.*

———

Selene came through the front door, breathless. "Did she come back?"

Elizabeth was fearful. "No! Rani went to look for her. But that was a long time ago!"

Selene tried to suppress her rising panic. It was nearly dark out now. *Where was Ulrika?* "We shall have to get help."

"Yes. The rabbi—"
"Hurry!"

=====

Rani realized that there was only one way out of this: she must somehow
divert the dog from Ulrika.

She searched the ground and, finding a rock, sharp and heavy, hefted
it in her hand.

If she could strike a lucky blow—hit the dog on the head and knock it
unconscious . . .

But what if it only landed *near* him and startled him into flying at
Ulrika?

I must make him turn around and come this way.

Rani's fingers tightened about the stone. The light was nearly gone; the
dog was creeping closer to Ulrika.

I'm an old woman, Rani thought. What chance have I of outrunning
the dog? He must come out this way and I must stand on this spot to throw
the stone.

"Stay very still now, Ulrika," she said in a tight voice. "I'm going to
throw a stone and frighten the dog away. Do you understand?"

Ulrika, who had followed the raven to this place and who had her
father's warrior blood in her, said without fear, "Yes, Aunt Rani."

I have seen the world, Rani thought as she raised the stone. *I have no
regrets* . . .

She threw the stone.

=====

The child's screams were heard many streets away so that by the time
Selene arrived at the alley, a considerable crowd had gathered around
Rani's body.

Ulrika flew into her mother's arms, sobbing, while Selene stared down
in shock.

Rani and the dog lay together; they had died in the same instant. Rani's
dress was bloody and torn. The string around her neck was broken, the
agate seal gone. Her belt lay loose upon the paving stones. The tube
containing the letter of credit was no longer there.

BOOK VII
ALEXANDRIA

CHAPTER 46

If you are ever confronted with a dire wound and are without proper medicines," came the soft-spoken voice from the center of the circle of women, "then you may fall back on the old formula of first applying something stinging and then something soothing. And you may use almost anything at hand."

Mother Mercia, the *alma mater* of the temple, listened as Sister Peregrina gave morning instructions in the sick ward. The women who were gathered around Sister Peregrina at the bedside were novices, in training to tend the sick. They were young, dedicated and earnest, dressed in long white robes and wearing the Cross of Isis on their breasts. And they were devoted to Sister Peregrina, who had come to Alexandria from Jerusalem three years ago.

Sister Peregrina was showing them wound care this morning, demonstrating on a patient who had been brought to the temple during the night —a young woman who had been the victim of an assault. Before Sister Peregrina's arrival in Alexandria, three years before, the young woman would have received little help, perhaps none at all. But today the small sick ward of Isis's great temple in Alexandria was known throughout Egypt.

Mother Mercia smiled with pride. How the sisterhood had grown because of Sister Peregrina! How richly the coffers were overflowing with the offerings of the grateful patients. And how pleased the Goddess must be to observe the dedication of these young women as they watched Sister Peregrina now demonstrate the Hindu cross-bandaging known as *svastika,* which was the Sanskrit word for "cross."

Mother Mercia never ceased to be amazed at Sister Peregrina's knowledge. She had introduced some rather peculiar yet efficient healing practices: such as suturing wounds with beetles, and putting green bread mold on wounds to keep infection out. And while the priestesses of Isis had long possessed the secret formula of Hecate's Cure, they had used it only to treat headaches and cramps; Sister Peregrina had shown them what the willow tea could do for fever and swelling. Even the master physicians from the nearby School of Medicine, the famed *therapeuta,* came to this sick ward to observe and listen.

It had been no accident, Mother Mercia was certain, that Sister Peregrina had come to the temple three years ago, offering to work in the service of Isis. The Goddess had brought her here. It was all part of a divine plan, the *alma mater* believed, because here was the evidence, before her eyes: This hall, once a warehouse, was now lined with beds, with the sun and sea air streaming in through windows, shedding light on sleeping women, on white-robed attendants, on flowers in pots that nodded in the summer breeze. A sick ward indeed! It was a far cry from the cramped little rooms where the sisters and priestesses had once given sanctuary to any sick and injured person who came for aid.

Mother Mercia gazed lovingly upon Sister Peregrina, thinking of her as the daughter she never had. She was a good woman, this much-traveled wanderer from the East—hence the name Mercia had given her: Peregrina, which means "traveler." But she was a strangely quiet and private person who kept part of herself locked away behind some secret door.

In those first months three years ago, when Sister Peregrina had come with her child to the temple to dedicate herself and her good works to the Goddess, Mother Mercia, hearing the sincerity in the offer, had given the mother and child sanctuary in the temple. And in those first months of getting to know each other, of evenings sitting in quiet conversation, of listening to Sister Peregrina's marvelous tales of Babylon and Persia, Mother Mercia had assumed the young woman would soon start to open up and speak of the private part of her life. The soul-mother of the temple was a gentle and compassionate woman whose patient manner seemed to invite confession. She put people at ease, allowed them to unburden their souls so that they left feeling relieved and cleansed. But, curiously, although Mercia was certain a dark memory was locked somewhere inside Sister Peregrina that would do well to get out, the admission never came.

After three years of sharing the pillared precincts of Isis's temple, of working together, of praying together, and sharing evenings in exchanging views, Sister Peregrina never went the one step further that would have unlocked her soul's door. And that she would be able to keep herself guarded for so long, that she should *want* to after all this time, puzzled Mother Mercia all the more. She really knew very little about her healing-mistress; nothing about how or why she had come from Jerusalem to Alexandria, penniless, offering herself to Isis, nor where she came from before Persia, nor even the history of the child Ulrika. And it was an irony not lost on Mother Mercia that the name she had given the young woman three years ago, Peregrina, was more appropriate than she had initially thought, for Peregrina, while meaning "traveler," also means "stranger."

"Mother Mercia," came a voice behind her. It was a young girl who had only recently come into the service of Isis. "You have a visitor. He is waiting outside."

"Thank you, child. I shall be there momentarily."

Before turning away, Mother Mercia paused to look at Sister Peregrina who was leading the novice nurses to the next bed. As Peregrina turned to face her students, Mercia frowned. There it was again—that brief, haunting familiarity.

The very first moment she had set eyes on Sister Peregrina three years ago, the *alma mater* had thought: *I know this woman.* And then, in the next instant, she had realized she didn't know her at all. Over the following three years there had been isolated instances, when Peregrina had gotten a look on her face, a tilt of her head, and Mother Mercia had felt that annoying tug at the back of her memory. What was it about Sister Peregrina that was vaguely familiar? Or possibly reminiscent of someone Mother Mercia once knew?

She shook her head now, as she had done those other times. The look was gone, the familiarity vanished. She turned and walked to the entrance of the sick ward where her visitor waited.

"Andreas!" she said in surprise, holding out her hands. "How good it is to see you again! How long has it been? Three, four years?"

Smiling, he came forward and took her hands in his. "How is it, mother, that you are younger and more beautiful each time I see you?"

She laughed. "Tell me now, Andreas. Are you in Alexandria to stay, or do you pass through like the khamsin wind?"

"I'm afraid this is only a brief stop. I have just a few days to visit with friends, and then I shall be bound for Britain."

"Britain! I have heard that is such a savage place! You are going on the emperor's business, I suppose?"

"What other business is there?"

They began to stroll around the garden. "You look well, Andreas. Living in Rome seems to have done you some good."

Andreas, much taller than the elderly *alma mater,* bent his head to smile at her, and his hair, completely silver, caught the summer sunlight. "Rome is good and Rome is bad. I love her and I hate her."

"And what is the latest news? Please tell me."

Andreas smiled; he was not the same person he had once been, long ago, back in Antioch—an angry, serious young man of thirty. Seventeen years of roaming the earth, of learning the world and the foibles of its inhabitants, had tempered the intolerance that had once made him so severe. The furrow between his eyebrows was still there, deeper in fact and permanently etched, but he smiled more freely and there were small creases about his eyes that told of good humor and forgiveness.

"And yourself, mother. How are you? I am told that you are now in competition with the School of Medicine. That you steal patients from them."

"You would be quoting Diosthenes, that old crocodile! Only *he* would speak of patients as if they were merchandise to be fought over. No, Andreas. Our little sick ward is no threat to the School of Medicine. For one thing, we treat only women and children. For another, we do not perform surgery."

They had come to the entrance of the ward, and they paused to look inside. Andreas was at once impressed with the rows of beds, the quantity of light, the apparent cleanliness of the ward. "How did this come about?" he asked, watching the group of novices at the far end.

"It was a miracle, Andreas. Truly. Three years ago a healer-woman from Persia appeared at our door asking to be granted work in the service of Isis. She is now our healing-mistress; she trains healing attendants so that they might be sent to other temples up the Nile."

"She came from Persia, you say?"

"She told me that she had traveled a great deal. To Babylon, even."

Andreas stared at the students grouped around a bed. He saw their teacher, standing with her back to him, bend over and do something to the patient. He watched as she gestured, then handed a bandage to one of the students. He was mildly intrigued.

But, as he watched her, Andreas's interest sharpened. "What is her name?" he asked.

"Sister Peregrina. She and her daughter live here in the temple compound."

He stared for a moment longer, then said, "For an instant . . . she reminded me of someone I once knew, long ago in Antioch."

Mother Mercia's eyebrows rose. So Peregrina affected others the same way! Perhaps it was her face, perhaps she had the kind of features that seemed to hold something familiar to anyone who looked at her. There were such people. That would explain it.

"Will you have supper with me one night while you are in Alexandria, Andreas?" she asked, as they turned away from the door.

"Ah, I cannot promise. My ship sails in a few days and there are so many people I need to see."

"Then have some wine with me now."

Andreas turned his back to the sick ward, and as he proceeded to recount for Mother Mercia the latest scandals of Empress Messalina, behind him, at the far end of the ward, Sister Peregrina was standing as still as a statue, her eyes closed, her hands outstretched over a sleeping patient. She was demonstrating the "touch" to her novices, but Andreas did not see it.

CHAPTER 47

Ulrika had done it again.

She had sneaked out of the classroom and run down to the harbor where the great Library stood. And once again she had taken a book without anyone knowing. If she were ever caught by the librarians, if her tutor ever discovered her creeping away from her lessons, if her mother ever found out—well, Ulrika knew she would be punished. But she did not care. This was a new book and she had to have it. Besides, she wasn't doing any harm. She would return it to the library by the end of the week and no one would be the wiser.

It was one of the wonderful new codex books—square leaves of parchment stitched together along one edge; so much more convenient than bulky scrolls that had writing on only one side and had to be held with both hands at all times. This book was a military memoir—one of many that recent wars had produced—and it was written by a Rhine commander named Gaius Vatinius.

Ulrika read secretively in her room, by the light of a solitary lamp. She devoured the words in the book as another girl might consume a forbidden sweetmeat. She was ravenous; and the more she read, the more hungry she became. To learn about her people, to know about the race she had come from.

But when Ulrika came to Vatinius's descriptions of the "northern barbarians," classifying them as animals, as soulless unthinking beasts, she tossed the book aside and sat up on her bed.

This book was like so many others she had read—steeped with Roman conceit and prejudice. This Commander Vatinius was no better than Julius Caesar, the man Ulrika hated most of all. It was Caesar who had first conquered the Germans and made slaves of them. His statues were everywhere in Alexandria; his assassination had made him a god. But Ulrika despised the first enemy of her people and mentally cursed him whenever she could.

Disheartened, she got up and went to her window, which looked out onto a small garden. She could smell the sea and feel its moist, beckoning caress, but she could not *see* it. This room was stifling; this massive temple, with its echoing cloisters and holy sanctuaries and cells of sleeping sisters, was bearing down on her like a great tomb. Ulrika could hardly breathe in the downy summer night. She wanted to have trees and sky around her; she wanted to be able to run, to be free.

This restlessness had begun recently, somewhere around the time of her first moon-flow, when she had turned twelve, six months ago. Before that, she had been a silent, withdrawn little girl who existed in a world of her own making, content to live in the little box of her mind where her only companion was her spirit-father. But then the change had come, and Ulrika felt as though a brazier had been lit inside her. She seemed to burn all the time, even on cold spring nights, or when summer storms beseiged the North African coast. Burning to get out, to *do* something.

Ghost companions were no longer enough for Ulrika.

———

Selene stepped out of the bath, dried herself, bound her damp hair with a white kerchief and put on a fresh dress. She straightened two necklaces between her breasts.

The first was the golden Eye of Horus, given to her seventeen years ago in the Grotto of Daphne. The second was Rani's turquoise stone, the gift from Nimrod ten years ago when they left Persia. And as she fingered it, Selene felt again the dark pearl of pain deep in her soul.

Before leaving her small apartment, Selene paused to sprinkle dust on the sacred fire of Isis that burned day and night by her door. She never forgot the Goddess. Three years ago she had been on the brink of despair

—homeless, hungry, a woman alone with a child. Alexandria, jewel of the Mediterranean, this perfect city of white plaster and alabaster one historian had described as being "so dazzling that one must shade one's eyes when walking the streets at noon, or be blinded," had let her down; Alexandria had betrayed her.

Selene had arrived in Alexandria with little money, having tried unsuccessfully in Jerusalem to find the banker to whom Rani had given her wealth; she had quickly found herself with no money at all. The rich, pampered and spoiled population of Alexandria had no need of a simple healer-woman, not with so many elegant, school-trained physicians about.

And then, after her inquiries at the School of Medicine about Andreas had proved fruitless, and her search for some evidence of her parents' having once been here had turned up nothing, Selene had had a revelation: "She came from the gods," her father had said. And Mera's dying words: "Remember to keep friendship with Isis." Selene had known then what she must do. She was in the hands of the gods. Without the ivory rose, without Andreas, she could not continue to pursue her greater dream. So she must put herself into the service of the gods and pray that they would choose the hour in which to illuminate her.

———

Selene found her daughter sitting by the window, staring up at the great bowl of night.

She paused to look at Ulrika. She was growing so fast these days! Already she was taller than some of the sisters in the temple. And her body was starting to fill out; there were new roundnesses here and there, strength was becoming evident in the arms and thighs. Ulrika's wind-like hair had grown paler, her eyes bluer. It was almost as if, Selene thought with a shiver, the German half of her blood were slowly taking over the other, Roman half. *She's growing away from me,* Selene thought suddenly.

And she was such a solemn girl. Why did Ulrika never smile? What went on behind those grave eyes? Was it Rani's death that had done it? Or, Selene tried to remember, had Ulrika always been such a serious child?

I must not lose her, Selene thought, as she entered the room. *She's all I have.*

"Rikki," she said softly.

The girl turned and regarded her mother with eyes too mature for one so young. *She's still a child,* Selene protested. *She should be giddy and frivolous like all the other girls her age.* But Ulrika kept away from the other girls, she had no friends, and Selene never knew what she was thinking.

Selene glanced at the bed, and Ulrika was immediately on her feet. She tried to block her mother's view of the book but was too late. "What are you reading?" Selene asked, stepping around her daughter and picking up the book. "You went to the Library again, didn't you?"

Ulrika nodded.

Selene put the book down without looking at it and sat on the edge of the bed. Gesturing for her daughter to sit next to her, she said, "Is it a good book?"

Ulrika hesitated, then said, "No," and joined her mother on the edge of the bed. "It's full of lies."

Selene sighed. She had known for some time that her own store of information was no longer adequate for Ulrika's needs. The girl had picked out every scrap of information Selene had ever known about Wulf and his people. Now her daughter was turning to other sources in her obsession.

In fact, they had not spoken of Ulrika's father in a long time. Selene could not even recall the last time. Could it truly have been as long ago as Jerusalem? Had Rani's death somehow plugged up the one avenue of communication left between mother and daughter? Selene felt herself become slightly panicked. *I should speak of him now,* she thought. *Now more than ever Ulrika needs to know the truth.*

But it was a terrifying step to take. So Selene merely said quietly, "Your father was a wonderful man, Rikki. I wish you could have known him."

A moment of silence hung in the room, and then tears gathered in Ulrika's eyes. And when Selene saw them, she took her daughter into her arms and they embraced for the first time since they had clung to each other back in Jerusalem at the end of that awful alley, with Rani lying at their feet.

"Rikki," Selene murmured. "I'm sorry. I'm so sorry."

"Mama," sobbed the girl.

But that was all they said. The barriers were still up, there was still too much pain and distance between them. *And what would the truth do now?* Selene wondered, as she stroked her daughter's hair. To tell her that her father did not die back in Persia, that he had set out for Germany not knowing Selene was pregnant, that he might be in his forest right now, unaware of the daughter who yearned for him. *I can't tell her, I cannot . . .*

"Come on rounds with me tonight, Rikki," Selene said, drawing back and brushing hair away from the girl's face. "Help me with my patients."

Ulrika stared at her mother for a moment, almost in surprise, and then another look, a dark one, with a hint of betrayal in it, of having been betrayed, closed over her face. The girl stood up and backed away to the window. "I . . . I'd rather not, Mother. I'm sleepy."

Selene looked at her daughter. *What have I done wrong? What clumsy thing have I done now?* Their moment of intimacy, of shared grief, so sweetly held, was snuffed like a flame.

"Very well," she said, standing up and crossing to the door. "You must not sneak down to the Library any more, Ulrika. The harbor is a dangerous place for girls. Do you understand?"

"Yes, Mother."

"We'll go together tomorrow, all right? We'll ask the librarian to give us the best book on the Rhineland. Would you like that?

Ulrika said, "Yes," and returned to staring out the window.

CHAPTER 48

Six new members!" Mother Mercia declared, as she refilled their wine cups. "Think of it, Peregrina. Our membership is now the largest it has been in the history of the temple. All because of you!"

Selene looked into the depths of her red wine and felt overcome with sadness. How Rani would have loved this! How differently things might have been had Rani not died! It had been Rani's dream to visit the School of Medicine. Perhaps Rani could have purchased a house here in Alexandria, for the three of them to live in; and then perhaps they would have gone regularly to the school, to learn from the great medical minds there. And then, too, perhaps, now that she had money, Selene could have persisted in her search of someone who might know something of her family. But, being penniless and homeless, Selene had been forced to come to the temple for help.

She had come close on occasion to confiding in Mother Mercia and asking her help, but the *alma mater* was a very unworldly woman. She had set foot inside this temple as a young girl nearly sixty years ago and had not once stepped outside. She received all the news of the world from infrequent visitors. Mother Mercia was the High Priestess of Isis; her mind was upon mystical matters. There was no way she could help Selene in her search, and Selene did not want to bother the good woman with her seemingly insoluble woes.

Nor had she told Mother Mercia about Andreas. After making inquiries at the School, and receiving head shakes, or misinformation ("Oh yes, Andreas! Short man, came from Gaul.") Selene had withdrawn into a private sadness. To lose him again—she had *so* hoped to find him here —so soon after the loss of Rani, had been more than Selene could bear. And so she had laid that greater dream away in a safe place. For now, she was able to serve the Goddess by putting to use the knowledge and skills she had collected in her travels.

"Many young women would like to join the sisterhood of Isis," Mercia was saying, "but many balk at the thought of spending their lives in such mundane chores as making incense or copying sacred scriptures. And so they stay away. But now we offer an employment that appeals: care of the sick. It seems to call to the natural healer that abides in the heart of every woman. Indeed, now I must turn applicants away." Mercia smiled. "And you are such a good teacher, Peregrina!"

"The credit is not all mine, mother. My students are very good. My only worry is that in their zeal they may do more harm than good. That is why the first rule I always teach them is: First, do no harm."

"Now that's interesting," Mother Mercia said, tasting her wine. "My old friend Andreas is often fond of saying that very—"

"Andreas! Do you know a man named Andreas?"

"Why, yes, I do. We met years ago when he was a student at the School of Medicine. I don't see much of him, he travels a lot. But whenever he comes to Alexandria—"

"Mother Mercia," Selene said slowly, putting her wine cup on the table. "*I* once knew a physician named Andreas. Years ago, in Antioch."

"Now that is a coincidence. He was remarking to me only the other day that *you* reminded him of someone he once knew in Antioch."

Selene froze. "He was *here*? In the temple? And he *saw* me?"

Mother Mercia gave Selene a puzzled look. "Is he the same man?"

"Where is he now? I *must* know."

"Whenever he visits Alexandria he takes a room at the School of Medicine. But I doubt he is still there. He was due to sail for Britain about now."

"Forgive me, mother," Selene said as she hurried to the door. "This is most urgent."

"Peregrina, wait!"

But she was gone.

———

Alexandria's broad avenues were crowded with evening strollers—people taking the air, hurrying to one of the many theaters and museums, idling away the hot night among the city's famous parks and fountains. Only a few heads turned as the young woman walked rapidly by, dressed in the white robe and headdress of a holy sister. Her sandals slapped the smooth pavement in cadence with her racing heart. Andreas, Andreas . . .

The School of Medicine stood along the corniche, looking out over the great arc of bay that ended in the Pharos, the great lighthouse that was known as one of the Seven Wonders of the World. The school was a massive creation of white marble and alabaster, all columns and colonnades and blazing with torchlight.

Selene cut across the broad lawns, ran past clusters of medical students in their white tunics and togas, and dashed up stairs that seemed endless. When she arrived at the magnificent double doors flanked by statues of the healing gods, Selene slowed down and caught her breath.

Given the vast collection of buildings and courtyards, and the large population of teachers, students and patients, the School appeared curiously subdued. As Selene entered the cavernous rotunda, she had a feeling of entering a place of worship. And in a way she was, for the gods were here: Aesculapius, Greek god of healing, and his two daughters, Panacea and Hygeia; Thoth, the ancient medicine god of the Egyptians; even old Hippocrates stood in a niche with an eternal lamp burning at his feet.

Selene came upon a caretaker sweeping the floor. She asked where she might locate a visitor staying temporarily at the school, and he directed her to the blocks of dormitories at the far side of the campus.

She ran again, unable to restrain herself. "I doubt he is still here," Mother Mercia had said. "He was due to sail for Britain about now."

Selene's heart felt as if it might burst. *Andreas,* her mind cried out. *Be here. Please be here . . .*

The chamberlain was a pleasant old Greek who seemed to find Selene's breathless appearance at the dormitories amusing. His little brown eyes twinkled as he bobbed his head and said, "Ah yes, Andreas. He's in the visitor's accommodations. A friend of yours, is he?"

"Please take me to him."

He led the way across a garden, along a serpentine path and finally up a stairway. He chatted constantly, but Selene was not listening. She kept her eyes forward, while her hands twisted each other, and her heart pounded.

At last they came into a corridor and Selene heard muffled voices behind closed doors: men's voices, and the sounds of music and laughter.

"Visiting professors stay here," the Greek said. "And former students, who like to come back and see the old school. Even some wealthy patients who don't want their presence here generally known. Why, last spring the governor's wife stayed with us while she recovered from a special operation that—"

"Which room belongs to Andreas?" Selene asked, trembling now and finding it difficult to breathe.

"Right here," the chamberlain said, and they came to a halt before a closed door.

The Greek knocked. There was no response.

He knocked again.

From up and down the hall came sounds of activity and life, but behind this door all remained still and silent. "Perhaps he's asleep," Selene said.

The man gave her an odd look, then put his hand to the knob and turned it.

They found an empty room. "He's gone," the chamberlain said.

Selene pushed her way inside, where she saw a bed, a chest, a table and chair. All were bare.

"You lookin' for Andreas?"

Selene spun around. A man was leaning against the door frame, drying his hair with a towel.

"Do you know where he is?" she asked.

"Left a few hours ago. Said he had a boat to catch."

"*Which* boat? Do you know?"

He looked her up and down, and shared a knowing look with the chamberlain. "Goin' to Britain was all he said. Couldn't tell you which boat it was."

As they watched her run down the hall and disappear, the two men exchanged a remark and their laughter rose into the hot night.

───

The last time Selene had been to the harbor was three and a half years ago, when she and Ulrika had walked down the gangplank with their bundles of possessions and small bag of coins. The harbor had bewildered her then and it bewildered her now, but she would not be daunted by the crowds, the forest of masts, the sailors and stevedores who called to her as she pushed by.

Selene ran out onto the quays and asked about this ship, that ship, hurrying from one dock to another, encountering ships' masters who didn't speak Greek, captains who were surly, shipping agents who were pressed for time. There were men high up in the riggings, or hung over ships' sides making repairs. Cargo was being loaded, unloaded. Gigantic sails were stretched out to be mended; animals huddled in crates; displeased passengers argued with ticket clerks. Selene stopped anyone she could and inquired about a boat for Britain, and she was told that the one on the end was about to leave, that she had just missed the one she wanted, that there wasn't one due to go out for weeks, all misinformation and false leads until her hope gradually wore down and she was left with a sinking heart.

Andreas had already sailed; she had missed him.

———

As she was crossing the temple courtyard, a postulant came hurrying up to her. "Mother Mercia wants to see you at once, Sister Peregrina," the girl said. "She has had everyone out searching the city for you."

Selene looked in the direction of Mother Mercia's apartment. Mother Mercia. Selene had run out, not giving a reason, and now it was past midnight. She was exhausted and filled with despair, and she wanted nothing more than to be alone. But she knew she must apologize, and explain.

Selene followed the postulant into the cloister with a heavy heart, and thought: *What shall I do now?*

She had come within minutes of being reunited with Andreas. Now she knew where he was, that he was still alive and still taking to the sea. What should she do?

Do I sail on the next ship bound for Britain?

The postulant held the door open for Selene and then closed it discreetly, leaving the healing-mistress alone with Mother Mercia and the visitor.

Selene stopped abruptly inside the door and stared across the room.

"Ah," said Mother Mercia, rising from her chair. "Here is Sister Peregrina now."

And Andreas turned around.

CHAPTER 49

I tried to stop you from running out, Peregrina," Mercia said to Selene. "I knew that a messenger sent by me would be faster and have more success in finding Andreas than you. And you see?" She smiled. "I was right."

"Andreas . . . " Selene said.

He stared at her in disbelief. Then he said, "Selene!" and suddenly she was no longer in Alexandria, a woman thirty-three years old, but back in Antioch, sixteen and wearing her first adult dress. She was standing on a rooftop with Andreas, a backdrop of summer stars behind him; he was standing close to her, taking her face into his hands, and he was saying quietly, passionately, his dark-blue eyes burning into hers: "You heal others, Selene, you can heal yourself."

Oh, Andreas, Selene wanted to cry. The years and the miles I have traveled since that day! The things I have witnessed and learned. The names I have borne: Fortuna, Umma, Peregrina. But I am still Selene, that girl of long ago!

She wanted to rush to him, she wanted him to open his arms and take her to himself, closing those years and miles, telling her that they didn't matter, didn't count. But instead he stood across the room looking at her with a stunned expression.

"I was in a tavern at the harbor," he said, his voice incredulous, "passing my remaining time in Alexandria with the captain of my ship, when the messenger from the Temple of Isis came in. I could not imagine what urgent business would call me here . . . but because it was Mother Mercia who called, I could not refuse. And when I arrived, she told me about Sister Peregrina, who thought she might know me."

He paused. Then he stared again, as if not believing his eyes. "Selene . . . It's been many years."

Andreas, at forty-seven, seemed to Selene more handsome even than she remembered. His hair was silver but the beard was still dark brown, and the eyes softer, the mouth no longer severe. "I've thought of you," she said.

"And I, you."

They fell silent again, staring, filling their eyes with each other. Mother Mercia, at first perplexed, then comprehending, marveled at the mysterious workings of the Goddess, and said, "I shall leave you two alone. You must have a lot to talk about."

"When I saw you in the sick ward the other day," Andreas said, after Mercia was gone, "I thought I recognized you. But then Mother Mercia said you were Sister Peregrina."

"I have been known by many names," Selene said softly. "I went to Antioch five years ago, Andreas. But your villa is no longer there."

"There was a fire, I'm told."

"You left Antioch," she said.

"As did you."

His eyes held her as he said, "I have seen you so many times in my memories, Selene, in my dreams, that I hesitate now to believe my eyes. Mother Mercia has told me about your work here. She told me how you came to be here, that you and your daughter live with the sisters. How strange life is, to bring us together again like this . . . "

Selene was lost in the intensity of his eyes. For seventeen years she had dreamed of this moment; she had enacted it in her mind so often and it had become such a permanent part of her thoughts that it sometimes seemed to have actually taken place. But now it was indeed happening, seeing him there, hearing his voice and knowing this was real, not a dream, Selene was suddenly at a loss for words. "Did you become a teacher, Andreas?" she asked. "The textbook you were going to write . . . "

A dark look came over his face, and bitterness crept into his voice as he said, "I have been sailing the seas and the oceans. I never finished the book."

"And now?"

"Now I am in the service of the Emperor Claudius."

Selene felt something in the air. The atmosphere was charged; there was a force in the room. Something was wrong. She felt dizzy. *Andreas!* she wanted to say. *The gods have brought us together at last! We can begin our work now!* But, inexplicably, she could not bring herself to say it.

Andreas! cried her mind. *Why didn't you find me? Why didn't you come after me on the Palmyra road?*

And then she realized: She didn't want to know the answer.

It struck her like a blow, the sudden realization of what she had been trying to deny for seventeen years—the inescapable truth that Andreas had not come after her.

We were two weeks on the road to Palmyra, she thought now, suddenly hurt and angry. *And I was three days sitting by that road with my dying mother. You could have come, Andreas. You should have come. But you never did.*

She turned away. "Why," Selene said in a breathless voice, "are you going to Britain?"

"Claudius has sent for me. He is in Britain and the climate does not suit him. He is suffering from ill health." Andreas's voice sounded hard; but his heart was weeping. These were not the words he wanted to say, but the memory of his pain, of his anger and bitterness of seventeen years ago, stilled his tongue. She had asked about the textbook. He could tell her that it died with the dream; that he had been a fool to think he could start life anew, that the punishment for his past crimes would cease.

Everything was different now; the love they had once shared had died then.

Selene had killed that love when she left the message at the gate, the message the girl Zoë had passed on to him—that Selene was going to marry someone else, a man who lived in Tyre.

As he stood staring at her now, fighting the impulse to take her into his arms, Andreas recalled how, not believing Zoë, he had gone that next morning to Selene's house and had found it empty. They have gone to the mountains early, he had told himself. They will be back in two days. He pictured himself going back again and again to that little house in the poor quarter, puzzled and confused, disbelieving, foolishly hoping, waiting, until the days and weeks and months rolled by and Selene never returned and he realized it had been true, that he had been love-blind a second time in his life and that Selene, like Hestia before her, had deserted him.

And if Andreas ever harbored one kernel of doubt, if his heart ever yearned, on that long and lonely voyage to China, to be reconciled with Selene and to learn that Zoë had lied, it was all dashed when he learned from Mother Mercia that Selene had a child, that Zoë had, after all, told the truth.

Selene looked down at her hands. This was all wrong. They were like two strangers. Where had the dream gone? Their beautiful dream of working together in medicine, of teaching, of healing. She wanted to weep for the terrible loss, for the broken dream, and finally, strangely, for the boy who had sailed with the amber-hunting ship and allowed his soul to be killed.

"Why did you come to Alexandria?" he asked suddenly, his voice tight.

Selene looked up and saw dark, angry eyes. *To find you,* she wanted to say. "To search for my family," she said. "I was told that my parents came from here."

"Your parents?"

"Mera was not my real mother."

Andreas looked confused. And then Selene remembered: She had begun the quest for her identity on the Palmyra road. Andreas knew nothing of it. All these years, he had not known how priceless the ivory rose was!

"Do you . . . " she began, suddenly afraid. *Had he sold it? Lost it? Is the only key to my identity and to my destiny gone forever?* "The ivory necklace, which I gave to you in Daphne. Do you still have it?"

A look passed briefly over his face, too quickly to have been read by Selene; a look of disappointment, of having expected, *hoped* she had been about to say something else. Then he said, "Yes."

He strode across the room, lifted a leather traveling bag onto the table and undid the straps. He reached inside. Andreas turned and held out his hand; the ivory rose lay on his open palm.

Selene stared at it. A small, white, perfect rose. Each petal meticulously carved. Cupped in his hand, which she saw was tanned and hardened. *It is I he holds there,* she thought, as she started to move toward him. *But he doesn't know it . . . Here it is. At long last. All the answers to identity and destiny . . .*

And she was afraid.

Someone tapped on the door, and Mother Mercia looked in. "May I join you now?" she asked. Then she was aware that Andreas was holding something out to Sister Peregrina, and that Peregrina seemed hesitant to take it. The *alma mater* was surprised by the stormy expression on Andreas's face; and when she looked at Peregrina, she saw the rigid posture, the manner of someone struggling for control.

How extraordinary, Mercia thought, as she came into the room. *A few minutes ago, when they first looked at each other, I could have sworn I saw love pass between them.*

"What is it, Peregrina?" Mother Mercia asked, coming to stand with Selene and Andreas.

"It's something my mother gave to me when I turned sixteen. But I gave it to Andreas." Selene picked it up with great care, laid it in her palm and stared down at it. "My mother," she said in a mystified tone, "the woman who raised me, told me that a clue to who my real parents were is in this rose."

Mercia looked surprised. "Inside it?"

Selene nodded.

"Aren't you going to open it?"

Selene hesitated. What was she going to find? What if, after all this time, she were to discover that the rose contained no answers at all? That Mera, in her simplicity and faith in the miraculous, had believed a dying man's fantasy?

She tried to open it, but the ceramic seal would not break.

"Here," said Andreas. "Let me."

His strong fingers snapped the seal and he tipped the contents of the rose into her open hands: the strip of linen from her brother's receiving blanket, a lock of hair, a gold ring. Instinctively, because she recognized these to be powerful tokens, Mother Mercia crossed herself.

It was the ring that drew their attention. Gently placing the other objects on the table, Selene turned the ring to the light. "There is writing," she said, "but I cannot read it. They are Latin letters."

Mother Mercia looked and saw it was a gold coin set into a ring, a coin stamped with the profile of a man; around its edge were Latin words that she, too, did not know how to read.

Andreas took the ring and held it up. His eyebrows arched. Forming a circle around the man's profile were words: CAESAR · PERPETUO · DICT

"What does it mean?" Selene asked.

"It's an old coin," Andreas said. "Struck many years ago, when Julius Caesar declared himself dictator for life. He was the first Roman to have his likeness stamped on a coin."

"Is that who this is?" Selene asked, taking the ring back. "Julius Caesar?"

"Yes. And the writing says: Caesar, Perpetual Dictator. The coin commemorates the occasion, which, I believe, took place some seventy years ago."

Selene looked up at Andreas. "What does it mean?" she asked. "Why did my father call this my destiny? Why did he say that I came from the gods?"

Mother Mercia gasped and whispered, "Your father said that?"

"What year were you born?" Andreas asked.

"Nearly thirty-three years ago. If you know what this means, Andreas, then tell me!"

"Thirty-three years ago," he said cautiously, "Augustus Caesar died, and Tiberius took his place. But it was not a smooth succession. There were conspiracies to stop Tiberius from becoming emperor. There were those who wished for the restoration of the Republic as it had been under Julius Caesar. There were those who thought the dictatorship of Rome should pass on only to the descendants of the man who had established it—Julius Caesar. Augustus, after all, had only been Caesar's grandnephew. There was a great deal of turmoil when Augustus died, and before Tiberius got control once and for all."

"But what does that have to do with me?"

"People were gotten out of the way, Selene. Anyone who could be a threat, who could lay legitimate claim to the succession, was eliminated by Tiberius."

Selene drew in a breath. "You mean . . . my *father?*"

"I don't see how, though," he said, frowning. "It's a known fact that Julius Caesar died childless." Andreas turned to Mother Mercia and saw that she was staring at Selene in a strange way.

Suddenly the priestess said, "I think I know the answer. Come with me."

Mother Mercia led Selene down a dim corridor, through archways and into a part of the temple Selene had not visited before. The walls were covered with murals of very ancient gods, looming figures of human bodies with animal heads, and column after column of ancient hieroglyphic writing. The walls were stained with mildew, plaster had fallen away, the air smelled stale. Selene realized that this was the very oldest part of the temple, its core. These walls had been built centuries ago, possibly thousands of years ago; they were already standing when Alexander claimed this land for his new city. This was the most sacrosanct part of the temple.

Mercia led Selene into a chamber thick with incense, and they found an elderly priestess, bent with age, devoutly tending the holy fires burning around the room. After dismissing the woman, Mercia drew Selene to face the statue that dominated the room.

The statue was incongruously new within these old walls, and appeared to have been placed here within recent memory. Mother Mercia pointed to the pedestal, which was inscribed with Greek lettering that Selene could read: THEA NEOTERA.

"New Goddess . . . " Selene murmured. Then she raised her eyes to the face of the statue and felt herself go numb.

She was gazing at what in many ways looked like her own face.

"Cleopatra," Mother Mercia said in a reverent tone. "The last queen of Egypt. The last living incarnation of Isis. Now I know why I once thought that I should know you, Peregrina. Do you see how you resemble her? They say she had extraordinary coloring—unusually white skin and hair as black as the night. You are like that, Peregrina."

Spellbound, Selene could not speak. She was held by that white face; she stood as still as if she, too, were carved from marble.

Mother Mercia turned to Andreas, who had followed them and who now stood behind them in the shadows. "You said, Andreas, that Julius Caesar died childless. That is not true. There was a son, Prince Caesarion, by Cleopatra, his Egyptian wife."

Andreas's voice was a deep rumble in the ancient chamber. "But the boy was killed. When Antony and Cleopatra were found dead by their own hands, Augustus ordered the execution of their two children, and of Caesarion."

Mother Mercia stared across the room at Andreas, her small, wise eyes communicating more than words could. She said: "I was a little girl at the time, and I remember when the Romans came. I remember when our last queen was put in her tomb. I remember that her children were slain. But there were rumors, Andreas. Stories of a slave being killed in the place of Caesarion, of a group of conspirators, still loyal to Julius Caesar, saving the prince and hiding him away. To raise him, to prepare him for the day when he would claim his rightful legacy in Rome. That was why Augustus ordered him killed. Caesarion was a threat to Augustus's claim to Caesar's office. But the prince escaped."

Andreas stepped into the circle of light. "Tiberius might have found out about it, I suppose. His spies and agents might have learned of Prince Caesarion's existence. Perhaps Tiberius dispatched soldiers. And they came to Alexandria, forcing Caesarion and his wife to flee. But the soldiers caught up with them in Palmyra . . . "

Selene stared up at the beautiful goddess. "Can it be?" she whispered. "Is this woman my grandmother?"

"Her full name," Mother Mercia said, "was Cleopatra Selene. And her brother was Ptolemy Helios."

The room suddenly seemed very hot. The smoke from the lamps was swirling around Selene's head; the cloying scent of incense pressed all around her. She could not breathe. She was being suffocated. Selene swayed. Then she felt a strong arm go about her waist and she leaned against Andreas.

When they were back in Mother Mercia's apartment, Selene shook her head and murmured, "I cannot believe it."

"There is the ring to prove it," the *alma mater* said, "and your name, and your remarkable resemblance to the queen."

Selene's voice came from far away. "The healer-woman who delivered me told me how my mother whispered my soul-name into my ear the moment I was born. What name did she whisper, Mother Mercia?"

The *alma mater* stared back at Selene, the answer hanging unspoken in the air.

"Am *I* Cleopatra Selene? And my brother, Ptolemy Helios?" Selene looked from Mother Mercia to Andreas. "But why did the soldiers slay only my father, and take my mother and brother alive? Was not my brother a threat to Tiberius?"

"I don't know why they were not slain," Andreas said. "They were definitely a threat."

Selene's eyes widened. "Then . . . am *I*?" she whispered. "Am I now a threat to the ruling family in Rome?"

They sat and listened to the deep summer night breathe softly around them. Beyond the temple walls, Alexandria slept; the salty kiss of the Mediterranean stirred palm trees and rippled the moonlit water.

Finally Selene said, "That is what my mother meant. As she lay dying in the desert outside Palmyra, she told me that Isis was my goddess. That She had a special interest in me."

"Your grandmother *was* Isis, Selene," said Mother Mercia. "Cleopatra was worshiped by millions in her lifetime. And your grandfather, Julius Caesar, was a descendant of Venus. The two goddesses are watching over you now, Selene. You have both royal and sacred blood flowing in your veins."

———

They stood in the courtyard in the sultry night air. Dawn was not far off; Venus would soon be rising over the tops of the palm trees.

Selene was numb. She knew she was not the same woman tonight that she had been that morning; that the world was no longer the same place. And Andreas . . .

"What will you do now?" he asked quietly.

"I don't know. I had thought . . . it would be so different. Finding out who I really was. What I was meant to do in life. I had pictured this moment in many ways. But not like this."

Andreas stood close to her; his breath warmed her face. But he didn't touch her, he didn't reach out as he wanted to. *Say the word, Selene,* cried his heart, *and I will disobey the emperor and stay here with you. We will find a place to hide, far up the Nile where no one can find us and we can live in love and peace. I will forget the past and the hurt and seventeen years of anger. Only say the word, Selene . . .*

She stood close to him. Selene knew that she had only to move slightly and they would touch. *Ask me to go with you, Andreas,* she thought. *Say the word and I shall leave Alexandria and the gods and my destiny, and follow you.*

"You have a great gift, Selene," he said quietly. "You are wasting it here in this city full of healers. You were born to do more important things. The temple sick ward can go on without you now; you have trained others to take your place. There is nothing in this world you cannot do."

He spoke softly but passionately. His eyes held her as surely as if his arms did. "You had a dream years ago, Selene, of creating an unsurpassed healing art, and taking it where it is most needed. You have that skill and knowledge now. You are unique. Take those gifts to where the greatest need is."

"And where is that, Andreas?" she asked. "Where shall I go?"

"Go to Rome."

"Rome!"

"The people there need someone like you, Selene. They need your skills and wisdom. You are lost here in Alexandria, like a diamond among thousands of pearls. But Rome, Selene. Rome needs you."

Rome, she thought, her head swimming. *City of my ancestors; the city that made my grandfather a god.*

And then Selene thought: *Are* they *there? My mother and brother. Were they taken back to Rome, alive? And are they alive still, today?*

"I have always had a feeling, Andreas," she said quietly, "that my healing and my identity are in some way linked. But just how has not been made clear to me. Will I find my answers in Rome?"

"Perhaps."

"And will you go back to Rome, Andreas?" she whispered. "After you have seen the emperor in Britain, will *you* go back to Rome?"

"I must go back, Selene. My home is there. My friends are there. I will return to Rome when Claudius permits me to. And we shall meet again, you and I . . . "

CHAPTER 50

Selene and Ulrika sailed on one of the mighty grain ships that regularly crossed the Mediterranean from Egypt to Rome. It was named *Isis*, a magnificent craft with a sweeping stern that rose up into a gilded goose head; it carried a thousand tons of grain and over six hundred passengers, and it made the voyage, pushing against the northerly winds, in seven weeks.

Several delays had set the departure back. First, there had been the exit pass everyone departing from Alexandria must secure from the governor —but he had been on an inspection tour up to the First Cataract of the Nile and unable to issue passes. Then there had been the argument over the fee, which Selene had thought outrageous: men were charged ten drachmae to leave Egypt, but for Ulrika it was thirty and for Selene, one hundred. There had been no fighting it; the law was created to discourage women from traveling. Mother Mercia paid the fees out of the temple treasury. Next it had been necessary to find a ship, which meant going up and down the waterfront and inquiring which was bound for what destination, and if there was room for two more passengers. Finally, there had been the problem with omens.

All ships' masters were superstitious men, but the master of the *Isis* was more so than most. On the day of the scheduled sailing his sacrifice of a bull to Poseidon had not gone well, so he postponed the departure. The second time, a crow had sat in the rigging and squawked. On the third scheduled day of sailing the ship's carpenter had reported having dreamed of black goats. And the fourth day had been passed by because it was the twenty-fourth of August, a universal bad-luck day. Selene and Ulrika had gone to the harbor each time, along with their bundles of possessions, in the company of Mother Mercia, to await the cry of the herald announcing their ship's departure, because ships never left on a fixed schedule. Each time they had returned to the temple, frustrated and anxious.

But finally the day had come when the winds were favorable, the date auspicious and the omens good. Ulrika and Selene stood on the deck waving until the shore fell slowly away and Alexandria could no longer be seen.

They slept on the deck by night, behind a curtain that separated the female passengers from the male, cuddled under blankets with their precious belongings tucked between them. By day they sat in the shade of the big square mainsail, where they ate, mended their clothes and conversed with other passengers. They were never idle. Once it was known that a healer-woman was on board, Selene was kept busy dispensing ginger root for seasickness and ointment for the inevitable gum blisters.

Ulrika passed the time watching the helmsman as he pulled on the tiller bars, or listening to the speech of sailors as they trimmed the lines and pumped bilgewater, or talking with the ship's carpenter as he fashioned spare oars and belaying pins. And when not marveling at this floating citadel that was like a self-sufficient little town, Ulrika spent many hours at the railing, gazing out over the Mediterranean with big solemn eyes and thinking how her father, years before, had crossed this very sea—as a slave in chains.

It was a smooth and uneventful voyage, and all the passengers cheered with relief when the port of Ostia was in sight. Fear of sailing was common the world over, and not a person on the *Isis* had neglected to wear the traditional gold coin around his or her neck these past seven weeks—a time-honored practice that, in the event of the ship going down in a storm, ensured that one's corpse would be buried by anyone recovering it.

As the *Isis* drew closer to the shore, Selene stood at the railing with her face to the wind. *Another new land,* she thought. *With new people, new customs. What will I find in Rome?*

And by what name shall I be known *here?*

Selene was filled with a sense that she was arriving at her last new shore; that her years of wandering were soon to end. *The gods will reveal their purpose to me here at last. My identity will finally be joined with my calling as a healer—but in what way, or how, I do not yet know.*

She thought of Mera, a humble woman from humble origins, who had lifted the ring of Julius Caesar from the hand of a dying prince. She thought, unexpectedly, of old Ignatius, who had fought the desert bandits to protect her, and whose miraculous transparent stone had given her fires on cold nights in strange lands. Selene even recalled Kazlah, whose favorite "medicine" had been a drink made of pulverized emeralds and rubies dissolved in wine, and which only made his patients sicker. What did he do with the secret of Hecate's Cure, she wondered. Did he finally turn it into a weapon against Lasha? And then there was Fatma, the wise-woman of the desert who had shared with Selene the secret knowledge of her ancestresses; now it was being brought to Rome. And Rani, who had sacrificed so much in order to be a healer—forsaking marriage and children, denying her femininity so that she could work in a man's world.

And she thought about her daughter, that remarkable result of her love for Wulf. *We will work together in Rome,* Selene thought. *I shall pass all my knowledge to Ulrika so that it will not die with me.*

Finally, she thought of Andreas.

It seemed to her that her love for him encompassed the vast Mediterranean sky, and plumbed deeper depths than the green water beneath her ship. She had lost him somehow; something had allowed their dream to die. But perhaps in Rome, when he returned from Britain, if the gods permitted . . .

Perhaps my life has been but a prelude to this moment, Selene thought in excitement, as the busy harbor came into view. *The gods have prepared me and now I am ready.*

CHAPTER 51

Rome is a dangerous city, Selene," Andreas had warned. "Especially for a woman on her own. Go to Paulina's house. She's an old friend and she will help you."

During the nine weeks since Andreas had spoken those words, as they stood by the temple gate saying goodbye, Selene had visualized the house of Lady Paulina as small and modest, and the woman herself to be like Mother Mercia. And so the villa on the Esquiline Hill and the lady who lived there came as a surprise to Selene.

This was their first day in Rome, a blue-and-gold autumn day, and Selene and Ulrika had gone straight to the Esquiline Hill. The street of Lady Paulina's villa was plain and unremarkable, fronted by one continuous wall with gates set at intervals, to hide from public view the fabulous houses of the rich. When Selene and Ulrika were admitted through one of those gates, they found on the other side a garden that was like a paradise, filled with fountains and trees and flowers. Selene and Ulrika were led into the atrium of the house, beyond which they could see the inner garden surrounded on all four sides by a pillared cloister with rooms branching off from it. It was the grandest house Selene had ever seen, and she wondered now about the woman who lived here.

"Paulina is a widow," Andreas had explained. "Her husband, Valerius, and I were close friends. She lives alone in the house he left her. She's lonely; I know she will welcome your company."

Music and laughter were coming from one of the rooms off the peristyle garden, and from that room a woman now emerged. She crossed the garden with aristocratic grace and entered the atrium with a self-possessed presence.

Lady Paulina Valeria was of medium height and slender build, with topaz eyes, and brown hair arranged on her head in rising rows of curls. Her skin was delicate and fair, as if she avoided sunlight; she appeared to be perhaps forty years old, much younger than Selene had expected.

Lady Paulina took in Selene's simple linen dress and the sandals of an Egyptian peasant in a single glance. Her gaze lingered a fraction longer on Ulrika—Selene thought for an instant that she saw a cloud of disapproval cross her face—then Lady Paulina said in Latin, "I am Paulina Valeria. You wish to see me?"

Selene replied in Greek: "My daughter and I are newly arrived in Rome. I am a friend of Andreas the physician, and he suggested I come to see you."

The topaz eyes flickered. "I see. Welcome to Rome. Is this your first visit here?"

"Yes. My daughter and I have just come from Alexandria and we don't know our way here. We don't know anyone, except for Andreas."

"Yes, Andreas. How is he?"

"He's on his way to Britain."

"I know. I saw him off at Ostia three months ago. Did he depart safely for Britain?"

"He set sail from Alexandria in good weather."

Paulina paused. Then she said, "Where are you staying?"

When Selene told her of the inn near the Forum, where she and Ulrika had spent the previous night after arriving from Ostia, Lady Paulina smiled without warmth and said, "Then you must stay here in my house. Inns are so expensive and unsafe, don't you think? As you are Andreas's friend, then you are mine as well. I shall have a boy fetch your things."

A slave was summoned to escort the new guests to their rooms, and before she left the atrium, Lady Paulina said, "You will stay for as long as you wish, of course. I insist." Then, glancing again at Ulrika, Paulina said, "How old is your daughter?"

"She will be thirteen next March."

Lady Paulina seemed to consider that, then she said, "This is a large house; it would be easy for a child to get lost in it. And my gardens in the rear are quite extensive. I am sure you will want to tell her not to wander. You will want to keep her close to your rooms."

As they followed the slave across the garden, they passed the room where the music was coming from, and Selene heard voices: "I can't imagine why Amelia married beneath her." "Because he's handsome and rich." This was followed by laughter, and then a woman's voice said, "Still, what of his family? He comes from a long line of *cheesemakers*. They may have money—new money, mind, not *old*—but they have no *name*. I think Amelia has quite demeaned herself. She's a laughingstock. Ah, here's Paulina. Ask her what *she* thinks of poor Amelia."

But when Paulina walked into the room the laughter died. Selene heard whispering and imagined the curious eyes of the guests following them past the open door.

As Ulrika walked with her mother through the garden, she looked right and left, marveling that all this belonged to just one person. And then she saw a boy, two or three years older than herself, raking dried leaves from the garden path. Ulrika stared at him. He had blond hair and blue eyes, and he was very tall. He looked up from his work and stared back, the rake forgotten in his hand.

Selene and Ulrika settled into the house of Valerius with an ease learned from their years of traveling and adjusting to new surroundings. Ulrika had said little since their arrival at Ostia—indeed, she had not spoken much since the night her mother had come to her room in the temple and announced they were leaving Alexandria. She finally washed her face, got into her night shift, said her silent prayers and slipped into the clean bed without saying a word.

She was thinking of the boy in the garden.

Selene, in the next room, tried for a long time to sleep but could not. Exhausted though her body was, her mind was wide awake. Was this her home at last? Rome? She was increasingly certain of it. She could *feel* it.

Her family was here, the mighty rulers of the Empire, men and women who were related to her by blood, who shared her ancestral line. And here, too, was Andreas's home, to which he must some day return from Britain. But what else did Rome hold for her? Selene's medicine box stood ready at the foot of her bed, a little travel-worn now, scratched and chipped, but stocked nearly to overflowing with all the remedies she had gathered in her years and miles of traveling.

"The people of Rome need you," Andreas had said. "They have no sick-tending places such as you have seen in other cities, no temple wards to turn to such as you created here in Alexandria, no haven for the relief of their pain. You will find your destiny in Rome."

Growing sleepy at last, Selene's thoughts went finally to Lady Paulina. What was she to Andreas, and he to her?

As her breathing grew deeper, slower, Selene saw Andreas in her mind; she felt the old aches awaken, a new rush of an old yearning, and above all, love.

CHAPTER 52

These people are our family, Rikki," Selene said with pride in her voice. "They are our cousins. We are of the same blood."

They were standing at the foot of the Palatine Hill, looking up at the terraces and porticoes and stands of cypress trees that marked the mansions and palaces of the aristocracy of Rome. Selene was trying, once again, to straighten out the tangled relationships, so that Ulrika might better understand.

"Augustus, the first emperor," she said, repeating what Andreas had told her that night in Mother Mercia's apartment, "was Julius Caesar's grand-nephew. His sister, Octavia, married Marc Antony and they had a daughter, Antonia. Antonia, after marrying Drusus, had two sons—Germanicus and Claudius. That same Claudius is now emperor of Rome. While he is a distant cousin, Rikki, he is our cousin nonetheless."

A short while later, they visited the Shrine of the Divine Julius, a pretty circular temple where he was worshiped as a god. Selene explained: "You see how Rome feels about your great-grandfather? It is *his* blood that rules the Empire, Rikki. And the people who are in power now, the Julio-Claudians, claim their right to rule by that drop of Julian blood in their veins. But your blood, my daughter, is pure; you are a *direct* descendant of the Divine Julius. His son was your grandfather." *And,* Selene added to herself, *because Julius Caesar was a descendant of the goddess Venus, so then is my daughter.*

Ulrika listened without speaking, her grave blue eyes taking in the taller-than-life statue of the man she despised, the man she was ashamed to call great-grandfather, the man who had first marched into Germany and made slaves of her father's people.

These were not her people and this was not her city. Instinctively, Ulrika turned away from the statue of Julius Caesar and set her eyes to the north. She kept them there, steady, determined.

═══

At first Selene had difficulty getting around the sprawling city, but soon, as she set out each day and walked until her old thigh wound ached, as she memorized the plan of the streets, the placement of the hundred monuments, and spoke with the people, Selene began to understand Rome.

She carried her medicine box with her everywhere she went and frequently stopped to give aid. As Andreas had said, there was nowhere for people to go in times of illness or injury. Rome was a wild place, Selene thought, its streets brutal, its people, crammed into airless and unsafe tenements, were like savages. As she walked narrow streets that never saw sunlight, Selene began to realize that there were *two* Romes: this dark, crowded one, where the unemployed thousands sat idly in the heat of late summer, drinking rations of government beer, grumbling, having nothing before them but short, hard lives; and the other, the one that existed behind high walls and locked gates, in those landscaped villas of the rich, like Lady Paulina, who seemed to move on another plane, a tiny population that ruled the world but took no part in it.

Selene soon learned to hurry home at sunset. Once the day began to recede and wheeled traffic was permitted into the city, another element of the population, dangerous and desperate, emerged. Selene quickly understood why windows were covered with iron bars and why doors were fitted with monstrous bolts. The Roman nights were filled with crime.

In time, Selene also learned something about her hostess: that, contrary to what Andreas had said, Lady Paulina was never alone.

There were always visitors and house guests at the villa, noisy dinner parties downstairs, evenings with philosophers and poets, and once a touring mime troupe had filled the garden below with music and applause late into the night. At sundown Paulina's slaves went about lighting all the torches and lamps, and soon the guests arrived with their bodyguards and the villa rang with laughter. Selene and Ulrika were never invited to join in, but they listened to it all from their bedrooms on the floor above, and sometimes Selene found her daughter kneeling on the balcony, peering down through the railing.

Selene rarely encountered her hostess; days would pass before she would glimpse Lady Paulina gliding across the peristyle garden. And since the day of Selene and Ulrika's arrival, the two women had exchanged few words.

Selene did not mind being excluded from the gaiety; she had work to do. Each dawn saw her leaving the house—without Ulrika, who preferred to stay at home—and each sunset brought her back, tired, limping, her medicine box depleted of some of its supplies. Evenings found her rolling bandages, sharpening scalpels, sorting herbs purchased in the Forum. Then, a bath and early retirement to bed.

Selene was ready. Her destiny, she was certain, lay waiting for her in this city—around the next corner, at the next turning; and she hoped she would recognize it.

CHAPTER 53

Ulrika snapped her head up. She saw a flash of blond hair duck back from the window. He had been spying on her again, the boy from the garden.

Ulrika laid aside her book, got up from the bed and crossed the room on tiptoe.

This was the fifth time this week that she had been aware of him watching her. How many other times, she wondered, had he spied on her and she did not know it? Sometimes, when she passed through the garden, she felt his eyes following her; and once, as she had walked to the street gate with her mother, Ulrika had seen the boy hiding behind bushes.

She crept to the door and looked out. The corridor was empty. Below, in the open-air garden, the slaves were beginning to light the torches in readiness for this evening's festivities. Ulrika frowned. She had been so absorbed in reading her book that she had lost track of the time. The sun was almost down; her mother was not yet back.

Stepping out of her bedroom, Ulrika looked right and left. Across the way, a door opened and two people emerged, Lady Paulina's current house guests, a senator and his wife. Ulrika watched them. The people who came to this house were always beautifully dressed; the men were smart and handsome, the women wore their hair in extravagant pyramids of curls. They talked in a special way—their Greek was pure and careful; even their laughter was different, polite and restrained. Ulrika was fascinated by Lady Paulina's friends; she also hated them.

As the senator and his wife descended to the garden below, Ulrika saw a movement out of the corner of her eye. She spun around in time to see the boy duck into a doorway.

"Wait," she said. "Don't run away." Ulrika hurried down the corridor and came to a closed door. She hesitated for a moment, then put her hand to the latch and opened it. Inside, she found a bedroom similar to her own, ready for an overnight guest.

"Please come out," Ulrika said as she walked inside. She stopped to listen. All she heard was the commotion of guests arriving downstairs. She called to him again, switching from Greek to Aramaic. "Can you understand me? Please don't be afraid. I'd like to talk to you."

She walked farther into the room. When she saw the window hangings stir even though there was no breeze, she said gently, "I'm your friend. I'm not one of these people. Please come out."

She kept her eye on the hangings. She saw the hem move. "I'm not going away," she said firmly. "I'm going to stay here until you come out."

———

Selene emerged from the tenement near the river, alarmed to see how late the hour had become. Earlier, a woman had begged her to come and look at her baby, which was listless and would not eat. Selene had spent longer with the infant than she had realized, and now found herself in this squalid quarter by the river, with the sun slipping behind the hills.

Gathering her medicine box close to her, she turned down the first street leading away from the Tiber and started to hurry in the direction of the Esquiline Hill.

Her way was suddenly blocked by a crowd surging around the corner.

The people were angry, shouting for "bread and circuses." Selene knew what was happening. She had seen several such spontaneous outbursts in Rome: the mob usually consisted of unemployed men, bored and restless, ignited into fury by the slightest provocation. The excuses were generally thin, but tonight they were protesting Claudius's absence from Rome and the dwindling supply of games and free food.

Selene stepped under a sheltering eave as the mob pushed by her, shaking fists, and cursing the people who lived on the Palatine Hill. Selene did not blame them; Rome's unemployment rate was outrageously high, and the government handouts supported a large proportion of the population, creating a jobless, uneducated, quick-to-rebel class. This was their entertainment for today, rushing through the city and antagonizing the soldiers, who were now appearing at the end of the street; tomorrow they would stream into the Circus Maximus and watch games, all the while gorging on free beer and food.

As the mob met head-on with the line of soldiers at the intersection, men on horseback appeared; they had baskets lashed to their saddles from which they rapidly produced live snakes, flinging them into the mob. At once the jam started to break up. People ran this way and that, screaming. It was over almost instantly, and soon the soldiers were gathering up their snakes from the deserted street.

As she stepped out from the protection of the doorway, Selene saw a man also step away from the wall, grab his side, teeter and fall to the ground. The soldiers ignored him, but Selene went to him and saw that he had been wounded below the ribs. A hasty examination told her that his injury was beyond her skill; he was bleeding too heavily. He would need tourniquets and deep ligatures, and a place to lie still.

When she raised her head, thinking to call to one of the soldiers, Selene saw that she was now alone with the injured man, and that the street had grown dark and quiet.

Then she remembered the island in the middle of the river, where the temple of the healing god Aesculapius stood, and that the bridge leading out to it was not far away. Selene struggled to help the weak and dazed man to his feet. With his arm around her shoulders, Selene staggered down the street, away from the direction of the Esquiline Hill and toward the river.

An old stone bridge connected the left bank of the Tiber with the boat-shaped island; its terminus lay near the entrance to the Theater of Marcellus around which a large crowd was milling, buying tickets for a night performance. Selene helped the stranger through the throng and onto the bridge.

She knew that the buildings clustered on the island, standing in silhouette against the last of the sunset, made up the precincts of the Temple of Aesculapius. She had yet to visit this local healing place, but assumed it would be like any other Aesculapian temple found throughout the Empire, and so presumed this man could find help here. But when she reached the other side of the bridge and, unable to hold him any longer, lowered the unconscious stranger to the ground, Selene straightened up and stared, stunned, at the sight that met her eyes.

Finally, the hangings stirred and the blond head appeared. Two wary blue eyes regarded Ulrika; the boy moved stiffly, ready to run.

"Please don't be afraid of me," Ulrika said, wondering why he was so timid. She held out her hand. "I'm your friend."

He came all the way out from behind the curtain, but kept his distance, watching her. Now Ulrika saw the reason for his fear: there were fresh whip marks on his upper arms, and scars on his wrists where manacles must have rubbed his flesh raw. This boy was new to slavery; he had not yet been "broken."

"Don't you understand me?" she asked, reverting to Greek. No, she realized in frustration; he was so new to slavery that he had not yet learned the language of his masters.

She studied him frankly. The boy was tall like herself, and long-limbed. He was young and gangly still, but already the shoulders were showing signs of the power they would soon have, and his arms were developing wiry muscles. His face, Ulrika thought, was beautiful. The eyes were large and set far apart, and his jaw had a nice angle to it. His nose was very long and straight. And he wasn't really afraid, Ulrika realized; he was mistrustful, and as untamed as a wild animal.

"I am Ulrika," she said, pointing to herself. "Who are you?"

He stared at her.

"Ulrika," she repeated, tapping her chest. "I am Ulrika." She took a few steps closer, but stopped when she saw him grow tense. She pointed a finger at him and gave him a questioning look.

Finally, he said, "Eiric."

Ulrika smiled. "Hello, Eiric," she said.

He did not relax, but she moved closer anyway, and when she was near, looked down at the pendant that lay on his chest. Her eyebrows arched. He wore the Cross of Odin.

Ulrika reached up for the leather thong around her neck and withdrew her own necklace. When he saw it, Eiric's eyes widened.

"Odin," he said in disbelief.

"Yes, Odin. My father gave this necklace to my mother before he died."

He searched her face again, taking in her pale hair and blue eyes, then he gave her a tentative smile.

"That's better!" Ulrika said. "Now I shall teach you my language and you will teach me yours, and we shall be friends because we are of the same people."

When she held out her hand and Eiric shyly took it, Ulrika felt a strange new thrill go through her. She forgot all about the lateness of the hour and that it was now night and that her mother had not yet come home.

———

Lady Paulina escorted the last of her guests to the street, kissed them good night and turned toward the house. A strange, hot wind came up suddenly, rustling dead leaves and stirring the dusty earth. Paulina drew her *palla* about her bare arms and hurried down the garden path.

As she passed through the atrium toward the stairs that led to her suite of rooms, she paused. Someone was sitting in the peristyle garden.

Walking out to the center of the garden, she saw that it was the child, Ulrika, sitting alone on a bench. Her face was shockingly pale in the moonlight.

"What are you doing out here?" Paulina asked.

"I'm waiting for my mother."

Paulina raised an eyebrow. "She's not home yet?"

Ulrika pressed her lips together and shook her head. It was midnight. She had been sitting here for hours, ever since Eiric had been roughly pulled away by the overseer of Paulina's slaves and marched back to the slave quarters. Unable to touch the supper that had been brought, as usual, to her room, Ulrika had come to the garden to wait.

Paulina hesitated. She had an impulse to sit next to the child and offer reassurance; but she fought it. "Do you know where your mother went today?" she asked.

Again Ulrika shook her head, struggling to keep back the tears.

The child is afraid to cry, Lady Paulina thought. *She doesn't want to show her fear.*

The impulse came over her again, to comfort the child; but Paulina was strong. Emotions could be conquered, she knew, if one fought hard enough. "Perhaps I should send someone out to look for her," she said crisply. "Some of my slaves."

Ulrika looked up. "Oh, would you?"

Paulina turned away from the young, bright eyes and regretted her moment of weakness. She should not have let these two stay here. It had only been for Andreas . . .

The gate opened then, and a moment later Selene came into the garden. "Mother!" cried Ulrika, jumping up and running to her.

Selene took her daughter into her arms. "Rikki! I'm sorry I worried you. There was no way I could get word to you."

Selene looked up at Lady Paulina who stood dramatically in a column of moonlight. There was the look of displeasure on her face, and something else—was it pain?

"Where were you, Mother?" Ulrika asked, drawing back from Selene's arms.

"I went to the Temple of Aesculapius."

"Aesculapius!" said Paulina. "Are you ill?"

"No, Lady Paulina, I was—"

"If you are ill, you may make use of my household physician. There is no need for you to go to that wretched island."

Before Selene could say anything further, her hostess said, "It is late. Your daughter is sick with concern."

Selene and Ulrika went up the stairs with their arms about one another. "Oh, Mother, you don't know how worried I was!"

"I'm sorry, Rikki," Selene said, as she massaged her aching thigh and placed her medicine box on the table. Her dress was stained and her hair had escaped from the white cloth that bound her head, but her face glowed. "Something wonderful happened tonight, Rikki."

While her daughter fetched hot water and filled a basin for her mother to wash in, Selene told her about the man who was hurt in the mob and how she had taken him to the temple on the island, and what a sight she had seen there.

"It was unbelievable, Rikki! There must be hundreds of people crammed on that tiny island. They take up every inch of space. And such wretched creatures! Far too many for the handful of brothers and priests to take care of. The High Priest, a man named Herodas, told me that because the numbers were so overwhelming, physicians from the city have stopped coming to help at the temple. The brothers are on their own.

"I was appalled! All those pitiful men and women—they are *discarded* slaves, Rikki. Apparently it is the practice in this terrible city to cart sick or injured slaves, or slaves too old to be of use anymore, to the Temple of Aesculapius, and abandon them there. The priests are overwhelmed. It has become a horrible place. And because of the dreadful conditions created by such a large and helpless crowd, those who would normally come to the temple to seek the God's healing are staying away. And so the temple's treasury is empty. That makes it even harder for the brothers to take care of the homeless slaves, and so conditions get worse and therefore the island has become more and more untouchable."

Selene took hold of her daughter's hands and drew Ulrika down to sit on the bed next to her. "Listen, Rikki!" she said. "It has come! It has finally happened! I know now the work I was born to do!"

Ulrika stared at her mother's face, at the flushed cheeks, the bright eyes. Ulrika had never seen her this way before, and was mesmerized by the power of her mother's passion. "As soon as I saw that island," Selene said, "I *knew*. It all came clear to me. I saw the *greater vision*, Rikki. I saw that this was the end of my long road, the reason for everything I have been through. Andreas was right! He was right, Rikki! My destiny lies here in Rome."

Selene's grip on Ulrika was beginning to hurt. Tremendous energy was flowing from her mother's hands into hers. And Ulrika was overcome.

How beautiful! she thought. How marvelous to be so certain, to *know* where one belongs. "What are you going to do, mother?" she asked, excited now, caught up in Selene's vision.

"I'm going to work on the island, Rikki. It can be restored to the refuge it was meant to be. That was why I was brought there, what I was made ready for. I shall take all the skills and wisdom my travels have taught me to that wretched island that has been forsaken by the gods."

Impulsively, Selene released Ulrika's hands and took her daughter in her arms. "We shall work together," Selene said. "And I shall teach you everything I know. I shall pass it on to you, daughter, so that the dream will never die."

CHAPTER 54

At first the priests and brothers were astonished by Selene's daily appearance at the temple steps, then suspicious of her motives and, finally, once convinced of her good intentions, boundlessly grateful.

"Many of the physicians of the city came and worked here," Herodas explained to Selene. "Some only one day a month, others more often, donating their services to the God. There was a time when we were proud of our temple and the God worked miracles. But then the crowding came, and you see . . . " He gestured in helplessness.

The interior of the temple was like other Aesculapian shrines: A long basilica with an enormous statue of the healing God was at one end, seated on a throne and holding his snake-staff; the rest of the space was empty, to leave room for the pilgrims, who would lie down hoping that the God would heal them in their sleep. This was called "incubation"—the *incubus* or the priest embodying the spirit of the God visited the supplicant in his sleep and prescribed drugs, diet or therapy. Covering the temple walls were the thank offerings of people who had been healed, stone or terra-cotta replicas of parts of the body that had been restored. But they were dusty, Selene saw, and many of them were very old. Only a few appeared to be of recent manufacture, including the effigy of a woman's head, indicating that the God had cured her of a head ailment. Selene understood why so few of the thank offerings were new: The crowds of abandoned slaves left no room for the regular pilgrims. A few priests and brothers moved among the sick, administering food and drink, but the sheer numbers made progress impossible.

"People who do not want to bother trying to heal a sick slave," Herodas explained, "or have no use for an old one, bring them here and leave them, like rubbish. And the law allows it. These poor wretches just lie here and die. There is nothing we can do about it, and now people from the city are staying away. I feel that they are deserting the God."

Herodas was an old man, small and fragile, with white hair and tremulous hands. He had been custodian of the temple through the reigns of four emperors; it grieved him to see how things had deteriorated.

"Will Claudius not help?" Selene asked, as they passed through the temple courtyard, where more people lay—men, women, terribly malnourished children.

"Claudius is blinded by that witch of a wife, Messalina, and also by his ambition to conquer Britain. He tells me to pray to the God and to make sacrifice!"

Selene was thoughtful; finally she said, "I will help."

Herodas looked at her with sadness. She was not the first idealistic healer to appear at the temple and declare noble intentions. And he knew one thing for certain: This young woman, with her marvelous medicine box and skills, would soon become discouraged and leave like everyone else.

CHAPTER 5 5

L ady Paulina took a last look at the necklace inside the box, assured
herself that she had made the perfect choice, then closed the lid and
gave the box to the messenger who stood waiting. The necklace,
made of rare pearls from the Red Sea, was a gift for the empress;
while Paulina did not care for Messalina, she knew nonetheless it was wise
to stay in that powerful woman's good graces.

After the runner had gone, carrying the gift to the Imperial Palace
where Messalina, in her husband Claudius's absence, was holding one of
her notorious parties, Lady Paulina considered the other gifts displayed on
the table.

This was the week of the Saturnalia, the five days in December when
Rome celebrated the annual winter birth of the savior-gods. Houses all over
the city were decorated with pine boughs; gifts were being exchanged; old
friends visited. Tonight Paulina was expecting eight guests, and the smells
of roasting pig and peacock filled the rooms of her villa.

Before leaving the atrium, Lady Paulina paused to close her eyes and
listen to the sounds of traffic beyond the villa's high walls. Her heart was
heavy tonight; she was going to have to make a special effort to be gay with
her guests.

My first Saturnalia without Valerius . . .

When tears threatened, Paulina struggled to compose herself. She was
of ancient and aristocratic blood, having been born into one of the oldest
and most patrician families of Rome and raised in the old-fashioned
atmosphere of Roman *gravitas,* the dignity and breeding that set the
aristocracy apart from the rest of the world. She must not let anyone see
her crumble like this. Valerius, if he were alive, would be disappointed.

Paulina opened her eyes and forced herself to check the gifts one last
time—a book of poems for Maximus, a gold-inlaid platter for Juno, a
tortoiseshell lyre for the wife of Decius. All in order, wrapped in colorful
cloths and tagged for opening later.

But there were no toys . . .

Paulina gripped the edge of the table and rode out the storm of threatening breakdown. Then she left the atrium and mounted the stairs to her
private rooms above. She planned to soak in a hot bath while waiting for
the guests to arrive, and give thought to the problem of what to do about
her unwanted house guests.

She wished Andreas had not done this to her. He had left her no choice but to give Selene and Ulrika shelter. He had even written to her from Britain, thanking her, presuming she had done as he had asked. And now Paulina was hard-pressed to think of a tactful way to get that woman and her child out of the house.

Especially the child.

Something had to be done about them soon. They had been in the house for over two months now. It was becoming unbearable. If it were just the mother, it would be all right—Selene was quiet and unobtrusive, going out at dawn to wherever it was she went every day, returning at sunset and remaining in her room thereafter.

But the child!

Ulrika liked to sit in the garden, she liked to talk to the slaves. She had even made friends among them. Her voice could always be heard, ringing off the walls, and Paulina never knew when she was suddenly going to come upon the girl—once she had even caught her in the library, going through the scrolls.

Paulina closed her eyes.

Ulrika's laughter, her presence, caused such pain . . .

She's nearly thirteen, Paulina thought. *Valeria would have been thirteen this month.*

Lady Paulina was brought out of her reverie by the entrance of a slave announcing the arrival of the first guests, Maximus and his wife, Juno.

Paulina opened her eyes. Maximus and Juno lived in retirement in a villa near Pompeii.

Of course! There was her answer.

Paulina was suddenly relieved—she had come up with the solution to her problem.

Maximus and Juno were forever asking her to come and spend a holiday with them at their seaside home. Well, tonight she was going to surprise them by accepting. By the end of the week she should be on the road to Pompeii, and this villa, naturally, would have to be closed for the duration of her holiday. The two house guests would have to find somewhere else to live.

———

Selene sat on her bed and stared glumly at her medicine box. It was nearly empty.

She stood up and walked to the balustrade that ran along all four sides of the second floor, overlooking the peristyle garden. From here she could smell the delicious feast below, and hear the music and laughter of

Paulina's friends. The party had been going for hours, and gave no sign of letting up.

Selene turned away.

How could Ulrika sleep through all that noise? she wondered. Earlier, Selene had looked into the adjoining bedroom and had seen her daughter's form under the covers, fast asleep in the dark. Selene had quietly closed the door. Why wake her? This Saturnalia was not for them. They had no gifts to exchange; there was no money to buy any.

Nor, she thought morosely as she looked again at her medicine box, *to buy supplies with.*

How could she have let this happen? How could she have been so naïve as to think that some miracle would save them? The High Priest had warned her that the God had turned a deaf ear. In her two months of working on the island, trying to cure some of the sick slaves, Selene had been certain that help would come. But now the temple treasury was empty and so was her own purse.

Selene had not told Ulrika of this new development. Why worry the child? And, anyway, how to explain it? *How do I explain that, in my foolish hope that the God would somehow provide, I spent the last of our money to buy medicines for the temple. And now even those medicines are gone.*

At least, nearly all were gone.

Selene sat down on the bed again and picked up the small jars one by one. Many were empty, a few half full, one or two completely full. In a few days these, too, would be gone.

And then what?

Selene rubbed her eyes. She was trying to think, trying to come up with a solution. How could she raise the money to purchase new supplies? She knew she could earn some by going out into the city with her healing skills. But to do so she needed medicines. And to buy medicines she needed money!

But Selene was thankful for one thing: Because of Paulina's generosity, Selene and Ulrika had a roof over their heads and meals they could count on. And there was clearly no limit to the length of their stay. *For as long as we need,* Selene thought, recalling Lady Paulina's words.

Thinking of this, looking around the lovely bedroom and reminding herself that she and Ulrika were in fact very lucky, Selene's gloom began to lift.

The important things in life—food and shelter—were theirs for as long as necessary.

In the dining room, Maximus was saying, "Poor old Claudius. They say that when his uncle Tiberius was emperor, Claudius begged to be given some office of state. So he was given the title of consul. But when Claudius asked to be given the *duties* of consul as well, old Tiberius is said to have replied: 'The salary I pay you is meant to be squandered on toys during the Saturnalian holidays.' "

Everyone around the table laughed, and Juno added, "Now he's emperor and squandering his money in Britain!"

"Whatever for, I wonder?" asked Lady Paulina, as she delicately washed her hands in a golden fingerbowl. "What could he possibly want in Britain?"

"Perhaps in Britain he cannot hear Rome laughing behind his back."

Lady Paulina shook her head and said, "Claudius is a good man, I think, with good intentions."

"Hmp! Everyone knows he became emperor by default. Found hiding behind a curtain when Caligula was assassinated. The Praetorians named him emperor because Claudius was the only surviving male adult of the Julian and Claudian families. There *was* no one else!"

"Still," said Paulina. "I think he is a victim. Claudius has been corrupted."

"And you need not name by whom!" Juno said.

"Can he truly be so ignorant of Messalina's activities?" another asked. "Is Claudius really unaware of what wickedness his wife is up to?"

"Claudius is too blinded by the wickedness he himself is involved in," Maximus replied, stuffing an enormous piece of honey cake into his mouth and washing it down with wine.

Across the table from him, reclining on a couch between Paulina and the famous poet Nemesis, Juno watched her husband with worried eyes. Maximus was not looking well tonight.

"If you are referring to Agrippina," Lady Paulina said, "I do not believe the rumors."

"I do," said Maximus. He paused to shift his great bulk on the couch and to wipe his sweating face. As he tossed a handful of spiced walnuts into his mouth, he said, "He visits her bed, I tell you."

"His own *niece*?" said the poet.

"You don't know Agrippina," someone said, quietly so that the servants and musicians could not hear. "She is a dangerous woman. She has only one thing on her mind: succession to the imperial throne for her son Nero. She will stop at nothing to achieve that end, even if it means committing incest with her uncle."

Juno, thinking that her husband's face was looking gray, said, "But there is Britannicus, Claudius's son. He will succeed his father."

"If he lives that long," Maximus said with a wheeze. His breathing was becoming labored.

Nemesis, the poet visiting from Athens, said, "Is Messalina as bad as they say? Are the stories true?"

Maximus wiped his face again; despite the cold December night he was perspiring heavily. "The stories don't tell the half of it!" he declared, reaching for a second helping of mushrooms. "I know for a fact that thirty men had her in one night."

"Outrageous!" said someone, laughing.

Maximus suddenly tried to sit up.

Another guest said, "Can Claudius even be sure that Britannicus is his son? If Messalina is as promiscuous as they say—"

Juno cried out.

Maximus had collapsed.

Paulina was on her feet. When she saw Maximus lying on his back on the floor, gasping and grimacing with pain, she sent a servant to fetch the house physician.

Juno was kneeling over her husband, her hands cradling his face. "What is it, my dear? What's wrong?"

"Pain—" he gasped.

"It's his stomach," one of the others said. "He ate too much."

"Make him vomit," Nemesis said. "It will relieve him."

Paulina looked down at Maximus in alarm. His lips were turning blue.

"He can't breathe!" Juno cried.

"Get the food out of his stomach, I tell you!" Nemesis dropped to his knees and started to pry open Maximus's mouth.

"Wait for the physician," Paulina said.

But an instant later the slave returned to say that the physician had gone out for the night.

"Give me a feather," Nemesis said. "Quickly!"

Paulina nodded to the slave, who ran out of the room.

"All that food," one of the guests said, wringing her hands. "It's possible, you know, to die from overeating."

"Be quiet," snapped Paulina. "Decius, remove your wife from the room."

Maximus was getting worse. His face was a shocking gray; his clothes were soaked with sweat. Strangely, Paulina noticed, he was not clutching his stomach but rather his chest.

When the slave returned with the feather, Nemesis took it and proceded to stick it down Maximus's throat.

"Wait!"

Everyone looked up to see a young woman come into the room.

"Selene!" said Paulina, surprised.

"Don't make him vomit," she said, kneeling opposite Nemesis. She pulled the feather out of his hand and tossed it away.

"Now see here—"

"You will kill him for certain if you make him vomit," Selene said. She bent over Maximus, felt his neck and wrists, examined his eyelids, then pressed her ear to his chest. "It's his heart," she said, straightening.

Juno's hands flew to her mouth.

Selene reached for her medicine box, which she had set on the floor by Maximus's head. When she had heard the commotion below and the report that the house physician was not at hand, she had grabbed her box and run down.

Now, she prayed frantically. *Let there be enough . . .*

Selene emptied some powder into her palm, studied it, mentally calculated the correct amount for Maximus's weight, then sprinkled it into the nearest cup of wine.

"Help me to get him to sit up," she said, looking up at the faces around her.

"What are you giving him?" asked Nemesis, who stood over her.

"Foxglove leaves. It will slow his heart and ease the pain."

"But I say it's not his heart." Nemesis turned to Paulina. "And foxglove is a poison. Everyone knows that."

The others looked at Paulina; someone else added, "We all saw how much Maximus ate."

"Please!" said Selene. She tried to lift Maximus to a sitting position, but he was too heavy for her. "It *is* his heart. Feel his pulse if you don't believe me!"

Nemesis gave her a contemptuous look. "Pulses carry air. They have nothing to do with the heart."

"You're wrong!"

"*Do* something," Juno cried.

For an instant Paulina stood in indecision. Then she turned to the slave and said, "Help her to get him to sit up."

Nemesis spun on his heel and walked away.

When everyone crowded around to watch, Selene said, "Move away, please. He needs air." Once Maximus was sitting up, Selene administered sips of wine to him.

When the cup was empty, slaves carried Maximus to a couch and laid him upon it. "Put pillows behind him," Selene said. "He'll breathe easier." Then she took his wrist in her fingers and felt the racing pulse. Sometimes the foxglove worked immediately, sometimes slowly, and sometimes not at all.

Nobody moved. All eyes were fixed on Maximus. He lay groaning, gulping air. Ten minutes dragged by. As she watched the rising and falling of his chest, Selene mentally prayed to Isis for help. Then, remembering, she also called upon Venus, the mother of her Roman ancestors.

A December gust blew through the room, stirring the pine boughs and causing lamps to swing on their chains, while everyone looked on in protracted silence. Selene looked at Maximus's nail beds; they were blue. Then she looked at his ankles, which were swollen. She realized with a degree of relief that, if he lived, Maximus had a heart ailment that could be controlled.

The villa on the Esquiline Hill grew strangely quiet, like the city beyond its walls, which was closing in on itself as citizens retreated behind locked doors and barred windows. Only the group gathered in the dining room of the Lady Paulina Valeria had no thoughts of sleep. They watched Maximus.

Finally, at long last, Selene felt the pulse begin to slow down. The others noticed that Maximus's breathing grew easier and that his color was beginning to improve. One by one they began to relax, and soon everyone was sighing and slumping onto the couches.

"He will need a great deal of rest," Selene said, as slaves prepared to carry the slumbering Maximus up to a bedroom. "But there is no reason he cannot live for many more years. He has the kind of heart weakness that can be managed with regular daily doses of foxglove."

―――――

"I don't know how to thank you," Paulina said. "Maximus is one of my oldest and dearest friends. If he had died . . . " She clasped her trembling hands.

Paulina and Selene were sitting alone in a small reception room off the atrium. A hot brazier gave off heat against the winter night, and the two women drank warm honeyed wine. The rest of the guests were asleep upstairs; Juno sat watch over her husband.

"Maximus almost died tonight," Paulina continued. "I saw it on his face, the shadow of death. How familiar I am with that look. How can I repay you for saving him?"

"Take an offering to the Temple of Aesculapius on the Tiberine island."

"A sacrifice, yes."

"Better, money for the priests and brothers."

"Whatever you wish. But you, Selene, how can I repay *you*?"

"You have paid me a hundredfold, Lady Paulina, by giving me and my daughter a place to stay."

"It's not so much," Paulina said, looking away.

"But it is. You see . . . we are totally without money. We haven't even a penny left."

Paulina gave Selene a startled look. "But surely—" she began. Then she said, "But where is it you go to everyday? You appear to work so hard."

When Selene told her, Paulina's eyes grew wide. "I had no idea," she said. "Nor did I know you were a healer. Andreas mentioned nothing of that to me in his letter."

Selene stared at Paulina. "You have received a letter from Andreas?"

"Only last week."

Selene felt a stab of pain. *Andreas knows I am here and yet he did not write a letter to* me.

But why should he? she thought. She no longer had a claim on him; he had returned the ivory rose to her. "How is Andreas?" Selene asked. "Is he well?"

"He complains of the damp and the cold of Britain."

And when is he coming back to Rome? Selene wanted to cry. But she remained silent. Andreas had written to Lady Paulina, not to her. Whatever his news, it was not intended for Selene.

"Might I ask," Paulina said politely, "how it is you know Andreas?"

Selene thought of her sixteenth birthday, the Dressing Ceremony, Andreas. She was overcome with melancholy. No matter how full her days were in the temple on the island, how busy her mind was with plans, there still remained that untouchable hollow space deep in her heart, the place where love lay unrequited and unfulfilled. And sleep though she did every night, heavily, her body exhausted from the day's labor, Selene's dreams were filled with Andreas, and she always awoke hungering for his touch.

"I met Andreas many years ago," Selene said quietly. "In Antioch in Syria."

Paulina's finely plucked eyebrows rose. "You have been friends for a long time then."

"Our friendship has followed a strange course. We met and parted years ago; we met again in Alexandria, quite by chance, this past summer."

"I see. But you are young. You were . . . a child, when you met Andreas?"

"I was sixteen. He taught me healing—as did Mera, the woman who raised me."

"So," Paulina said with admiration, "you are a *femina medica.*"

Seeing Selene's puzzled expression, she explained: "That is what we Latin-speakers call our medical women. I number a few *feminae medicae* among my acquaintance, although they are mainly *obstetrices,* which is to say, midwives. Where did you train?"

Selene gave Paulina a summary of her life, beginning with her childhood years in Mera's instruction, and concluding with the Temple of Isis in Alexandria. But she left out much—Queen Lasha, Wulf, Rani, learning of her descendancy from Julius Caesar. And the intimate aspect of her relationship with Andreas.

As she listened, Paulina studied Selene with a thoughtful look. And when Selene went on to tell of the appalling conditions she had found on the Tiberine island and the plight of the Aesculapian priests and how Selene believed that the gods had brought her to that temple for a purpose, Lady Paulina felt suddenly sad. To have such ambition in life, she thought, to have such a future to look forward to! My eyes once blazed with hope and visions, as hers do now. But that light died years ago.

"I envy you," Paulina said.

Selene was surprised. How was that possible? Lady Paulina had everything: this beautiful house, the best social standing, so many friends, her life full of parties and gaiety.

As if reading her thoughts, Paulina said quietly, "I married young, and my husband and I lived a full life together. He died last year. I have not yet adjusted to being alone."

Each time she spoke her husband's name, Paulina added, "May the gods rest his soul," an old custom designed to keep the dead from rising. The Romans, Selene had discovered, were a very superstitious people; they believed that uttering a dead person's name raised his ghost, but that adding the ancient spell, "rest him," kept the restless spirit in the grave.

"I used to like the night quiet," Paulina continued, "when I sat at my weaving or writing letters, knowing my husband was nearby, in his study. But now I am afraid of the night. The dark hours seem so long, so very much like death . . . "

"How did your husband die?" Selene asked gently.

"It was a very long and terrible process. He was slowly eaten away by the *cancer,*" Paulina said, using the Latin word that means "crab." The name was given to the disease because cancer often grows in a crab-like shape, and the growth is usually hard like a shell. "One after another, physicians came into this house, and none could save him. In the end, Valerius begged to be freed. Finally, Andreas gave him painless release . . . "

"I'm sorry," Selene said.

Paulina lifted swimming topaz eyes. "Now I fill my nights with my friends. I cannot bear to be alone."

"You had no children?"

"We had one. Her name was Valeria. She died five years ago."

Paulina's grief was like a sharp stone she might have swallowed and which had become lodged behind her breastbone. It stayed there night and day, as a reminder, and nothing could make it go away. All the parties and visitors and music, all the dinners and torches blazing to push the night away, all the witty people and Greek poets—nothing could dislodge that sharp stone behind her breast and send it down into her stomach where she knew it would eventually dissolve.

Because nothing compared with the death of a child. Seven-year-old Valeria had lain there with her poor hairless head on the pillow, smiling to give her parents comfort, to reassure them as they faced the terrible journey she was soon to make, and Paulina had seen that it was not just the little girl who was dying. Paulina had seen the young girl Valeria might have been, the woman of twenty, the mother she would never be. Layers of faces, all transparent and overlapping, had smiled up from that pillow; and Paulina had watched them all die.

She wiped away a tear and said, "We tried to have other children, Valerius and I, but for some reason I could not conceive again. And I wanted children so much, just so very much . . . " Paulina took a moment to compose herself, using a linen handkerchief to dry her eyes. Then she said in a firmer voice, "When he lay dying, Valerius made me promise I would marry again. But I am forty years old, Selene. I am too old to bear children now."

"You could adopt."

Paulina shook her head. "Valerius wanted us to. There was the son of a distant cousin. The parents were killed when a theater collapsed. Valerius wanted to take him in, but I hadn't the strength. You see, my little girl had just died. And I wanted my next child"—she pressed her hands to her breast—"to come from here."

Selene listened to the coals crackling in the brazier and pondered the strange tides that governed people's lives. She was recalling Fatma, those many desert summers ago, and how she had at first rejected the child of her body. But Selene had been able to help Fatma. What could be done for Paulina?

Then, curiously, she remembered something she had once witnessed in

Persia, and which Rani had explained was not an uncommon phenomenon in the East. Childless women taking orphaned babies to their breasts, and producing milk.

As Selene was about to tell of this strange but true miracle, for she had seen it herself, the night silence was broken by shouts in the corridor and the sound of running feet. Then Ulrika suddenly burst into the room.

"They said you were in here," she said breathlessly to her mother.

Selene jumped to her feet. "Rikki!"

A man came running in behind her and made a grab for the girl's arm. "Caught you again," he growled. Then, seeing Paulina, his mistress, he mumbled, red-faced, "She's been bothering the slaves, ma'am."

"Rikki," Selene said, "I thought you were asleep in bed."

Ulrika's face was also flushed, but with defiance, not embarrassment. "You saw my pillows under the blankets. *I* wasn't there."

Selene stood speechless. Could this wild thing be her daughter?

"I've done it a lot," Ulrika went on, twisting her arm free of the man's grasp.

"I'll say she has," the overseer said.

"Lucas," Paulina said, rising to her feet. "What is this all about?"

"She's made friends with one of the slaves, ma'am. Visits him at all hours and they talk gibberish together. I've told her before to stay away."

Selene stared in shock at her daughter. Ulrika's face seemed to be swelling with tears, but no tears came. Ulrika never cried, Selene realized; in fact, Selene realized in dismay that Ulrika had not cried in years, not since she was a baby, with the exception of the night Rani had died, and that other, brief moment when they had held each other in Alexandria.

"He's my friend," the girl protested. "I'm teaching him to speak Greek."

Selene turned to Paulina and said, "I apologize for this. I had no idea it was going on."

Lady Paulina turned to Ulrika and asked gently, "Who is the boy you visit?"

The girl gave her a truculent look and stayed silent.

"It's Eiric," the overseer said. "One o' the new ones from Germany."

Lady Paulina continued in a kind tone, "Why are you teaching him to speak Greek?"

"Because he doesn't understand anybody," Ulrika blurted out, her lip quivering.

"He understands all right," barked Lucas. "He's stubborn. Plays dumb. So you have to clout him to get work outa him."

Ulrika wheeled around. "That's not true! He doesn't *understand.* So you *whip* him! You hit him all the time and treat him cruelly." She turned pleading eyes to Lady Paulina. "They beat him to make him understand. It isn't *fair.*"

Selene continued to stare at her daughter. Tears were beginning to stream down Ulrika's cheeks. Tears for an unknown slave-boy?

Lady Paulina looked at the overseer. "Is this true?"

He seemed to shrink before her. "The boy's more trouble'n he's worth. He should be got rid of."

"I shall decide that," Paulina said abruptly. "Our slaves are not to be mistreated, Lucas. I have warned you before." She turned to Ulrika and her look softened. "You need not worry for the boy's sake. He is young. He will learn our language in good time."

"But he's teaching me, too. He's teaching me to speak *his* language."

"And what language is that, Ulrika?"

The girl glanced at her mother, then said quietly, "The language my father spoke."

Selene put a hand to her forehead. "Ulrika," she said wearily, "what you have done is wrong. Lady Paulina does not want you going all over her house. You're going to have to stop—"

"But Eiric is *German,* mother. He doesn't care about Julius Caesar. And neither do I!"

"I see no harm in it," Paulina said with a smile, not seeing the shocked look on Selene's face. "When his daily duties are done, you may visit Eiric if you wish—and if your mother permits it." To Lucas she added, "They can meet in the orchard, and they are to be chaperoned. But not by you."

Ulrika stared at the Roman woman she had been hating for so long and suddenly said, "Oh, thank you! I promise I shall be good from now on."

"I confess, Selene," Paulina said when they were alone again, "that having your daughter here causes me some pain. Her presence is a constant reminder of my lost Valeria, rest her."

Selene was nursing a pain of her own; she would never forget the look on Ulrika's face as she denied her great-grandfather's blood. "I shall restrict my daughter's movements from now on," she said.

"Not at all! I am being foolish. I am not facing up to my fears as I should. Ulrika may go anywhere in this house she chooses. She's a lovely child."

They walked through the atrium and into the roofless garden, where the cold, hard stars of winter looked down. Drawing her *palla* about her, Paulina said, "I can never be grateful enough to you, Selene, for saving the life of my friend. In the morning I shall send a thank-offering to the Aesculapian priests. And for you"—her eyes misted with emotion—"you and Ulrika must stay with me for as long as you want and never think of leaving."

Selene smiled. A miracle had occurred here tonight. Of all the medicines gone from her box, there had been just enough foxglove left to save the life of Maximus. The God had provided after all.

CHAPTER 5 6

As soon as she saw her, Selene knew the girl was going to die.

"Make her as comfortable as possible," Selene said to the religious brother who was the caretaker of the little makeshift ward. "I must pray on it."

Selene was going to pray to the God for strength and steady hands; she was not going to pray, as the brother thought, for a decision on what to do. That decision had already been made, as soon as the girl had appeared on the steps of the temple, dying from prolonged labor. There was no doubt what must be done—the law was clear. Written centuries ago, the *Lex Caesare* decreed that if any woman died while pregnant, the living child was to be immediately cut out of her abdomen. This poor girl, whose name no one knew, was certain to die; but the baby inside her lived and must be given a chance to survive.

Selene was fearful. She had never before performed a Caesarean-law operation.

Wearily, she made her way along the path that led from the small outbuilding to the temple. Since childbirth could not be allowed inside the basilica, as it would defile the sacred ground, the brothers had hastily transported the semiconscious girl to one of the smoke-houses Selene had converted into a sick ward. And there, beneath that low roof, with pigeons cooing under the eaves and barely enough light to see by, Selene was soon going to try to cut the living baby from its dead mother.

The inside of the temple was a little cleaner now—Herodas had been able to hire help for the maintenance of the God's house—but it was still too crowded, and the priests and brothers were still overwhelmed by the numbers of slaves that continued to be discarded on the island. This was not, after all, the Temple of Isis, which had a rich treasury and a sisterhood made up of the daughters of nobles; this was the old and neglected Temple of Aesculapius, overburdened and understaffed by a handful of dedicated but limited brothers.

The visions that had driven Selene in December, when Paulina and Juno had made generous contributions to the temple, had not materialized.

Money was all well and good, but what Selene had learned in the months that followed was that money was useless if there was no manpower available. The temple needed the work of muscles and backs and determined human hearts. But the problem was that the island had become untouchable; few men could be hired to keep the precincts clean, to cook the food and do the washing. Fear of the sick, fear of the bad air surrounding the temple and fear of the evil spirits of illness and death kept people away.

Selene did not blame them: their fears were justified. But could they not learn from previous lessons? Roman health officials knew all about the benefits of sanitation and hygiene—sewers, flushing toilets, street drainage all existed in the city. And they had drained the marshes near the river in an effort to put an end to repeated epidemics of malaria; everyone knew that this sickness, "bad air," in Latin, was caused by foul emanations from stagnant water. The marshes had been drained and filled in with soil and built upon, and, as hoped, the malaria had disappeared. And as a secondary bonus, they had also rid themselves of the annoying mosquitoes which lived in the marshes.

So why then, Selene thought in frustration as she now made a sacrifice of spring flowers to Aesculapius, didn't the Romans apply the same energy to this wretched island? Why didn't they come and clean it up and restore the temple to its former glory?

Because, she thought bitterly, one cannot expect compassion from a people who delight in carnage.

Unbidden, a terrible memory came back, the remembrance of a day not long past, on the festival of Anna Perenna, ancient goddess of the full year, when special games had been held in the Circus Maximus.

The entire city had turned out to honor the Goddess, and Selene had decided to make it a special holiday for Ulrika and herself as well. They had joined the throng streaming under the arches into the Circus, and had marveled at this immense structure, the largest of its kind in the world and famous as far away as Persia for its chariot races.

Selene and Ulrika, having never been to the Circus before, stared with wide eyes as they climbed to the top tiers where they sat under a canvas awning, jostled by the boisterous crowd, infected with the excitement. They had brought with them a basket of eggs and cheese and bread, and a flask of watered wine. Ulrika had laughed for the first time since Selene could recall, and the two of them, like the rest of the thousands of spectators crammed into the rising rows, had barely been able to sit still.

Finally, there had come the fanfare, then the Gods and Goddesses had been brought into the *harena* to the passionate roar of the crowd. Following them were priests, civic dignitaries, performers, and lastly the emperor and empress, whose appearance had sent the crowd into a frenzy. The show began with circus riders who, standing astride pairs of horses, raced around the *harena*—so-called for the Latin word "sand," which covered the Circus floor. It was a wonderful spectacle and made Selene and Ulrika clap and laugh. Next came the tumblers and acrobats, all beautifully costumed; clowns ran to and fro across the sand.

Another fanfare announced the next segment of the entertainment, and two men strode out wearing helmets and loincloths, carrying shields and swords. The crowd went wild. From the excitement of those around her, Selene guessed that the two men were famous, although she had never heard of them; money rapidly changed hands as wagers were made up and down the seats, and it seemed that the tallest of the two men was the favorite, as Selene overheard talk of his remarkable record of a hundred wins.

When the fighting began, the crowd grew even wilder. The swords clanged; muscles glistened. Selene and Ulrika watched at first in curiosity, then in growing horror.

The screams of the crowd reached a crescendo when one of the gladiators, the tall favorite, fell to the ground and was immediately pinned down by the foot of his opponent. The victor looked up to the emperor's box, where the vestal virgins were making a hands-down gesture, and before the startled eyes of Selene and Ulrika, the man ran his sword through his fallen opponent. Then he bent and pulled off the victim's helmet, revealing a handsome face and blond Germanic braids.

Selene and Ulrika sat in numb shock as they watched the victor receive his prize of gold; the body of the other man was dragged away.

Up and down the length of the Circus, thousands of people screamed and shouted and stamped in blood-lust; vendors went up and down the aisles with food and souvenirs; money changed hands as wagers were paid off. Selene and Ulrika were still in a daze when the next show began— iron doors were raised and a hundred or so wretched creatures stumbled out, blinking in the sunlight. They were a pale, bedraggled group of men, women and children. Across the way, more iron doors went up and a pack of starved looking tigers rushed out. As the mob shouted, "Jews! Death to the Jews!" Selene seized Ulrika's hand and together they ran out of the Circus.

Now Selene knew why there was no help for her island. How could she expect to find pity in the hearts of such people? People who discarded sick human beings as if they were rubbish.

"We shall never find a solution," Herodas had said, "as long as such a practice is allowed. For that is the crux of our problem on this island: too many people. If only the emperor would listen."

The emperor is a greedy and selfish man, Selene thought, as she stood before the statue of Aesculapius.

Three times she had petitioned to see him; three times she had been refused. Not even Paulina had been able to use her influence. Now that the emperor was back in Rome, he was too obsessed with pursuing his personal pleasures to listen to the problems of the people.

Claudius back in Rome . . .

Then where is Andreas?

Lady Paulina had made inquiries among her friends at the Imperial Palace, but no one seemed to know where Andreas was.

I know where he is, Selene thought. *He has found a ship bound for another horizon . . .*

Selene shook her head. She had come before the God to ask guidance in the Caesarean operation, not to place her private woes at His feet. She must concentrate on the here and now. As Herodas had said, "It is like trying to sweep back the ocean tide with a broom." Her plan to convert this island into a sanctuary for the sick and injured of Rome had not come to pass; there was still no place for people to go.

"Lord Aesculapius," Selene murmured through the smoking incense and dancing shadows, "Father of Healing, guide my scalpel tonight. Grant me the wisdom and strength to bring that doomed child to the light.

"Mother Venus, whose devoted daughter I am, watch over that poor girl, make her exit from this world a painless one, and give the child to me."

Lastly Selene called upon the spirit of the Divine Julius, her grandfather —and her secret.

If, six months ago, Selene had arrived in Rome with the intention of being reunited with her family on the Palatine Hill, all those hopes died when she heard tales of their treachery and greed. The Imperial family, as Andreas had warned, were indeed a dangerous group. All of Rome whispered of Messalina's scheming ambition to have her son Britannicus succeed Claudius as emperor. The empress would put any obstacle out of the way; she already had. There were stories of mysterious deaths and unexplainable disappearances of people who, in one way or another, had crossed Messalina.

With each passing day and each new rumor coming down from that hill, Selene's wariness grew. They fought and scrapped like cats, the Julio-Claudians; they would not welcome the sudden appearance of the only legitimate descendant of Julius Caesar. For her own safety, Selene decided to keep out of their way; moreover, for *Ulrika's* sake she must keep quiet. The great-granddaughter of Julius Caesar was now of childbearing, heir-bearing age.

Selene's final, most reverent prayer went to the Goddess, the Mother-of-All. Selene appealed for the soul of that young girl coming to so tragic an end. And she added, as she always did, a special plea for the safekeeping of her own mother and brother, dead or alive, wherever they might be.

———

"I think, Aunt Paulina, that I shall want to have a lot of children."

Ulrika was sitting in the sunny garden watching Lady Paulina gather peonies and yellow iris. They were out here almost every afternoon these days, now that the spring blossoms were bursting with color; Ulrika would sit beneath the pomegranate tree while Lady Paulina moved among her hedges and bushes, looking like one of the graceful marble statues that inhabited the garden. They were friends now, the thirteen-year-old and the lady, ever since that night back in December. Paulina had come eventually not only to tolerate Ulrika's presence but to welcome it, and Ulrika now looked upon Paulina as a second mother, as Rani had once been.

"Having just one child," Ulrika continued, "seems cruel. I should worry that my baby was lonely. So I have decided that I shall have many babies, to keep one another company, or"—her face grew serious—"I shall have none at all."

Paulina, remembering to pick some pomegranates for Selene, who used the rind in certain medicines, came to stand beside the tree. "You will need a husband first," she said with a smile.

"Oh yes. But I shall be very careful about that. He must be someone very special."

How well I know that, Paulina thought wistfully. Valerius was special, when we first met so long ago. Oh, to be young again like Ulrika, and have all those exciting things still ahead. All that is behind me now. I could marry, yes, but it would not be fair to deny children to the man who would be my husband.

Paulina sighed and looked up at the deep, transparent sky. *If I could have children,* she thought, *I would want to marry someone like Andreas. Possibly Andreas himself . . .*

"Yes," Ulrika was saying, her face twisted in a pretty frown, "I cannot marry just anyone. I have royal blood in me. My father was a prince."

Paulina looked down at the tawny head. She worried about Ulrika. The child had a wild, defiant streak in her. And she often lapsed into periods of silence, her eyes grave and thoughtful. She was much too serious, Paulina thought. And how she had attached herself to that slave-boy, Eiric! How she practiced speaking German at every opportunity, and always talked of her dead father! It was as if Ulrika were lost, were looking for someplace where she belonged.

"And then, of course," the girl went on, "there is my other side, too. I suppose I shall have to take that into consideration as well. I don't like it that my great-grandfather was Julius Caesar, but it seems important to other people and it might be important to my husband."

Paulina smiled absently as she dropped the yellow-red fruit into her basket. Then she paused, her arms still reaching into the branches, and looked down. "What did you say, Ulrika? About Julius Caesar."

"He was my great-grandfather." Ulrika took a pomegranate out of the basket and began to peel back the tough rind.

"Why do you say that?"

"Because he was. His son was my grandfather. That makes him my great-grandfather, doesn't it?"

Paulina lowered her arms. "His son?"

"He was a prince, too. Prince Caesarion. He was my mother's father."

Lady Paulina stared for a moment, then said, "Ulrika, are you making this up?"

"Oh no. The *alma mater* told my mother back in Alexandria. She told us all about how Queen Cleopatra was my mother's grandmother, and that Prince Caesarion was hidden away and a slave killed in his place, and then the soldiers did kill him in Palmyra on the night my mother was born."

Slowly lowering herself to the bench next to Ulrika, Paulina said, "That seems hard to believe. Your mother has never mentioned it to me."

"She keeps it a secret. But she wears Julius Caesar's ring around her neck. He conquered Gaul, you know, and Germany. I don't want him to be my great-grandfather, but—"

"Ulrika," Paulina said, taking the girl's hand. "Does anyone else know about this?"

"Only Mother Mercia. And there was a man who came to the temple. Andreas."

Paulina looked into the wide, honest eyes, as blue as the April sky, and saw that the girl spoke the truth. "Ulrika," Paulina said carefully. "Listen to me. Your mother is right. It must be kept a secret. You must never tell anyone, Ulrika. Promise me."

As the girl solemnly promised, Paulina squeezed her hand. If word of this should reach Messalina . . .

———

"She is at death's threshold," the holy brother said quietly.

There was no need to cleanse her surgical instruments in the fire, Selene knew, for the girl would be dead and have nothing to fear from the evil spirits of infection. But it did not seem right, somehow, to put unclean instruments into her flesh, so Selene took care and prepared herself and her equipment in the same way she would for any operation.

Special lamps had been brought in from the temple's Holy of Holies—the sacred flames of the compassionate Panacea and Hygeia. Apollo had been brought in, too; his benevolent form stood in the gloom, the snake-staff of healing in his hand. Sacred herbs had been hung on the doors and windows; the mystical signs of Isis and Minerva were drawn on the walls. The brothers were calling upon all the powers they knew to aid Selene in her formidable task.

They believed in her, the priests and brothers of Aesculapius. Contrary to Herodas's prediction months ago, Selene had not failed them. She had not become discouraged and given up. In fact, she was working harder than ever. Unfortunately, her relentless energy was not enough.

Selene had come to them with glorious plans. She wanted to divide the temple precincts into different areas, each according to a certain ailment, as she had seen practiced in the Roman *valetudinarium*. She wanted to replace the pallets with real beds, such as were used in Persia, and to train special nursing attendants as the Hindus did. She tried to make use of running water and to flush away refuse and offal; she tried to stock fresh new bandages and cleanse all instruments in sacred fires. But when a hundred sick and dying are lying in the dirt all around the temple grounds, when flies fill the air with their drone and the terrible smell from the island reaches the city and keeps away people who might otherwise help, and when there is no more room to bury the endless dead, no room to separate infants from dying old people, to maintain a quiet place for those who need it, to provide sunlight for others . . . One woman and all her wonderful plans can be of little help.

But where Selene *did* help, where she sometimes succeeded, was in cases like this one. This poor girl had dragged herself to the island in the hope that the God would help her, and now Selene was at least going to give the baby a chance. If the whole island was an *infernus* of darkness, the brother thought, then at least one small lamp burned here.

Selene and the brother sat on either side of the recumbent girl; their eyes never left the slowly rising and falling chest. At the very instant of death the scalpel would be used. But it must not be before, else she would cut into a living woman; nor too late, for the baby would die in the womb.

At the precise moment when the last breath left the girl's body . . .

The brother laid a hand on the warm breast and felt no pulse. "It is done," he whispered.

Selene took up the scalpel, called upon all the gods and goddesses she knew, and began.

C H A P T E R   5 7

Selene knew she was taking a big gamble.

She realized that she did not know Paulina well enough yet to predict how she was going to react; nor had their friendship developed to the point where Selene could take the liberties she was going to attempt tonight. But she had no choice. She could not leave the baby to die.

Last December, after Maximus had left the villa restored and well, Paulina had insisted Selene move into the honored guest rooms of her house. They were at the back of the villa, away from the noisy street, and opened onto the orchard that climbed the hill. Selene hurried there now, her bundle pressed close to her chest. A quiet dinner party was going on in the dining room off the garden; a philosopher was reading from his latest work. After the guests were gone, Selene would invite Paulina to her room.

Sweet Mother-of-All, Selene prayed, as she hurried past the dining room unseen and up the stairs to her apartment, *let Paulina's heart be softened at the sight of this helpless babe. Let the maternal love that is locked inside her spring forth.*

That was what Selene was gambling on: that one look at this tiny infant would release Paulina's natural mothering instincts—instincts she had worked hard for five years to suppress.

If not . . .

Then the baby will be mine, and I shall raise him as my own son.

But it was Paulina who needed the child, Paulina who sometimes looked longingly at Ulrika and yearned for her own, Paulina whose life was empty and who refused to take a second chance at marriage because of her childlessness. Quite possibly, Selene hoped, Paulina's taking the baby would then spur her to allowing herself to marry.

Paulina, though forty and middle-aged by Roman standards, was nonetheless a handsome woman, well-bred, charming, and full of unchanneled love. Such virtues did not go unnoticed among the unattached males of the Roman aristocracy; there was no end to the would-be suitors who sought Paulina's company. But, Selene had observed, whenever intimacy threatened, Paulina pulled away and the friendship was discouraged.

Paulina's life could be changed by this baby, Selene thought excitedly, as she laid it on her bed and propped it up with cushions.

Selene paused to look down at him. He was a lovely little boy with a round head of black hair. And healthy, too. His young mother had surely eaten well during her pregnancy. Selene had noticed other strange things afterward: the good quality of the girl's dress, her soft hands and feet— she had been no peasant or slave, possibly even high-born. Why had she not had the baby at home?

When the last of the dinner guests left, Selene sent a slave to ask Lady Paulina to come up. And when, a short while later, Paulina appeared, dressed in one of her most elegant *stolae*, her cheeks flaming from the mercurial happiness of the evening, Selene invited Paulina to sit, and proceeded to tell her the story of the nameless girl and the Caesarean-law operation.

When she came to the end, Selene turned away from Paulina, who was puzzled over why she was being told this, and picked up the sleeping bundle.

"I brought him home with me," Selene said, turning. "I kept the baby."

Paulina did not speak; she kept her eyes on Selene's face as if refusing to acknowledge what lay in Selene's arms.

"He is beautiful, so perfectly formed, so sturdy. I could not let him die." Selene came to kneel before Paulina and drew the blanket away from the little face. "See what a handsome fellow he is!"

Paulina looked down. "Yes," she said.

"Here." Selene held the baby out to her.

But Paulina did not move. "You will want a wet nurse for him. I shall hire one for you."

"The baby isn't for me," Selene said slowly. "I brought him home for you."

"What?" whispered Paulina. "What did you say?"

"Just take him in your arms—"

Paulina shot to her feet. "You must be mad."

"Take him, Paulina. Hold him."

"Have you lost your mind? You thought *I* would take him?"

"He needs a home."

"Not *my* home!" Paulina walked a few steps and spun around. "I would never have believed this of you, Selene. That you would expect me to take this . . . this . . ."

"Homeless child!" Selene rose to her feet, clutching the baby. "Look at him, Paulina. He's just a baby!"

"A baby from the gutter. A baby no one else wanted."

"*I* wanted him."

"Then you keep him."

"But, Paulina—"

"Why did you do this, Selene?" Paulina began to tremble. "How can you be so cruel?"

"I couldn't abandon him, Paulina."

"Why not? Rome is littered with unwanted babies. Why should you care about this one?"

It was true, why should Selene care when she had seen so many, exposed to the elements to die—girl babies, cripples, bastards.

"Because I gave him life," Selene said softly. "I gave birth to him."

"Then *you* keep him. You be his mother."

"But why can't you take him, Paulina? Just tell me so I can understand."

"I have told you before. I don't want another woman's cast-off child."

"She didn't cast him off, Paulina. She *died.*"

"I want my baby to come from *here.*" Paulina wrapped her arms around her waist.

"But none can come from there."

"Then I shall have none." She turned to walk out.

"Paulina, listen to me!" Selene ran after her. "Listen! You can nurse him yourself. You can hold him to your breast and give him life. Isn't that almost the same as bringing him forth from your own body?"

Paulina reached for the door latch. "Now I know you are mad."

"Paulina, listen to me! Let me tell you what I have seen. In the East. Women who have never been pregnant nurse newborn babies. It is possible, Paulina."

"Do you take me for a fool?"

Selene seized Paulina's arm. The baby, lying in the crook of Selene's other arm, slept between the two women. "It is true. I have seen it with my own eyes. When a baby suckles a breast, milk will eventually come. I have *seen* it, Paulina."

Paulina hesitated for an instant; her eyes flickered. Then she pulled her arm free and walked out.

========

Ulrika stood with her hands on her hips, looking down at the baby and wondering what all the fuss was about. Her mother had called him beautiful. Ulrika thought him rather funny looking. And he was so utterly useless.

She sighed and turned away from the bed. The April night was full of delicious perfumes; it seemed to the thirteen-year-old as if all the flowers in the world were growing in Paulina's garden. Ulrika went to the balcony and looked out at the dark orchard that swept up the hillside. The air was warm and alluring.

Last December, when Maximus had his attack and the house physician had not been at home, Paulina had sold the Greek slave and asked Selene to be the house healer for herself and her large slave staff. So Selene was down in the slave quarters now, tending a fever, and Ulrika had been told to watch the baby. She did not mind doing it—he was helpless, after all. Still, there was not much to do. All he did was sleep, and she was so restless.

"Your new brother," Selene had said.

Ulrika did not quite know what to make of it. Her mother seemed sad about it. Then why had she brought him home? And he hadn't even a name yet. What on earth were they going to call him?

A sound in the orchard brought Ulrika out of her thoughts. It was a familiar sound, a whistle. It meant that Eiric was free and waiting for her.

Eiric. Ulrika's heart raced.

She looked back at the bed. The baby was still asleep.

She turned to the orchard again. She saw an arm waving.

Biting her lip in brief indecision, Ulrika waved back to Eiric and ran for the stairs. The baby was clearly going to sleep for *hours*. Her absence would never be noticed.

========

"Do something about it!" snapped Paulina in a rare show of anger. "Find someone who can keep it quiet."

The baby had been crying for nearly an hour; its little wail was heard throughout the whole house, and so far none of the slaves Paulina had sent had been able to quiet it.

She paced her room in a rage. This was one of Selene's tricks, Paulina told herself. A ruse to get her to accept the baby. But she would not do it, she would not be beguiled.

"Where is she?" Paulina asked, when her slave returned.

"There is a fever in the slave quarters," the whey-faced woman said. "Mistress Selene said she cannot leave. She said her daughter is with the baby. She said there is sugar-milk for the baby to drink."

"And *is* the girl with him?"

The slave shook her head in fear. She had never seen her mistress so angry.

Finally, Paulina took up her *palla*, wrapped it about her shoulders and swept out of the room.

In Selene's bedroom she found four women desperately trying to quiet the screaming infant. They were passing him around, rocking him, bouncing him, dangling things in front of his face.

"Leave," Paulina said, and they hastily replaced him between the cushions on the bed and rushed from the room in relief.

Paulina pressed her trembling hands to her ears. His cry was unbearable. It was a screech, a frantic call for attention. Valeria had done that, when she was just days old . . .

Paulina walked stiffly to the bed and looked down. Tiny feet and fists waved in the air; the face was screwed up tight and red. Paulina's body shook. She knew that all she had to do was take the first step and the rest would follow.

She looked around. The feeder lay on the table, something Selene had put together—a teat made of loosely woven linen. By the collapsed look of the nipple, Paulina guessed that the slaves had tried to give it to the baby without success.

"Inept women," she muttered as she picked up the feeder. Then she thought: *It needs something sturdier, something his mouth can hold on to.*

The shrieking was starting to hurt her ears. Paulina returned to the bed and looked down in a mixture of pity and resentment. Selene should have left him to die. It was what anyone else would have done. To have performed the Caesarean had been folly. Paulina shook her head. Selene could be quite unthinking sometimes; she never paused to consider consequences.

"There, there," she heard herself saying. And her arms, almost against her will, reached down.

Paulina really looked at the baby this time. She was surprised. He was so small. She had forgotten how small newborn babies were.

"There, there," she said again and drew him to her. The crying stopped.

"Well now," said Paulina. She began to walk, marveling at the feel of him in her arms, the warmth coming through the blanket, the little knobs and depressions that were his soft bones and flesh, the face still puckered from its recent journey into the world. And eyes, little round things, unfocused and searching.

It reminded her—

Memories and feelings, long forgotten, came flooding back.

"You shouldn't have been left alone," she murmured. "What can Selene have been thinking, to leave you alone with that irresponsible Ulrika?"

Paulina picked up the feeder and went to sit in a chair. But, as she had thought, the teat was worthless. So she pulled it off the phial, dipped her little finger into the sugar-milk and put her fingertip to the baby's mouth. He sucked at once.

She did it again, and again. "We shall think of something better than this," Paulina said, rocking him. But for now it kept him quiet. He would need more nourishment than this, and something better than a bottle.

"I'll tell Selene she must hire a wet nurse," Paulina said absently, rocking him, her little finger going from bottle to mouth.

She settled back in the chair and felt a familiar warmth spread through her, a sweet laziness she had known but few times in her life. She hummed an old melody Valeria had liked.

The baby jerked his head away. He started to cry again.

"There, there," Paulina said softly. She unclasped one shoulder of her dress and brought the fabric down. The small head turned instinctively and began to nuzzle.

The instant the baby's lips went around her nipple, Paulina felt the sharp stone of grief behind her breastbone, where it had been lodged for nearly six years. She felt it begin to dissolve, as she had known someday it would.

"Your name will be Valerius," Paulina said. "And you will be a noble little man . . ."

CHAPTER 58

The leadership of the Roman Empire was based on a curious paradox: although the Imperial family ruled with absolute power, answering to no one, they nonetheless required the approval of the people in order to rule. The people of Rome cared little for palace intrigue, for the constant plotting over power, and were content to let the Julio-Claudians be masters of the world so long as they continued to provide free food and spectacles.

That was the reason for the River Festival this afternoon, a celebration in honor of the god Tiber, who gave water and life to Rome. It was to be the grandest entertainment Claudius had thus far staged in his seven years as emperor, and the entire population of the city had turned out for it.

Up and down the length of the river, the banks were packed with spectators. Temporary grandstands had been built for dignitaries and favorites of the Imperial family, while the most illustriously named—the Metelli, Lepidi, Antonii—enjoyed seats near the Imperial platform itself, close to the water's edge. This was where Selene and Lady Paulina sat, as excited as the thousands who stood or sat along the river for as far as the eye could see, all anxiously awaiting the start of the Procession of the Gods.

Selene and Paulina were attended by slaves, and like everyone else this late October afternoon were dining on a picnic they had brought. Their basket contained roasted fowl, corn bread, olives and cheese, and a flask of cold wine. Selene was glad she had come. The summer, with its terrible heat and fevers, had been especially bad for the island in the Tiber. The death rate had risen dramatically, and even more slaves had been abandoned on the temple steps. Paulina's contributions of money were of little help. No one would come to the island. And Selene's efforts to gain an audience with the emperor had been fruitless. She was beginning to wonder if Herodas was right: Had Aesculapius finally abandoned His holy house?

Selene had been surprised when Paulina had accepted the emperor's invitation to attend the festival. In these past six months, Paulina's hours had been so filled with taking care of Valerius that she had suspended all social activities. But then Paulina had explained her reason for wanting to attend: Andreas might be there, she had said.

Six months ago, after the night Selene had brought the baby home, Paulina had made a confession: "I would not remarry, because I thought it unfair to refuse any man the right to an heir. But now I have a baby, a son, to give to my husband. I *want* to marry now, Selene. And I will tell you a secret: I have always been fond of Andreas."

They had been good friends for years, Andreas and Paulina's husband Valerius, ever since Andreas had come to Rome and joined the court as one of Caligula's personal physicians. Paulina had spent many evenings with the two men, had visited the seaside with them, attended parties and games. They were fond of each other, Andreas and Paulina, and were well suited. He had never been married, but surely, Paulina hoped, now that he was forty-eight and without an heir, he would want to have a family?

"I have waited a year from the date of my husband's death, as required by law," Paulina had said. "Now I am free to marry. Who better than Andreas?"

Who better indeed? Selene asked herself, as she watched the activities on the Imperial platform. The family was there, but some seats were still vacant. Andreas's ship had been due to arrive at Ostia in the last few days; would he be here today?

The baby stirred in its mother's arms and began to fret. Paulina unclasped her dress, and soon little Valerius was nursing beneath the modesty of Paulina's *palla*.

Selene never failed to wonder at the magic and power of the maternal breast. The Bedouin woman Fatma had rejected her baby until she had spent a night with it bound to her bosom. And Paulina, like the women in the East whom Selene had seen, after a few days of nursing, alternating between dry breast and wet nurse, had at last produced milk; Paulina was now as attached to this infant as if it had indeed come from her own body. It was thin and insufficient milk, but enough to bond mother to baby. Valerius still required supplemental feedings, but these feedings with Paulina were not so much for nourishment as for reinforcements of love.

Paulina and Selene had come up with a story to account for the baby: Little Valerius was the son of a distant cousin, the heir to a very noble and ancient bloodline, whose parents had died in an epidemic. Paulina had paid a good deal of money for bogus papers to be written up; but now the boy was registered with the officials and legally carried the proud and aristocratic Valerian name.

Selene lifted her face to the river breeze. It carried myriad scents, from the smoky cookfires of the spectators up and down the banks to the heady perfumes of the noble ladies around her. Paulina, when they had arrived earlier, had introduced Selene to them: Cornelia Scipionis, a descendant of the great Scipio Africanus; and Marcia Tullia, the great-granddaughter of Cicero.

"Selene," Cornelia had said slowly. "What an unusual name. Who is your family?"

"Selene is a *therapeuta*," Paulina had said quickly. "She trained in Alexandria. You heard of Maximus's attack last December?"

"Indeed we did!"

"It was Selene who saved his life. She lives with me now. I sold my house physician and Selene has taken his place."

"Those Greeks!" Marcia Tullia had declared. "Very much overrated, I say. The quality of slaves isn't what it used to be." Then she leaned over and whispered something in Paulina's ear. Selene had heard Paulina say quietly, "No, Selene is not my slave. She is a freeborn Roman citizen."

Selene had come to accept the fact that, in Rome, one's name meant everything. Pedigree mattered more than character, ancestry more than accomplishments. Those sitting near her, eating their picnics and waiting for the Festival to begin, were descended from the founding families of Rome, the patricians, and they guarded their circle fiercely.

"—quite down on his luck," Cornelia's husband was saying to the man next to him. "Nonetheless, he *is* an Agrippa and so we couldn't let him sell his house to a Syrian! Oh, the buyer has money, but absolutely *no* family . . ."

Behind Selene, two women were talking: "And of course, when she found out he had lied, that he hadn't a drop of Gracchus blood in him, well, she had no choice but to divorce him. Although she took it very hard. She claims to have been in love with him."

Marcia Tullia's laugh made Selene look around. "An actor!" the socialite was saying. "What a fool she was to fall in love with an actor! She's lucky her father only banished her."

Cornelia, with a dour look, added, "They should both have been put to death. It is her father's right."

Seeing Selene's perplexed look, Paulina leaned close and said, "It's against the law for the descendants of senators, even great-grandsons and great-granddaughters of senators, to marry actors, or anyone whose father or mother had been an actor."

Paulina took Valerius from her breast, discreetly fastened her dress and handed the baby to a slave. As she was adjusting her *palla,* she looked past Selene and said, "Oh! There's Andreas!"

He was making his way toward them, his white toga and silver hair catching the light of the dying sun. He was constantly being stopped by people clasping his hand and welcoming him back to Rome; it gave Selene time to compose herself, to command her racing heart.

It seemed to take him forever to reach her. Their eyes met long before he was near, and they held as he walked up, so elegantly dressed, so distinguished and refined, the Andreas of Antioch, of her memories, of her heart.

"Hello, Selene," he said.

She looked up into his smile. "Hello, Andreas."

"Well!" said Cornelia's husband, rising from his chair. "Back in Rome at last, are you?" The two men shook hands.

"How was Spain?" Marcia Tullia asked. "Dreadful at this time of the year, I understand."

Selene looked away. Spain. He had been in Spain.

"What forsaken backwater will your next mission take you to, Andreas?" said Paulina.

He strode to her and took her hands in his. "You look well, Paulina," he said warmly. "How are you getting on?"

Selene did not mistake the concern in his voice, the searching look in his eyes as Paulina replied, "I am well, Andreas. Thank you for your letters."

"I am told you have a son."

"He could be Valerius's son, he is so like him."

"Are you in Rome for long?" Marcia Tullia asked.

"I am," he said, releasing Paulina's hands. Andreas turned and looked at Selene. "I am here for good now." He paused. "And you, Selene," he said, coming back to stand over her and smile down. "How are you getting on?"

"I thank you for sending me to Paulina," she said. "This would have been a difficult year for me without her kind help. My daughter and I are well."

A shadow passed briefly over his face, then he was smiling again.

"When did you get back to Rome?" Paulina asked.

Andreas started to say, "My ship docked only this morning," but then he was being greeted by someone else, who shook his hand and took him away.

Selene stared out over the river. The breeze picked up, causing her to shiver. When she looked over her shoulder, she saw Andreas surrounded by more people; he was the center of attention. She should not have been surprised to see him take a place on the Imperial platform, and yet she was. Andreas sat on the emperor's right.

Selene looked at the Imperial family. From this proximity, Claudius did not seem to Selene as repulsive in appearance as his detractors claimed. He was lame and his head twitched, but he was not terribly ugly nor did he look to Selene to be particularly evil. Then she saw that the couch next to him was unoccupied. Where was the empress?

The sound of trumpet fanfare brought everyone's attention to the river. From far downstream a roar could be heard, the crowd welcoming the start of the Procession of the Gods.

There came a slow and steady drumbeat from far away. The crowd fell silent; all eyes were fixed on the bend in the river. After a moment, the prow of a majestic barge came into view. The drum was the sound of the *hortator* striking a rhythm for the rowers below decks. As the barge came fully around the bend, a thousand archers, cunningly concealed throughout the crowd on the banks, let arrows fly into the air, and from them streamed colorful tails and pennants. The late-afternoon sky was briefly obliterated by a canopy of multicolored cloth. The crowd roared.

Sitting on the magnificent barge was the god Tiber, portrayed by an actor with long hair and a beard. In one hand he held an oar, symbol of the seafarers who passed over his waters, and in the other, a cornucopia, symbol of his fertility. He stood on a bed of false waves; sprays of water shot up now and then through the deck of the barge. Tiber was surrounded by naked water nymphs, who threw great handfuls of food to the crowds on the banks. The people went wild; they surged forward, pushing those in front into the river.

A smaller barge came next, but it only carried the caged she-wolf that was always on view on the Capitoline Hill, symbol of the founding of Rome. Two infants were in the cage with her, representing Romulus and Remus, but instead of suckling the wolf as they were supposed to, one sat screaming and the other lay listlessly. It was apparent that the wolf had been drugged to prevent her from attacking the babies, because each time she tried to stand, she staggered and fell. Not the effect the designer of the float had intended, but the crowd roared all the same.

Trumpets blared again and a very strange boat appeared around the bend. It was piled high with stones to look like a mountain, and atop this "mountain" stood a man, naked except for a pair of enormous feathered wings strapped to his back. The crowd recognized him at once. "Icarus!" they shouted. "It's Icarus!"

The man, clearly not a volunteer but a slave forced into the role, stood shaking on his tower, afraid to look down. "Fly, Icarus!" the mob shouted. "Fly! Fly!"

It was obvious his orders had been to jump when the barge reached the Imperial platform, but the man was too terrified to move. So the helmsman of the barge, hidden behind the "mountain," scrambled up the pile of rocks and pushed the slave from behind. Icarus plummeted into the river and was dragged under by his monstrous wings. The crowd howled with delight.

Selene looked away. The people with whom she was sitting were not as undisciplined as the mob; they nodded their appreciation, while continuing to eat their picnics and converse among themselves.

She glanced back over her shoulder and saw Andreas looking at her.

The next float was a beautiful one, the product of an artistic eye. An artificial forest grew out of the deck—trees and bushes and even a running waterfall. And at the center of the sylvan paradise stood a lone white horse, calmly grazing. Like Icarus, he also had giant feathered wings strapped to his body; they stood straight up and caught the copper hues of the setting sun.

Pegasus sailed serenely past a hushed crowd; so simple and pure was the scene that everyone was compelled to silence.

But their boisterousness resumed when the next barge appeared, bearing two dazzling young people who rode chariots of silver and gold. They were Selene, goddess of the moon, and her brother, Helios, the sun, who drove a blazing chariot and who had spikes of fire coming out of his head. Selene was a blinding vision of silver, representing the moon's heavenly light; her gown was silver and her arms were sprinkled with silver dust.

When they came abreast of the Imperial platform, Sun and Moon bowed to Claudius. All of Rome cheered.

"Rather novel," Cornelia Scipionis said. "I must hand it to the clever old devil. This far outshines his usual games."

Marcia Tullia added: "Claudius has won the people for another year."

The next float carried Laocoön, the unfortunate priest of old who had broken his vows of celibacy and thus had brought about the fall of Troy. The Laocoön of myth had been strangled by two enormous serpents; this Laocoön, a slave sitting alone on a small raft being towed by a rowboat, grappled with a giant python that clearly was about to kill him.

Cheering from downriver told those near the Imperial platform that a particularly impressive float was coming next, and presently a dramatic tableau emerged around the bend.

Two people, an actor and an actress, stood frozen and still as statues. The girl was very pretty, with long hair streaming over her naked body; she stood with her arms upraised and one leg extended slightly behind her, as if she were running. The young man "pursuing" her was also beautiful and naked, with arms outstretched as if to embrace her. What made the crowds cheer was the remarkable illusion that the girl was slowly being turned into a tree: leaves extended from her fingertips, her arms were covered with bark, laurel branches were sprouting from her hair. The mob knew who she was: Daphne, changing her form in order to escape the lust of Apollo.

Selene looked back at Andreas again, and her eyes met his. Was he, too, remembering their day in the Grotto of Daphne, so many years ago?

More boats and barges sailed by, bearing gods and goddesses, heroes and heroines of myth, historical figures, each more imaginative and fantastic than the last, with ingenious contrivances such as a volcano spewing flames and a chariot drawn by swans flying up from the earth.

Day gave way to night and thousands of torches were lit up and down the Tiber, reflected on the river's surface. Pipes and harps were heard above the steady rumble of a celebrating crowd. Free bread and sausages were distributed among the mob, and tickets to the chariot races tomorrow. The night grew cool but the temperament of the crowd grew hot. "Claudius!" they cried, as each new boat or raft appeared. They were drunk, they were happy, and they loved their emperor. For today.

Selene glanced frequently at Andreas. He often looked her way and their eyes met and held, but several times she found him speaking intimately with Agrippina, Claudius's beautiful niece, and laughing with her.

Finally the crowd, on signal, fell silent. Not a sound was heard up and down the river, except for the crackling of torches, the water lapping the banks.

A stately barge, the largest yet, with sides painted gold and a hundred golden oars rising and dipping into the water in unison, sailed slowly around the bend. Its golden sides blinked and shimmered in the torchlight; its reflection turned the river to molten gold. All eyes watched it slowly glide on the current; the night wind whipped hair and togas, snapped flags and pennants. No one moved or made a sound.

The barge was divided into two settings, different from each other but blending in the center in an artful metamorphosis. The front half had been built to create an illusion of the sea, with rocks and waves and arching dolphins. Rising out of this sea was a magnificent white shell, with two little boys standing on either side of it; the shell was twice their height, and as the barge drew near, people recognized them as seven-year-old Britannicus, Claudius's son, and eleven-year-old Nero, Agrippina's son.

The second half of the barge, everyone saw as it came into view, was a spectacular woodland, abundant with roses and myrtles, swans and doves. The barge sailed silently, and as it drew near to the Imperial platform, the crowd started to shift restlessly. So far, other than the two boys clad in loincloths and little wings, there were no other players on the barge.

The float rocked to a halt on the water, tethered by unseen anchors; it stood in the torchlight, a silent mystery.

As the crowd started to murmur and whisper—had something gone wrong?—the two boys stepped away from the shell and moved to the bow of the barge. A hush fell over the crowd again. A new sound was heard over the cold night air, a distant creaking, like cogs and wheels turning. And when they saw the giant shell start to open, the mob gasped.

One half of the shell came down slowly, like a drawbridge, and when its shadow fell away from the interior, the crowd saw what the shell contained. They went wild. Two hundred thousand throats roared their delight as Venus, Rome's favorite goddess, appeared inside the shell.

A beautiful young woman, with skin like moonlight and golden hair tumbling over her bare breasts, stood dramatically on that artificial sea. The serenity of her face was illuminated by torchlight; she was breathtaking.

"It's Messalina," people started to say. "It's the empress!"

Selene stared at the twenty-two-year-old empress, fascinated. She knew that Messalina had been fourteen when she married Claudius, and he forty-eight; and that she came from old and distinguished families—the Domitii and the Messalae. But that Messalina was lascivious and cruel was, as far as Selene knew, all rumor and hearsay.

Nearby, someone was saying, "I know for a fact that it is true. Messalina puts on a blond wig and goes out at night to the most disreputable brothel on the waterfront and gives herself away for free. They say she is insatiable!"

Selene looked at the beautiful empress, of whom it was said she killed her lovers when she was through with them, and whom all of Rome knew had had several women of the aristocracy put to death out of jealousy; recalling that Messalina was the great-granddaughter of Octavia, the great-niece of Julius Caesar, Selene thought: *We are related.*

When she had stood majestically in the shell long enough for everyone to appreciate the goddess's "birth," Messalina stepped down from her pedestal and began to act out a pantomime. Somewhere belowdecks a musician played a pipe, and to the musical accompaniment a myth unfolded. A young man suddenly appeared on the wooded half of the barge, and the crowd knew him at once: He was Silius, reportedly the handsomest and most ambitious man in Rome—and Messalina's lover.

While "Adonis" on his side of the barge mimed idle ignorance of the drama about to unfold, Venus went through the theatrical motions of playing with her two sons, Eros and Anteros. When Eros, little Britannicus and Messalina's son, produced a small bow and arrow, everyone knew what was going to happen. It was a favorite myth, the accidental piercing of Venus's breast with Cupid's arrow, and her glimpsing Adonis before the wound healed. The crowd knew how this story was going to end: with Adonis getting gored by a wild boar and his spilled blood creating a new flower, the red anemone.

But the drama did not get that far. Venus struck a pose and Eros raised his bow and arrow. A little unstable on the gently bobbing barge, young Britannicus took a step back to steady himself, and, to everyone's surprise, fell off the boat.

There was a moment of stunned silence; then the mob burst out laughing. The boy was splashing frantically and his wings were spread out comically on the water.

Then Messalina screamed, "He cannot swim!"

At once, several men dived into the water. There was much confusion, as they each wanted the honor of saving the Imperial heir; but the light was poor, and they got so tangled in the mooring lines of the barge, that, by the time the boy was dragged onto the river bank, he was unconscious and not breathing.

"Do something!" shouted Messalina. The men took Britannicus by the heels and began to swing him.

Andreas was out of his chair and jumping off the platform. As he ran by, Selene saw how dangerously close the boy's head came to the ground. She had also seen, from her advantageous position, what no one else had: Britannicus had been pushed off the boat by Nero.

Andreas reached the bank and took Britannicus from the men. Putting the boy down on his back, Andreas proceeded to pump the lifeless arms.

The entire population of Rome looked on in unearthly silence. Messalina stood shivering in Silius's arms. Claudius, on his platform, appeared dazed. Everyone saw the water spill from Britannicus's mouth, but still he did not breathe.

"He's dead!" Paulina whispered in disbelief.

Selene was on her feet and running down the bank. Without a word to Andreas, she knelt by Britannicus, took his head between her hands and began to blow into his mouth.

Andreas sat back, mystified. Everyone looked on in bewilderment. Selene puffed several times into the boy's mouth, then paused to watch his chest. It did not rise and fall. She bent over him and pressed her ear to his rib cage; she heard the frail beating of his heart. She blew into his mouth again, rhythmically, stopping only to see if he breathed on his own. The night seemed to stretch far above her into eternity, and the minutes seemed to drag into hours.

Selene grew desperate. But when she listened to his heart again, she heard a rapid, thready pulse, and it matched her own. She felt the thousands of eyes upon her, and Andreas, watching. *Live,* shouted her mind as she breathed into the boy's mouth. *You must* live!

Then she saw the flame. It came on its own; she did not call it up. Her soul flame, rising suddenly from the deepest part of herself, burning as brightly as the cresset torches around her. And when she saw it, she felt its warmth, its reassurance. Selene reached inside herself and brought the flame up into her chest and out through her mouth. Her eyes were closed;

her body relaxed. Her lips closed over Britannicus's like a kiss, and she breathed the soul flame into his body.

Live now, whispered her mind. *Take me into yourself and breathe with new life.*

When she saw, behind her closed eyes, the soul flame lengthen and stretch and arc through her lips and down into the boy's mouth, to connect there with a smaller, brittler flame, Selene knew he was going to live.

Finally, as the crowd was starting to stir impatiently and Andreas had laid a hand on her arm, Selene sat back and Britannicus coughed.

The cheering was thunderous as the boy was carried away and Selene brought up to the Imperial platform.

Claudius had to hold his hands up for a long time before the mob fell silent, and when all was finally hushed, he said in a quaking voice, "You have saved the life of my son, and the heir to Rome."

Now that she was close to him, Selene could see the ravages of time and disease on the emperor's face. Claudius was only a few years older than Andreas, and yet he looked to be a hundred. He was also visibly shaken.

"What is your name?" he asked.

"I am Selene, lord."

Claudius's lips jerked at the corners. "Don't call me 'lord,'" he said quietly. "It smacks too much of monarchy. Caesar will do." In a louder voice he said, "You worked a miracle here tonight. It is a sign from the gods."

Everyone cheered.

Claudius waited for the tumult to die down, then he said, "For what you did there can be no reward great enough." Selene heard the trembling in his voice and saw the tears forming in his eyes; Claudius had very nearly lost his only son. "Name your reward," the emperor said. "You will see how Rome appreciates her heroes."

"Thank you, Caesar," Selene said. "I want nothing for myself, but would ask that Divine Caesar take the Tiberine island under his personal protection."

"What's that? The island? Why?"

She described the conditions there, the overworked priests and brothers, the population of discarded slaves, and when she was through, the emperor said, "How do you know all this?"

"Because I work there, Caesar. I am a healer." Selene glanced at Andreas, who stood behind the emperor, and she saw that he was smiling at her.

"A healer!" said Claudius. "And that is how you were able to restore life to my son. Your wish will be granted, Selene. The island will come under Imperial protection. My ministers will go there tomorrow and see what has to be done. I am one man, as you can see, who cannot afford to offend the god of healing."

Selene smiled. "Thank you, Caesar."

"Selene, eh?" he said. "Is that your full name? What of your family?"

She hesitated. "My full name is Cleopatra Selene."

"Cleopatra Selene! How is that?"

"I was named for my grandmother, the last queen of Egypt."

In front of her, arranged on the platform around Claudius, members of the Imperial family and the Empire's highest dignitaries looked at Selene with astonished faces. Behind her, ranging over the river banks, on balconies and rooftops, hundreds of faces watched and waited. All that could be heard in the silence was the snapping of pennants in the breeze, and the hissing of the torches.

Claudius said, "I had not thought any descendants of the queen survived. And what is your family on the other side?"

Selene lifted her necklace over her head, slipped the gold ring off and handed it to Claudius.

He brought it close to his eyes and squinted. "Eh? This ring belonged to the Divine Julius. Or one like it." He looked up at Selene. "What does it mean?"

"My grandfather was Julius Caesar."

A shock began to ripple through the crowd, starting with those nearest who could hear, traveling out like a rock thrown into a still pond and causing a chain reaction, until even those farthest downstream were murmuring among themselves.

"I speak the truth, Caesar," Selene said in a loud voice. "My father was Prince Caesarion, the son of Cleopatra and Julius Caesar. He was not killed when the God Augustus had ordered it, but was taken away and put in hiding, a slave being slain in his place. In the year of Augustus's death, Tiberius sent a patrol to kill Caesarion; he fled from Alexandria to Palmyra with his wife, and there I was born."

Claudius studied her for a moment, then said slowly, "My uncle Tiberius had many enemies. He was insecure in his rule. I am aware that he claimed to have heard of the existence of Caesarion, the only living descendant of Julius Caesar, and that, fearing competition for the rulership of Rome, dispatched soldiers to have the man slain. But no proof was ever brought back that the man they killed was Caesarion."

"*There* is your proof, Caesar," Selene said, pointing to the ring. "As my father lay dying, he gave it to the midwife who had just delivered me, and he told her it was my legacy."

Claudius eyed her skeptically. "When was this? In what month?"

"It was August, in the first year of the reign of Tiberius."

Claudius nodded. He was a historian and a scholar; his head was full of dates and events. "That was the time, as you say. Still, you could have had this ring made."

"I could have, but I did not."

"It is still no proof. Have you other proof?"

She paused. "None, Caesar."

"Anyone who can vouch for you?"

"I can, Caesar."

All heads turned to Andreas, who stepped forward. "She speaks the truth. I was in Alexandria when Selene learned the truth of her ancestry," he said. "It was only last year. Before that, her own identity was unknown to her."

"And what proof is there in Alexandria?" Claudius asked.

"Her resemblance to Queen Cleopatra. The likeness is exact."

As Claudius studied Selene a moment longer, a noise began at the periphery of the mob, just a soft rumble at first, but growing louder, rising to the night sky, riding a tide of waving arms as the shout was taken up and carried to the Imperial platform. The crowd chanted in a four-beat rhythm: "JUL-ius CAE-sar, JUL-ius CAE-sar," over and over, accompanied by fists thrusting into the air.

Selene turned around and looked over the crowd in wonder. All up and down the river, illuminated by torches and campfires, thousands upon thousands of Romans were waving their arms and chanting, "JUL-ius CAE-sar."

"It seems," Claudius said dryly, "that Rome believes your claim."

He pursed his lips and scanned the restless spectators. He did not believe Selene's story, but clearly the mob did; Claudius, seeing how anxious the people were to adore her, saw at once the profit in granting them a new idol. In embracing her himself, he would be taking one more step toward cementing their favor. So the emperor laid a hand on her shoulder, turned her around to face the crowd and cried in a loud and clear voice, "See how Rome welcomes the granddaughter of Julius Caesar!"

Then, closer to her ear, he said, "You will sit by my side for the rest of the Festival. Tonight, when the celebrations are over, come to the palace. No one but you must touch my son."

———

Britannicus recovered quickly from his brush with death, and after a bath and hot supper went obediently to bed. One by one, people left the room:

Claudius and Messalina, Agrippina and her sulking son, the imperial physicians, attendants and slaves, leaving Selene alone with the boy and with Andreas, who stood leaning against a pillar with his arms folded.

It was deepest night, and the bedchamber glowed softly in the light of lamps hanging from the ceiling. Selene sat at the bedside, her eyes on the boy's sleeping face.

"How did you know to do what you did?" Andreas asked, when the last of the footsteps were heard retreating down the hall. "I have never seen it before."

"I learned it in Persia," she said, feeling Britannicus's forehead. "In some respects, Hindu medicine is far in advance of ours."

"The people are saying you're a goddess."

"The people need someone to worship. Tomorrow it will be someone else."

Andreas pushed away from the pillar and walked around the elegant bedchamber. "I was pleasantly surprised to find you at the Festival tonight," he said. "I had thought I had missed you."

"Missed me?" she said, turning around. "What do you mean?"

"I went to Paulina's house this afternoon and you weren't there."

Selene gazed at him, marveling at his power, his magnetism. "Are you in love with Paulina?" she heard herself ask.

His eyebrows arched. "I love her, yes. But as a friend."

"You arrived in Rome this morning and went straight to her house."

"To see *you.*"

She stared. "I don't believe you."

"Ask the servant at the gate when you get home. When my ship came in, I had only one thought: to see you."

"Why did you never write to me?"

"I tried," he said softly. "Many times."

Selene squeezed her hands tightly together. "Why did you go to Spain instead of coming directly back to Rome?"

"Claudius sent me. He wanted a matter investigated and I was the only man he trusted. I had no choice."

There was something in the air, charged and urgent; Selene could feel it: it came from Andreas, from herself. *Let it go,* said her mind. *You are strangers now. Too much has happened. Keep the wounds closed. Keep the pain away.*

But she could not help herself. Those dark gray-blue eyes were too compelling; the past had too strong a hold on the present. "Andreas," she said quietly. "I want to ask you something. I shouldn't, I suppose. I should let it go and forget it. After all these years . . . "

He came closer. "What is it?"

"Did you . . ." She looked down at her intertwined fingers. *If he says no, if he says no—* "Did you ever go to Palmyra, Andreas?"

He looked puzzled. "Palmyra?"

Selene wished she had kept her silence. There was safety in not hearing the truth.

"Why should I have gone to Palmyra?"

Selene reached out to feel Britannicus's forehead.

"I left Antioch, yes," Andreas said. "To search for you. But not in Palmyra. I went to Tyre."

Selene turned around.

"Why should I have gone to Palmyra?" he said again.

She rose to her feet and faced him. "I left a message for you at your house. Didn't you get it?"

"Yes, I did. But what has that to do with Palmyra?"

"My note," she said. "I explained it in the note."

Andreas frowned. "What note? The girl who took the message told me you were going to Tyre."

"Tyre!"

"To get married."

Selene was thunderstruck. "Married! And you . . . believed it?"

"That was the message you left!"

"It was not. I told the girl to tell you that my mother was taking me to Palmyra. I wanted you to come after me. I left you a note written on a shard."

"I received no note," he said. "The girl said you told her you had decided to marry someone else."

"Andreas! That was a lie!"

"Why would she lie?"

"She must have been in love with you."

Andreas tried to recall the girl who had taken care of him near the harbor, a sad-eyed wraith who had moved around his house like a ghost. She had died that same summer, of a weakness of the marrow caused by her life of hardship and deprivation. Malachus had loved her, Andreas remembered now.

Andreas reached for Selene and took her by the shoulders. "You say it was a lie, and yet you did marry!"

"I never did."

"Your daughter—"

"Her father and I were never married! He was someone I met a long time after I left Antioch, a man who—"

Andreas silenced her with a sudden kiss, and her arms went up around his neck.

He buried his face in her hair and murmured, "I searched for you. I went to Tyre, to Caesarea. I lived only to find you again, Selene. The pain of your leaving me was nothing compared to the pain of not having you. I thought, if I found you, I would fight for you, win you back. I had no idea where you had gone."

"All those terrible months in Lasha's palace," she sobbed, kissing his eyes. "And in the desert, running, hiding, following the river. And in Persia—your face was always before me. I prayed that someday you would find me."

"I have found you at last and I won't let you go. I have never loved anyone, Selene, as I have loved you. You taught me to dream again, to hope again. You restored my self-esteem to me. But when you vanished, the dreams and the hope died. I returned to the sea . . . "

"We can dream again, Andreas! Together! We can begin where we left off, at the Grotto. You will write your books, you will teach, and I—"

They kissed again, and clung to each other to assuage the pain of all the years so cruelly lost. Then Andreas led Selene away, to the rooms in the palace where he lived.

BOOK VIII
ROME

Then here it was. The Domus Julia—the "Julian House"—a sanctuary for the sick.

Empress Agrippina held the curtain of her litter open just wide enough to look out without being seen. She had paused on the left bank of the Tiber to watch the activity on the island, where the Domus Julia was being built, and now she was thinking: *That woman has the arrogance to give her folly the name of one of Rome's oldest and noblest families—and Claudius, the idiot, has sanctioned it.*

Agrippina's grasp on the curtain tightened. She knew what Julia Selena was up to—her acceptance of that name was proof enough of her ambition. The name, Julia Selena, had been given to Selene by the people of Rome on the night of the River Festival, five and a half years ago. How humble Julia Selena had pretended to be after saving Britannicus's life! How modestly she had received the homage of the mob! But Agrippina knew the truth. She knew that Julia Selena was no less ambitious to control the throne of the Roman Empire than she, Agrippina, was.

In the four and a half years that Agrippina had been Claudius's wife, ever since Messalina's execution for bigamy shortly after the River Festival, Agrippina had moved with only one purpose: to become the mother of an emperor. In her consuming obsession, she had gotten herself married to her uncle, been declared his legal consort, and had managed to persuade

Claudius to formally adopt her son, Nero, as his own, thus placing him, because he was older than Britannicus, in direct line of succession. Anyone who posed even a remote threat to Agrippina's plan was put out of the way. She had seen to it that her son was the only legitimate Julio-Claudian left, and that the people would have no choice but to accept him after Claudius's death.

But now, it seemed, there was a new obstacle!

Agrippina watched the activity on the island like a cat watching the progress of a mouse. There were the work gangs, the marble cutters, the draughtsmen, the artisans and architects, all bustling in and out of the half-completed Domus, scaling its scaffolding like bees around a hive. Mindless drones, Agrippina thought, attending upon their queen. And where was "her highness" this morning?

Agrippina opened the curtain a little wider and scanned the island.

At the southern end stood the ancient and modest Temple of Aesculapius. Surrounding it were gardens and the small outbuildings—storage sheds, smoke huts—that Julia Selena had converted into temporary sick wards. And dominating the island was the partially built Domus, its granite columns and marble arches reaching to the sky, hinting of the magnificence to come, the splendor that was going to outshine the great buildings of Rome—the Theater of Marcellus, the Temple of Agrippa—and thereby establish the Domus Julia as the most beautiful and famous building in the Roman Empire.

A house for sick people!

Agrippina signaled to the litter bearers to move closer to the river bank. She was hoping to glimpse Julia Selena and see for herself if what her informants had told her was true.

From this vantage point, the empress could see the garden pathways and the dry fountains and the shrubbery lying in winter dormancy. Soon the island would burst forth with life and would lie like a garland cast from some god's brow to the center of the old, gray river, brightening Rome with flowers and greenery. That had been Julia Selena's doing. In all her memory, Agrippina could not recall the Tiberine island having been anything but an eyesore. In five and a half years, Julia Selena had managed to turn the island into a paradise.

It was because of Claudius's new decree, written right after the night of the River Festival, stating that any slave abandoned on the Tiberine island, and who was cured, was to be set free.

The result, of course, was quick and predictable. No one dared insult the emperor and his new project; people suddenly started to respect the old island. And not a few slave owners saw the financial waste of discarding slaves and seeing them later restored to health and allowed to leave the island, free.

Almost overnight, the wholesale abandonment of slaves on the island ceased. As the Aesculapian brothers took care of those already there, and discharged them as freedmen, the crowding came to an end. Soon the grounds began to clear, the outbuildings emptied and the island started on its road to recovery. Money poured in from wealthy benefactors anxious to curry the emperor's favor; walls and roofs were repaired; gardens were planted; fountains were installed. The regular pilgrims began to reappear, and with them, physicians from the city. Everyone declared that the God had returned to the island, and that it was the granddaughter of the Divine Julius who had brought Him back.

The Romans were a pious and superstitious people; they respected ancient traditions, feared the gods and venerated their ancestors. Which accounted for Julia Selena's stupendous popularity. Ever quick to idolize a hero, the people of Rome had put Julia Selena on an improbable pedestal, not only because of her Julian lineage—which, like Caesar before her, connected her directly to the goddess Venus—but also because of her outrageous "good works."

Agrippina grasped the curtain so tightly that it almost tore.

Why couldn't people see through Julia Selena's charade? An asylum for the sick, indeed! Where they stayed for as long as they needed and were taken care of by trained attendants. There was no such thing in all the world. It was a ruse, Agrippina knew; this sanctuary island and the obscene Domus rising up to the clouds were a trick to cement Julia Selena's place in the people's hearts.

So that her *son, and not mine, will be the next emperor* . . .

At last she saw her. Dressed in the white linen *stola* she was known for, her head veiled, the familiar ebony box hanging from her shoulder. Julia Selena emerged from one of the small stone buildings and headed down a path toward the construction zone at the northern end of the island. And close on her heels was her "shadow," the everpresent simpleton named Pindar who had appeared one day on the island and who was now forever seen at Julia Selena's side.

Agrippina narrowed her eyes. She watched Julia Selena approach the Domus; she saw how all the work ceased and how the men called out to her, from high atop walls, from deep in the plaster troughs. The tricky March wind, which had been blowing from the west, shifted suddenly and came bearing down from the north. It was only for a moment, but long enough for Julia Selena's *palla* to flutter away from her body and expose the new fullness of her figure.

Agrippina let the curtain fall. She had seen what she had come to see. Her informants had told the truth. Julia Selena was pregnant.

As the empress gave orders to the litter bearers and was carried away from the river bank, her mind began to work. Julia Selena had been no threat to her in these five and a half years; but now she was dangerous, and Agrippina was going to have to act.

Julia Selena's child—and the Domus—must not be allowed to survive.

CHAPTER 60

As always, whenever Ulrika came here to Lady Paulina's house, she told herself that she was not looking for Eiric.

If she ever did encounter him, and their eyes met, she ignored the sudden racing of her heart. Ulrika might admit having had a sisterly affection for Eiric when she was twelve, seven years ago, but she certainly was not in love with him now. It was unthinkable.

Ulrika frequently came to Paulina's house, which was not far from her own on the Esquiline Hill, where she lived with her mother and Andreas, her stepfather; she came because she was fond of little Valerius. She taught him lessons, played with him; they each filled an emptiness in the other's life. This afternoon Lady Paulina was giving a grand party, and Ulrika was now searching for the little boy.

She found him hiding in the peristyle garden, waiting for the first guests to arrive. Ulrika sneaked up on him, grabbed him, and swung him high in the air. Valerius squealed and kicked his heels.

"Oof, little brother!" Ulrika said, putting him down. "You're getting too heavy for this. You're six years old now, nearly a grown boy."

But when she tried to straighten up, Valerius kept his arms about her neck and wouldn't let go. "Don't leave me, Rikki," he said.

She knelt before him and brushed the hair out of his eyes. Valerius had a sweet face, with fat cheeks and worried eyebrows. *Why is he always so afraid?* she wondered.

Lady Paulina was a good mother, but she was busy, and did not always recognize the needs of a little boy. Ulrika recognized them. She, too, had spent her baby years getting lost under adult feet.

"Don't you want me to go to the party?" she asked.

"Oh, I don't mind the party, Rikki. I just don't want you to marry Drusus."

Ulrika's face clouded. At such times the two might have been brother and sister, two serious faces mirroring each other's frowns. But then Ulrika smiled quickly and said, "No matter whom I marry, little brother, you will always come and visit me."

"But I won't *live* with you."

"You don't live with me now, do you?"

Valerius pushed out his lips. This was different. Rikki lived just down the street and she was here nearly every day. Somehow, he sensed that marriage would change everything, although he wasn't sure how. "You'll have a little boy of your own and forget me."

"Oh, little brother!" She pulled him into her arms and hugged him. "What doomsday thoughts fill your head!"

Yet she did not deny it. No matter whom Ulrika eventually married, she would move away and, she hoped, have children of her own.

Suddenly Ulrika was annoyed with Paulina. She should not say such things in front of the boy. It was not as if there was any likelihood that Ulrika would consider marrying Drusus. That, too, like the absurd idea of being in love with Eiric, was unthinkable.

As she led the boy from the garden back to the nursery, Ulrika thought of Drusus.

He was very good-looking, the son of a knight, wealthy, and with ambitions to become a senator. And he was young yet, only twenty-three, unlike many of the hopeful prospective suitors who came to Ulrika's house. However, like all the other eligible men who called, Drusus did not mind that Ulrika was nineteen, already old by contemporary marrying standards; they overlooked the age factor because of the many advantages of marrying Ulrika: she was beautiful, offered a considerable dowry, and shared her mother's illustrious ancestry. Ulrika was, in fact, one of the most sought-after young women in Rome.

But how could she explain to her mother and Paulina that she was not ready for marriage, that she felt moved by an inexplicable energy, a restlessness she could not put a name to? Ever since her twelfth birthday back in Alexandria, Ulrika had felt a strange heat deep in her soul, like a brazier that had been lit and was burning for some special purpose.

But what purpose? she asked herself as she returned Valerius to his nanny.

Ulrika felt driven, but she did not know toward what. She felt born to action, but had so far heard no call. She loved working on the island, shared her mother's interest in medicine and healing. But still, Rome felt as stifling as Alexandria once had; it did not seem big enough to contain her nameless ambition. And what was Ulrika's ambition? Was it perhaps to follow in her mother's footsteps and travel the world with a medicine box?

Perhaps it will be revealed to me someday, Ulrika thought, as she encouraged Valerius to eat his lunch. *As it was once revealed to my mother. And perhaps it will be soon . . .*

Sounds of the first guests arriving downstairs made Ulrika raise her eyes to the window of the nursery. It looked out on the orchard that covered the hillside behind the villa; she saw the April sunshine and her heart ached.

She was thinking of Eiric.

Her mind went back to the early days, when she was first living in this house as Paulina's guest and she and Eiric sneaked out to the orchard to learn each other's language. They had been shy and uncertain then— Ulrika new to Rome, Eiric new to slavery. The Greek and German words had been spoken softly beneath the orange and lemon trees; Ulrika had traced letters in the dirt with a stick, teaching Eiric to read his own language for the first time. Then there had followed a comfortable familiarity; bored with their lesson, they had played in the orchard. Eiric teased her and pulled her braids; Ulrika made fun of his breaking voice and the fuzz sprouting on his upper lip. They chased each other and threw rotten fruit. Those had been happy, uncomplicated days.

But then, the summer she was fifteen and he seventeen, they had been playing tag. Ulrika stole Eiric's sandal and he chased her through the trees. He caught her, they scuffled, laughing. Ulrika stumbled and fell back on the ground. They wrestled for a moment, and then, impulsively, Eiric put his mouth over hers. Ulrika, startled, pushed him away. She said his manners were atrocious, and she called him a barbarian.

Eiric had sulked after that. He refused to speak German with her; he called her a child and told her to leave him alone.

Ulrika had been miserable for weeks afterward. She did not understand her feelings, why she had reacted that way, why she had said such cruel things. She began to have strange, disturbing dreams, about physical loving, and whenever she came to Paulina's house she watched for Eiric.

And finally there had been the terrible incident two years ago, on the night of her seventeenth birthday.

"Rikki," said Valerius, tugging at her dress. He was finished with his eggs and bread.

She smiled at the solemn face. "Promise me you'll be good, little brother," she said. "Mind Nanny and take your nap, and I shall bring you a treat later."

As she went downstairs, to meet Paulina's guests, Ulrika told herself that her restlessness must be due to what had happened during the early years of her life. All those miles traveled and explored, living in tents and inns, never calling one place home—surely that was when the seed had been planted, the germ that now made it impossible for her to know what lay in her future.

Through the gates that opened onto the street, Ulrika glimpsed three horses drawing up. And she saw Eiric, in his fine tunic, his hair shining golden in the sun, handling the horses.

There had been a party for Ulrika here at Paulina's house two years ago. There were guests, jugglers and mimes, birthday presents. All through the day she had surreptitiously watched for Eiric, hoping he would appear. But he never did and Ulrika decided he must be sulking. It was like Eiric to do that. And then she convinced herself that she didn't want him there anyway, that he would probably embarrass her with his uncouth ways.

That night the whole house had been wakened by a commotion in the garden. Lucas, overseer of the slaves, was dragging Eiric in. There were fresh whip marks on his back, his face was bruised, his hands were manacled. Lucas explained to Lady Paulina that the boy had been caught riding in the hills toward the coast, running away.

It was a serious offense for a slave to run away, because in removing his body from his master's house, he was in fact stealing someone's property. As Eiric had also taken a horse from the stable, his crime was doubled and Lucas therefore recommended death, as a warning to the other slaves.

Ulrika had interceded. She had begged Paulina to be lenient. Paulina had hesitated. In a society where the chained outnumbered the free, it was vital that the masters maintained the upper hand. No one would ever forget the bloody uprising led by Spartacus years ago, but because Ulrika pleaded so desperately, and because it was her birthday, Paulina had reluctantly given in, with the provision that a second offense would be punished without appeal.

As everyone went back to bed and Eiric was freed from his chains, Ulrika went to him smiling, expecting him to be grateful. Instead, he had glared at her, angry at her interference, and had stalked away.

They spoke rarely after that. When accidentally passing in the house, Ulrika met him with cool indifference, and Eiric's blue eyes smoldered with resentment.

He's beneath me, she reminded herself now as she felt her traitorous body ache for him. *How could I love such a brute?*

"Aunt Paulina," Ulrika said, as she joined Paulina in the peristyle garden. "I've put Valerius down for his afternoon nap."

"Thank you, my dear," Paulina said, taking Ulrika's hand and squeezing it. "There are times when I think he thinks *you* are his mother, and not I."

"Aunt Paulina, you know by now that mothers are never appreciated as much as they should be," Ulrika said. Then, remembering Rani, she added, "But aunts always are!"

They laughed together, and then Ulrika said, "Speaking of mothers, has mine arrived yet?"

Paulina shook her head. "You're not surprised, are you?"

"My mother has not been on time for anything in this past year. She has become absolutely obsessed with the Domus."

"She is to be envied," Paulina said quietly. "The Domus is the final realization of your mother's lifelong dream. When it is completed and begins housing the sick, she and Andreas will commence a great work."

"I want her to rest more," Ulrika said, "now that she is going to have a baby."

"Yes," said Paulina. She was happy for Selene; the baby had been so desperately wanted. And Andreas was overjoyed. Paulina had long ago recovered from the momentary disappointment she had felt upon hearing of Andreas's and Selene's plan to marry. She had seen how they belonged to each other, that Andreas had in fact been Selene's long before Paulina knew him, and, accepting that, resting content with the memory of her own husband and her happy years with him, and focusing her love and attention upon the baby, which had been a gift from Selene, Paulina had been able to lay aside her private fantasy of marrying Andreas and wish her friends joy.

Just then three men rode up on horseback, and, by their appearance and manner, they were men of importance.

As she watched them dismount, Ulrika also watched Eiric, whose job it was to handle the horses. His face had that hard look she knew so well, which meant that a cold hatred was boiling inside him. Ulrika knew that Eiric despised his conquerors. In seven years he had not been completely "broken," and his back still sometimes felt the sting of the lash.

A chamberlain stood in the garden to announce the names of the arriving guests. It turned out that the three who now strode through the gate were military men. The first was a notable centurion; the second was a famous tribune.

And the third was the victor of the Rhineland, Commander Gaius Vatinius.

CHAPTER 61

I'm afraid I can't help you," Selene said, when she had finished examining the young woman. "I don't know the cause of your barrenness, nor can I recommend a treatment for it."

The patient was a twenty-five-year-old woman of the upper class who had been married for nine years and was still childless. She was one of many such women who came to Selene, seeking advice on conception.

After the woman left, Selene walked to the tiny window and looked out, breathing in the refreshing April air. All winter, the small wards had been sealed to keep out the cold, and, in old Roman tradition, bread had been burned continuously in every room to cover up the smell of stale air. But spring had come at last; the island was in full bloom; and the river sent cleansing breezes through the sick wards.

Selene placed her hands on her abdomen, marveling at the miracle contained in her womb.

The events of the night of the River Festival, five and a half years ago, had instantly admitted Selene into Rome's most elite circles, and while she had observed that the ailments of the Roman aristocracy were no different from the ailments of the rich in any other city, she had discovered one puzzling exception: The Roman upper class was afflicted with a mysterious barrenness.

When Selene had started socializing with Roman nobility, she had noticed that many couples were without children, and she had assumed that it was their wish. But then, unexpectedly, the women had started coming to Selene for help in conceiving.

Selene had asked Andreas about it, but he had had no explanation. What was even more curious was that the barrenness did not seem to afflict the lower classes. They continued to turn out large families and to leave unwanted babies on temple steps. Only those living in the mansions on the hills, it seemed, were plagued with a stubborn inability to reproduce.

At first, Selene had regarded it as an interesting phenomenon, but soon the problem had become a personal one. After the wedding, in that October five and a half years ago, Selene and Andreas had tried to have a child, but for five years had had no success. Selene had begun to fear she was somehow infected like the others, that the unknown thing plaguing the wealthy women of Rome had invaded her body. Because she had proof of her own fertility—Ulrika.

It had become a cause for great anxiety until, at last, in January, Selene had felt the familiar signals in her body.

This miracle baby was more for Andreas than for herself. She knew how badly he wanted a child of his own. He had never put it into words, but it was in his eyes, every time they made love, each month when she shook her head. He was fifty-four years old and without an heir. It meant so much to him now, Selene knew: there was the villa in the hills to pass on, and the wealth he and Selene had accrued, and the massive encyclopedia on medicine he was writing, now so near to completing. A portion of it all would go to Ulrika, of course, but if Andreas had a son . . .

And with the birth of this baby, Selene thought as her eyes settled on the half-built Domus rising above the rooftops, *my bond with Andreas will be complete. We shall be a true family.*

As for her other family, the one that lived in the Imperial Palace, Selene did not much care for them. As for the family lost long ago, her mother and twin brother, Selene had finally resigned herself to the fact that they must be dead. "No proof was ever brought back from Palmyra," Claudius had said on the night of the River Festival. Which could only mean that the young mother and her newborn son had not survived the journey to Rome.

Selene tried to read the hour on the sundial in the garden. She must be getting to Paulina's house; the guests would be arriving soon. But she could not tear herself away from the sight of the white skeleton of the Domus Julia standing against the blue April sky.

It expanded Selene's soul to see the slow birth of that magnificent structure—the final realization of her quest.

The Domus was being built to Selene's specifications, it was going to be the perfect refuge for the sick, and a medical school to spread knowledge. The men who worked on it now, and the staff who would later operate it, and the students who would come and the one thousand patients who would occupy its beds, would not know that, in the Domus Julia, they saw something of the Persian *chikisaka*, of the Roman *valetudinarium*, of the Essene *infirmaria*, of the School of Medicine in Alexandria. There were going to be special wards in the Domus, and chapels for all the gods and a surgery with a dome opening to the sun. Andreas had designed classrooms, a small anatomy theater and a dormitory for his medical students. Pipes were being laid now, to bring in fresh water, to carry away wastes. The Domus was being built with an eye to practicality, and to beauty as well, because Selene believed that tranquillity of the

soul helped to heal the body. When completed, the white rotunda dominating the building, larger than any in existence, would gleam in the sun,
visible for miles around, a monument to health and healing. The Domus
Julia was going to be unique in the world, and it was going to stand, Selene
was certain, for eternity.

She saw at last how her identity was linked with healing, for there stood
the evidence: the Domus Julia, the "Julian House." Only as the granddaughter of Julius Caesar could Selene have brought such a vision to life.
This was what she had seen in her delirium on the Euphrates—*alabaster
walls shining whitely in the sun.* And it was also the realization of the
dream she and Andreas had dared to give birth to back in the Grotto, the
dream of working together for a mutual cause.

As Selene turned away from the window, she caught sight of Pindar
hurrying along the path. He had a worried look on his face.

Pindar was such a regular feature of the island—he lived here, he tended
the grounds—that people barely noticed him. Just as Selene was no longer
aware of her constant "shadow"; she had become quite used to him.

No one knew exactly when he had started coming to the island; he had
simply appeared one day, sweeping a garden path. He was doing odd jobs
—scraping algae from fountains, trimming hedges—when Selene finally
asked who he was. And it turned out that no one knew.

Pindar appeared to be in his thirties, but he had the look of a boy. It
was because of the way his tunic hung on his lanky frame, Selene had
realized; it wasn't straight, the hem was always crooked and material was
always bunched in the belt. His sandals were always laced wrong, and his
hair was forever falling over his face in a boyish mop. His face was strange,
too: though a grown man's, it was oddly without lines or adult character,
and his smile was curiously endearing.

He had seemed harmless enough, never spoke, never asked for anything,
just did chores around the temple precincts and so was allowed to stay.
Then one day a man had come to fetch him away. His name was Rufus,
and he was the boy's father.

"He don't mean no harm," Rufus had explained to Selene, as Pindar
resisted his father's effort to take him off the island. "The boy's like that.
Once he sets his mind to something, there ain't no changing it. Don't
know what got into his head, though. I've fetched him off this island must
be a hundred times, and he keeps coming back."

Rufus was a man of nearly sixty, big and brawny, with battle scars on
his face and gray in his beard. His tunic was homespun and he smelled of
onions. They were poor, Selene had realized, this peculiar father and son
—one not educated, the other simpleminded.

"He can stay," Selene had said. "He's actually a help to us."

"He'll sleep here, miss, if you let him," Rufus had said in plain relief. "Y'see, I'm a fuller and I work all day. Pindar needs minding. People have treated him badly, him being simple and all."

"No one will be cruel to him here, I'll see to that."

And so the curious boy/man had stayed. He was always seen near Selene, diligently performing some chore and smiling at anyone who passed by. Today, as he came hurrying along the path, Selene saw that the dog was with him.

The saving of that dog had spoken volumes to Selene about Pindar's nature.

There were quite a few dogs on the island, running about, watch-dogging, clearing out rats and rabbits, and they were fed on scraps. But there was this one, a square-headed hound with the look of an old bear, who was painfully thin, his ribs sticking out through dull fur; and everyone had assumed he was ailing and soon to die.

Soon to die, yes, but not from an ailment.

It was Pindar who had opened the hound's mouth and had seen the broken and worn-down teeth and had understood at once that the poor dog simply couldn't chew what was thrown to him. In the midst of plenty, the dog was literally starving to death. So Pindar had taken some bread and gravy drippings, mashed them into patties and fed them by hand into the old dog's mouth. It had been a long and tedious process, and it still continued, six months after the dog's recovery; but recover he had, and today the dog bounced along the path behind his master—a pair of lookalikes, Pindar and the dog. Everyone named him Fido, the popular name in Rome for dogs, being Latin for "faithful."

Seeing Selene at the window, Pindar gestured frantically. He was rarely agitated, and so Selene knew that something must be wrong. And as she drew her *palla* around her shoulders, a chilling intuition told her what it must be.

She arrived at the construction site to find the work at a standstill. The workmen had left the interior of the roofless building and were standing around outside, shifting nervously.

"What is it?" Selene asked Gallus, the foreman.

He was a large man with husky shoulders and the muscles of a gladiator, but when he came up to Selene there was meekness in his manner. "It's happened again, mistress," he said.

Selene compressed her lips. This would be the fourth time in three weeks! Who was committing these acts of sabotage?

"Where is it?" she asked.

He pointed to the Domus. "Inside. The men won't go back in. Some've already quit and left the island. They're saying the project is cursed."

Selene shot him a look. She had warned Gallus about fostering such talk among the men.

Lifting the hem of her dress off the ground, she stepped over the rubble and tools and entered the building. There was a layer of fine dust everywhere from the veneer of Carrera marble the marble cutters were beginning to apply to the walls. It covered scaffolds, surveyors' equipment, even the architects' table. Selene headed for the very center of the building that, in several months' time, would be marked by a statue of Venus, standing directly beneath the center of the rotunda. The floor would be marble, but now it was concrete, and it was littered with debris.

Selene stopped abruptly. She pressed her hand to her mouth and looked quickly away, fighting down her nausea before returning to the doorless entrance of the Domus.

"Where did it come from?" she asked the foreman.

"One of the workmen found it buried in one of the walls. He said the plaster was still fresh. It must have been done during the night."

Selene closed her eyes for a moment, trying to block out the memory of the vile thing she had just seen. Then she said, "Where were the guards?"

"They insist they were awake, mistress. And all the lanterns were lit. We've tripled the watch since . . . "

Since last week, when a black goat was found hanging on one of the pillars.

Selene could not believe it. These acts apparently were the work of someone *inside*—a member of the work gangs, perhaps, or one of the many draughtsmen and surveyors. Three hundred men were working on the Domus; it could be any one of them.

"Get it out of there," she said. "Burn it."

But the foreman did not move.

"I said to remove it."

"I'm sorry, mistress," Gallus said, "but that's a wicked thing in there. It's the work of demons. If I touch it, what'll happen to me?"

"Oh, Gallus, it's only a—" Selene could not bring herself to say it. In a quieter tone, she said. "Someone is trying to slow down the work on the Domus, don't you see that? Someone is trying to frighten us. We mustn't let that happen. That thing in there, Gallus, is only an *object.*"

"It's black magic."

Selene saw the men start to move uneasily. She said, "*I'm* not afraid of it," and turned to go back inside.

But Pindar laid a hand on her arm and gave her a worried look. He started to push past her, but she said, "No, Pindar. I will do it. I have to show them that I am not afraid."

She found two sticks and managed to wedge the thing between them. When she emerged into the sunshine with it, holding it out from her body, the men fell back and made the sign against the evil eye. Selene hurried to the sloping back of the island and let the sticks and their burden drop into the river.

When she returned to the men, she tried to hide her trembling beneath her *palla*. "It's gone," she said. "There is nothing to be afraid of."

"It's witchcraft," Gallus said. "Someone's put a curse on this project, and it's going to fall on us."

"Get back to work, all of you."

The men looked at one another.

"I said get back to work."

Selene saw how their eyes shifted to Gallus, watching him for a sign, and how Gallus hung back, afraid. So she marched up the littered steps of the Domus and picked up an enormous hammer. As she lifted it over her head, she cried, "Then I shall do the work myself! I will not have the Divine Julius insulted this way!"

Several of the men stepped forward and took the heavy tool from her hands, reminding her of her delicate state, protesting that they honored the Divine Julius and his granddaughter. Then, like scolded children, they went reluctantly back to work.

———

"I shall next be having to call in priests and have an exorcism performed. It will be the only way the men will continue working in the Domus."

Ulrika, walking through the garden with her arm linked in her mother's, said, "Who could be doing such a thing?"

Selene shook her head. She was looking at the brightly lit dining room where Paulina's guests were mingling, but she did not see them. She was seeing instead the obscene object she had thrown into the river that afternoon, and was wondering what terrible things tomorrow would reveal.

They came upon three military-looking men, standing stiffly in the garden and debating a point of battle strategy. They paused to introduce themselves to Selene, and when Commander Vatinius spoke, Selene looked at him, startled.

She studied him for a moment; to her surprise he was extraordinarily handsome. She said, "Commander Vatinius? Have I heard of you, sir?"

The tribune laughed, showing white teeth in a tanned face. "If you have not, mistress, then you have ruined his day! Gaius would be shattered to think that there was one beautiful woman in Rome who did not know who he was!"

She ignored this other man and stared at Gaius Vatinius. His eyes were deep-set over a large, straight nose; his handsomeness was severe, his manner arrogant. The hint of a smile played around his lips.

"Are you, by any chance," Selene heard herself ask, "the Gaius Vatinius who fought some years ago on the Rhine?"

His smile deepened. "You *have* heard of me, then," he said quietly.

Selene closed her eyes. *Wulf,* she cried, *what happened? Did you never get back to Germany? Oh, Wulf! You never had your revenge* . . .

Gaius Vatinius then looked at Ulrika. His eyes moved up and down her body, lingeringly; the next moment, a slave was announcing the serving of dinner, and the three men excused themselves and turned toward the house.

"Mother," Ulrika said, seeing Selene's pale face. "Are you all right?"

"Yes. I'm all right."

"You're thinking of the Domus."

"No." Selene was breathless.

Ulrika looked at the three military men entering the dining room. "Did they upset you?" she said. "Was it Gaius Vatinius?"

Selene forced a smile. "I'm not upset, Ulrika. I'm all right. Shall we go inside?"

"Who is this Gaius Vatinius?"

Selene avoided her daughter's eyes as she said, "He once commanded the legions on the Rhine. It was years ago, before you were born."

There were four tables set, each bordered on three sides by couches. The placement of guests followed strict protocol, with the honored ones reclining on the left edge of each couch. The fourth side of the table was open to allow slaves to come and go with food and drink.

As they walked into the dining room, Andreas came up behind his stepdaughter, slipped an arm about her waist, and murmured, "I see Paulina has invited Odius and Odia tonight."

Ulrika laughed. It was their private joke. Neither cared for Maximus and Juno.

She squeezed his arm and gave him a conspiratorial look. Ulrika loved her stepfather. In the beginning, she had thought Andreas an intruder, but then, during the wedding ceremony in Ostia, when her mother had stood in the flame-colored veil and Andreas had slipped the iron band onto the third finger of Selene's left hand, Ulrika had been so moved by the look of love in his eyes that she had been won over.

Andreas was a good man, kind and soft-spoken. And he was brilliant.
His encyclopedia was nearing forty volumes, and promised to be the most
complete work on medicine ever written. Ulrika often helped Andreas
with it, as he worked in the garden of their estate in the hills. She wrote
as he dictated, or she proofread and offered suggestions; and he always
listened to her and respected her advice.

"But who are those three?" he asked her, nodding toward the military
men, whose tunics and togas were scarlet and gold, and who had an air
of owning the house.

"Soldiers," Ulrika said, and went to take her place on the third couch.

The place of honor at this table went to Commander Gaius Vatinius.
Selene, acting as hostess, reclined on the couch to his left, Ulrika was
opposite her mother. In between were Maximus and Juno, the centurion,
and Lady Aurelia, an elderly widow.

Roasted pheasant, dressed in its feathers, dominated the table, surrounded by a variety of dishes from which the guests helped themselves
with their fingers. The conversation of thirty-six people filled the room and
nearly drowned out the solo performance of a musician playing his pan-
pipes in the corner, while a staff of forty slaves moved about the room
efficiently and noiselessly.

Ulrika could not take her eyes off Gaius Vatinius.

"I tell you, it is deuced bothersome," he was saying to his table companions. "We signed peace treaties with the barbarians during the reign of
Tiberius, and now they are breaking them. Caligula had plans, you know,
to cross the Rhine and conquer the 'free' Germans. If only he had carried
it through, I should not now be faced with the tiresome task of going
back!"

When he saw Ulrika staring at him, Gaius Vatinius fell silent and stared
in his turn. He did not fail to appreciate her unusual beauty—the tawny
hair and blue eyes. A glance at her left hand told him she was unmarried,
which surprised him, as he guessed she was past the age.

He gave her his best smile and said, "I am boring you with military talk."

"Not at all, Commander," Ulrika said. "I have always been interested
in the Rhineland."

His eyes moved to her breasts, and lingered there as he said, "Perhaps
you would be interested in seeing my library on the subject."

Lady Aurelia said, "Why can't they settle down and be civilized? Look
what we have done for the rest of the world. Our aqueducts, our roads."

Ulrika looked over at her mother and was startled to see how white she
was. Selene was not eating; her wine went untouched.

"They've been peaceful for a long time," Commander Vatinius explained, "but now it seems they are being incited by a rebel leader."

"And who is that?" Maximus asked.

"We don't know who he is, or what his name is. We've never even seen him. He came from nowhere, all of a sudden, and is now leading the Germanic tribes in fresh uprisings. They strike when we least expect it, and then vanish into the forest. Patrols sent out to search for his camp never come back. The situation is getting worse, so Pomponius Secundus, the governor of Germany, has called me back to take command of the legions."

Gaius Vatinius sipped his wine, paused while a slave wiped his lips for him, then added with confidence, "I shall find that rebel leader, and when I do I shall make an example of his execution as a warning against others who might have rebellious thoughts. I intend to put a stop to this mischief once and for all."

Ulrika said, "And what makes you so certain, Commander, that you will be successful this time?"

"Because I have a special plan. It was no accident that the emperor chose me to command the Rhine legions. I am a master strategist. And this campaign calls for superior strategy."

Ulrika stared at him. This arrogant braggart was planning to go back to her father's people and subjugate them once and for all!

She smiled at him as she said, "I have read that the barbarians are cunning, Commander Vatinius. What could you possibly have in mind that would assure you of such a certain victory?"

He returned her smile with one that sent a message to her, an invitation that was impossible to mistake. Then he said, "A plan that cannot fail, because it hinges upon the element of surprise."

Ulrika forced herself to appear calm, as if interested only in a theoretical way. Reaching for an olive, she said, "I would think that by now the barbarians are wise to every form of strategy the legions use, even those intended for surprise."

"This plan will be different."

"How so?"

He chuckled and shook his head. "You wouldn't understand. These matters are best left to men."

But she persisted, smiling flirtatiously. "I have read my great-grandfather's memoirs of his conquests," she said, subtly reminding him of the great general Julius Caesar, whose descendant she was. "Military talk does not bore me, Commander."

"It bores me," said Lady Aurelia, who then addressed herself to Selene. "Julia Selena, my dear. How goes the work on your new building?"

Selene blinked; her thoughts had been far away. "I beg your pardon?"

"Your new building. The Domus. Is it going well? I must confess that I find it difficult to imagine what it will be like. It appears to be such a grand establishment. Why fill it with sick people? And besides, I should think that the sick are best cared for in their own homes, by their own families."

"Many have no homes, no families. Take yourself, Lady Aurelia. You are a widow. You live alone, do you not?"

"But I have a physician among my slaves."

Selene discounted that. Many of the so-called slave physicians were ill-trained and could do little more than tie a crude bandage. But Lady Aurelia would not understand; nor did the majority of Rome's population understand what Selene and Andreas were hoping to accomplish on the island. Because there was nothing like the Domus anywhere in the world. But, once its doors were open and the healing and teaching began, Selene knew, the people would quickly grasp its importance.

"Commander Vatinius," Ulrika said, drawing his attention back to herself. "Do you intend to make use of military engines in your campaign against the barbarians?"

He regarded her for a moment; then, flattered by her persistent interest in his plan, and mildly impressed with her ability to comprehend it, he said, "That is precisely what the barbarians will be expecting. But I have in mind a different plan of attack. This time I shall fight fire with fire."

She gave him a quizzical look.

"You see," Gaius Vatinius said, "in order to conquer the barbarians once and for all, it will be necessary to take them completely by surprise. What they will be expecting are military engines, and that is exactly what I shall send against them."

Ulrika's eyes widened. "A ruse?"

He nodded. "The emperor has granted me complete freedom in this campaign; I have the authority to call up as many legionaries as I require, as much siege machinery as I will need. And this is what the barbarians will see. The catapults and movable towers, the mounted troops and infantry units. All very organized and very Roman. What they will *not* see," he said, pausing to taste his wine, "are the guerrilla units, trained and led by barbarians themselves, deployed throughout the forests *behind* them."

Ulrika stared at Gaius Vatinius. Fight fire with fire, he had said. He was going to use her people's own form of warfare against them. While mustering themselves to fight the Roman engines and cavalry—a decoy—her people were going to be attacked from behind.

She looked away. She looked down at her hands, where she felt her pulse throbbing in her fingertips. And she thought: *It will be a slaughter . . .*

CHAPTER 62

The night had turned cold. Ulrika, wearing only her nightdress, pulled her woollen cloak about her shoulders before stepping outside.

Paulina's house was dark and silent. The guests had left long ago, and now everyone slept. Maximus and Juno, whose house was far away, slept in the next room, and Ulrika's parents, agreeing to Paulina's request that they stay the night, were three doors down. Ulrika crept silently along. When she knocked and her mother opened the door, she found Selene fully dressed and not at all surprised to see her daughter standing there.

"I thought you might come," Selene said, closing the door behind Ulrika. Coals burned in a brazier, and two chairs with footstools were positioned close to it. As Selene sat down and motioned for Ulrika to join her, she said, "Andreas is asleep. We can talk."

They sat in silence for a while, both staring into the glowing charcoal, and then Selene finally spoke. "You want to know about Gaius Vatinius," she said softly.

"He upset you, Mother. It was obvious. All through dinner. And you left early. Tell me. What has he to do with my father? Was he the one who . . . ?"

Selene turned and faced her daughter. "It was Gaius Vatinius who burned your father's village to the ground and who took your father away in chains. In the years we were together, your father often spoke of returning to Germany and taking revenge upon Gaius Vatinius."

"I see," Ulrika whispered. "Father never lived to fulfill that vow. To kill *that* man. The man I just had dinner with."

"Ulrika." Selene took hold of her daughter's hand. "It's in the past. It happened many years ago. Let it go, Ulrika. Put it out of your mind."

"I feel as though I have betrayed my father."

"But you haven't!" Selene glanced at the closed door that led to the bedroom, then said in a lower voice, "You didn't know who Gaius Vatinius was. And it was your father's fight, not yours."

When Ulrika felt the grip tighten on her hand, so tight that it hurt, she looked into her mother's eyes. "There is something else," Ulrika said. "Something you haven't told me. What is it?"

Selene withdrew her hand and looked away.

"*Is* there something more?" Ulrika pressed.

Selene nodded.

"Tell me."

Selene faced her daughter again, pain showing in her eyes. "It is something I should have told you long ago," she said in a tight voice. "I meant to. I didn't think I could explain it to you when you were little, but I always thought . . . when you were older. Rani was always urging me to tell you. But each time, the moment wasn't right."

Selene's hands twisted in her lap. "Ulrika, I told you that your father was killed in a hunting accident before you were born. That was a lie. He left Persia. He went back to Germany."

Ulrika frowned. "He didn't die? He went back to Germany?"

"At my insistence. We had been in Persia only a short while when we heard that Gaius Vatinius had been there before us. We were told he was on his way to Germany. I urged your father to go, to hurry after him, while I stayed behind in Persia."

"And he went? Knowing you were pregnant?"

"No. He didn't know I was pregnant. I didn't tell him."

"Why not?"

"Because I knew he would have stayed with me then, and after the baby was born I knew he would never go back to Germany. I had no right to interfere with his life, Ulrika."

"No right! You were his wife!"

Selene shook her head. "I was not. We were never married."

Ulrika stared at her mother.

"He already had a wife," Selene went on, not meeting her daughter's eyes. "He had a wife and a son back in Germany. Oh, Ulrika, your father and I were never meant to spend the rest of our lives together! He had his destiny in the Rhineland, and I was searching for Andreas. We had to go our separate ways."

"He left Persia," Ulrika said slowly, "not knowing you were pregnant. He didn't know about me."

"No."

Ulrika was suddenly filled with wonder. "And he doesn't know about me now! My father doesn't know I exist!"

"He can't still be alive, Ulrika."

"How can you say that?"

"Because if he had reached Germany, your father would have found Gaius Vatinius and carried out his revenge."

Horror filled Ulrika's eyes. She said softly, "And Gaius Vatinius is alive. I shared his table tonight . . . "

Selene reached again for her daughter's hand, but Ulrika pulled away. "You had no right to keep it from me," she cried. "All these years have been a lie!"

"It was for your own sake, Ulrika. As a child, you wouldn't have been able to understand. You would have been angry with me for letting him go. You wouldn't have understood why I did it."

"I'm angry with you now, Mother. I haven't been a child for a long time. You could have told me years ago, instead of letting me find out this way." Ulrika stood up. "You robbed me of my father, and then you let me grow up thinking I adored a dead man. And tonight, Mother, tonight you sat there while I talked with that monster."

"Ulrika—"

But she was out the door.

———

Ulrika lay staring up at the ceiling, listening to the distant rumble of night traffic in the city streets. Her head throbbed. She had cried only for a short time, and then she had started to think. Now, as she lay on her back, her eyes peering into the darkness, she tried to sort out her feelings, but she could not. There was pain and disappointment, and the feeling of having been betrayed. But there was pity also, for her mother, for the young woman back in Persia, carrying a child and sending the man she loved away from her for his own sake. Ulrika's admiration for her mother's sacrifice, and then for the way she had bravely borne the secret all these years for a child's sake, clashed with her resentment at not having been told the truth. She thought of her father, who surely had been alive while she was thinking of him in her early years. And in Jerusalem, when Ulrika had followed the raven, perhaps her father had still been alive then. Alive, and not knowing that he had a daughter at the other end of the world.

Ulrika fell into a brief sleep and she had a dream. She dreamed she got out of bed, went to the window, climbed out and landed barefoot in snow. Tall pines grew all around her and clouds whispered across the face of the moon. She saw tracks—big paw prints in the snow, leading away into the woods. Ulrika followed them; she could feel the moonlight on her shoulders. Presently she saw a large shaggy wolf with golden eyes. She sat down in the snow and he came up and lay beside her, putting his head in her lap. The night was pure, as pure as the wolf's eyes gazing up at her; and she could feel the steady beat of his heart beneath his ribs. The golden eyes blinked and seemed to say: *Here is trust, here is love, here is home.*

Ulrika woke up, surprised to find herself in bed, and was momentarily confused by the spring perfume on the night breeze. She went to her window and looked out. The ground was white; it stretched away up the hill like a blanket of snow. Then Ulrika realized they were petals from the flowering fruit trees, pink and orange blossoms, fallen like snow and looking white in the moonlight. She peered ahead through the trees and she saw something move.

It was Eiric.

She crept along the peristyle hall and out through the back gate to the orchard. Her feet had walked this familiar path for seven years, but not as often lately as earlier, when her feelings for Eiric had been straightforward and uncomplicated.

She walked to where he sat. His back was to her, hard and muscled. He wore a thin gold band around his head; his blond curls touched the tops of his shoulders. He was beautiful.

Ulrika thought that if she felt any more love for him her heart would burst.

"Eiric," she said.

He spun around, and was on his feet. They faced each other in the moonlight.

And then she was in his arms. The feel of his body hard against hers made her dizzy, the pressure of his lips on hers, the warmth of his tongue. She tried to touch every part of him with her hands. Eiric kissed the tears off her cheeks and stilled her sobs with his mouth. He murmured to her in German; she plunged her fingers into the golden curls on his head.

The petals cushioned her bare back as she took Eiric's weight upon herself. She glimpsed the moon between overhead branches. The pain was going. She felt it being pushed out of her. The anger and resentment and feeling of betrayal receded before the force of Eiric's passion.

"We'll run away together," she whispered. "We'll hide. I love you. I love you."

Eiric did not speak. He already knew what he had to do. There would be no running away together, hiding in shame, no being brought back in humiliation, no punishment for the two of them. This was something he must do on his own. He must prove himself to her.

Then he would come back and take her away, with honor, to where she belonged, where they both belonged. North.

CHAPTER 63

Rufus marched across the bridge like a soldier under orders. Word of what was happening at the Domus, wicked tricks meant to scare off the workers, had reached his ears, and it inflamed him. Rufus was not going to sit by and allow someone to frighten Mistress Selena. Something had to be done to stop it, and Rufus was the man to do it.

The island lay quiet in the spring moonlight. It seemed to be slumbering beneath a blanket of snow, but then one saw the hundreds of pink and orange petals that had fallen to the ground, looking white in the night. Torches burned at the temple entrance, but otherwise few signs of life showed. Except at the construction site, which dominated the far end of the island: Many lights blazed there, and men sat around campfires with clubs at their sides.

Rufus strode toward the Domus with a determined step. For what Mistress Selena had done for him and his son Pindar, Rufus could not show enough gratitude. The poor boy had been mistreated for years, the target of rotten fruit and eggs, of children's cruel taunts, of practical jokes. Pindar was simple, that was all; he didn't have the Evil Eye, as people said.

Pindar could not help being simple. It was on account of his having been taken from his mother too soon after he was born. The gods knew how hard Rufus had tried to save the poor girl, but there she was, yanked out of childbed and into the cold desert wind.

They had all agreed, Rufus and the other soldiers, that it wasn't right, slaughtering the young mother and her babe. They had killed the Roman —that was enough. But what harm could old Tiberius see in that pitiful pair? So the soldiers who had been sent out of the Palmyra post had made a secret pact: The girl and her baby should be spared. And Rufus himself had kept another secret all to himself, not even shared with the others— that he had seen the midwife hiding in the corn bin, clutching another newborn babe.

It had been a messy business—breaking in and executing the Roman. Of course, the soldiers had not known why they were doing it, they were just obeying an order from the new emperor, Tiberius. Still, even tough legionaries stuck in a remote outpost like Palmyra drew the line some- where. So the mother and baby had been spared.

But the mother had not lived to reach the post; she had died on the road, and there they had buried her. But the baby had lived long enough to make it to the full breasts of Rufus's young wife, who herself had just had a baby and who had sufficient milk for two.

Rufus reflected on that bittersweet memory of long ago as he neared the Domus, silhouetted majestically against the April stars. Poor Lavinia, so young, so fragile, had not been cut out to be a soldier's wife and live a rugged existence; she and their baby had died of the childbed fever that had taken so many young mothers and babies that summer in Palmyra. But the foundling had survived. Rufus had seen the hands of the gods in that miracle: They had replaced his lost son with another. So he had named the boy Pindar, not knowing his real name, and had settled down to raising him as his own.

It was queer how Pindar had taken to Mistress Selena. After years of abuse, Pindar had learned to stay away from people, to make himself as unobtrusive as possible. But then, one day in the Forum, as Rufus and his son had been looking through a sandal-maker's stall, Pindar had abruptly left his father's protective side and hurried off after a strange woman passing by. She had disappeared in the crowd and Rufus had found Pindar near the Curia steps, frantic and distraught.

And then, days later, Pindar had somehow found the lady again, on this island. And after that, there was no keeping him away.

Well, Rufus thought now as he searched the workers' encampment for a head man, dumb animals were supposed to have that special sense, knowing who had a kind heart and sticking by them. Perhaps Pindar, in his simpleness, had been given that dog's knowing. Because that was how he stayed by Mistress Selena—as Fido stayed by him.

And then there was the resemblance. It was almost uncanny. Maybe others didn't see it, but Rufus had noticed it at once—the similarities between the faces of Mistress Selena and Pindar. That could also explain why the boy was drawn to her. He saw a face he could trust.

Rufus came to a halt and surveyed the scene. There were plenty of guards on duty at this late hour, but not one, he saw, sat inside the half-finished building. And he thought that very odd. Shouldn't they be on guard *inside*, where the next nastiness was likely to happen?

———

Selene was out of breath by the time she reached the construction site. She was tired on this crisp, early morning. There were violet shadows beneath her eyes. She had not slept after her talk with Ulrika the night before, and now Selene was worried.

She had intended to go straight to Ulrika's room this morning and have a talk with her daughter, perhaps spend the day with her, explain things.

But then a messenger had come from the island to report that there was something wrong, and so Selene had left the house at once.

The men were standing around, scratching their heads, looking at one another. "What is it this time?" Selene asked, as she came up.

Mordecai, the Egyptian architect, approached her with a baffled expression. "The men are ready to start work, mistress. But the foreman is nowhere to be found."

"Gallus?" Selene said as she looked around. The men stood in clusters: marble cutters, plasterers, bricklayers. Their faces were puffy from the night's sleep, many still held their breakfast beer.

"Has anyone searched for him?" Selene asked.

"We've sent men into the city. He wasn't at any of his usual places. His wife said he didn't come home last night."

Selene frowned. Was this another terrible trick to stop work on the Domus? As she was about to send a messenger to the construction guild, to find a replacement foreman, shouting came from inside the Domus.

Everyone turned to see Rufus hurrying out of the entrance. He cried, "Mistress! Come and see!"

She felt a chill and thought: *Not again!* But, as she dared not show fear in front of the workers, she followed Rufus inside, bracing herself for what she might find.

"Look, mistress," he said, pointing up.

There, among the temporary rafters and beams standing against the morning sky, a white dove was flying around.

Selene stared in amazement. The bird went from girder to girder, fluttering up and down throughout the wooden scaffolding, without once flying up to the open sky and away. The dome had not yet been built over the rotunda; the house was roofless. And yet the dove did not fly away!

Then Selene saw something green in its beak, a sprig of myrtle.

"It's a sign, mistress!" Rufus boomed loud enough for those outside to hear. "A sign from the gods."

One by one the men came up the steps and peered inside, fearful of what they might find. But when they saw the dove fluttering overhead, they came all the way in and gazed up in wonder.

"It's a sign from Venus," said Mordecai the Egyptian, for myrtle was the tree sacred to that goddess.

"And therefore a sign from Caesar," cried another man.

Soon, all the men were talking and nodding and coming further into the Domus.

When the noise of many voices filled the vast, roofless rotunda, Rufus

leaned close to Selene and murmured, "Gallus is gone, mistress. He won't
be coming back."

She looked at him. "Why not? Where did he go?"

Rufus did not reply; and Selene had her answer. When she looked again
at the dove, this time more carefully, she saw what none of the others had
noticed: that the sprig of myrtle was tied to the bird's beak, and that a very
fine string was attached at one end to its feet, at the other to a central beam
overhead.

Suddenly understanding and impressed, Selene turned to Rufus and
said, "This is indeed a sign from the Divine Julius. It tells us that work
on the Domus must continue. However, I am without a foreman."

"I shall go to the guild at once, mistress."

"Perhaps, Rufus," she said, staying him, "you would take the job?"

"Me? Bless ya, mistress, I'm just an old retired soldier. And a fuller when
I can find the work."

"It pays well, and you'll have meat three times a week."

Rufus's scarred old face wrinkled in a grin. "It'd be an insult to you if
I didn't at least give it a try."

By the time she was taking the path back to the temple, labor on the
Domus had resumed and the Tiber rang with the music of hammers and
chisels.

There was a small stone building, no bigger than one room, that had once
stored wine and smoked meat. Selene had converted it into a small office
for herself, where she kept scrolls and records, and met with visitors. Ulrika
was there now, waiting for her.

The young woman's face was also drawn from a sleepless night, and she
stood stiffly before her mother, like a stranger. "I came because I want you
to tell me everything," she said.

"Everything about what?"

"I want to know everything that Gaius Vatinius did to my father's
people."

"What do you mean?"

"My father told you, I know he did. Now *I* want to know."

"Ulrika, it was so long ago."

"I want to know what happened. It's my right. My legacy. I want to
hear it all just as my father told it to you."

Selene shook her head. "It was terrible, what that man did. The fighting
in the forests was bad enough, but there was mutilation of the bodies,
desecration of the holy tree shrines . . . and there was torture."

"Go on."

"Why, Ulrika?" cried Selene. "Why must you know?"

"Because I want to see what my father saw, I want to feel in my heart what he felt. If he had stayed with us in Persia, he would have told me these things himself. I would have grown up knowing his pain. Now you must pass these things on to me."

Selene stared at her daughter. Then she said, "The women were raped. Your father's wife was taken to the tent of Gaius Vatinius. There were other men with him. Your father was forced to watch."

Ulrika's face was stone-like. "You said he went back to her. She must have lived through it."

"She was barely alive when he was taken away."

"And his son?"

"Wulf said that Einar had been tortured. He was just a little boy. He was still alive, too."

The April breeze that came through the open window brought with it the sounds of the busy dockside across the river. The clanging and hammering of the men working on the Domus could also be heard. The Domus Julia—Selene's dream after all these years, reaching up to the sky.

"My brother," Ulrika said. "I have a brother named Einar. How old was he? Did my father tell you?"

Selene tried to think. "I believe he said he was ten years old. Ulrika, why can't you let it die? It was so long ago!"

"Because my father is still alive."

Selene's eyes widened. "Why do you think that?"

"He's the rebel leader Gaius Vatinius was talking about last night. It's my father who is leading the uprisings in the forest."

"You can't believe that! Ulrika, it's been nineteen years!"

Ulrika walked past her mother to the window. She felt as if she had aged a lifetime overnight. And she knew that nothing would ever be the same again. She also knew now her purpose in life, what the restlessness had meant, why Rome could never satisfy her. In the early dawn hours, as she lay in Eiric's arms, Ulrika had seen her future as clearly and brightly as she now saw the half-constructed Domus Julia. She knew what she must do. If it was not her father leading the new rebel uprisings, then it was her brother, Einar. But Ulrika would never know if she did not go and try to find out for herself.

"I'm leaving, Mother," she said at last, turning around. "I'm leaving Rome."

"Leaving! But why? Where will you go?"

"To Germany."

Selene's hand flew to her mouth.

"I'm going to search for my father."

"Ulrika, no!"

"He needs me, Mother. I realize that now. I realized it as soon as I knew that my father must be the rebel leader Gaius Vatinius has been ordered to liquidate. I must warn them of his plan, Mother. Gaius Vatinius will have a big surprise, because my people will be ready for him. And I'm going to help them fight. I can give them medical help."

"Please," Selene whispered. "Please don't go."

Ulrika hesitated for an instant. A look swept over her face, her body faltered for a moment, then she was in control again. A threshold had been crossed; there was no going back.

At the door, Ulrika turned and said quietly, "You spoke of the parting of the ways for you and my father, that you had always known the fork would come in the road. Now you and I must part, Mother, because we have separate destinies. Goodbye, and may the gods, yours and mine, watch over you."

Selene opened her mouth to speak, but instead she went wordlessly to her daughter and took her into her arms. Ulrika clasped her mother hard, with a finality in her embrace that explained what words could not.

Selene drew back and pulled her necklace over her head, but as she tried to press it into her daughter's hands, Ulrika said, "No, Mother. This is *you.*" She pointed to the Julius Caesar ring. "Give this to the little brother or sister you are now carrying. He or she will grow up Roman, will grow up to be proud of Great-grandfather. My spirit calls me to the northern forests. I have nothing to do with this place. Odin goes with me as I go to my father."

A sob escaped Selene's throat. "It is so far away, Rikki! And so dangerous! Your home is here in Rome, with me."

But Ulrika shook her head. "Mother, you of all people must see why I have to go. You spent your life searching for your identity and your destiny. Now I must seek mine."

Selene watched the door close behind her daughter, then she slumped into her chair. For a fraction of a second, she had the impulse to jump up and stop Ulrika. She wanted to hold her, to keep her here in Rome, by her side as she had been for the past nineteen years. But in the next instant Selene remembered something: Many years ago, Mera had tried to subvert Selene's destiny by taking fate into her own hands. It had been in Selene's stars to live her life with Andreas, but Mera had not been able to accept it. And so she had twisted Selene's road to suit her own vision.

That was what Selene was tempted to do now—stop Ulrika from following her chosen path. And she could not. Twenty-two years ago, Mera had not been able to let her daughter go. But on this April morning Selene must.

C H A P T E R 64

Ulrika had to hurry. Last night, Gaius Vatinius had said he was leaving for Germany in five days, taking with him a legion of sixty centuries—six thousand men. Ulrika must reach the Rhineland before Vatinius did.

She stopped first at the Forum, where hundreds of little shops and booths were set up in a busy marketplace. There, she had a woodcarver make a replica of the Cross of Odin that hung around her neck, and wrapped it in a square of linen. Next she stopped at her house on the Esquiline Hill. Andreas was in his study, working on his medical encyclopedia. Ulrika fought the impulse to go in and say goodbye to him. But there was no time; he would understand.

In her room she hastily put together a traveling pack. Her sturdiest clothes went in, with an extra pair of sandals, toilet articles, money, a spare cloak. Then she took things from her mother's medical stores: jars of medicines, bags of herbs, Hecate's Cure, a box of green bread mold, rolls of bandages, scalpels, sutures. From her mother's jewelry box Ulrika took the turquoise stone that had once been Rani's, and she strung it on her own necklace next to the Cross of Odin that had come from her father. Lastly, Ulrika tiptoed into the library and took two books: *Materia Medica* by Pedanius Dioscorides, and *De Medicina* by Celsus.

Down the street, Lady Paulina was not at home, so Ulrika did not have to explain her presence at the villa. She went straight to the slave quarters.

Eiric was not there.

She had come to tell him to get ready. But he was nowhere in the house, in the orchard, the gardens. And no one had seen him since dawn.

And then she knew: Eiric had run away.

He had told her nothing about it. He had gone on his own. And she knew why. That had been the reason for the grim look on his face after they had made love, and the thoughtful silence into which he had retreated. He had been planning to run away all the time, and had kept it a secret.

For me, she thought. *He did it for me.* But Ulrika had an idea where Eiric would run to—north, to his people. She would find him, she was confident of it. In Germany Ulrika would be reunited with her father, her brother and the boy she loved.

Finally, Ulrika hurried up to the nursery and dismissed the nanny so that she could be alone with Valerius.

"Little brother," she said, kneeling before him. "I've come to give you a present."

"You never came to my room last night, Rikki," the boy said. "I waited and waited, but you never came after the party."

"I'm sorry, Valerius. But I wasn't feeling well. I know I promised to bring you a treat, but isn't this a better surprise?"

When she opened the cloth, his eyes grew wide. "It's the same as yours!" he cried, reaching for the cross.

As Ulrika draped the necklace over Valerius's head, and smoothed the T-cross down on his chest, she said solemnly, "This is a very special present, little brother. It *is* just like mine, and that makes us very close. It means that, no matter how far apart we might be someday, we shall still always be joined by this cross."

He laughed, admiring the necklace he now wore. "We'll never be apart, Rikki. You only live down the street!"

She held back her tears. "Listen to me, little brother. Look at me, and listen. This cross is very important. You must keep it always. And then someday, if you ever need me—" Her voice broke.

"Why are you sad, Rikki?"

She gathered him into her arms and held him fast. "Listen to me, Valerius! You must promise me something. You must promise me that, if you should ever need me, no matter where you are or how old you are, send this cross to me, and I shall come, from wherever I am."

His voice was muffled by her hair. "But where will you be, Rikki?"

"I shall let you know when I can, little brother. If not, ask Aunt Selene. The cross will find its way to me, Valerius, and I shall come to you at once, wherever you are. I promise."

Sensing the gravity of the moment, the boy said, "And if you ever need *me*, Rikki, send me your cross and I will come to *you.*"

Ulrika drew back and looked into the little face that was always showing fear, and she saw for the first time the shadow of the man upon it, the man Valerius would grow up to be, handsome and brave. "Yes," she said in wonder. "If I ever need you, little brother, I will send my cross as a signal."

She left the nursery before he could see her tears. Ulrika picked up her bundle where she had left it in the garden, looked up at the position of the sun, then struck off down the Esquiline Hill in the direction of the Ostia road. She was wearing sturdy boots and carried enough money in her belt to get her to her destination. And from her left shoulder hung her medicine box.

Ulrika walked quickly, knowing the gods were with her.

CHAPTER 65

You are the woman called Marcella?"

"I am."

"You perform midwifery on the Tiberine island?"

"I do."

Empress Agrippina nodded to the slaves in the room, and they all left, closing the door behind them. Marcella, suddenly alone with the empress, and not knowing why she had been summoned here to the Imperial Palace, shifted nervously.

"I am told," Agrippina said, as she took a seat, leaving Marcella standing, "that you will be the one to deliver Julia Selena's baby. Is that true?"

"Yes, lady. She has asked me to. I have thirty years' experience in midwifery."

"When is the child due?"

"In two weeks."

"There is something I want you to do."

Marcella grew more anxious. She had heard stories about this wicked woman, terrible tales of people disappearing, innocent people who went to their deaths never knowing what crime they had been accused of. And so when the Imperial summons had come, Marcella had been frightened.

Agrippina reached for a small purse on the table by her hand and held it out. Marcella took it, puzzled.

"When her labor begins," Agrippina said, "you will send everyone else away. Make sure you are alone with Julia Selena when the baby is born, is that clear?"

The midwife nodded.

"And if the child is a boy, you will smother it until it is dead, and then you will tell Julia Selena that her child was stillborn."

Marcella gasped. "Lady! I cannot do that!"

Agrippina fixed green eyes on her, eyes which drove people to their knees, and she said, "You will not question it. You will do it."

"But, lady—" Marcella began. Then she stopped. It suddenly became clear. A boy whom the people recognized as the heir of their beloved Julius Caesar would be an obstacle to Agrippina's ambition for her son, Nero.

Marcella dropped the bag of gold onto the table, drew her plump body up proudly and said, "I will not do it."

Agrippina sighed. "I had hoped you would not be tiresome. I was told you are an intelligent woman. I see now that you are not." The empress clapped her hands and a slave came in.

He dropped some scrolls on the table and quietly left. Marcella looked at the scrolls, and her blood ran cold.

"Do you know what these are?" Agrippina asked.

Marcella shook her head.

"They are testimonies, sworn on the goddess Bona Fides, of people who were witness to your various acts of treason."

"Treason!"

"Do you deny them?"

"I most certainly do. I've never had a treasonous thought in my head!"

"Unfortunately for you, that is no defense. Are you prepared to face these charges in a court of law?"

"I am. My friends will swear to my loyalty to Rome, and to the emperor."

A finely drawn eyebrow went up. It filled Marcella with dread. She glanced at the scrolls again. Who had signed? Who had betrayed her? Whom had the empress frightened into committing perjury, just as she was now bullying Marcella into committing murder?

"You see?" Agrippina said. "You would not stand a chance in a court of law. And the punishment for treason, as you know, is death."

Marcella stared at the scrolls.

"Now then," Agrippina said as she rose and came around to face the midwife. "That gold is only half payment for the job. When you have done what I ask, you will receive the second half—and these scrolls, to do with as you please."

Marcella found the courage to speak. "I don't believe you," she said. "Those scrolls are blank."

"Oh, satisfy yourself, by all means! Inspect them."

She picked up one and untied its string with fumbling fingers. Marcella read the charge, and the signature at the bottom, of the baker who had been her neighbor for years. She read another, and another. They all accused her of saying treasonous things against Rome, the Senate, the Imperial family.

The empress watched the midwife's face slowly collapse. Just so had the man Gallus's face once folded in resignation. Gallus had been Agrippina's man on the island, in the strategic position of foreman on the Domus project. He had done well for a short while; he had nearly brought work to a halt. A few more "bad omens" and not a man in the Empire would have touched that building. But then Gallus had somehow been found out. Someone loyal to Julia Selena had spied on him, caught him in the act of witchcraft. A dove was supposedly sent from Venus, blessing the Domus; and two days later Gallus's headless body was found floating on the river.

Agrippina had had to turn to other measures. But none were successful. Julia Selena's popularity was her protection; also, she enjoyed the friendship of Claudius. He liked Julia Selena, and had an interest in the Domus. Agrippina was not yet more powerful than her husband; she had to move carefully. Although the Domus was near completion, there was still time. The problem of the baby, however, was more urgent.

"Well?" she said to the midwife.

Marcella dropped the last of the scrolls on the table and said with bowed head, "I shall do as you ask."

———

The city lay under a blanket of heat. There was no breeze to stir branches and pennants; even the river seemed sluggish. Because summer was such an incendiary period in Rome, with the oppressive heat sparking rebellions and riots, the Games at the Circus were almost nonstop.

Today, the populace was being distracted by slaughters in honor of the god Augustus, for this was the month named after him, just as July had been named for the Divine Julius. A fabulous naval battle was going to be staged in the arena: two mock navies, complete with ships and catapults, floated on an artificial sea, and they were to fight to the death. Because of this, the streets of Rome were nearly deserted as Selene and Pindar made their way slowly along Sacred Street.

Andreas had asked her not to go out, but Selene was determined. Today marked exactly four months since Ulrika's departure, and thus far there was no word, no news of her. So Selene was going once again to the shrine of the Divine Julius to make sacrifice to her grandfather and ask him to keep watch over Ulrika.

Pindar was with her, anxious and watchful, frequently taking her elbow;

and he carried her medicine box. Selene was very pregnant, she walked awkwardly and had to pause often to catch her breath. The baby had turned yesterday; now it lay low in her abdomen, head-down in its cradle of pelvic bone.

The shrine of Divine Julius stood on a square of grassland that was ornamented with a fountain and hedges. The building itself was small, circular, with columns all around it. There were no outbuildings; the priests lived elsewhere. Inside, there was only the statue of Julius Caesar, a flame burning at its feet. The priests were not there today—they were in their reserved boxes at the Circus.

Selene slipped into the welcome coolness with relief. She put her hand on her lower back and thought that perhaps she should have listened to Andreas. He had wanted her to come in a litter. But it seemed such a short walk; and the morning had started out cool.

She gazed up at the remote expression on her ancestor's face and wondered if he was indeed present in this little temple. Wondered what he made of her, his granddaughter.

"Divine Julius," Selene murmured as she placed flowers at his feet. "Please watch over Ulrika, your great-granddaughter. She denied you, but she is young. She needs to find her way in the world, as I had to find mine. She will return to you one day."

Selene felt ponderous and content. Things were going as planned. Since Rufus had taken over as foreman, back in April, work on the Domus had moved with speed. The dome was completed; all the walls and columns and arches were finished. Now the work crews concentrated on the finer touches—door latches, window grills. In only two months, it was estimated, the Domus Julia would be ready to admit patients, the classrooms opened to medical students.

Selene closed her eyes. She felt as if she stood on a brink. Such a long road so far traveled; and yet a longer one seemed to stretch before her. Soon, her work with Andreas would begin.

She felt a sudden spasm, and it was followed by a warm wetness between her legs, and, immediately afterward, by a cramp in her lower back.

It's too soon, she thought, as the cramp traveled around and encircled her abdomen.

"Pindar. I must sit down. Help me. See if there is—" Another cramp, sharper, shot around her waist.

Pindar took hold of her arm and helped her to the back of the shrine, where, behind the statue of Julius, there was a large stone chest to hold incense and robes for the priests. Selene sank down onto the chest and laid her hands on her abdomen. Before she could take a breath, another contraction came, stronger than the others, and she felt the ominous shifting of her bones.

"Fetch Marcella," she said breathlessly. "I shall go home."

Pindar shook his head.

"Go!" she said, pushing him. "There's time. I'll be all right. I shall walk slowly. Run, Pindar!"

He hesitated for a fraction of a second, then spun on his heel and ran out of the shrine. Selene saw his silhouette briefly fill the doorway, the August sun haloing him, creating an optical illusion that made her blink—rays of light seemed to surround him, as they did in depictions of the god Helios—then he was gone, lumbering down the steps, leaving her alone.

The next contraction doubled her over. Selene folded up and gripped the hem of her dress with both hands. A cold sweat sprang out all over her body, contrasting with the hot pain.

The next contraction was a band of fire around her body. For an instant, everything went black; Selene went blind. She was blind and deaf and aware only of a terrible, burning pain.

It wasn't like this with Ulrika, her mind said from the dark corner it had receded to. *Something is wrong.*

She tried to stand. A wave of pain toppled her; she sank to her knees, then lay on her side. She began to pant. Her dress, cold and wet, clung to her skin. She waited. The next pain seemed to begin in her heart, a slow catapulting of fire, spiraling down like a shooting star and exploding in her pelvis.

She cried out.

Then she lay for a while, just breathing, calling her body back together, to gather strength to withstand the next assault. The pain was hideous.

"Help," she whispered, but she thought she screamed it.

This one is killing me. I am going to die.

Selene felt herself slipping away from the shrine. She saw the marble feet of her grandfather fall away from her as she tumbled down a dark tunnel, where all that awaited her were bands of hot pain.

The floor was cold and hard, but Selene was engulfed by a black fire. Minutes widened into hours, and those stretched into days and into eternity. She had lain there forever, it seemed; Pindar was only a distant memory.

Then she saw feet running toward her; Divine Julius changing his mind, coming back to help her. But it was Pindar, and he was babbling in his child's way about being too scared to run all the way to the island to fetch Marcella. He couldn't leave his mistress alone. He was crying and trying to lift her up.

Selene was horrified; he had only been gone a minute.

"Something's wrong," she whispered.

He put his big hands under her arms and pulled her back behind the statue, and Selene was further surprised to realize that she had been crawling. *To where?* she wondered.

She saw Pindar break the lock on the stone chest and lift the lid. Through another wave of pain, Selene's oddly detached mind thought: *He mustn't do that. It's sacrilege.*

Then she remembered why she had been crawling. To get out of the shrine, because childbirth would defile this holy sanctuary.

But why? she thought, as she felt the next wave of pain rush toward her, crest and cover her. *This is the miracle of life; the gods themselves invented it.*

The spells between contractions, during which Selene breathed and reasoned, grew shorter until she rode a continuous tide of pain.

And then she *was* pain, because it had devoured her and carried her away to some dark place that was before time and existence. Pindar was doing something—pulling out scarlet robes and belts of gold. "Mustn't . . . " she said.

He was sobbing, he was frightened, but he was determined to stay by her and help. A pillow for her head, a cushion beneath her pelvis. Selene looked up at the domed ceiling of her grandfather's temple and felt the warm summer air on her legs as Pindar drew her dress back.

She thought of Ulrika's birth, tried to recall what it had felt like. But it had been nothing like this. There was the great, soft bed and the warm wine Rani gave her to drink, and the old Zoroastrian priest who had delivered a thousand babies. Ulrika had seemed just to walk out of the womb and into life.

Ulrika is like that, Selene thought, as she took herself away from her tortured body. *Wherever she is now, whether fighting at her father's side or just waiting for the snow to fall, Ulrika will always reach out for life.*

There was another pain now, a different one, lower down, a tearing, knife-like pain. It frightened her. Then Pindar's hand was lying gently on Selene's forehead and it produced a curious, unexpected balm.

I am too old, she thought. *Ulrika was born nineteen years ago, when I was still young . . . My body has hardened; it is protesting this eruption. I am dying . . .*

"I'll keep it," she whispered. "I won't push it out. I'll keep my baby inside me and carry him for the rest of my life."

Selene screamed.

Pigeons flew off the overhead rafters, fluttered, caromed off walls, then settled back down.

Selene screamed again.

Something *was* wrong. She could feel it, and Pindar could see it. She was fighting it. He tried to tell her not to. He tried to calm her, to relax her. He tried clumsily to order her to draw back and let it happen by itself, that her struggling was doing harm.

But the pain made her fight, and her fighting worsened the pain. Selene realized in fear and panic that she was indeed going to kill herself, but she couldn't help it, the pain, the pain . . .

And then loving arms went around her and soothing words slipped into her ear. "It's all right," she said to the faithful simpleton, who was holding her and crying on her shoulder.

Pindar rocked her like a baby and Selene thought it was the nicest thing in the world. Her mind wanted to scream along with her throat, but instead it thought: *He knows what I need, better than Marcella would know. I need someone up here, not down there. Someone to share my pain, to cut it in half, lift it from me.*

And then, all of a sudden, she saw it.

Her soul flame.

Only once before had the flame appeared unbidden, without having been called up, and here it was now, unexpected, burning brightly like a comet, such a welcome sight that Selene ran to it and embraced it, as Pindar was embracing her.

Then she realized: It wasn't *her* soul flame. This was another's. It was different, cooler, sweet, a younger flame. Then she knew that it was Pindar's, and it quivered and danced as she held it.

Selene started to cry, then to laugh, and then she said, "Here it is." There was one final push of pain and all the liquid fire ran out of her.

CHAPTER 66

Ghosts walked with her.

Selene could sense their presence in the gentle, early autumn air. Spirits who had gathered to guide her, to share her moment of triumph as she walked through the Domus, which was empty now, on this October afternoon.

The work gangs had been dismissed a week ago. Cleaning crews had then swept through, to polish, to make the healing house shine. The

Domus smelled of wood oils and beeswax, of fresh tallow and herbs; the marble floors gleamed like seas, the white ceilings were as yet unsmudged by lamp smoke. The Domus Julia—new and young and ready to begin its great purpose.

Pindar walked behind Selene as she made her final inspection. He was carrying Julius, her three-month-old son. He watched his mistress slowly cross the great rotunda that dominated the building, looking up, her body slowly turning, an expression of wonder on her face as if she were seeing the Domus for the first time. He followed her through the many rooms: the wards with their beds, the storage vaults, gymnasium and library, Andreas's classrooms. Pindar's vision did not include what Selene's did— the patients, the nursing attendants, the doctors and teachers. He could not imagine the bustling life that would, after tomorrow, fill these hollow chambers with noise and energy. Only Selene saw it, as she had seen it in nineteen years of dreams, since Persia, since Dr. Chandra and the Pavilion.

That was when the Domus Julia had really begun to be built, during those evenings in Princess Rani's rooms. And she walked with Selene now, that wise old friend, a tender, wistful presence that had come to congratulate, and to goad a little.

"Patients must be kept awake and cheerful," Rani had argued many times with Selene.

"Patients need to sleep," Selene had countered.

It was one of the few points they could never agree upon; but Selene had won. Above the entrance of the Domus, these words were inscribed: SLEEP IS THE PHYSICIAN OF PAIN. A reminder to staff and visitors to tread quietly on these marble floors.

That there would be many visitors to the Domus, Selene did not doubt. For months the people of Rome had buzzed with curiosity about the building going up on the north end of the island. A sanctuary for the sick? Not a temple, where one pays a penny to the priest and spends the night, but a place to be taken care of, like a home, where someone cared. The people of Rome had never heard of such a thing, could not visualize it, could not imagine how it was going to be. The little temporary wards on the island, which had taken care of sick and injured while the Domus was being designed and built, were nothing compared to this.

Tomorrow, during the grand celebration to mark the opening of the Domus Julia, the citizens would be free to wander the rooms and halls and discover for themselves what mysteries were housed beneath the bone-white dome.

Selene paused in the library. Shelves of scrolls and codex books lined the walls from floor to ceiling. Here were ancient magic and spells brought from Egypt, a medical treatise from faraway China, a compendium of the folk healing of Britain. And, the crowning treasure, Andreas's massive medical encyclopedia—fifty volumes, completed in time for the festival opening tomorrow. Andreas had labored long and hard on that work; it contained the total knowledge of Roman and Greek medicine, from herbs to surgery, from botany to anatomy. In a few days, after the celebrations were over, he would take his book to a publisher and have it copied, so that physicians and medical students in cities the world over might benefit from it.

Selene heard a gurgle; she turned around to see Pindar rock Julius back to sleep in his arms.

Selene could not help frowning. Ever since that frightening episode with Marcella a few days after the baby was born—Julius suddenly ill, turning blue—Pindar would not let the baby out of his sight. And Marcella, who was found dead the next day in her bath, her wrists cut, a suicide note asking for forgiveness . . .

Were the rumors true? Was Agrippina furious over the birth of Selene's son? Had she really been heard to declare that she thought the birth in the shrine of Divine Julius to have been staged? On purpose, to ratify the baby's place in the Julio-Claudian line? It had been a propitious event, Selene did not deny it. The priests had even overlooked the ancient taboo of defilement, saying that the birth of the baby in the Divine Julius's temple was a good sign. But Selene had not planned it that way!

She might have died there, at the foot of her grandfather's statue, had it not been for Pindar.

It was strange, how Selene felt toward him now. There was an inexplicable bond between them, one she could put no name to. Pindar had delivered her baby, he had held her during a time of crisis, and so she felt the sort of warm affection for him one feels for a close friend or relative. And yet . . . there was something more, something she could not bring into sharp focus.

Selene shook her head. There was so much to fill her mind today! She trembled like a bride, she felt as if she were sixteen again. *The rug merchant would have been taken to a place such as this,* she thought, recalling how it had been when she was indeed sixteen. Back in Antioch Selene had been so helpless, so frustrated; the man would have died had it not been for Andreas. That was not going to happen in Rome, Selene assured herself. Because now there was the Domus Julia.

Mera was walking with her, too. Selene could sense her amazement, her bewilderment to see healing on such a large scale. There was approval in Mera's spirit, but Selene felt also a touch of wariness, as if that old-fashioned woman were saying: *Can it work? Is the world ready for this?*

The only spirit Selene did not sense at her side was Wulf's. Did that mean he was still alive? Was he, after all, the rebel leader in the German forests? Did Ulrika find him; were they reunited at last, and fighting side by side?

Selene wrapped her arms about her waist and hugged herself. Tomorrow it would all begin. Tomorrow would mark the end of her long odyssey. Tomorrow would see the sunset of an old age and the dawn of a new one, as prophesied. Tomorrow—

"Selene!"

She turned.

Andreas came in, breathless. "Paulina," he said. "She's been arrested!"

They hurried to the Capitoline jail, leaving Pindar on the island with the baby, and after some inquiries learned, to their shock, that Paulina had not been put in the usual city jail but was incarcerated in the dungeons below the Circus Maximus.

"Great gods, why?" Andreas said.

The official consulted his ledger and shrugged. "She's been accused of treason."

"Treason!"

"Why the Circus?" Selene asked, clutching Andreas for support.

The man flipped through some wax tablets, rosters of scheduled executions, and said, "She's been condemned to die with the Jews."

Selene felt faint.

There was a new sect of Jews who called themselves Nazarenes, and who had refused to worship the emperor as a god, a treasonable act. Already examples had been made of them in the Circus, they had been pitted against wild dogs and bears; tomorrow there was going to be a spectacle that Claudius was known to favor—the traitors were going to be put on crosses in the arena, covered with pitch and burned alive.

"But Lady Paulina has had no trial!" Andreas said.

And he received a look from the jailer which said: No trial for *that* prisoner.

"But *why?*" said Selene. "Paulina isn't one of them! Claudius knows that."

"Weren't the emperor ordered her arrest," the man said. "She was picked up on Lady Agrippina's orders."

Out on the busy street, Selene said, "Andreas, I don't understand. Why would Agrippina have Paulina arrested on charges she must know are false?"

Andreas squinted into the setting sun, and said, "You go and comfort Paulina. Tell her we will see to it that she is released at once."

"Where are you going?"

"To Claudius. My guess is, he knows nothing about this. He'll write an order for her release."

Selene had to make her way through the busy Forum to get to the Circus Maximus on its south side, and, once there, had to argue and plead with a series of guards before she was finally granted a visit with Paulina.

Her friend was in a cell by herself, sitting rigidly with her hands flat on her knees. When she heard footsteps coming down the stony hall, Paulina turned to the grill in the doorway and saw Selene's face. She rose as gracefully as if she were admitting a guest into her house.

"Paulina," Selene said, gripping the bars of the grill. "We just heard. Andreas has gone to the emperor."

Paulina drew near, and Selene saw a pale, shocked face. But she also saw the familiar Roman *gravitas*, the inbred patrician dignity that set Lady Paulina apart from the rest of the prisoners, who wept and cursed.

"It happened so quickly," Paulina said in a level voice. She held herself with pride, her chin raised. "Praetorians walked into my house, showed me the order for my arrest and took me away. I managed to tell a slave to get the news to you."

Selene stared into Paulina's topaz eyes, and she saw the fear beneath the glaze of courage. "But why?" Selene said. "Who is your accuser?"

"That I do not know. I was taken to the empress, and she showed me some scrolls, testimonies, she said, of witnesses to my treason."

"Forgeries!"

Paulina compressed her lips. "Agrippina has no doubt bribed or bullied my friends into committing perjury. I shall not even be allowed a trial. I am to . . . die tomorrow. In the arena."

Selene stared at her friend in disbelief. This could not be happening. It was all a nightmare; soon she would wake up in the Domus, in the pure and white sunlight. And the sounds she heard—the sobbing, the begging behind the doors of other cells—were all part of the terrible dream. "But did she say *why*, Paulina? She must have wanted something for her to have you brought to her. What did she say?"

For the first time, Paulina's façade cracked. She had to lower her voice, the better to control it, and she said, "She made one demand."

"What is it?"

"That I persuade you to renounce your claim to Julian blood."

There was one tiny window set high in the wall of Paulina's cell, and through it now streamed the molten-metal tones of the dying day. There was a strange smell in the air, a singed, scorched smell, and from far away came shouts of fire.

Selene watched the copper sunlight slowly retreat across the stone floor, as if it were being pulled back like a tide; she inhaled the faint smell of smoke, listened to the distant cries of the *Cohortes Vigilum,* Rome's fire brigade; she pictured their buckets, leather hoses, and inefficient hand pumps. She had seen them at work many times, those brave volunteers, battling fire more fiercely than if they fought an invading army, for fire was Rome's biggest fear, the city's greatest threat.

What was burning now? Selene wondered.

"I see," she said at last, quietly, and suddenly she *did* see. Paulina's few words made it all clear. The witchcraft in the Domus, the baby's inexplicable illness while in Marcella's care, Marcella's baffling suicide. The hand of the empress had been behind everything. To stop Selene from some imagined plan to steal the throne of Rome.

She dares not touch me, Selene thought, *but she can hurt me through my family and friends.*

"And how am I to perform this act?" Selene asked.

"In front of the people," Paulina said quietly. "You are to declare that it was all a lie. That you are not a descendant of Julius Caesar. And you are publicly to give the ring to Agrippina."

"And for this she will let you go?"

Paulina was silent.

"Then I must do it, Paulina. Because of me, you face a terrible death. I am responsible. It is up to me to get you out."

Paulina brought her face close to the bars and said, "But there is more . . ."

"More! What more can I do!"

"Agrippina wants you to publicly denounce your healing as witchcraft."

Selene stared at her friend.

"And to denounce the Domus Julia as an evil place."

Horror filled Selene's eyes. How had it come to this? From that humble little house in Antioch's poor quarter—to *this*? To disclaim an ancestor whom I only recently learned of is one thing. But to denounce my sacred calling, to deny the dream I share with Andreas!

Selene looked up at the little window in the wall and saw that daylight was gone. Night was sweeping over Rome; smoke was in the air, growing thicker. The voices of other prisoners were also filling the air with their frightened shouts to be let out; they too were smelling the smoke, and beginning to panic.

"It will not come to that," Selene said. "Andreas has gone to see Claudius . . ."

She stopped, suddenly realizing that Andreas had been gone a long time.

"Selene," said Paulina. "You must get away from Rome. Agrippina's power grows daily and the time will come when the mob will not be able to save you. I know that woman. She will turn them against you. The people are fickle, Selene. They follow any new star that is rising. Today it is you, tomorrow they will drag you down. Get out of Rome, Selene. Take your baby and go far away."

Selene regarded her friend with wide eyes. "But . . . The Domus! It's everything I have lived for. How can I leave it?"

"Do you think Agrippina will suffer it to stand? She'll find a way to destroy it, and you with it, and those you love."

"But if I renounce my ancestry!" Selene cried. "Surely that's enough. If I show her that I have no intention of challenging her son's succession to power, surely Agrippina will leave us in peace."

But no—Selene saw that, even as she spoke the words. Once she renounced her heritage, Selene knew, there would be nothing left to protect herself and her son. By her own hand she would be turning the mob against herself, playing right into Agrippina's hands.

Paulina reached through the bars and grasped Selene's wrist. "Go," she whispered urgently. "Tonight, this minute. Take Andreas and the baby and flee to some safe place far away."

"I will not leave you, Paulina!"

"And take my son, Selene. Take Valerius with you. Once I am dead, he will not be safe. Raise him as your own."

By now the other prisoners were banging on their doors and screaming to be let out. Selene and Paulina looked up at the little window. A new light glowed there, like a second sunset, and the smell of smoke was getting stronger.

A guard came through the iron door and shouted at the prisoners. "The fire ain't nowhere near here!" he boomed. "Y'ain't gonna burn up. So be quiet!"

When he went back behind the door, leaving it ajar, Selene heard a new voice join the din: it was Andreas, arguing with the jailer. Selene went to look and saw the man frowning over a piece of paper; Andreas was saying, "You're familiar with the emperor's seal. There it is. Release Lady Paulina immediately or suffer the consequences."

As the jailer scratched his head in indecision—the prisoner was *Agrippina's*—Andreas shot Selene a warning glance. She stayed behind the door.

Finally the man relented and said, "Awright. It's supposed to come from the empress, but . . . "

As soon as the door was unlocked, Paulina hurried out. The three walked away quickly, but not so fast that they would draw attention to themselves. When they were at the entrance, stepping out into the smoky night, Andreas said, "We must leave Rome at once. Claudius is dead."

"*What?*"

"He was at dinner when I went to see him about Paulina. He was drunk and insisted I sit with him. Agrippina urged a second helping of mushrooms upon him, ones which his taster had not tasted, and it was those that did it. But listen." He took Selene's arm and held it tightly. "Agrippina is saying that *I* poisoned him. She has ordered my arrest."

"No!"

"I managed to get out of the palace unseen, but Agrippina is in supreme power now. She will act in Nero's place until he is an adult. We must leave Rome tonight."

"My son—" Paulina said.

"I've made arrangements with a sea captain who is due to depart tonight. It's our only hope. The roads leading out of the city will all be watched. The ship sails within the hour."

"Andreas," Selene said. "Go with Paulina to her house. Collect Valerius and . . . money, Andreas. We will need money. I'll go to the island for Julius. We'll need to take some things—provisions, medicines. I must give Herodas instructions about the Domus. I'll meet you at the docks."

They parted on the dark street, Andreas and Paulina to go to their villas on the Esquiline Hill, Selene to hurry to the island.

But when she reached the riverbank she stopped short, her eyes wide with disbelief.

The Domus was on fire.

A fire brigade was there, but it was obviously completely useless. The Domus was too large, the island too cramped to allow them room to work. People were starting to gather on the banks to watch the flames shoot high into the night. As Selene ran past, she heard: "Never did have good luck. Remember back in April? I always thought this place wasn't meant to be. Whoever heard o' such a thing? A house for the sick . . . "

No, no, no, thundered her heart as her sandals thumped along the stone bridge.

The heat from the fire reached this end of the island, driving patients and priests from the temple. Many plunged into the river, others fled across the bridge, jamming it, trampling those who fell. Such a roar the fire made! It was as if an angry, blazing lion crouched on the island and roared its hot breath to the sky.

Selene was pushed back by the mob. She fell twice and picked herself up. It was an awesome sight, the burning Domus, like an incandescent new sun, lighting the night sky for miles around and sending ash and cinders raining down upon the city.

Selene felt the hot air sear her lungs. She dipped her *palla* into a fountain and drew it, dripping, over her head. With the wet cloth held to her mouth, she pushed ahead to the Domus.

Where were Pindar and the baby?

She found Rufus first, lying beneath a block of fallen stone. His head was cracked, but his eyes were open, reflecting the golden flames.

When she knelt at his side, the old veteran managed enough breath to say, "Take care of m'boy. You're Pindar's family now," and then he died.

Others were trapped beneath fallen rubble. Selene saw one man run like a flaming torch and topple into the river, charred.

She stared at the conflagration as if hypnotized. The entrance to the Domus was like a fiery mouth. She thought of everything that was inside —the books, her medicines.

Andreas's encyclopedia.

Her medicine box.

Selene was forced to turn back. Explosions were erupting all over the building as gases within the masonry heated and expanded. Even the fire brigade was abandoning the island now. And the crowds on the river banks were growing. They cheered and shouted and passed around jugs of wine. It was as if they were at a spectacle, as if this were entertainment.

Selene ran to the rear of the Domus, where the fire was less intense. "Pindar!" she shouted.

The windows glowed like demons' eyes; smoke rolled out from doorways.

"Pindar! Where are you!"

A cinder fell on her dress, igniting the hem; she stamped it out. An explosion overhead sent rubble and ash down over her head. She flung up a protective arm.

The baby! Where was the baby?

"Pindar!" she called in desperation, but her voice was lost in the roar of the inferno.

Then a man, one of the holy brothers, had her by the arm and was trying to pull her away. "Have you seen Pindar and the baby?" Selene cried.

"They were inside when the fire started, mistress! They never came out! Come away, mistress!"

"Pindar! Julius!"

She fought with the brother until he released her and fled, his hands over his head against the falling debris.

Selene ran around the perimeter of the Domus, searching for a way in, but all was blazing.

"Pindar—" she sobbed, tripping and falling to the ground.

She made her way back to the main entrance, where tongues of flame licked the columns of the massive porch. The heat was like a solid wall; it pushed her back in great waves. Then, overhead, there was an explosion. The stone lintel bearing the inscription SLEEP IS THE PHYSICIAN OF PAIN blew apart, and chunks of marble came down like hail.

Selene looked up. She raised her arms. Too late. A rock the size of a fist struck her head and she fell, onto the seared grass and into darkness.

Andreas and Paulina hurried along the streets winding up the Esquiline Hill, looking back over their shoulders to see what was burning. But each time their view was blocked, by buildings, by garden walls, by tall cypress trees. Fires in the city were common in August; barely a day went by without the acrid smell of smoke and a fine rain of ash filling the hot summer air. But when they reached their own street on the summit, they were able at last to see. And they froze.

"It's the island!" Paulina whispered.

"Selene is down there!" Andreas turned to Paulina and said, "Listen. The ship is the *Bellerophon*, the captain is a man named Naso. Get Valerius and go there at once."

"But—"

"Quickly, Paulina! Have you a slave you can depend on?"

She was breathless. "Yes . . . "

"Take everything of value that you can carry—jewelry, money. And hurry!"

"Let me come with you, Andreas."

"No! I'm going back, to get Selene and the baby. We'll meet you at the ship. Hurry, Paulina. Naso is sailing on the tide."

"Surely he will wait for you!" she cried.

"I've told him not to. Once you and Valerius are on board, then he will be in as much danger as we are. If Selene and I don't come in time, you must sail, Paulina! And we shall find our way out of the city as best we can. Go now!"

Andreas watched Paulina hurry through her garden gate, then he turned to run back down the street in the direction they had just come from.

He stopped short. The empress's guards were coming around the corner. Andreas ducked into an archway. He looked up and down the dark street. Before him, the sky glowed orange against black night and stars. Smoke from the fire was rising to the hills; his eyes stung and tears blurred his vision.

When he saw two of the guards stop at Paulina's gate, Andreas left the archway and crept along the wall until he came to its end, where a narrow alley led between two villas to the next street over. Andreas ran down the alley, found a place where low-hanging tree branches drooped over a wall, and jumped, pulling himself up and over.

He found himself in the rear garden of Paulina's villa, near the slave quarters, and he could hear, far on the other side of the house, the soldiers breaking down the gate.

Paulina met him as she came running out of the house with a sleepy Valerius in her arms. Andreas took the boy and led her quickly back to where the tree hung low over the garden wall.

"My slaves!" Paulina said. "Agrippina will have them all killed!"

"Climb!" Andreas said to Valerius, as he helped the boy up the tree. "Up and over. Wait on the other side and help your mother down. You're a man now, Valerius. You have to take care of her."

The six-year-old snapped to life and scaled the tree like a monkey. When he saw that Paulina was getting safely up the tree, Andreas said, "Remember. It's the *Bellerophon*. And hurry!"

Then he turned and ran back to the slave quarters where he found the slaves huddled in fear. "Come!" he said. "Run!"

But they didn't move.

"Run!" he shouted again.

They stared at him like dumb animals, paralyzed with fear.

When he heard the gate crash down, followed by the stamp of sandaled feet running through the front garden, and the shouts of soldiers, Andreas turned and ran to the wall. He was up the tree and dropping down into the alley on the other side just as the soldiers burst into the rear garden.

———

When Selene came to, the grass all around her was on fire. She coughed in painful spasms; her eyes stung with tears. She tried to cover her face, but her *palla* had blown away. She staggered to her feet, and looked around, dazed.

"Help!" she cried.

Then she looked up. On a pedestal high over the massive porch, a gigantic marble statue of Venus was threatening to topple.

"Help!" Selene screamed.

Andreas heard her as he ran across the bridge. He saw her in the ring of fire and saw also, directly above her, the statue of Venus starting to break up.

"Help!" Selene screamed again.

Andreas found a toga snagged on a bush, abandoned in someone's flight. He plunged it into a pond and then ran with it, sopping wet, to the ring of flames. Flinging the wet toga over his head, Andreas darted into the fire, grabbed hold of Selene's arm, threw the other end of the wet garment over her head and shoulders and ran with her.

Just as Selene was pulled away from the spot where she had lain, the statue of Venus came crashing down.

When they reached the bridge, Selene drew back suddenly. "The baby!" she cried. "We have to find the baby!"

Andreas looked around. Every building was on fire; the entire island was lost. "It's no use, Selene!" he shouted. "We must save ourselves!"

He held her hard and pulled her along, sobbing, onto the bridge and away.

———

They ran down streets dark and filled with smoke, coughing, supporting each other. To their left, the formidable walls of the Circus Maximus stood in the ghostly haze of smoke, its arches and columns illuminated by the fire's glow.

Selene fell several times but Andreas held her up, his arm tight about her waist. He knew that the guards, having found his house empty, would have gone next to the island. And by now they would be searching the city for them.

Let them search the roads out of the city first, Andreas prayed.

But even as he prayed, he knew the hour was too late. Naso would have set sail by now.

They came upon a break in the buildings, a small park with a little circular temple in the center—the shrine of Divine Julius. As Selene and Andreas ran past, they heard a dog barking. Turning, they saw Fido come loping out of the temple.

And behind him Pindar, carrying the baby.

"Pindar!" Selene cried, running to them. She took Julius into her arms, crying with relief, and listened to Pindar's stumbling account of how the dog had smelled the smoke before any human had, and had barked the alarm.

Then Selene saw the box that hung from Pindar's shoulder—her medicine box, which he had grabbed in his flight—and she hugged him and kissed his tear-streaked cheeks.

"Come," Andreas said. "We must hurry."

The docks were nearly deserted, everyone having run upriver to watch the fantastic fire, but, to Andreas's relief, the *Bellerophon* was still at anchor.

As they hurriedly climbed aboard, Naso said, gruffly, something about, "Too old to be running scared from some mad empress," and then he shouted orders for the lines to be cast off.

Selene and Paulina ran to each other and embraced. Fido bounded along the deck to Valerius and licked his face. And Andreas stood at the railing, watching as the dock slowly moved away.

———

Hours later, just before dawn, they finally entered the open sea.

The ship, which was carrying wine to Mauretania on the distant North African coast, and one of the last to cross the Mediterranean before winter closed down all shipping, was a sturdy craft with one big sail and a hearty crew. Naso assured his fugitive passengers that they were safe now, in the bosom of Poseidon.

Although the others stood at the stern to look back and watch the distant glow from the fire against the sky, Selene stood alone in the bow, looking forward. She held Julius in her arms, and her necklace brushed his body; she had hung on it good-luck tokens gathered over the years: his ancestral ring, and the ivory rose, resealed and carrying the lock of Prince Caesarion's hair, the piece of blanket belonging to the twin brother Selene thought she had never found.

Finally, Andreas came to stand with her, and then Pindar. Paulina left Valerius where he had fallen asleep on the deck, using Fido as his pillow, and came to join the group.

They looked ahead into the starry darkness and black, endless sea, a silent group, shocked, bedraggled, weary. They listened to the boards creak in the water and they thought of everything they were leaving behind.

Paulina began to weep softly and Pindar put an awkward arm about her shoulders. Andreas sought Selene's hand, to give her strength, and to take strength from her. The vision of the burning Domus would be stamped forever upon their memories.

Behind them, dawn was beginning to break, and already its promise of a new day was stealing across the water.

"We must take heart," Selene said at last in a tight voice. "We must be thankful that we escaped with our lives, and that we are all together. We shall go to where Agrippina cannot find us. We shall find a new home, a place where we can begin anew—" Her voice broke. "Where our children can grow up in peace and freedom from fear."

She drew in a breath. "We shall build another house of healing, one that will stand through the tests of time. It is what we were born to do."

As she stood next to Andreas, and leaned against him, Selene realized that this was but one more new beginning in the series of new beginnings that had made up her life. *I have been Fortuna of Magna,* she thought, *Fortuna of good luck and happiness; I have been Umma the "mother"; Peregrina, the stranger and traveler; Cleopatra Selene, descended from queens; and Julia Selena, daughter of the gods. But I am in the end who I started out to be—Selene the healer-woman.*

Although she was grief-stricken over the loss of the Domus, she knew that her dream had not died with it. She had come to the end of her long odyssey, and her two quests had been fulfilled: to find her roots, her identity, and to build a place of healing where people could go.

She stood on the deck, surrounded by her family and the people she loved, and watched as Venus disappeared with the dawning of a new day.

The ancient Western world had no word meaning "hospital." The first such institution as we know it was founded in Rome in the year 394 by the Christian benefactress Fabiola. A modern hospital stands today on the Tiberine island, on the foundation of the ancient Temple of Aesculapius, and it is operated by an order of religious brothers.

The emperor Claudius did write a law freeing slaves who either ran away to or were abandoned on the island. And his wife, Agrippina, who was later murdered by her son, Nero, is remembered to this day by a city on the Rhine which was named for her: Colonia Agrippina—better known as Cologne, Germany.

Several theories have been put forth to explain the epidemic of sterility among Rome's upper classes during the Imperial period, an affliction that lowered the birth rate of free citizens, and which has been described as one of the eventual causes of the fall of the Roman Empire. Modern historians have shown that the Roman upper classes might have suffered from lead poisoning, absorbing lead from water carried in lead pipes, from cups and cooking pots containing lead, from the lead in their cosmetics, and their wine, which was boiled in lead-lined pots. The lower classes did not enjoy such luxury items, but cooked in and drank out of lead-free clay pots.

Chronic lead poisoning causes sterility in men, miscarriages and stillbirths in women.

The various folk remedies mentioned throughout *Soul Flame* are derived from ancient sources; there are modern explanations as to why they were successful:

The application of green leaves to open wounds does prevent gangrene, as the chlorophyll contained in the leaves inhibits the bacteria that causes it.

The application of fleece is a very old remedy for skin problems; it contains lanolin, an ingredient found in most modern hand lotions.

Green mold as an infection-preventative is a centuries-old folk remedy; the mold, as found on bread and used in cheesemaking, contains the bacteria *Penicillium.*

Hecate's Cure is still used today. It is derived from the bark of willow trees, which contains salicylic acid, more commonly known as aspirin.

SCATINAVIA

NORTH
SEA

ATLANTIC OCEAN

BALTIC SEA

GOTHS

York

BRITAIN

Londinium (London)

GERMANIA

Elbe

BELGICA

Rhine

RHINELAND

NORICUM

Seine

Lutetia (Paris)

LUGDUNENSIS

HELVETII

GAUL

ALPS

Burdigala (Bordeaux)

Lugdunum

Po

AQUITAINE

PYRENEES

Arelate

ILLYRIA

Salonae

Massilia

Ebro

Narbo

ITALY

ADRIATIC SEA

Caesarea Augusta

CORSICA

Rome

Thessa

HISPANIA

BALEARIC IS.

Tarentum

Brundisium

SARDINIA

Corduba

Carthago Nova

SICILY

Syracuse

Carthage

NUMIDIA

MARE INTER

MAURETANIA

AFRICA

0   100   200   300   400   500 Miles

D E S E

Jean Paul Tremblay